A
MARRIAGEABLE
MISS

Dorothy Elbury

®™ MILLS & BOON®

First published in Great Britain 2009
Paperback edition 2010
Harlequin Mills & Boon Limited,
Eton House, 18-24 Paradise Road, Richmond, Surrey TW9 1SR

© Dorothy Elbury 2009

ISBN: 978 0 263 87568 3

Harlequin Mills & Boon policy is to use papers that are natural, renewable and recyclable products and made from wood grown in sustainable forests. The logging and manufacturing process conform to the legal environmental regulations of the country of origin.

Printed and bound in Spain
by Litografia Rosés, S.A., Barcelona

A
MARRIAGEABLE
MISS

For Dodie B, Jojobub and Tom Bloggs, with love.

Chapter One

Tossing aside yet another polite reminder of a still unpaid account, Richard Standish, now 6th Earl of Markfield, leaned back in his chair and stretched his aching limbs, wearily surveying the mounting pile of similar requests on the desk in front of him.

It hardly seemed possible that a mere six months had elapsed since his cousin Simon's fatal accident, as a consequence of which, Standish had unexpectedly and, most reluctantly, found himself in possession of the ancient title. Having resigned his commission the previous year, following Napoleon's decisive defeat at Waterloo, the ex-dragoon major had returned home to his own small estate, fully intent on realising a long-held aspiration to revive the Standish Stud which, in his grandfather's day, had been highly regarded in horse-breeding circles.

Unfortunately, his sudden acquisition of Markfield's vast acreage, along with its accompanying tenant farms and labourers' cottages, had very quickly put a brake on his purchasing powers, owing to the numerous calls on his rapidly diminishing funds. Not that the expense of the estate itself was in any way responsible for his present financial crisis since, thanks to the competent management of his late grandfather's land agent, Ben Hollis who, for the past fifteen years or so, had been allowed a more-or-less free hand in the running of the place, this concern was largely self-supporting.

The real headache, from the new earl's point of view, was the appallingly run-down state of Markfield Hall, the family mansion house, which had been built to celebrate Sir Edmund Markfield's elevation to the peerage in 1698. In its prime, the Hall had been much revered as an outstanding example of classical architecture but, due to severe neglect on the part of the 4th earl, the late Simon Standish's father, two of the chimney stacks were now dangerously unstable, several parts of the roof were open to the elements and rain had caused considerable damage to much of the Hall's fine oak panelling.

Following Simon Standish's untimely death, the newly ennobled Richard had been appalled to discover how carelessly the previous two occupants had treated the magnificent old mansion house. Not that he had any real desire to take up residence there himself, since he much preferred the more modern comforts of his own house at Westpark—which, until his grandfather had made it over to Richard's father Henry, upon the occasion of his marriage, some thirty years earlier, had originally formed part of the much larger Markfield estate.

Nevertheless, as his grandmother, the dowager countess, had been swift to point out to him, 'The Hall has always been regarded as a symbol of the family heritage—to simply stand by and watch it crumble into ruins would be an act of pure sacrilege!'

Accordingly, more in deference to his ageing grandmother's wishes than to his own requirements, Richard had set in motion an extensive refurbishment programme but, since it had then transpired that the estate kitty contained insufficient funds to bear the brunt of the mounting expense, he had found himself obliged to furnish the cost of the operation out of his own pocket. Having already invested most of his capital in setting up his fledgling stud farm, this additional burden on his finances had been more than enough to cause him concern. Added to which, it now seemed that he had seriously underestimated the likely cost of the venture and, as he stared glumly down at the column of figures before him, he could not help thinking that the project was getting to the stage where it could only be likened to some enormous millstone hanging round his neck! Where in Hades he was going to find enough money to finance the spiralling expenditure was proving to be an ever-increasing quandary. He had already been forced to sell off two of his most promising mares, both in foal to the one-time champion Gadfly, and now it was beginning to look as though he might well have to sacrifice his prize-winning stallion, too!

Distracted as he was by the weight of his problems, the distant sound of the front door bell failed to impinge itself upon his consciousness and it was only the opening of his study door some ten minutes later that eventually roused him from his deliberations.

'Her ladyship has arrived from London, my lord,' came the sepulchral tones of Kilburn, his butler. 'She has instructed me to inform you that both she and Mr Standish are awaiting your presence in the drawing room.'

Stifling a groan, Richard laid down his pen and pushed back his chair.

'Have some tea sent in and tell her ladyship that I will be with her directly,' he instructed the man as, getting to his feet, he shrugged himself into his jacket and ran his fingers hurriedly through his dishevelled hair. After casting a perfunctory look at his reflection in one of the glass-fronted bookcases at the doorway, he made his way across the hallway into his drawing room, whereupon he was greeted by his grandmother's ringing tones.

'Oh, here you are at last, Richard! Charles was just about to come in search of you!'

'Dreadfully sorry to have kept you waiting,' said Richard, bending down to kiss the old lady's surprisingly unlined cheek before turning to acknowledge his cousin. 'Have you eaten?'

'We stopped off for a quick bite at the Red Lion in Wimble-don, as usual,' said Charles, returning his smile. 'But Grand-

mama was keen to get on and view the latest improvements—
I see they've started stripping the roof of the west wing.'

Mindful of the tiler's recent statement of account, Richard
gave a cursory nod. 'The work is progressing more quickly than
I had anticipated. I rather fear that, if the bills keep coming in
at their present rate, I may well have to call a temporary halt in
the proceedings.'

'Oh, surely not, Richard!' protested the dowager, laying
down her teacup with such force that its contents spilled over
its rim. 'I have only just this minute finished telling Charles that
the Hall is beginning to look almost as it did when I first went
there as a bride over sixty years ago! Your poor grandfather
would be so disappointed if he could hear you!'

'It's a question of juggling the finances, dear heart,' returned
her grandson, as he moved over to the sideboard to pour drinks
for Standish and himself. 'I already have a mountain of bills to
pay and I must keep enough in the kitty for day-to-day
expenses. However, if we are lucky enough to pull in good
harvests on both estates, I dare say it might be possible to start
on the east wing in the autumn.'

'If only your Uncle Leo had paid heed to my warnings after
that dreadful storm, the poor old Hall wouldn't be in this state
now!' said Lady Isobel, with a plaintive sniff. 'I begged and
begged him to attend to the roof damage, but would he listen?
Oh, no! Said he had better things to do with his money. And
your cousin Simon was little better. I can only thank God that
neither of you is a gambling man!'

'An occupation for fools and tricksters, in my opinion,'
replied Richard, shooting a warning glance at his cousin, whose
cheeks had reddened at the dowager's remark. 'Have no fear,
Grandmama, I promise you that neither Charles nor I has any
intention of following either Simon's or Uncle Leo's example.'

Lady Isobel frowned, but said nothing. Having suffered the
loss of so many males in her family under somewhat unfortunate circumstances, she took considerable consolation from

the knowledge that the current Lord Markfield had few, if any, of his predecessors' bad qualities and was determined to restore the estate to its former grandeur.

Furthermore she was confident that once Richard was set on a course of action almost nothing would change his mind.

Glancing across at him now, as he stood chatting to Charles, the youngest of her grandsons, her eyes softened. The 6th earl certainly cut a fine figure and was very personable to boot. If only he could be persuaded to take himself a wife and start setting up his nursery! Having reached the ripe old age of eighty-one years herself, she was well aware that her time was running out and she dearly wanted to hear again the joyful sounds of childish laughter ringing through the old Hall before she eventually met her Maker.

'You'll stay for dinner, of course?' Richard was asking his cousin.

Placing his empty glass down on the tray, Charles shook his head. 'Better not, old chap,' he replied. 'I promised Mother I'd be back in time to dine with her. It's been over a week now and you know how fidgety she's apt to get if I'm away for more than a few days at a time. I'll look in tomorrow, if I may?'

'Of course—you're always welcome, as I hope you know.'

After escorting his cousin to the door, Richard returned to his grandmother's side. Sitting himself down on the sofa next to her, he leaned back and stretched out his legs, a slight frown on his forehead.

'Take heart, my boy,' Lady Isobel said bracingly. 'At least you don't have to face up to a complaining invalid every time you come home. How Charles finds the patience to deal with that woman is quite beyond me. I have never been able to understand what your Uncle Andrew ever saw in her, for she was always completely useless as a cleric's wife!'

Richard, whose own mother had died when he was just seven years of age, gave a rueful smile. 'Well, it's not as though he can ignore her, is it? Besides which, he's obliged to come down to Southpark to attend to various estate matters.'

'To see how much is in the coffers, you mean!' returned the countess, with some asperity. 'He would do far better to get himself a wife and run his share of the estate as it should be run, instead of gallivanting about town!'

Well aware of what was about to follow his grandmother's observation in regard to his cousin's marital state, the earl, shifting uneasily on his seat, compressed his lips and waited.

'And, much the same applies to you, Richard, my boy,' she then went on. 'Apart from anything else, *you* have the succession to consider! Four changes of title in eight years should be more than enough warning to you. What if you were to die without issue?'

'Well, I did manage to get through an entire war pretty well undamaged,' he felt constrained to point out. 'I dare say I'm good for a few years yet! But, as to marrying, there's time enough for that—besides which, I have far too many other problems to deal with without adding the complications of courtship to the list.'

'That would depend on your requirements, surely?' returned his grandmother. 'In my experience—which is hardly limited—the acquisition of a wealthy wife tends to solve a good many problems!'

Richard stared at her in amazement. 'You're surely not suggesting that I should choose a wife on the strength of her dowry?'

Lady Isobel lifted one shoulder in a graceful shrug. 'It's hardly uncommon, amongst those of our standing, my boy. Always provided that the gel comes from good family stock, of course.' Pausing for a moment, she then continued, in a seemingly offhand manner, 'Added to which, a sizeable injection into those dwindling funds of yours would enable you to concentrate your efforts on that new horse-breeding programme you keep on about. I cannot think of anything that would please your grandfather more than knowing that you had brought the Standish Stud back into the forefront of horse-racing circles once again—he was deeply hurt that not one of his sons showed any interest in what had always been his pride and joy!'

One quick glance at her grandson's expression assured the countess that she had hit the vital spot. 'All those empty stables over at Markfield are just crying out to be restocked,' she added persuasively.

For a moment, Richard regarded her in silence, the hint of a frown sifting across his brow. 'I'm beginning to get the feeling that you won't be satisfied until you see me actually standing at the altar. Indeed, it wouldn't surprise me if you'd already drawn up a list of this Season's likely candidates—the usual progression of whey-faced schoolroom misses out on the catch, I dare say!'

'And *I* dare say that you might expect to do rather better than that!' laughed the countess. 'You are a Standish, after all! All you really need is some suitably endowed young female of acceptable breeding who fancies herself as a countess. Sadly, it would seem that this Season's selection has very little of interest to offer. Why, only the other day I was talking to my stockbroker—trying to find out if any of my shares were worth more than a fig—and he was telling me— *Oh!* Good heavens! I do believe I may have hit upon the very thing!'

Giving little credence to the idea that the dowager might be seriously considering involving herself in his selection of a bride, Richard was, however, somewhat confused by her sudden change of topic. 'Thinking of selling some of your shares?' he queried. 'I doubt if we have enough between us to cover even half of what's needed to fix that roof.'

His grandmother shook her head impatiently. 'Wheatley—my broker—I hear that he has been touting around for a leg-up into the *beau monde* for his girl for over a year now.'

'You're not about to suggest that I shackle myself to a Cit's daughter, I hope!'

As she eyed him uncertainly, Lady Isobel's brow furrowed. 'Whilst it is perfectly true that Giles Wheatley is a man of business, he also happens to be positively dripping with lard. Besides which, it just so happens that the girl's grandmother was a Coverdale.'

'I'm afraid the name means nothing to me,' said Richard, giving a careless shrug. 'So, what's she like—this daughter, I mean? She must be something of an anathema, since your man hasn't been able to palm her off for a twelvemonth or more!'

'That's as may be,' returned the countess, with some asperity. 'She is, however, her father's only heir and, apart from the fact of her dowry being something in the region of fifty thousand pounds, it would seem that her background is reasonably sound. In point of fact, if I remember correctly, I was slightly acquainted with her grandmother, Lady Joanna Coverdale, before she became Countess of Ashington. Be that as it may, it seems that Lord Ashington disowned their daughter—Louisa, I believe her name was—when she eloped with his accountant's clerk—who is now my very wealthy stockbroker, Giles Wheatley. They—the Ashingtons, that is—died in a carriage accident shortly after the gel ran off and, since the estate was entailed to some distant cousin in the Antipodes, the daughter was left with nothing.' Pausing reflectively, she then added, 'Nevertheless, it seems that the pair did very well for themselves over the years, although it appears that Wheatley's wife and son both died a couple of years ago. Can't say that I have ever set eyes on the girl herself, but she is sure to have been brought up in a very proper manner, her mother being who she was.'

'Well, there must be something deucedly odd about her,' remarked her grandson, who was not at all happy with the direction in which this conversation was heading. 'Plenty of fellows would be willing to sell their souls for fifty thousand!'

'Perhaps she is just difficult to please?' ventured the countess. 'Her father is certainly wealthy enough for her to pick and choose—not that she will have been presented with a particularly inspiring set of individuals, if the usual set of fortune-hunters is still out on the prowl. You are sure to have far more chance with her than any of those ramshackle bucks.'

'You are too kind!' the earl ground out. 'However, I am not sure that I care to join the ranks of such dubious company.'

Lady Isobel picked up her teacup and sipped tentatively at its now lukewarm contents. 'Well, it's entirely up to you, of course. However, I cannot help thinking that a readymade bride would certainly absolve you from having to go through all that tiresome business of formal introductions and correct procedures at Almack's and so on.'

Although the idea of being obliged to contemplate marriage at all at this point in his life was sufficiently galling, without the added prospect of being saddled with a bride whose attributes had, it would seem, already failed to capture the interest of several previous suitors, the earl's hitherto sceptical dismissal of his grandmother's suggestions was now beginning to be replaced by the uncomfortable feeling that the dowager might actually be correct in her summation of the situation.

He was well aware that few men of his station married for love, an amicable mutual tolerance between the two parties being all that was usually required—and there was always the possibility that this Wheatley girl might not be quite as unprepossessing as she sounded, after all! It would mean giving up his occasional visits to Rachel Cummings, of course, although, in the event, that might not be such a bad thing, since that lady was beginning to develop rather expensive tastes of late—those ruby earrings he had recently presented her with had been a trifle extravagant, given his current financial position. Aside from which, the temporary cessation of his carnal delectations was a small enough price to pay for the restoration of the Markfield estate! Indeed, the very idea of being able to devote all his own resources to re-establishing the Standish Stud was beginning to prove an almost irresistible inducement.

Picking up his glass, he strode over to the window and stared pensively across the wide expanse of fresh green lawn that swept down to the river, which separated Westpark from its parent estate of Markfield—so very different from the baked and arid plains of the Iberian Peninsula where he had spent much of the past six years. The lush green landscapes of the English countryside were, as he knew, entirely dependent upon the weather, rainfall in particular. Just as rain could affect the outcome of a battle, so also could it affect the success of a harvest. He was well aware that his plans to utilise the returns from the forthcoming harvest to settle his outstanding bills lay very much at the mercy of the weather. And, given that they were still only in April, he was also shrewd enough to recognise that some of his creditors might be less than willing to hold out until August. Meanwhile, just the rumour of a possible alliance with a wealthy spouse could be all that was needed to deter further financial harassment. It would certainly make good sense to have, as it were, a second line of defence. After all, he then reasoned, it should not be too difficult to bring any such temporary relationship to a close, since it appeared that the female in question was merely out to gain herself a title and he was quite certain that there were any number of other fellows around who would be more than happy to fulfil that requirement.

As a Field Officer he had been used to choosing courses of action based on the information to hand and when timing was of the essence.

There was little doubt that this present situation required such an instant decision.

Draining his glass in one swift gulp, he swung round to face his grandmother.

'Very well, you may go and see your Mr Wheatley and inform him that I'm willing to throw my hat into his ring.'

Chapter Two

'Do come away from the window, Lottie, I beg of you,' implored Helena. 'It is not at all seemly to be seen twitching at the curtains in that manner!'

'But are you not in the least bit interested in seeing what he looks like?' queried her cousin Charlotte, reluctantly turning away from her self-appointed vigil at the window that over-looked the front doorstep.

'Not in the slightest,' returned Helena, with a weary sigh. 'He will be much the same as all the others—rude, conceited and feigning an interest in me simply in order to get his hands on my dowry. If it were not for the fact that it upsets Papa so, I should have refused to go through this charade again. He seems incapable of understanding how very demeaning it is for me.'

As she watched Helena continue to ply her needle in silence, Lottie could not help but feel a certain sympathy for her cousin's unusual plight. The Wheatleys' runaway marriage had left their daughter stranded between the two distinctly separate worlds of upper and middle class. The young men of her father's acquaintance considered her too far above their touch and those who moved in the circle on which her mother had turned her back all those years ago were not of a mind to consider the girl at all. Not until Mr Wheatley had, by word of mouth, advertised his present intention, that was, and, as Lottie well knew, this obsession of his had developed only as a direct result of dear Aunt Louisa's death.

'Perhaps I could try talking to him,' she offered hesitantly. 'If I explained how very much you have taken against the whole idea since that unpleasant business with Lord Barrington—'

'No, Lottie! Please do not!' urged Helena, her clear blue eyes widening with concern. 'Papa got into such a dreadful state over that incident and you know that Doctor Redfern said that it was not good for him to be upset—his heart will simply not stand up to another attack.'

'But what will you do this time?' asked her cousin, perplexed.

An impish smile spread over Helena's attractive features. 'Oh, have no fear,' she replied complacently. 'I shall be sure to think of something. Fortunately, these town dandies—the ones with whom I have come into contact, anyway—hardly seem to be blessed with much in the way of intelligence, so it does not take a genius to find a dozen ways to send them packing!'

'It is a good thing Uncle Giles does not realise what a minx his daughter is turning into,' chuckled Lottie, as she resumed her seat at the window and picked up her book.

'I just wish that I could persuade him that I have no desire to wed,' sighed her cousin. 'It is not as though I have any need to find a husband but, ever since Jason's death and then poor dear Mama following him so soon after, Papa has had this bee in his bonnet about failing to give me my rightful place in society. I ask you! As though you and I could not rub along very nicely together if only he would allow us to do so!'

And, as the well-remembered image of her teasingly light-hearted elder brother once more invaded her thoughts, Helena's eyes grew moist. Just four short years had passed since Jason had gone off to war, so handsome in his scarlet regimentals and so full of confidence. Sadly, a mere six months later, he had been shipped home so grievously wounded that, even with his mother's devoted care, there was never any real chance of his recovery and, although he had clung courageously to life for several weeks, he had eventually slipped away.

Mrs Wheatley's careless disregard for her own health during her son's illness had resulted in her contracting the bout of pneumonia from which she had never recovered. The shock of his wife's death, less than a year after that of their beloved son, had exacerbated Mr Wheatley's prevailing heart condition, obliging him to take to his bed on more than one occasion since her passing.

From Helena's point of view, these enforced periods of rest had enabled her father to spend rather too much time dwelling upon what he considered to be an unacceptable uncertainty regarding his remaining child's future. His late wife's ostracism from her social circle had always weighed heavily with him, and he had continually held himself to blame, despite Mrs Wheatley's laughing insistence that, having happily relinquished her own title all those years ago, such things mattered not a jot to her. However, now that Helena was all that he had left in the world, Mr Wheatley was determined to do his utmost to—as he saw it—retrieve the situation for her sake.

Recognising that, after the death of her mother, Helena would be in need of a female companion and disliking the idea of bringing a stranger into his house, Mr Wheatley had invited his sister's eldest daughter, Charlotte, to make her home with them. Lottie, being one of a family of seven children, had been more than delighted to accept her uncle's offer, for with it had come the promise of a room of her own and a generous quarterly allowance, as well as an opportunity to move into a social circle that, whilst not being of the highest, was certainly considerably removed from that of her own country-vicarage upbringing.

However, despite being more than two years older than Helena, Lottie lacked her cousin's fine judgement and presence of mind, possibly due in part to the fact that she had not had the benefit of the highly expensive schooling that the younger girl had received and, although Helena loved her dearly, she was frequently obliged to take Lottie gently to task in order to curb her somewhat impulsive behaviour.

Disregarding Helena's constant pleadings that she had no wish to marry into high society and was perfectly happy to remain as she was, Mr Wheatley, concerned that his daughter had reached the ripe old age of twenty-two without so much as a single suitable offer, had made up his mind to take matters into his own hands. In reaching this conclusion, it had pleased him to ignore several tentative proposals he had received from various of his city acquaintances on their sons' behalves since, despite his own relatively humble beginnings in the world of commerce, his aspirations for both of his offspring had always been somewhat more high-flown. Hence his current ambition to secure his daughter's elevation.

Observing that her cousin was, once more, deeply absorbed in her sewing, Lottie was unable to resist taking the occasional quick peek out of the window along the path that led to the front gate, in the hope of catching sight of this new contender for Helena's hand. Being an inveterate reader of romantic novels, she had developed the notion that it was simply a matter of time before Mr Right would ride out of the blue and capture her beloved cousin's heart. For, quite apart from the fact that Helena was possessed of the most generous of natures and—as a result of having lost her brother in so tragic a manner—given to devoting much of her free time to the welfare of the many crippled or displaced soldiers who roamed the capital daily, she was, without doubt, an extremely attractive young woman. With shining russet-brown curls that framed the creamy complexion of her face, expressive violet-blue eyes and the neatest of noses, she was, in her cousin's eyes at least, quite without equal. Lottie, although she had inherited her mother's light-hearted and easygoing personality, had also been, somewhat unfortunately perhaps, blessed with her father's somewhat Romanesque features and, well aware that she herself lacked the physical attributes of her storybook heroines, had long ago given up any thoughts of meeting her own Prince Charming. Instead, finding herself not entirely unsympathetic towards her uncle's attitude regarding his daughter's continued single state, she was quite content to spend a good deal of her time indulging in her own private fantasy that, any day now, the ultimate *beau idéal* would arrive and sweep Helena off her feet.

Therefore, when her eyes did finally alight upon the carriage that drew up at the gateway to the Wheatley house, she was obliged to push her disappointment firmly to one side. For, instead of the showy, dashing carriage of the sort with which each of Helena's three previous potential suitors had equipped himself, today's visitor had arrived in nothing more than a common hackney carriage!

'I perceive that Lord Markfield has arrived, Nell,' she began, her tone non-committal but then, as the earl's rangy figure hove more closely into her view, her eyes brightened and she leant forward with deepening interest.

'Lottie, please!' urged her cousin. 'If the gentleman should happen to look up and catch you staring, it might well give him the impression that I have been eagerly awaiting his attendance! With Papa in his present frame of mind, I swear that it will be difficult enough to turn this one off but if, in addition, I have to cope with the fellow's puffed-up supposition that I am on tenterhooks to meet him…!'

'I'm sorry, Nell,' said Lottie contritely, as she pulled back from the window. 'I don't think he saw me—but I have to tell you,' she added, in a breathless rush, 'he really is most awfully good-looking!'

'And, very probably, just plain awful!' replied Helena tartly, folding away her sewing and getting to her feet. 'Nevertheless, I suppose I shall have to go and tidy myself up in readiness for when Papa summons me to meet the odious sycophant!'

Richard, who had indeed caught a glimpse of Lottie peering down at him from the window of the morning room, suffered a moment's irresolution as he approached the house but, steeling himself, he remembered his grandmother's words about the Standish Stud and, striding purposefully up the steps to the front door, pulled at the bell knob.

He was ushered into what appeared to be a study and was pleasantly surprised to find that he was not confronted with the brash, modern furnishings that he had, for some reason, associated with the *nouveau riche*. Instead, the room was filled with comfortable, well-worn pieces that he recognised as being of very good quality.

Seated at the large mahogany desk that dominated the room was a rather stout gentleman with a florid complexion. At Richard's entrance, he rose to his feet and offered his hand.

'Your lordship,' he said, inclining his head. 'I am very pleased to meet you.'

Mr Wheatley's voice, Richard noted, as he took the seat that his host had indicated to him, was nicely modulated and, relieved that the man was exhibiting neither servility towards his rank nor—and what he had dreaded more—the superior air of one who has all the cards at his disposal, he accepted the drink that Mr Wheatley offered him and leaned back in his chair.

'You will no doubt have some questions that you wish to put to me,' he ventured slowly. The man's first impression of him, he knew, would be vital and, since he had made up his mind that, come hell or high water, he would do everything in his power to succeed in this undertaking, he forced his lips into some semblance of a smile.

Mr Wheatley waved his hand dismissively. 'That will not be necessary, your lordship,' he replied. 'I have already made it my business to enquire into your background and find myself more than satisfied with your credentials. Let us proceed.'

Extracting a single piece of paper out of a folder, he placed it down on the desk in front of him and began, 'In my taking what you might well consider to be this rather extraordinary course of action to find my daughter a suitable husband, you must realise that I have only her best interests at heart. She will be in possession of a considerable fortune when I am gone and I am sure that you will understand why I feel that it is my duty to ensure that she is not taken advantage of by some unscrupulous scoundrel.'

'Naturally,' replied Richard smoothly. 'As her father, I would expect nothing less of you.'

'I have drawn up this agreement,' continued Wheatley, nodding to the sheet of paper under his hand. 'It contains the main qualities that I require in any prospective candidate for my daughter's hand—you will, no doubt, have heard that you are by no means the first such contender. I myself do not consider that these requirements to be particularly onerous but, for some reason, it appears to be increasingly difficult to find someone who is able to fulfil my expectations.'

Urging Richard to cast his eye over the several clauses therein, he pushed the sheet of paper across the desk. 'It will save time if you read the thing yourself, my lord,' he said. 'If there are any points that you do not understand or on which you are not prepared to agree, we need not waste any more of each other's time.'

Richard picked up the document and began to peruse it. It appeared to be a contract of sorts—an agreement that was to last for a period of three months, during which time the candidate for Miss Wheatley's hand would be required to introduce her into his circle of friends—given that her father found them acceptable—acquire the necessary entry and escort her to as many of the Season's upper-class functions as the time allowed. During this period, all expenses would be met, including that of furnishing the applicant with a suitable wardrobe, should he be in need of such refurbishment.

Whilst it was clear that the proposed schedule was one that might be achieved with very little difficulty on his part, he still could not help feeling that, by entering into such a calculated agreement, he would be in grave danger of signing away the last vestige of his self-respect. There was no question that the cost of the renovations at Markfield Hall had reached a crisis point and to be given another chance to try and re-establish the Standish Stud would be a dream come true but, as the Bible said, *'For what shall it profit a man to gain the whole world, if he loses his own soul?'*

Very gradually, a deep frown began to develop on his forehead as he contemplated the document and he was just in the process of questioning whether he could really bring himself to sign such an ignominious agreement, when an odd sound from across the desk caught his attention. Looking up, he encountered Wheatley's frozen grimace. The man's face was sweating profusely and he seemed to be having difficulty breathing; his hands were frantically tearing at his intricately tied neckcloth, in a vain endeavour to loosen the offending article.

At once, Richard leapt to his feet. 'My dear sir,' he gasped in dismay, 'are you ill?'

In answer, Wheatley's eyes bulged, a weak gurgle issued from his lips and, to his visitor's consternation, he slumped forwards on to his desk, his outflung hands knocking over the inkstand and scattering his pile of papers in all directions.

Anxiously casting around for the bell-rope, the earl located it on the wall next to the marble fireplace and, having given it two hefty pulls, hurried back to Wheatley's side where, gently lifting the man's wrist away from the pool of ink into which it had fallen, he felt for some signs of life.

He was just beginning to discern a faint thready pulse beat when the door opened and a footman entered.

'You must send at once for a doctor,' barked the earl, without looking up. 'Your master appears to have suffered some sort of attack.'

With a horrified gasp, the servant backed out of the room and hurried away to carry out the order.

Richard, meanwhile, was doing his best to make the old gentleman more comfortable. He had managed to untie the knot in

Wheatley's neckcloth and was endeavouring to unwind the linen band when he found himself violently thrust to one side, almost causing him to overbalance.

'What have you done to him?' an irate female voice demanded.

'Hold hard, madam!' he protested, ruefully rubbing his elbow, which had struck the corner of Wheatley's high-backed chair in the foregoing scuffle. 'I must assure you that Mr Wheatley's collapse was not of my making!'

'Get out!' snapped Helena, as she knelt beside her father's chair trying to get some response from her unconscious parent. 'I beg of you—just go!'

Biting back the sharp put-down that had been on his lips, the earl, having quickly reached the conclusion that his presence seemed to be causing more of a hindrance than help, turned sharply on his heel and made for the open door. Clicking his fingers at the footman in the hall, he retrieved his hat and gloves and, without waiting to be helped into his greatcoat, left the house without a backward glance.

Chapter Three

'And she refused to allow you to explain yourself?' exclaimed Lady Isobel in amazement, having listened to her grandson's recital of the afternoon's extraordinary events.

'She told me to get out,' replied Richard curtly. 'In the circumstances, I could hardly argue with the girl, now could I?'

Striving to hide her disappointment over the fact that her resourceful scheme had gone so badly awry, the dowager pursed her lips. 'I take it that you were not impressed with the gel? Was she as ill favoured as you had supposed?'

'I was hardly given the opportunity to study her in depth.' The earl shrugged. 'I merely caught sight of her peering out of an upper window as I was arriving—she looked to be a plain, gawky sort of creature and, of course, she had her back to me in the study, so I was unable to determine the full extent of her charms. However, her manner did seem to be singularly unattractive and I have to say that it came as no great surprise to me to learn that she has already managed to frighten off no less than three aspiring suitors.'

'Such a pity,' sighed the dowager. 'All our hopes dashed at the first hurdle.' Then, eyeing her grandson speculatively, she added, 'Although, it would be perfectly in order for you to pay a further visit to enquire as to how the poor man does.'

'I would just as soon not, if it's all the same to you,' returned Richard tersely. 'That agreement that your Mr Wheatley wanted me to sign was quite enough to put me off, thank you very much. The fellow seems to be looking for a veritable gigolo! I'll have you know that I still have some pride left!'

'Then we must hope that your resolve remains just as implacable when the bailiffs start to dun us for money that we don't have,' returned Lady Isobel with a resigned sniff. Then, after a slight pause, she continued in a somewhat plaintive tone, 'And, of course, I shall not press you, my boy. It is your heritage, after all. I, myself, will soon be dust and ashes!' And, dabbing affectedly at her eyes, she gave a heavy sigh. 'I had, of course, always supposed that I would be buried in the Hall's own chapel, alongside your dear dead grandfather!'

Well acquainted with his grandmother's affectations, Richard had long ago learned when appeasement was the better part of confrontation. Furthermore, since the latest request from one of his creditors had been couched in a somewhat more belligerent manner than those received previously, it was reasonable to assume that should one creditor decide to take immediate action, the rest would be sure to follow like a pack of wolves, spelling financial disaster.

'Very well, you old harridan, I will give your blessed scheme another try!'

'That is very sensible of you, Richard,' said his grandmother, brightening. 'One ought not to allow one's personal feelings to interfere with the ultimate objective. Besides which, it is infinitely possible that you might find that the Wheatley gel has hidden talents.'

'Possible, but highly unlikely,' Richard ground out, as he made his way towards the salon door. 'But, since it is, apparently, her father's money that I need to keep in my sights, I suppose I shall have to do my best to try to worm my way into the creature's good books—regardless of her decidedly unattractive disposition.'

But, as he left the room, his jaw tightened and, under his breath, he murmured to himself, 'Dear God above! What sort of a fellow is this business turning me into?'

The next morning, however, the earl was not a little surprised to receive a note from Miss Wheatley asking him if he would be so good as to call into Cadogan Place that afternoon. Although he had decided to comply with his grandmother's suggestion, this timely invitation now meant that he would no longer have to return to the house 'cap in hand,' so to speak, for which reprieve he was profoundly thankful.

Therefore, it was in a considerably lighter frame of mind that, sharp on the dot of three o'clock that afternoon, he presented himself at the Wheatley house, whereupon he was straight away shown up to a pleasantly appointed sitting room on the first floor.

At his entrance, two equally elegantly clad young ladies turned to greet him; Miss Wheatley, he presumed, as he executed his bow, being the aquiline-featured, mousy-haired female whom he had spotted at the window on his previous visit. However, upon raising his eyes, he met the challenging stare of her very striking companion who, having returned to her own seat, indicated that he should take the chair opposite.

'It was very good of your lordship to come,' said this chestnut-haired vision, in a clear, mellow tone of voice which, noted the earl, his temporary loss of composure now restored, was quite as attractive as its owner and who, it was now becoming increasingly obvious to him, was in fact the daughter of the house.

'Not at all, Miss Wheatley,' he eventually found himself saying. 'It is my pleasure, I assure you. I would, of course, have called in any case, to enquire after your father's health. I trust that he suffered no serious hurt from yesterday's unfortunate incident?'

'Thank you for your concern, my lord,' she replied coolly while, at the same time, beckoning Lottie to come forwards. 'I

am happy to say that he does, indeed, seem to be on the mend—
please allow me to introduce my cousin and companion, Miss
Charlotte Daniels.'

Rising to his feet, Richard bent his head and raised Lottie's
outstretched hand to his lips, which unexpected gallantry
caused that young woman's cheeks to turn bright scarlet and
her heart to flutter quite atrociously. Bobbing a swift curtsy, she
returned hurriedly to her seat where, still overcome, she took
refuge in her book.

Finding herself somewhat irritated, not only as a result of
her cousin's gauche behaviour, but rather more so by Markfield's extravagantly high-flown gesture, Helena, who had been
agreeably surprised when the earl had walked into the room,
was beginning to think that he was no better than any of her
previous would-be suitors.

When she had arrived in the study on the previous afternoon
to find him bent over her unconscious parent, other than
pushing the visitor to one side, she had given him scant regard.
Lottie had, of course, regaled her with enthusiastic descriptions
of his dark, wavy hair, shapely limbs and broad-shouldered
elegance, all of which Helena, for the most part, had ignored.
In fact, had it not been for Mr Wheatley's insistence that she
should write and ask Markfield to pay another call, there, as
far as she was concerned, the matter would have rested.
However, loath to cause her father any unnecessary anxiety in
his present fragile state, Helena felt that she had no choice but
to obey his instructions that, since his own consultation with
Markfield had been all but finalised before his seizure, she
herself should complete the interview, which merely needed the
earl's signature on the document. Once this was obtained,
Helena knew that she was then committed to yet another dreary
round of accompanying the man to any tedious function to
which he had managed to procure an invitation. Having already
undergone similar ordeals with Markfield's three predecessors—as undistinguished a set of no-hopers as one might ever

expect to come across—the prospect of wasting still more of her time in another such pointless exercise filled her with the utmost despondency.

Nevertheless, after she had taken stock of her visitor, Helena found herself experiencing the oddest sense of disappointment that this latest contender for her hand had shown himself to be just as shallow as his peers.

Richard, having resumed his seat, was waiting patiently for his hostess to offer some explanation for her note. He knew that it was hardly likely that she had invited him here to apologise for her untoward behaviour on the previous afternoon and, since he had already expressed his regret over Wheatley's mishap, he was beginning to feel that, other than the usual trite remarks about the weather, there was little that he could add to the conversation.

Uncomfortably aware of his intent gaze, Helena felt a warm flush creep across her cheeks and, vexed that his scrutiny should have such a remarkable effect upon her normally calm demeanour, she braced herself to carry out her father's wishes and decided to go straight into the attack.

'May I take it that you have read these requirements?' she enquired, gesturing to a small table nearby upon which lay not only the dreaded document from Wheatley's study but, in addition, an inkwell, a sandpot and a pair of newly sharpened quills.

'Oh, I hardly think that this is a suitable subject—' he began, somewhat taken aback at such a direct approach to what was, after all, a rather delicate matter and one that was, insofar as he was concerned, strictly between the girl's parent and himself.

'Nonsense!' she interrupted briskly. 'It is as much my affair as it is your own! Besides which, my father has expressed the wish that the business should be completed without further ado and so—if you are of a mind to agree to his terms…?'

Frowning, the earl flicked his eyes over to Helena's companion who, he saw with some exasperation, was gazing at him in breathless fascination. Getting to his feet, he crossed the short distance between himself and his hostess and, lowering his voice, murmured, 'I am inclined to think that a little more privacy might be in order for a discussion such as this, would you not agree?'

As the barely discernible scent of his lemon-verbena cologne wafted across her nostrils, Helena felt her pulses quickening, immediately causing her to reach the conclusion that this clearly practised popinjay seemed to be attempting, in her father's absence, to gain some sort of advantage over her undoubted lack of experience in handling transactions of this kind. An indignant spurt of fury ran through her and, leaning well away from his undeniably compelling magnetism, she waved her hand dismissively.

'That will not be necessary, your lordship,' she said, in as airy a tone as she could conjure up. 'You may rest assured that my cousin is perfectly well acquainted with my father's plans for my future.' And, picking up one of the pens, she held it out to him. 'Will you sign first or shall I? My father has given me his authority.'

For, possibly, the first time in the whole of his twenty-nine years Richard found himself at something of a loss. It was becoming increasingly apparent to him that Lady Isobel's stockbroker's daughter was no ordinary title seeker. Indeed, the young lady appeared to have all the necessary qualities one might look for, if one were truly in search of a wife and, in any other situation, he might well have been tempted into getting to know her better. Nevertheless, since he considered his word far above any mere signature on a document, and despite the impending disastrous consequences of his actions, he was certainly not about to enter into any sort of written agreement.

'Lord Markfield?'

Conscious that both of the ladies were watching his movements intently, the earl's lips tightened. 'I fear that I shall have to decline your father's offer, Miss Wheatley,' he said abruptly. 'I find that I am, after all, unable to meet his—requirements.

Please forgive me for wasting so much of your time.' With which, he executed a stiff bow and turned to leave the room.

In consternation, Helena leapt to her feet and attempted to bar his way. 'But you cannot mean to leave!' she gasped. 'That is—I gave Papa my word that I would soon have the matter tied up—may I be permitted to know what has caused you to change your mind?'

Looking down at the girl's lovely face, with her exquisite blue eyes now so full of concern, Richard experienced a sharp pang of regret that he had not met her under more favourable circumstances. Immediately putting aside that obstructive thought, however, he made some attempt to formulate an adequate reply to her question.

'I have not exactly changed my mind, Miss Wheatley,' he began. 'As it happens, it was not fully made up in the first place.'

'Am I to take it then that you have been offended by my forthrightness?' she faltered, suddenly conscious of the fact that she should, perhaps, have waited until the earl had signed the agreement before she set about demolishing his pretensions.

A swift smile creased his face. 'No such thing, I promise you,' he assured her. 'Your candour is most refreshing.'

Although deeply perplexed, Helena found herself strangely unwilling to allow him to leave before she had discovered the true reason for his *volte-face*.

'Then, *why*?' she persisted, steadfastly ignoring the sound of her cousin's sharp intake of breath.

Richard hesitated momentarily then, with a slight lift of his shoulders, said, 'The fact of the matter is, Miss Wheatley, that I find I am having considerable difficulty in coming to terms with the idea of being—bought off—if you will excuse the expression!'

She flushed. 'But I was under the impression that that was the whole point of the scheme!' she rejoined. 'Your title for my hand—or rather—the fortune that goes along with it! Why did you offer yourself up if you find the whole idea so repellent?'

Shaking his head, the earl stepped away from her. 'I fear that it is far too complicated a matter to go into here, Miss Wheatley so, if you will excuse me, I will bid you "good day" and thank you again for your patience.'

'No, wait, please!' exclaimed Helena, now in some desperation. The thought of having to tell her father that she had failed to carry out his mission did not sit readily with her and, racking her brain for some sort of inspiration, a possible way out of the dilemma occurred to her. 'I do have another suggestion—if you will hear me out?'

Richard gave an impatient shrug. 'Naturally, I will listen to what you have to say, Miss Wheatley,' he said wearily. 'But, I must assure you that it will not alter my decision.'

'You cannot possibly know that until you have heard what I am about to suggest!' she flashed back at him. 'Now, do sit down and hear me out, I beg you.'

Stifling the smile that was threatening to form, the earl returned to his seat where, leaning back, he folded his arms and waited expectantly. He was not a little intrigued as to why the lady should be so anxious to stay his departure since, as far as he had been able to gather from his grandmother, she had given every one of her previous suitors very short shrift before he had been sent on the rightabout. Not that he numbered himself among such fly-by-nights as Barrington, Arnold and Farley, he was quick to remind himself. In fact, having spent some time considering the various snippets of information that the dowager had imparted, it had not taken him long to arrive at the conclusion that Miss Helena Wheatley was, possibly, not altogether enamoured of her father's plans for her future and might well have been going to considerable lengths to sabotage them. Her initial coolness towards him on his arrival had reinforced this belief and had, in the end, gone some way in strengthening his resolve to quit. Although he was achingly aware of the highly parlous state of his affairs, he could see no reason for compounding an already shameful situation by setting himself up as a target for general ridicule.

Helena took a deep breath. 'I completely understand your reticence, my lord,' she began. 'But you must understand that I cannot bring myself to tell my father that his efforts have been to no avail. I have, however, come up with a sort of compromise—a solution that may prove to be of benefit to both of us.'

One of Richard's brows rose imperceptibly. It was becoming clear he had not been wrong in his surmise. However, he opted not to comment and waited for Helena to continue.

'You must correct me if I have gained the wrong impression, my lord,' she said. 'But it is my understanding that, whenever a gentleman's name is linked to that of an heiress, his creditors seem perfectly content to hold back from their demands—banking, no doubt, on the possibility of acquiring a good deal more in the way of extra interest and so on?'

The earl stiffened. 'You are remarkably well informed, Miss Wheatley,' he drawled. 'But I still do not see…?'

'I was merely trying to point out that there are certain advantages to be gained from even a short-term relationship—two or three weeks, for instance?'

At Richard's continued expression of incomprehension, Helena then leaned forwards and, clasping her hands together, entreated him, 'What I am asking you, my lord, is whether you would be willing to consider fulfilling some of my father's requirements for that length of time—just long enough for him to recover sufficiently for me to explain the situation to him?'

'To which particular requirements are you referring?' he asked suspiciously.

'Well, for instance, if you would be prepared to escort me to just one or two simple affairs—you would have no need to sign anything, of course—I could tell Papa that you did not deem it necessary to put your signature to the document until you find yourself obliged to ask him to furnish you with extra funds—any expense you do incur I can easily reimburse you out of my own pocket.'

'I trust that I have not yet sunk to the level that would require me to accept money from a lady,' said Richard firmly, as he rose once more to his feet. 'I am sorry, Miss Wheatley, but, in my opinion, the whole idea is totally impracticable!'

Her lips trembling, Helena stood up and faced him. 'I do not believe so, my lord,' she replied in a toneless voice. 'But, thank you for hearing me out—I shall not take up any more of your time. Please allow me to see you to the door.'

Taking one look at her set, white face, the earl was filled with remorse. 'I am sure that, when you have explained to your father, he will understand the situation, my dear,' he said kindly, finding himself reluctant to leave the girl in such a dismal frame of mind.

'Then you clearly do not know my uncle!'

Charlotte Daniels, outraged at Markfield's casual dismissal of her beloved Helena's suggestion, had thrust herself between the pair and, ignoring her cousin's exclamation of dismay, proceeded, in no uncertain terms, to berate the astonished earl.

'How can you be so insensitive!' she exploded, wagging her finger under his nose. 'Is it beyond you to see that Helena is out of her mind with worry about her papa? She will not tell you, so I shall!'

'Lottie, please!' begged Helena, attempting to pull her cousin aside. 'His lordship wishes to leave!'

'Not until I have said my piece!' countered Lottie obstinately and, turning back to Richard, she informed him that, contrary to what Helena had given him to understand, Mr Wheatley was, in fact, a very sick man and this latest attack had been described by his physician as extremely grave. If there were to be any hope of a recovery for him, he would be required to remain in his bed for at least two weeks, during which time it was vital that he had no excitation of any sort.

'And, if you imagine that being told that you have left without signing his precious document does not qualify as excitation,' she finished scornfully, 'then I must tell you that you are fair and far out!'

Somewhat taken aback by the unexpected onslaught, Richard's eyes travelled slowly from the scarlet-faced female in front of him over to Helena's frozen expression. The rigid set of her shoulders told him how deeply mortified she was by her cousin's interference.

'You really should have told me how serious your father's condition is,' he said gently.

She gave a little shrug. 'Would it have made any difference, my lord? It is clear that you had already made up your mind to refuse his offer before you arrived.'

'That much is true,' he was obliged to acknowledge, as he stepped towards her and reached out to take her by the hands. 'Nevertheless, Miss Wheatley, I must point out that being in receipt of such important information might well have caused me to give more serious consideration to your own request—I would not be altogether happy to find that your father's recovery had suffered any sort of setback as a result of any action of mine.'

At the gentle pressure of his fingers on her wrists, Helena seemed to feel her heart skipping several beats and, colouring faintly, she stammered, 'It was not my intention to make you feel under any sort of obligation, sir.'

Raising one eyebrow, Richard gave a rueful grin. 'That may not have been your intention, Miss Wheatley,' he said softly, 'but that is exactly how I do feel and—if you believe that it will help your father's case—you have my promise that I shall do my best to advance your little scheme!'

Chapter Four

'Good heavens, Rick! Please tell me that you are joking!'

Carefully placing his glass on to the table in front of him, Charles Standish leaned forwards and stared at his cousin in astonishment.

'You can't mean to tell us that you're actually prepared to go ahead with this chit's bizarre proposition?'

Wincing at the other man's somewhat discourteous reference to the far from chit-like Miss Wheatley, Richard took a deep breath and began, once again, to explain to his three companions the reason for his unexpected change of heart.

Standish and the earl, along with Sir Peter Braithwaite and the Honourable Geoffrey Fairfax, both ex-army colleagues of Markfield's, were seated in the smoking room of Brooks's, currently their preferred choice of venue.

'Do pay attention, old man!' groaned Braithwaite, as he signalled to the barman to bring another bottle. 'Rick has already told you twice that the caper is merely for a couple of weeks and, it does seem to me that, as his friends, it is up to us to rally round him. Putting the word around that he could be about to shackle himself to this Wheatley girl might well stave off the bulk of his creditors while he regroups his resources.'

Then, turning to Richard, he asked sympathetically, 'What

would you have us do, old chap? I take it that you mean to have a stab at getting this Miss Wheatley accepted by the *ton*? Is the girl really up to it, do you suppose? It can be a pretty gruelling experience, you know—I understand that my cousin had a devilish hard time of it last year—in spite of the fact that Emily Cowper is one of her godmothers.'

Richard sighed. 'I realise that it is going to be far from easy, but I aim to give it my best shot. Grandmama has asked if I could bring Miss Wheatley to meet her this afternoon…' He paused for a moment, then continued manfully. 'However, since I accompanied her ladyship up to town in her barouche, I appear to have a slight problem regarding a decent conveyance. Would it be too much to ask if you could spare me the loan of one of your carriages, Peter?'

'Take your pick, old friend,' returned Braithwaite immediately. 'There is no one I would rather trust with my cattle than yourself. We can cut across to the mews right now, if you are of a mind?'

Not to be outdone, Fairfax, taking out his pocket book, added, 'If you give me the young lady's address, I shall get the mater to send an invite to her to attend her next soirée—Cadogan Place, you say? Pretty respectable part of town, at any event.'

'You really are the best of fellows,' said Richard, much moved by his friends' generosity and greatly relieved to know that they were prepared to give him their wholehearted support in this outrageous venture. And if, in addition to salving his guilty conscience to some degree, the undertaking also had the effect of staving off some of his creditors temporarily, then that could be no bad thing. As things stood at the moment, even two weeks' grace would bring about a brief but welcome respite, given that the estate's next quarter-day was just around the corner, heralding a much-needed input from its tenant farmers.

The earl's arrival at the front doorstep of Cadogan Place that afternoon was more than enough to cause Charlotte who, despite Helena's pleas, had taken up her usual position of 'look-out' at the window of the first-floor morning room, to jump up and down in absolute glee the minute her eyes fell upon the spanking pair of matching bays and the shiny maroon equipage to which they were harnessed.

'Oh, Nell!' she squealed, quite overcome, as she took in Markfield's appearance. Clad in a superbly cut jacket of blue superfine and pale grey pantaloons, his tasselled black Hessians polished to perfection, he leapt lightly down from the driving seat, tossed the reins to the waiting groom, mounted the short flight of steps two at a time and knocked briskly on the front door. 'He really is just too divine!'

'I trust that you do not intend to swoon at his feet as soon as he comes in,' sighed Helena who, truth to tell, had herself been itching to peep out of the window. 'What sort of carriage has he arrived in this time?'

'I believe it is what is known as a phaeton—oh!' Deeply disappointed, Charlotte spun round and confronted her cousin. 'But it only seats two, Nell—I understood that I was going to accompany you to visit her ladyship?'

'That was my intention,' admitted Helena, somewhat crestfallen. 'I must confess that I had not expected to have to beard the dragon on my own.'

She was now in something of a quandary, having rather taken it for granted that the dowager's summons must, as a matter of course, include her companion. More to the point, she could not help feeling that, in view of the recent Barrington incident, her father would not be altogether pleased to hear that his daughter had gone off in a carriage to an unknown destination with a relative stranger. However, she had little time to dwell on this perplexing matter, since Hayward was, at this very moment, ushering Markfield into the room.

As she rose to her feet to greet him, the swift appraisal she managed to give him before he bent over her hand caused her to experience a not dissimilar sensation to her cousin's but, striving to maintain the ladylike detachment that her mother had spent a good many years instilling into her, she merely inclined her head and bade the earl 'good afternoon.'

He, in turn, was equally gratified as he took in Helena's appearance. In an elegantly cut walking-dress of vivid turquoise that enhanced the blueness of her eyes, its fine, soft wool seeming to mould itself to her undeniably shapely form, it was clear that, if this outfit was an example of those she had in her wardrobe, she would have little difficulty holding her own in any company to which he might introduce her. Its fit and finish were clearly stamped with the unmistakable mark of one of Bond Street's very high-class modistes.

'I trust that I am not too early?' he enquired. 'If you are ready, I think that we should be on our way before the traffic gets too heavy—as you are no doubt aware, a good many people are inclined to make for the Row at about this time and I would prefer to skirt the park well in advance of the crush that usually forms at the gates.'

'I have but to collect my bonnet and pelisse,' replied Helena, uncomfortably aware of Charlotte's eyes boring into her. 'However, I understand that the carriage you have brought seats only two people, and I am not altogether sure that my father would find it acceptable for me to accompany with you without my female companion.'

Richard blinked back his astonishment but then, having registered her obvious discomfiture, he raised his hands in resignation. 'Well, I fear that it will be rather a tight squeeze for three of us on the driving seat, but if it is what you would prefer, then, of course Miss Daniels is very welcome to ride bodkin.'

Helena hesitated for just the briefest of moments before replying, then, 'No, really, my lord,' she said firmly, 'I am sure that will not be necessary. My father is, after all, very well acquainted with her ladyship. He could not object to my travelling alone with you.'

A tight smile appeared on Richard's face. 'A simple journey

from Cadogan Place to Curzon Street in broad daylight can scarcely be considered as clandestine,' he felt constrained to point out. 'Especially given that we will be in an open carriage with a groom in attendance at all times. I would hardly have suggested it otherwise, I assure you!'

Suddenly feeling rather foolish, Helena turned away to hide her confusion. 'No, I must suppose not,' she faltered, as she made for the door. 'And now, if you will excuse me for a moment, I will fetch my things and join you downstairs.'

Ignoring Charlotte's scowl of disapproval, Richard saluted both women and made for the stairs. His forbearance was amply rewarded, however, when, less than five minutes later, Helena descended, adjusting the buttons on her York tan gloves. His eyes lit up in admiration as they registered the close-fitting pelisse, its fabric and colour an identical match to her walking dress, along with a charming chip-straw capote bonnet, daintily trimmed with turquoise velvet ribbons and toning ostrich feathers.

'A most fetching outfit, if I may say, Miss Wheatley.' He smiled, as he handed her up into her seat. 'Very reminiscent of the famed Madame Devy, unless I am much mistaken?'

Helena shot him a surprised glance. 'You are very well informed, sir. An unusual talent in a gentleman, if I may say so.'

Swinging himself into the driving seat beside her, Richard laughed. 'I have to admit that, as a general rule, ladies' couture is not actually one of my stronger points.' Nodding to the groom to let go of the horses' heads, he flicked the reins and steered the equipage into the flow of traffic. 'It just so happens that my grandmother is one of the Devy's most devoted customers— has been for a good many years, so she tells me.'

As the phaeton swung out of Cadogan Place into Sloane Street, Helena, her thoughts being quite distracted by the pressure of Markfield's muscular thigh against her own, was momentarily lost for words. She considered trying to inch herself away from his very masculine nearness, but feared that the gentle swaying of the highly sprung vehicle would hardly lend itself to such a hazardous manoeuvre.

Keenly aware of her sudden reticence, Richard cleared his throat and tried again. 'My grandmama tells me that Madame Devy is in great demand. I understand that she is known to be rather choosy about accepting new clients. You must consider yourself very fortunate to be one of the favoured few.'

'I am aware that Madame is very well regarded nowadays, of course,' Helena eventually managed. 'The truth of the matter is that she is one of my father's oldest clients and has been making my gowns since before I left the schoolroom. But you are right,' she added hastily, fearing that he might have considered her offhand remark somewhat conceited, 'I am most gratified that she is still willing to keep me on her list.' A little smile leapt unbidden to her lips. 'Although I sometimes suspect that the fact that my father is always very prompt in his payment of her accounts may have more to do with her eagerness to fit me in, rather than my ability to advertise her skill in the *haut monde*.'

Richard flashed her a curious glance. 'But surely that is exactly what you have been doing during these past few months? I rather gained the impression that the whole purpose of your father's agreement was to ensure that you are brought out into society.'

Carefully evading his gaze, Helena toyed with her reticule. 'As it happens, my lord,' she answered reluctantly, 'Papa did not decide to have the contract drawn up until after he had agreed to receive you.'

Silently digesting this disquieting piece of information, the earl's brow furrowed but, since the press of traffic was becoming more intense, he found himself obliged to devote his full attention to the road ahead, in order to steer clear of a miscellany of poorly driven vehicles, the drivers of which were all seemingly intent upon hogging the entire carriageway. Consequently, it was several minutes before he was able to formulate his response.

'Am I to understand that none of my—predecessors was asked to sign that extraordinary document?'

At the clearly discernible frostiness of his tone, Helena stiffened and leapt at once to her father's defence. 'Papa was formerly of the opinion that a gentleman's word was his bond,' she replied guardedly.

Disturbed at the notion that the stockbroker had considered it necessary to treat him more exactingly than he had dealt with the previous suitors for his daughter's hand, Richard's jaw tightened but, trying to keep his tone non-committal, he enquired, 'May I ask what it was that occasioned him to change his mind in that respect?'

Her discomfiture increasing, Helena shifted uneasily in her seat. 'He took exception to one or two of the individuals to whom I was introduced.'

'I take it that you are referring to Lord Barrington and his colleagues?'

At Helena's nod, a wave of relief swept through the earl's body, but, sensing her discomfiture, he made an effort to lighten the conversation.

'Then, please allow me to assure you that neither your father nor yourself need have any qualms about the suitability of my friends,' he said. 'Their backgrounds are impeccable, you have my word.'

Thankful that he had not seemed to regard her father's change of tactics as in any way a personal slight against himself, Helena allowed herself to relax. 'I do not doubt it, your lordship,' she returned. 'I would hardly have agreed to accompany you in this manner had I believed otherwise.'

Inclining his head in acknowledgement, Richard offered her a brief smile before going on to say, 'I trust that you managed to explain to your father why I did not feel able to sign his contract.'

'N-not in so many words, my lord,' she was obliged to admit. 'His physician has insisted upon administering a mild opiate to Papa, in order to prevent him from becoming over-excited.

I simply told him that you had agreed his terms. But, you need not concern yourself, sir,' she hastened to reassure the frowning earl, 'as soon as he is well enough to discuss the matter, I shall tell him the truth, of course.'

In point of fact, since she had every intention of finding an easy way to extricate herself from this latest attempt of her father's to launch her into society, she was hoping that the necessity of divulging her perfidy would not arise. But then, as the phaeton inched its way through the press of traffic that was waiting to enter the park gates and she found herself mesmerised by the earl's highly impressive manipulation of the reins, it was not long before it occurred to her that it would be, perhaps, rather a pity if Markfield should happen to be tarred with the same brush as Viscount Barrington and his ilk. From the little she had seen of his lordship, he did seem to be quite a cut above some of his peers and he had certainly shown her a good deal more courtesy than any of his rivals had done. Nevertheless, as she was quick to remind herself, the only reason that he was here, driving her in this very showy equipage, was not because he had any real interest in developing any sort of acquaintanceship with her, but merely because he was no less eager than his predecessors to get his hands on her father's money.

'This is certainly a very fine carriage, Lord Markfield,' she ventured, after some moments of silence.

'Isn't it just!' replied the earl, with a swift grin. 'Not mine, however, I'm sad to relate—courtesy of a most generous friend!'

'It is not difficult to understand why he should place such trust in you, my lord,' she returned, drawing in her breath in admiration as Markfield neatly feathered the vehicle out of the path of an oncoming and rather badly driven curricle.

Resolutely ignoring the insolent gesture that the curricle's young driver offered him as he flashed passed, the earl acknowledged Helena's compliment with a swift smile.

'You are very kind,' he said. 'Although I am bound to admit

that the traffic is somewhat heavier than I had anticipated. One gets the impression that the whole of London is heading for the park.'

'I believe it's what they call the "fashionable hour"—although I have it on good authority that it more usually lasts for three or four!' returned Helena, her attention being momentarily diverted by a noisy altercation taking place some distance ahead. 'We, ourselves, seldom have any need to frequent this part of town at this hour.' And then, as the highly decorative attire of a passing whipster caught her eye, her cheeks suddenly dimpled. 'Although I must say that it is not hard to see what attracts them all!'

As yet another poorly driven vehicle rocked across their path, Richard, who was finding that it required all of his, not inconsiderable, driving skill to manoeuvre Braithwaite's equipage out of harm's way, was unable to reply. But then, when he had finally edged the curricle safely past Apsley House into the relative serenity of Park Lane, his attention was suddenly distracted by the unexpected sound of his passenger's smothered laughter. Unable to resist the temptation to see what might have caused such merriment, he took his eyes off the road long enough to glance across at her and was immediately struck by the sudden glowing animation on her face.

Her laughing eyes indicating the source of her levity, Helena, covering her lips with her gloved fingers, in a vain effort to control her rising mirth, whispered, 'Do look at that fellow's collar—he can hardly turn his head—and the size of his buttons—they must be quite three inches across! How perfectly ridiculous!'

As his own gaze lit upon the bizarre appearance of one of the occupants in a passing carriage, Richard was unable to prevent himself from joining in her amusement. 'I gather that it's considered quite the fashion amongst some of the young swells,' he said, with a quick sideways grin. 'But, surely, you must have come across some even more outrageous styles during your recent outings about town?'

Helena's smile faded. 'Not really,' she replied reluctantly. 'Two of my previous escorts proved to be rather a staid pair of individuals and the last one—Viscount Barrington—seemed to prefer to do his entertaining south of the river.'

'You were not taken to Vauxhall Gardens, surely?' Richard choked, well aware of the somewhat questionable reputation that the once-popular pleasure gardens had acquired during his absence from the country. 'I am hardly surprised that your father should have raised objections!'

'At the time, neither of us was aware of the unsavoury rumours,' she replied carefully, irritated that the conversation had once again returned to a subject that, in her opinion, was best consigned to history. 'Lord Barrington assured my father that it was a most respectable place and, since there were to be two other young ladies in his party, Papa bowed to what he called "his lordship's better judgement".'

Well able to imagine the kind of 'young ladies' who were known to frequent the usual supper parties given by the ramshackle viscount, Richard managed to bite back his groan of dismay. 'From the tone of your voice, I must assume that it was on one such occasion that your father found his trust to be somewhat misplaced?'

'Oh, I am perfectly sure that the resultant gossip cannot have failed to reach your ears, my lord,' she said curtly. 'No doubt your acquaintances have done their best to make capital of the event.'

'Let me assure you that I do not normally hold listening to gossip among my faults, Miss Wheatley,' replied Richard, somewhat incensed that she appeared to number him amongst Barrington's cronies. 'But on this occasion, I have to confess that, when my grandmother informed me that she had heard that you once threw a glass of wine into his lordship's face, I found myself inclined to commend your perspicacity.'

'Threw a glass of wine!'

For a fraction of a moment, Helena found herself to be

almost incapable of coherent speech but then, to Richard's utter astonishment, her eyes suddenly gleamed and her lips began to twitch. 'Is that what the wretched fellow put about?' She chuckled. 'Well, I have to say that I am sorry to disabuse you of such a delightful notion, my lord, but I fear that the incident was not nearly so dramatic. The plain fact of the matter is that I was finding his lordship's attentions rather too—how shall I put it?—*assiduous* for my liking and, after having repeatedly asked him to desist from his attempts to molest me, I felt constrained to give him a rather hefty shove which, in the event, I fear, caused him to tip his own drink all down his shirt front!'

Richard's face lit up and he let out a shout of laughter. 'Good for you, Miss Wheatley—I wish I had been there just to get a glimpse of the look on his face!' But then, as he considered the implications of Helena's story, his eyes grew serious. 'He must have been very angry with you—he did not try to harm you in any way, I trust?'

'I have to confess that I was far too mortified to wait for his reaction,' admitted Helena, with a slight smile. 'I simply vacated the supper booth and made my own way back to the pier. I was obliged to offer the ferry-man quite a large sum of money to bring me back across the river but, as it turned out, the man was most obliging. He insisted upon leaving his scull to take me to the hackney-carriage stand, for which I was very grateful, since I am afraid that I have had little experience of hiring such vehicles. He told me that he had young daughters of his own and even waited until he had seen me safely into what he assured me was "a respectable jarvey's rig".'

The earl shook his head, uncomfortably aware of the innumerable ways in which disaster might well have befallen an unaccompanied young lady in such a dubious area.

'You clearly had the saints on your side that night, Miss Wheatley,' he exclaimed, as he swung the phaeton into the quieter environs of Curzon Street and finally brought it to a halt in front of Standish House. 'Your father must have been beside himself when you turned up in a hired hack—no wonder he decided to draw up that contract! Although, upon reflection, it seems to me that the unfortunate episode should have been more than enough to put him off his whole scheme altogether.'

'Oh, you need have no fear, sir, Papa knows that I am well able to take care of myself,' she replied airily, her eyes following the earl's movements as he leapt down from his perch and proceeded to walk round the carriage to hand her down.

At Helena's somewhat naïve remark, Richard hid a smile, as he led her up the steps to the front door. It seemed to him that Miss Wheatley's rather suburban upbringing had failed to cover some of the less palatable aspects of society life. But then, as soon as Bickerstaff had ushered them into the salon, where his grandmother was waiting in attendance, he was obliged to dismiss the matter from his mind in order to concentrate on the impending interview.

In spite of herself, Helena could not help feeling just the tiniest twinge of nervousness as she approached the rather autocratic-looking old lady, who was seated on a high-backed chair at the far side of the room. Not that it mattered in the slightest what the countess thought of her, she hastened to assure herself, since— assuming that she managed to play her cards with sufficient skill—any association between the two of them would, hopefully, be very short lived. Nevertheless, she found that she could not control the little tremor of anxiety that ran through her as Lady Isobel raised her lorgnette and proceeded to inspect her minutely from the top of her head right down to the tip of her toes.

'Well, don't just stand there, girl!' commanded the dowager. 'Come over to the window and let me get a proper look at you!'

Torn between, on the one hand, a fierce desire to retort that she had no intention of being ordered about in such a peremptory manner and, on the other, a deeply instilled supposition that the young were under some sort of obligation to tolerate the idiosyncrasies of a generation much older than themselves, Helena swallowed her resentment and walked over to face the countess.

'That's much better! Now, turn around!'

Stifling her indignation, Helena did as she was bidden but, as Markfield's pensive face hove into her view, she could not resist casting him a fulminating glare. How dared he bring her here to be treated in such an insulting manner! This fiasco was turning out to be even worse than she had feared it might!

In growing disbelief at his grandmother's discourteous treatment of her guest, Richard watched in awe as Helena, exhibiting nothing of her innermost feelings, stood graciously erect, her chin raised high, and suffered the dowager's continued appraisal of her person with, he was bound to admit, the most incredible forbearance.

'Excellent!'

With a satisfied nod, Lady Isobel then bade Helena take the seat opposite her own. 'Very good posture and admirable self-control, I see!' she chuckled. 'I do believe the gel will serve, dear boy!'

Helena, somewhat taken aback at the countess's words, sat down on the sofa indicated and said nothing, having made up her mind to run whatever gauntlet the dowager had in mind for her with as much dignity as she was able to muster and then, when the two of them were done with their self-indulgent theatricals, to make her escape as soon as it was decently possible.

'She does have a voice, I take it?' the old lady then queried, frowning in disapproval at Helena's continual silence.

'Grandmama, please!' protested Richard. 'Don't you think you have embarrassed Miss Wheatley quite enough for one day?'

'Embarrassed her?' exclaimed the countess, raising her eyebrows. '*I*? The gel don't look in the least embarrassed!' And, leaning forwards, she tapped her folded fan on Helena's knee and asked briskly, 'Am I embarrassing you, child?'

'Not in the least, ma'am,' replied Helena coolly and, having suddenly caught sight of the glint of amusement in her hostess's faded blue eyes, instantly made up her mind that even if they were intent upon making some sort of game of her, she would refuse to allow either of them to intimidate her. Having already found her own way home on that earlier occasion with little difficulty, the vagaries of public transport were now much less of a mystery to her and she was quite confident that she would have no trouble hailing a cab in broad daylight in this prestigious area.

Lady Isobel nodded her approval. 'Come along then, child. What have you to say for yourself?'

'I am not altogether sure what you would have me say, ma'am,' returned Helena calmly. 'I was under the impression that I was invited here to take tea with you, not as a servant seeking some sort of position in your house.'

At the dowager's snort of laughter, Richard's eyes gleamed with admiration. It was not often that he had the privilege of witnessing at first hand the rather unusual spectacle of someone standing up to his formidable grandparent. And, with such serene assurance, he noted appreciatively. Past experience had taught him that any attempt on his part to try to modify Lady Isobel's quirkish interview technique would merely cause her to behave in an even more outrageous manner and, since Miss Wheatley seemed to be holding her own rather splendidly, he felt that any undue interference from him looked to be quite unnecessary.

'Do you know something, my dear,' the countess then announced, wagging her finger at Helena, 'I do believe that you have quite the look of your grandmother about you.'

'M-my grandmother?'

Despite all of her good intentions, Helena's attention was caught and, leaning forwards, she asked eagerly, 'You were acquainted with my grandparents, ma'am?'

Lady Isobel raised one shoulder briefly. 'Barely at all, child— I met your grandmother—Joanna Coverdale, as she then was— at several functions during my own "come-out". She married her earl at much the same time as I captured my own and, after that, for one reason or another, our paths seldom crossed. However, I do seem to remember that she had a very forthright way with her—not dissimilar to your own, I would say!'

Helena bit her lip. 'I am afraid that I know very little about my mother's family,' she said slowly. 'My brother and I were discouraged from asking questions about them and it was only after Mama died that my father took it into his head…' She stopped, suddenly recalling her previous resolve not to allow herself to become embroiled with this rather disturbing family. Glancing over at the ormolu clock on the mantelshelf, she saw, to her relief, that the obligatory half-hour for an afternoon call had almost run its time and, rising to her feet, she dipped a small curtsy to her hostess, saying, 'I see that it is time I was on my way, your ladyship. It was most kind of you to allow me to come and visit you, but I—'

'Nonsense!' interrupted the countess. 'You cannot possibly go yet. If I am to bring you out, there are a good many things that I need to know about you.' Then, turning to Richard, she exhorted him to ring for Bickerstaff to bring in the tea things, adding, 'And then you may take yourself off while Miss Wheatley and I have our comfortable little coze!'

Reluctantly sinking back into her seat, Helena watched in dismay as the earl rose to his feet to carry out Lady Isobel's request. After casting what she could only assume was meant to be a smile of apology in her direction, he quit the room, leaving her to the mercy of his formidable grandparent.

'What do you think of him, then—my grandson?'

Taken unawares by the countess's sudden question, Helena felt herself flushing. 'I—I cannot say that I have known Lord Markfield long enough to have formed any worthwhile opinion of him, ma'am,' she replied cautiously.

'Oh, stuff, gel! You must own that he is rather a handsome beast and quite out of the common! A far cry from those other cheerless profligates to whom you gave their marching orders, I'll be bound!'

'He certainly seems to be a very pleasant gentleman,' faltered Helena, desperately wishing that the subject of the conversation would return quickly and deliver her from this extraordinary woman's searching cross-examination. Whilst it was not at all difficult to fathom out what lay behind Lady Isobel's fulsome panegyric regarding her grandson's superiority, Helena had no intention of allowing the dowager to browbeat her into any form of commitment to him. As far as she was concerned, it was merely a matter of trying to keep up appearances for the short duration of the two to three weeks which she was certain would be ample time for her father to recover sufficiently to receive the news that Markfield was yet another unsuitable candidate for his daughter's hand.

'Pleasant! Humph!' For some moments, the dowager regarded her visitor with an inscrutable expression, then, 'You must understand, my child, that none of this business has been at Markfield's instigation. Due to other members of our family having failed to stay the course, my poor grandson—almost the last in his line—has been forced to compromise his own position in order to try to redeem what I can only describe as a grievous dereliction of duty on the parts of his uncle and cousin.' Lifting her handkerchief to her eyes, she dabbed away a non-existent tear. 'A very noble sacrifice, as I am sure you will agree, Miss Wheatley?'

'Oh, indeed!' Helena choked back the gurgle of laughter that threatened. 'Most noble.' Then, after hesitating for the briefest of seconds, she asked curiously, 'Forgive me if I have mistaken the matter, ma'am, but I was given to understand that your ladyship had quite an extended family living in Ireland?'

'Ha!' exclaimed the countess, nodding her head in triumph. 'My daughter's family. So you were sufficiently interested in Markfield to have done your homework, it seems!'

Helena shook her head. 'Not I, ma'am,' she replied evenly. 'I believe you must have conveyed that information to my father yourself—you have been one of his most valued clients for a good many years, I know. He certainly seems to hold you in some regard, which is, no doubt, why he was willing to consider Lord Markfield's petition.'

The countess gave a haughty sniff. 'As well he might, my

girl! Standish has been a name to be reckoned with for over two hundred years. You should be thanking your lucky stars that you have been afforded such an opportunity for advancement. Most of the gels in town would jump at the chance to snaffle Markfield and, without so much as lifting your finger, here he is, yours for the taking!'

At Helena's lack of response to this pompous assertion, a puzzled frown crossed her face. Fixing her young visitor with a penetrating look, she let out a sigh and her tone softened. 'Come, my child. Unless I have mistaken matters, you seem to be entirely reluctant about the whole affair. Surely the boy cannot have done anything to offend you?'

Chapter Five

Helena was at somewhat of a loss. The very last thing she had wanted to do was to enter into any sort of heart-to-heart discussion regarding either Markfield's enforced application for her hand or her own feelings about the matter. At the same time, the oddest thought was beginning to occur to her that, despite the apparently crusty exterior, her hostess was, in all likelihood, a good deal more bark than bite. However, no sooner had this surprising conclusion crossed her mind than it was followed by the equally disturbing thought that, unless she extracted herself from this interview very quickly, she might well find herself confiding in the old countess and seeking her counsel.

To a certain extent, Richard had not been far out in his assessment of Helena's limited social awareness. Her mother's illness and totally unexpected death, following hard on the heels of the loss of her beloved brother, had left the then nineteen-year-old, poised on the threshold of womanhood, without the benefit of an older woman's guiding hand. Although it was true that she had eventually managed to take over her mother's reins, insofar as the running of the Wheatley household was concerned, Helena still desperately missed the older woman's calm wisdom and forbearance. The fact that she was well able to deal with such matters at all was, for the most part, due to the unwritten precepts that the nobly born Louisa Wheatley had instilled into her from childhood.

At a time when other young women of her circle were involved in the frantic round of assemblies, routs and concert parties, Helena, for two consecutive years, had been in deep mourning and, apart from the occasional morning visits to the few close friends that she had acquired, all social activities had been, necessarily, curtailed. Even after the arrival of her cousin Charlotte, it had been only on the rarest of occasions that her father could be persuaded to pay a visit to the theatre and—unless one chose to count the twice-yearly country dances that were held in the hall of the village where her Uncle Daniels was rector—Helena's total experience of assemblies had been limited to the rather sedate functions given by one of her father's business acquaintances.

As it happened, although she had no intention of apprising Lady Isobel of this particular aspect of her life, she and her cousin spent most of their mornings helping out at a soup kitchen just off Chelsea's Cheyne Walk. Following her beloved brother's tragic death, Helena had found herself deeply affected by the sight of the scores of destitute and badly maimed ex-servicemen who roamed the streets of the capital at the end of the war. Consequently, when Jenny Redfern, who was sister to the Wheatleys' family physician, had first told her about the ambitious scheme that she and a few like-minded friends were in the process of setting up in the basement of a disused chapel in Justice Walk, Helena had instantly offered her support and services to the project. Since then, both she and Lottie had taken on the task of helping out at the soup kitchen in accordance with the necessarily tight rota that the sisterhood had drawn up.

Uncomfortably aware that the countess was still awaiting an answer to her query regarding the conduct of her grandson, Helena cast around for what she thought might be considered a suitable reply.

'I am sure that Lord Markfield has been everything that is proper, your ladyship,' she managed eventually.

'And yet you are still far from happy with the situation, are you not?' persevered the countess, eyeing her visitor closely.

'None of it is of my choosing,' admitted Helena, tentatively testing the water. 'But, as my father has no doubt informed you, he is most anxious to see me settled and I, for my part, have no wish to cause him displeasure.'

The dowager gave her a perceptive look and nodded. 'How does your father do, child? I understand that he has Thomas Redfern in attendance?'

Helena nodded and gave a slight smile. 'He tells me that my father is progressing favourably, ma'am,' she replied. 'We hope that he will be back on his feet in a matter of weeks.'

'During which time I imagine that you will be keen to ensure that he is not discommoded in any way?'

'That *is* why I am here, ma'am.'

Helena held her breath, waiting for the expected castigation, which, to her surprise and considerable relief, did not ensue. Instead, the countess studied her in silence for some minutes before nodding her head once more.

'Exactly as I supposed, my dear. And now, it would seem, it is time for both of us to lay our cards on the table.'

At Helena's puzzled expression, she leaned forwards in a conspiratorial manner, saying, 'I do believe that you and I will deal very nicely together, Miss Wheatley—I take it that I may call you Helena?' Without waiting for her visitor's answering nod, she went on, 'No doubt we each of us have our own agenda but, as I see it, the plain facts of the matter appear to be that *we* are doing our best to stave off our creditors for the moment and—correct me if I am wrong—*you* are intent upon avoiding an unwelcome marriage.'

'Any sort of marriage, actually,' said Helena, gazing at the countess in bewilderment.

At her interruption, Lady Isobel waved her hand dismissively. 'Either way, I believe that we can still serve each other's purpose perfectly well. Unless I am much mistaken, it seems abundantly clear to me that, despite your father's continued efforts to secure you a husband, you, my gel, have been doing your level best to bring about the failure of these plans.' She cast Helena a penetrating glance. 'Would you agree that this is a reasonable appraisal of the situation?'

Her cheeks turning pink, Helena gave a reluctant nod. 'It is true that I tried to discourage them, but—' At her hostess's quelling frown, she checked herself. 'I beg your pardon, ma'am, pray continue!'

'Humph! I can see that I shall have my work cut out!' retorted the dowager. 'However, notwithstanding all the various rumours that have circulated since your father set upon this course of action, I must admit to being not a little curious to hear your side of the tale. How, for instance, did you come to throw your wine over Barrington?'

With great reluctance, Helena related once again the events that had led to that particular suitor's dismissal. Following which, finding herself unable to parry the countess's close questioning, she was then obliged to divulge the various ploys that she had used to extricate herself from the previous two suitors for her hand.

The first candidate to fancy his chances at securing the Wheatley fortune had been the thirty-five-year-old Viscount Farley, whose approach to hygiene left a great deal to be desired. Both soap and water were, it seemed, complete strangers to his toilette; instead, he preferred to douse his person with an overabundance of the highly pungent patchouli oil. In addition, due to his nauseating habit of taking great pinches of snuff throughout the entire day, every one of his neckcloths, shirtfronts and handkerchiefs was permanently stained with an unappealing yellowish tint. Fortunately for Helena, Mr Wheatley, having found that his daughter's objections were entirely justified, had himself been quite willing to give that gentleman his *congé*.

Hard on Farley's heels had come the foppish and appallingly

henpecked Sir Percival Arnold, who had been bullied into putting his name forward by his impecunious widowed mother, an arrogant and overbearing woman possessed of remarkably poor taste and even worse manners. Regrettably, for Helena, the overly fastidious Sir Percy had proved somewhat more difficult to detach, due to his mother's constant vigilance.

However, since Lady Arnold's idea of introducing the Wheatleys into society had proved to be limited to inviting them to attend her dreary card parties, at which most of the guests seemed to be as socially unconnected as was their hostess, Helena had, eventually, been able to persuade her father that it was clear that no amount of consorting with the Arnolds was ever going to be likely to serve his original purpose. Mr Wheatley, who had been less than happy to have to dismiss yet another petitioner, had been placated only by his daughter pointing out that, at least, he would no longer be obliged to suffer Lady Arnold's outrageously patronising remarks. And so, much to his mother's shocked indignation, Sir Percy, too, had been given his marching orders.

The slightly questionable events to which her most recent suitor had taken her had done nothing to increase her regard for the so-called 'upper classes' and had merely borne out her belief that its members were decidedly lacking in decorum. Furthermore, she was well aware that her mother, had she lived, would have been less than happy to have permitted her daughter to attend such affairs.

Unfortunately, although Mr Wheatley's subsequent disbelief and outrage, when confronted with the result of Viscount Barrington's scandalous behaviour, was more than sufficient to eradicate the earlier disappointments from his memory, it also seemed to have the effect of making him more determined than ever to achieve his goal.

'Hence your father's determination to draw up this contract that Markfield has described to me, I take it?' nodded the countess, when the now highly embarrassed Helena's reluctant

explanations came, at last, to a close. 'Well then, in the further-
ance of your own strategy, it surely goes without saying that
my grandson's presence at your side will be more than sufficient to shield you from the unwanted attentions of any other
would-be suitor. Therefore, if you agree to have Markfield
escort you to some of this Season's more prestigious events, I
will take it upon myself to sponsor your début into society.'

Helena's brow furrowed. 'It is very good of your ladyship,'
she faltered. 'But I fail to see why you should wish to concern
yourself with my difficulties.'

The countess gave a graceful shrug. 'Your difficulties are
hardly my concern, child,' she replied indifferently. 'My objective is the safeguarding of the Standish heritage for future generations and it would appear that this scheme is, at present, our
only hope. To that end, insofar as I am concerned, such time as
we can buy ourselves can only be to our advantage. Any
received impression that Markfield might stand to benefit from
your father's fortune would do our cause no harm at all and, at
the very least, should win us sufficient time to garner whatever
resources we still have available.'

Although she managed to keep her features perfectly
composed, Helena could not help but feel a little surge of satisfaction at Lady Isobel's words. The countess, it was clear, was
simply proposing an arrangement very similar to that which she
herself had put to Markfield barely two days ago. The only difference being, of course, was the fact that her ladyship was
looking at the situation from her own particular point of view.

Having quickly assessed her position, Helena soon came to
the conclusion that, at this juncture, it would serve her purpose
very well to appear to go along with whatever suggestions the
countess put forward. In any event, until she had managed to
figure out precisely how to rid herself of Markfield in such a
way as to satisfy her father's exacting requirements, she realised
that she had very little choice in the matter.

However, before she was able to formulate an adequate

response to the countess's proposition, there came a tap on the door, followed by the arrival of the butler bearing the tea things. The countess's insistence that she should make herself useful pouring out the tea was sufficient to occupy Helena's attention for the next few minutes, since she was well aware that her hostess would be assessing her competence at performing this mundane but vital function.

Fortunately, from the slight smile that appeared on Lady Isobel's lips as Helena placed the cup and saucer carefully on to the small table at her hostess's right hand, it would seem that the dowager had been able to find nothing of which to disapprove.

'It would appear that your mother taught you well, my dear.' Inclining her head, the countess indicated her satisfaction. 'Perhaps I have been overly harsh in my appraisal of you—your manners clearly leave nothing to be desired. In point of fact, it does seem to me that you would have very little trouble in passing yourself off amongst the *beau monde.* Come now, Helena, what do you have to say? An offer such as this is hardly likely to come your way again.'

Helena gave a brisk nod. 'I am prepared to go along with what you suggest, ma'am. Shall we say for a period of two or three weeks, perhaps?'

The countess threw up her hands in astonishment. '*Two or three weeks, child!* If we are to make any sort of an impact, it will require two months, at the very least!'

'I had not intended that I should make an impact, your ladyship,' replied Helena, dismayed. 'I assure you that I would be perfectly content to attend the occasional assembly and, possibly, a couple of visits to the theatre.'

'That might satisfy you, miss,' countered the dowager, with some asperity, 'but it would hardly serve our purpose. For this scheme to have any effect, you and Markfield will need to be seen together everywhere—at the opera house, in the park, at Almack's—in fact, at any worthwhile social function to which

I can procure an invite. Make no mistake, my gel, entry into society is by no means as simple as you seem to suppose!'

'I had not supposed it to be simple, ma'am,' protested Helena, growing more and more apprehensive by the minute. What had started out as a straightforward ploy to protect her father from unnecessary stress was beginning to turn into a predicament of a rather different nature. With the strings of control now firmly in the countess's hands, Helena was conscious that it would take a good deal of ingenuity on her part to find a way to extricate herself from this entanglement.

'And if Lord Markfield does not agree?' she ventured, clutching at straws.

'With what might I not agree?'

With a guilty start, Helena spun round to see Markfield himself crossing the room. Uncomfortably aware that she had now entered into yet another pact, a faint flush spread across her cheeks. Would Lady Isobel divulge the details of their recent conversation to her grandson, she wondered but, more to the point, would he let slip that the scheme to which he had already given his agreement committed him to a far shorter duration than that which the dowager was demanding? Crossing her fingers, she forced a smile.

'Her ladyship has been making some suggestions as to how we might proceed,' she said lightly, turning again to the countess. 'Perhaps you would care to elaborate, ma'am?'

'Mere details,' replied the dowager, shrugging diffidently. 'However, it has just this minute occurred to me that, had I chosen to keep up my acquaintance with the Ashingtons, Miss Wheatley's mother, Louisa—who, you must remember, was a peeress in her own right—could well have been my goddaughter. Since it is highly improbable that there is still anyone around who might be likely to dispute this point, I believe that this is the story we should put about.'

He frowned. 'Surely a good many of your acquaintances may well wonder why this fact has never come to light before?'

Lady Isobel glared at him and pursed her lips. 'Do stop being so difficult, Richard!' she retorted. 'You really cannot expect someone of my advanced age to keep a track of every one of her numerous godchildren! It was only when Miss Wheatley's name was drawn to my attention that I recalled the connection. That this should have occurred at the same time as you succeeded to the title is pure coincidence.'

For one moment, Helena wondered if she could have misunderstood the countess's words for, if she had not, it would appear that her ladyship was already well into the process of believing her own fabrication. Stifling a smile, she could not resist glancing up at Markfield, in order to gauge his reaction to his grandmother's performance. To her astonishment, the earl, too, seemed to be having some difficulty in controlling his own mirth. But then, as he caught her eye on him, he winked and gave her a quick grin, causing a sudden quiver of agitation to cascade through her. Blushing, she dropped her eyes and tried to concentrate on the countess's continuing remarks.

'In any event,' her ladyship was saying, 'it is hardly as though anyone would take it upon themselves to challenge me!'

'That's certainly true,' chuckled her grandson. 'Who would dare? I swear I have seen both dukes and generals quail at one word of disapproval from you!'

'Enough of your sauce, my lad!' Eyeing him balefully, the countess wagged an imperious finger at him. 'If you have a better idea, then I am sure that both Helena and I would be glad to hear it.'

His lips still twitching, Richard shook his head and held up his hands in a playful gesture of surrender. 'Consider me at your command, ma'am. In matters such as these, I bow to your greater expertise.'

After eyeing him suspiciously for a moment or two, the countess turned her attention back to Helena, who had been watching the interplay between Markfield and his grandparent with increased interest. It seemed clear to her that, despite the light-hearted sparring that went on between them, the two of them had considerable respect and affection for one another. This rather surprising discovery had the effect of strengthening her growing belief that this particular aristocrat was something of a cut above the likes of the motley crew with whom she had had the misfortune to associate previously. All things considered, she decided, a few weeks in his company could scarcely do her any harm and would certainly afford her father plenty of time to recover from his latest attack. Deep in contemplation, she suddenly became aware that Lady Isobel was addressing her once more.

'You do ride, I take it?'

Helena barely had time to nod her head before the countess was firing other questions at her, concerning her ability to converse in French, stitch a sampler, play the pianoforte and dance a waltz.

'Not that you will be allowed to do so to begin with, of course,' added her ladyship, of the last, which Helena was obliged to admit that she had not come across, since dancing, along with the rest of her tuition, had virtually ceased at her mother's death.

'No matter—when the time comes, Markfield shall instruct you.'

Flicking another glance at the now-seated earl, Helena found, to her surprise, that his eyes were fixed searchingly upon her face, no doubt trying to gauge her reaction to his grandparent's intense barrage. At his clearly concerned expression, her lips curved in an involuntary smile. Their eyes locked and, for one breathless moment, during which time the whole world seemed to shudder to a standstill, she found herself incapable of rational thought. Her heart pounding, she forced herself to tear her eyes away from his mesmerising gaze, furious with herself for having been so foolish as to allow her carefully constructed guard to drop.

All at once, Richard's spirits rose. Taking a deep breath, he relaxed and, leaning back in his seat, reasoned that the future did not, after all, look nearly as bleak as it had a few hours earlier. Indeed, in the light of the extraordinary discovery that his grandmother appeared to be somewhat taken with her stockbroker's rather unusual daughter, it was becoming increasingly clear that the bulk of his potential problems might well be on the way to being resolved. Such was Lady Isobel's reputation amongst the *haut monde* that, with her at the helm of the project, it was highly unlikely that this particular ship would run aground. Added to which, the idea of spending more time in Miss Wheatley's company seemed, for some strange reason, to be growing more appealing by the moment.

Chapter Six

Lottie was almost beside herself with a combination of worry and impatience. She had been standing at the window for almost half an hour and when, at last, Markfield's carriage hove into view, she was out of the morning room and down the stairs in a trice, all agog to learn how Helena had fared at the hands of the imperious Lady Isobel Standish.

Reaching the hallway just as Hayward opened the front door, however, she perceived that Lord Markfield, having brought Helena to the doorstep, was now in the process of saying his farewells. Uncomfortably aware that any overly inquisitive behaviour on her part would meet with her cousin's disapproval, Lottie quickly withdrew from their line of vision but, since her curiosity was by this time almost at bursting point, she found that, by straining her ears, she was just able to catch the earl's words.

'I must thank you again for exercising such admirable self-restraint, Miss Wheatley,' he was saying. 'I fear that my grandmother can be—how shall I put it?—a little overbearing at times. I trust that she has not caused you to have second thoughts about our agreement?'

'Not at all, sir,' came Helena's reply. 'You must allow me to disabuse you of such a notion. I have every reason to believe that the countess and I came to understand one another perfectly well.'

'In that case, may I take it that you are not averse to attending this soirée she has suggested on Friday?'

'But, of course,' returned Helena evenly. 'If her ladyship truly believes that she will have no difficulty in procuring so many guests at such short notice, then it is hardly for me to cry craven.'

'You continue to surprise me, Miss Wheatley,' said Richard, a slight smile playing about his lips as he executed a bow and turned to leave. 'With your permission, then, I shall call for you at eight.'

Realising that her cousin was shortly about to make her entrance, Lottie turned tail and hurried back up to the morning room where, picking up the book that she had recently discarded, she resumed her seat in an attempt to give even the most critical observer the impression that she had been involved in that activity for quite some time. She was, however, considerably taken aback when, just a few short minutes later, Helena opened the door and, with barely a glance in her cousin's direction, made straight for the window, clearly intent upon catching a glimpse of Markfield's departing carriage!

'His lordship appears to have made a considerable impression on you,' she observed wryly, laying her book aside. 'May I assume that your visit could be deemed to have been something of a success?'

Suddenly conscious of her extraordinary actions, Helena turned briskly away from the window only to find herself facing a somewhat speculative expression in her cousin's eyes.

'As a matter of fact,' she replied defensively, as a becoming flush suffused her cheeks, 'it actually turned out to be a good deal more interesting than I had expected.'

Lottie's face lit up. 'How so?' she demanded eagerly. 'You were gone such an age that I began to fear they had abducted you for some huge ransom!'

Helena laughed. 'Silly goose! It is clear that you read far too many inferior novels,' she said, as after peeling off her gloves she made for the door. 'But I promise that I shall tell you everything as soon as I have been in to see Papa—he will be anxious to know how I got on.'

'You had best not go in to him just at the moment,' her cousin advised her worriedly. 'I peeped in only a short while ago and he was fast asleep. Digby has spent most of the afternoon trying to keep him calm. Uncle Giles is so very keen that this Markfield fellow should come up to scratch, Nell, that I fear you will be hard pressed to persuade him that he has any unacceptable failings.'

'I rather doubt that he has,' murmured Helena absently, but then, as she registered the attentive gleam in her cousin's eyes, she collected herself and added hurriedly, 'But none of that matters for the present. His lordship has already given me his promise that he will go along with the scheme and his grandmama also seems to have entered into the spirit of the thing most enthusiastically!'

She then proceeded to describe the more salient details of her interview with Lady Isobel, causing Lottie to express, in turns, various degrees of dismay, affront and amazement at the countess's high-handed treatment of her beloved Helena.

'You are so brave, Nell!' she breathed, when her cousin had finished. 'I could not have borne to have been spoken to in such a way! She sounds the most awful harridan!' A sudden thought struck her and she paled. 'I suppose I shall have to meet her if I am to accompany you on any future visits!'

Helena let out a little chuckle. 'Oh, come now, Lottie,' she cried. 'You only have to call to mind old Mrs Pettigrew in your village! You remember how *she* always tries to mortify everyone with her overbearing behaviour, while you and I both know that, at heart, she would really like to make friends, but simply doesn't know how to set about it. Look how quickly she came round when we offered to exercise her dog when she was laid up with the gout. In my opinion, her ladyship is merely a rather grander version of our Mrs Pettigrew!'

Lottie looked bewildered. 'But the countess must have loads of friends if she is going to invite them all to this party of hers!'

'Plenty of acquaintances, no doubt,' replied Helena, with a decisive nod. 'And hangers-on, too, probably, but I take leave to dispute that many of them are actual *friends!* As a matter of fact, the countess struck me as being rather a lonely old soul. Once you get past her hoity-toity grand manner, you will find that she is very little different from the likes of Mrs Pettigrew.'

'If you say so,' said Lottie, not at all convinced by her cousin's argument, but then, changing the subject, she asked anxiously, 'Am I to accompany you on Friday, do you know? I imagine that you would be expected to have some sort of a chaperon.'

Helena was silent for a few moments as she considered Lottie's words but then, shaking her head, she felt bound to admit that the etiquette involved in this particular issue was somewhat outside her sphere. Although the matter had seldom arisen, it was perfectly true that, since her cousin had joined the Wheatley household, Lottie's inclusion into any invitation, heretofore, had always been taken for granted. But, as Helena was well aware, small gatherings of her father's business acquaintances, accompanied by their wives and assorted progeny, could hardly be compared with what Lady Isobel was likely to have in mind for the coming Friday.

'I dare say I could ask Lord Markfield,' she said eventually but then, recalling her earlier embarrassment over the *faux pas* regarding the carriage ride, she heaved a reluctant sigh. 'But it is sure to give him even more reason to think us complete flats!'

At Helena's crestfallen expression, a puzzled frown appeared on Lottie's brow but she forbore from commenting on her cousin's remark. Instead, she felt constrained to point out that, since Lady Isobel appeared to be so eager to sponsor Helena's début, surely she was the person from whom any such advice must be sought.

Her face clearing, Helena reached out and grasped hold of Lottie's hands. 'But of course! How foolish of me not to have thought of that myself! Oh, Lottie, what an absolute gem you are. I shall write a note to her ladyship at once.'

* * *

Later that evening, however, as she sat at her father's bedside and studied his grey, lined features, Helena found herself filled with serious misgivings regarding her continued deception of the sick man.

'Now, my jewel,' he was saying, his voice a husky whisper, 'you must promise me that you will not allow this little setback of mine to interfere with any arrangement that the dear countess cares to make on your behalf. I feel myself growing stronger by the day and I find it extremely comforting to hear that you are not entirely averse to Lord Markfield's suit. I was beginning to fear that we would never find the right husband for you!'

Helena attempted a careless laugh and patted his hand.

'Good heavens, Papa! Anyone would think that you were anxious to get rid of me!'

The old man regarded her warmly. 'Dear child.' He smiled. 'You know full well that that is not the case—I am merely concerned for your future well being. And, in the short time I was able to study his lordship, I do have to say that he struck me as being a very fine gentleman.'

'Oh, I am sure you are right, Papa,' replied Helena, uncomfortably aware that these were almost the exact words that her father had used in his appraisal of each of the three previous contenders for her hand. However, conscious of the physician's recommendations that her father must enjoy absolute quietude, she refrained from any mention of those earlier conversations. Instead, having realised that the invalid was beginning to exhibit signs of fatigue, she gently disengaged her hand from his grasp, rose to her feet and bent to kiss his forehead.

'You must rest now, dearest. Doctor Redfern has promised to come and see you tomorrow morning. I would not like him to think that you had been overtaxing yourself.'

'You are a such a good girl, Helena,' murmured Mr Wheatley, as he closed his eyes but then, almost at once, he forced his heavy lids apart and blurted out, 'You will remember to have Markfield sign that contract, won't you—I must have his promise…!'

'Pray do not excite yourself, Papa,' interjected Helena, utterly dismayed at her father's sudden reference to the still-unsigned document, since she had been all but convinced that the dreaded subject had finally slipped his mind. 'I am dealing with the matter, you have my word!'

As she let herself out of his bedchamber, however, fresh qualms began to assail her and she spent a very unsettled night wrestling over the combined difficulties of, not only fending off her father's awkward questions but also, wondering how on earth she was going to come up with an acceptable excuse for terminating her association with the earl who, insofar as she was able to judge, appeared to be well nigh faultless!

The following day, having spent the morning helping out at the Chelsea soup kitchen, as was their usual practice, the two girls arrived home to find that, not only had the countess's reply to Helena's query been delivered during their absence but, in addition, a beautifully boxed posy of violets and primroses had arrived, courtesy of Lord Markfield.

To Helena's relief—although rather to her cousin's consternation—Lady Isobel indicated that, given that she was suitably gowned and coiffured, Miss Daniels's presence on Friday evening would be quite in order.

'Well, even she will have difficulty in finding fault with our appearance,' glowered Lottie, upon reading her ladyship's words. 'Most of those lovely evening gowns that you had Madame Devy make for us last year have barely seen the light of day, let alone graced the rooms of the rich and famous, so I certainly shan't shame you in that respect!'

Helena, who had been rapt in contemplation of the floral tribute, spun round in astonishment. 'Shame me? Good Heavens, Lottie! What are you saying? How can you possibly think that I would ever be ashamed of you—you are my dearest friend!'

'That's as may be, at present,' replied her cousin, only slightly mollified. 'But, just you wait! The minute you start moving in those exalted circles, you should not be surprised to find yourself surrounded by a great many new friends—especially once news of Uncle Giles's fortune gets about! Added to which, there is another matter that has been bothering me. If you really intend to allow her ladyship full rein in the setting up of these engagements, it cannot have failed to occur to you that they will all be organised to suit her convenience, not your own. It seems to me that you are going to find yourself in something of a social whirl—morning visits, afternoon calls, theatre parties and so on. How will we be able to fit in all our other commitments? We shall scarce have a moment to ourselves!'

Helena merely laughed, saying, 'Oh, come now! Surely you are worrying unnecessarily? We had no problem fulfilling our duties at the chapel when I was staving off the other three, so I fail to see why you think that it should prove any more difficult this time.'

Shaking her head, Lottie eyed the little posy reflectively. 'As I recall, Nell,' she pointed out, 'you were somewhat more averse to those particular gentlemen's attentions than you seem to be to Lord Markfield's—as well as doing your level best to find ways of extracting yourself from your various engagements with them. This time, it does seem to me that you are a good deal more eager to give the matter rather more than its fair share of your attention!'

A rosy glow crept across Helena's cheeks. 'W-whatever can you mean, Lottie?' she stammered uneasily. 'You must know that I only fell in with her ladyship's plans because it seems to me that, with Papa still so poorly, I really have very little choice in the matter.'

Lottie shrugged. 'Very true, my dear. But I can't help wondering exactly how you intend to ditch this particular peer!'

Helena flinched and a little shiver ran down her back. 'It is far too early to be thinking about that, Lottie,' she retorted.

'For me to pull out at this stage would be nothing short of disastrous. Besides which, Papa would never countenance such a thing at present.'

'You are right, of course,' returned Lottie sagely. 'Besides which, Lord Markfield is, without a doubt, far and away the best of those who have responded to Uncle Giles's offer and, apart from the fact that he has such extraordinarily perfect manners, you have to admit that he has to be the most devilishly handsome creature that you have ever come across!'

In order to hide the beginnings of yet another tell-tale wave of colour that ran across her face, Helena hurriedly bent to gather up her outdoor things and swept towards the door, declaring, 'If you are about to descend into talking utter nonsense, Lottie, it is clearly time to bring this conversation to a halt! Allow me to assure you that his lordship's looks, handsome or otherwise, are of very little concern to me.'

This grand exit, however, did nothing to diminish the guilty niggle within that warned her that there was, perhaps, a certain amount of truth in her cousin's words.

With a pensive frown on her face, she made her way up the stairs towards her bedchamber and would gladly have dismissed Lottie's remark had she not been obliged to admit to herself that she was finding the earl's attentions rather pleasing. His choice of flowers, for instance, could not have been more delightful—he could hardly have known that she had always preferred the fragile beauty of these woodland blossoms to their more exotic hothouse sisters.

She stared down at the small piece of pasteboard in her hand and turned it over hoping, against reason, to find some sort of message. But only the stark flourish of the single word 'Markfield' sullied the card's pristine surface. Laying the card down on to her dressing table, she buried her nose into the posy, dreamily inhaling its delicate fragrance. A soft sigh of pleasure escaped her lips as, with closed eyes, she found herself back in the woods near her uncle's vicarage where, as children, both she and Jason had spent many happy hours wandering at will with their country cousins.

Her eyes moistened as she recalled those carefree, far-off days and, not for the first time of late, she found herself wishing that she could find some way to persuade her father to give up his broking practice and move out of town. A plentiful supply of clean, fresh air, coupled with a stress-free existence in some peaceful rural backwater, she thought, surely must do wonders for his rapidly failing constitution.

Blinking away her tears, she fetched a glass from the night-stand and, after filling it from the water jug, she carefully arranged the posy of flowers within it, before returning the glass to its original position beside her bed. She was gravely contemplating the delicate loveliness of the pale blossoms, cradled in the dark velvety softness of their cool green leaves, when it suddenly came to her that the Earl of Markfield was, in all likelihood, the owner of such a country idyll. This thought had no sooner entered her head than it was immediately succeeded by the staggering realisation that, should she care to encourage his lordship's suit, rather than setting out to sabotage it, she might well, within a matter of mere months, find herself absolute mistress of an estate that would provide an ideal setting for her father's recuperation.

Almost as quickly as this somewhat fanciful notion conjured itself up, however, it evaporated into thin air, Helena having been obliged to recall Markfield's initial reluctance to involve himself with her proposal. Added to which, hadn't the dowager countess also made it perfectly clear that, as far as she was concerned, any association between Helena and her grandson was intended to be purely temporary and would continue only as long as it proved beneficial to Markfield's cause?

A small frown furrowed Helena's brow, as she realised that the reins of power did seem to have passed firmly into in her ladyship's hands, rather than remaining with herself, as she would have preferred. But why, she wondered, should this disconcert her so? Having achieved, more or less, what she had set out to do, she knew that she ought to be glad that there would no longer be any need for subterfuge and, more to the point, perhaps, it was reasonable to assume that the actual termination of the relationship would be settled by mutual agreement. It was, therefore, most vexatious for Helena to discover that, whenever her thoughts lighted upon the inevitability of the affair's eventual conclusion, she was conscious of the oddest sensation of regret. This mounting state of uncertainty was not aided by the fact that she then found that she was actually looking forward to her next meeting with the earl!

Grimacing at her reflection in the looking glass, she patted her hair into place and changed into her house slippers, ready to join her cousin in the dining room. As she was making her way down the stairs, however, a rueful smile began to play about her lips, for she had suddenly been beset by the most disquieting thought that, unless she kept her wits about her, despite all of her carefully conceived plans, she might well be about to find herself being beaten at her own game!

Richard, presently ensconced in the library at Standish House, was also wondering if he had been entirely wise to involve himself in what was turning out to be a rather more complicated set of circumstances than that for which he had originally bargained.

As a slight frown furrowed his brow, he found himself reconsidering the recent conversation he had had with his grandmother, whereupon his thoughts immediately flew to Helena, whose appearance, as he remembered quite vividly, had made a not inconsiderable impact on his senses. Under any other circumstances, this discovery would have proved something of a challenge to his healthy, masculine libido; the girl was undeniably attractive and, as she had recently demonstrated, more than capable of holding her own.

Then, as he once again recalled Helena's impressive stand

against the countess, Richard's lips began to curve in an involuntary smile. In fact, the more he considered the events of the afternoon, the more there appeared to be about Miss Wheatley than he had, at first, surmised. Had he not been so heavily occupied with his present difficulties, several rather interesting possibilities might well have presented themselves. A roguish glint came into his eyes and his smile deepened.

A tap on the door interrupted his reverie and, turning his head, he observed Charles entering. With a welcoming smile, he gestured to the drinks tray on the table at his side and told his cousin to help himself.

After pouring himself a large brandy, Standish took a seat opposite the earl.

'Just dropped in to ask how things went yesterday afternoon,' he said. 'Didn't think I ought to mention it to the old girl—wasn't sure if you'd told her that I was already "in the know", so to speak.'

'According to Grandmama, the more people who are "in the know", as you put it, the better,' replied the earl, as he leaned across to replenish his own glass. 'Apparently, the sooner word gets round that my bank account could be in line for a massive injection of cash, the quicker I shall be able to get on with the job in hand—wouldn't want to pop off and leave you holding the can!'

'Pop off!' Charles stilled and let out a startled gasp. 'What in God's name put that idea into your head?'

Richard gave a wry smile. 'Grandmama's words, not mine, I assure you. It seems that she's worried that I might turn up my toes before I've had a chance to produce the next in line! It would appear that she doesn't hold out much hope of either one of us achieving that objective before *she* breathes her last!'

'Good God, Rick!' exclaimed his cousin, with a grimace of distaste. 'When did this morbid conversation take place, may I ask?'

'After I got back from seeing Miss Wheatley home. She—Grandmama, that is—having spent the time mulling over the various pros and cons of the situation, is now firmly of the opinion that it would be no bad thing if I were to actually *marry* the girl!'

'And how did you react to that particular observation?'

'I reminded her that I have a good few more pressing matters to attend to before I'm ready to take that particular course of action,' replied Richard, grimacing. 'Nevertheless, as things stand, since I still have a mountain of bills waiting to be paid, I dare say it will do no harm to appear to be going along with this mad idea of hers—at the very least, it will, hopefully, serve to keep the creditors at bay!'

'I just wish that I were in a position to help you, Richard,' returned Charles awkwardly. 'When we were all at the club yesterday, I was rather afraid that I'd given you the impression that I regarded the whole thing as a joke, but I do want you to know that if there *is* anything I can do, you need not hesitate to ask.'

'Don't doubt that I am well aware of that, old chap!' averred Richard fervently, reaching forwards to grasp his cousin by the hand. 'Without your support, I can't imagine how I would ever get through this business.'

For several moments the two men sipped meditatively at their drinks then, suddenly, Richard's face lit up with a mischievous grin. 'Oh, by the way! I omitted to warn you to be on your guard. It seems that our dear grandmother could well be about to start gunning for you, too.'

Standish blanched. 'Not me, man! The day I take another woman into my home will be the day you can have me declared insane. As though one clinging female wasn't more than enough for me to cope with!'

Richard smiled sympathetically. 'And how is dear Aunt Adelaide, these days?' he asked.

'Much the same, I fear,' grunted his cousin. 'Always suffering from the vapours or some other blessed complaint known only to the female of the species! Costs me a fortune in doctor's bills and not only that, but whenever I do make the effort to go back home, she never lets up for a minute! Wanting to know where I've been, who I've been with and what I've been doing—you know the sort of thing! As much as I love the place, I find it impossible to remain at Southpark above a day or two—which is why I prefer to spend so much of my time up in town.'

Four years younger than both Simon and Richard, Charles Standish had never really enjoyed the benefits of the close friendship that had developed between his two older cousins and, although they had both done their best to incorporate the little boy into many of their juvenile adventures, the wide age gap had proved a considerable disadvantage. By the time the eight-year-old Charles was packed off to join his cousins at school in Rugby, the older two were already seniors and disinclined to hang around with a fresher. Added to which, they had both left Cambridge even before Charles had sat the entrance examination—Richard to join his father's regiment in Spain and Simon having been sent down for unspecified behaviour in regard to the dean's two teenage daughters.

Having learned that Charles, following the death of his father, the Very Reverend Andrew Standish, had renewed his acquaintanceship with the late Simon and had joined in a good many of that young man's nefarious activities, it had come as no surprise to Richard to discover that the real reason his young cousin spent far more time in the capital than he did at his country estate was due to his rather unhealthy addiction to gambling. Apart from which, it would seem that—probably as a result of his having been encumbered with the excessive demands of an habitually ailing mother since shortly after his twenty-first birthday—the young man had developed into something of a misogamist. Whilst it was true that he engaged in mild flirtations and had the usual number of extraneous affairs—in much the same way that Richard had run his life before the meeting with Giles Wheatley had threatened to overset his carefully laid plans—it seemed that Standish always went to extreme lengths to avoid having his name linked to any one female in particular.

Thanking Providence that *he* still had sufficient nous to retain some control over his life, Richard leaned across and poured his cousin another drink.

Chapter Seven

'And now, your Grace, you must allow me to present Miss Helena Wheatley,' came Lady Isobel's ringing tones.

Helena, dipping her curtsy for the umpteenth time, had lost count of the number of dukes, marquises, earls, generals and the like—along with their respective ladies—to whom she had already been presented that evening. Fortunately, however, it was becoming apparent that the crush of people making their way up the grand staircase towards the receiving line was, at last, beginning to show some sign of lessening. Having been standing at the countess's side for well over an hour without a moment's pause, she found herself marvelling at the older woman's remarkable fortitude, since the suffocating heat from the multitude of candelabra all around them was beginning to cause her own head to ache quite abominably. A swift glance to her left informed her that Lizzie, too, was looking rather drained. She managed to flash her cousin a quick smile of encouragement but, suddenly catching sight of Markfield's eyes on her, a soft flush rose in her cheeks and she at once resumed her former position.

He, having spent the best part of the afternoon trying to juggle his rapidly depleting finances in order to accommodate at least some of the waiting tradesmen, had been so preoccupied with his task that he had failed to notice the passage of time and, as a result, had arrived at Cadogan Place several minutes past the appointed hour.

Helena and Lottie, their evening cloaks in place, had been ready and waiting for some time. Having gone out into the hall to check the dial on the long-case clock for the third time, Helena, refusing to consider the possibility that the earl might fail to keep the appointment, had begun to wonder if she could have misunderstood his instructions.

Although he had apologised most profusely for having kept them both waiting, Richard's mind was still too full of his own troubles to pay any great attention to Helena's appearance and, thankful that they had, at least, had the foresight to don their cloaks in readiness for his arrival, he had handed the girls quickly into his grandmother's barouche, instructing the coachman to drive like the wind. Apart from murmuring the customary polite exchanges, any further bids at conversation on his part had been limited to banal observations regarding the unusual clemency of the weather.

His thoughts had still been otherwise engaged when, having escorted his guests up the steps into his grandmother's residence, he had stood aside to allow the waiting footmen to relieve them of their cloaks. But then, as his gaze had travelled idly towards the pair, his breath had seemed to catch in his throat and he had found it impossible to drag his eyes away from the entirely unexpected vision they beheld.

Helena, her wide blue eyes shining with a combination of excitement and trepidation, stood silently waiting his directions. She was clad in a gown of straw-coloured satin, the deceptively simple cut of which merely served to accentuate every delicious curve of her body; her hair, caught back with a pair of diamond encrusted combs, fell about her shoulders in a cascade of shining chestnut curls.

For several moments, due to his inability to take a full breath, Richard had been lost for words. Luckily, the arrival of Lady Isobel, who had appeared at the top of the stairs, demanding to know what could be keeping them, had saved him from further ignominy.

'Come quickly, do!' she had exhorted them. 'Several of our guests have already arrived!' And after focusing her lorgnette swiftly over the two girls' appearance, she had pronounced herself satisfied, even going so far as to commend Lottie on the bronze shot-silk of her gown—and thereby earning that young woman's undying reverence—by adding, 'I was rather taken with that fabric myself, my dear. It becomes you very well.'

And so had begun the tedious process of meeting and greeting the seemingly endless procession of the more than one hundred acquaintances who had turned up to inspect the countess's protégée and which, from Richard's point of view, was proving to be one of the most agonisingly frustrating evenings he had ever spent. He was prepared to wager that, from the very moment that they clapped their eyes on her, Helena would have no difficulty in winning the instant approval of at least fifty per cent of the gathering. Sadly, as he well knew, any real success that she might be accorded would depend, to a certain extent, upon the wives of that aforementioned fifty per cent but, more especially, upon the mercurial caprices of the small, but notoriously hard-to-please, group of elderly tabbies who ruled the roost at Almack's. They alone would dictate who would and who would not be accepted into their 'magic circle'.

Turning his head, he allowed his eyes to feast once more on Helena's lovely face and found himself hoping against hope that she would find favour. He was, however, no man's fool and was well aware that it would take a good deal more than mere beauty to endear her to some of this present company. That her mother had held a peerage in her own right would raise her standing by some degrees, it was true but, even when coupled with her obvious charms and attractively modest manner, there was simply no getting away from the fact that Helena was still nothing more than the daughter of a city stockbroker which, had not the man been almost as rich as Golden Ball himself, would have placed her well beyond the Pale!

Just then, as the light from the huge overhead chandelier struck the diamond pendant that dangled from its chain around Helena's slender neck, Richard's attention was immediately caught by the brilliant sparkle that emanated from the jewel. Blinking, he flicked his eyes away from the flashing gemstone, only to have them fasten upon the gown's low-cut neckline, from which swelled, in all its enticing glory, the provocative fullness of her creamy bosom.

Swallowing hard, he forced himself to drag his eyes away, mentally castigating himself for allowing even the hint of such a tempting possibility to invade his mind. As if he didn't have more than enough on his plate with which to deal! He let out a sigh, realising that, even with the full weight of his grandmother's determination behind the scheme, this whole affair appeared to be turning out to be an uphill battle—and in a good many more ways than one!

Thankfully, the line of visitors was, at last, reaching its end and, having correctly interpreted a signal from the countess, Richard moved to her side and was informed that, since the most important of their guests had already arrived, it was now time for them to start circulating.

'And do make sure that you stick close to Helena,' she exhorted him, under her breath. 'The word needs to get around that you and she are on the verge of forming a romantic liaison. Especially now that everyone has had the opportunity to take a good look at her, for the last thing we want is to have some aspiring fortune-hunter attaching himself to the gel!'

'As if one had not already done so!' Richard murmured drily.

'Fiddlesticks!' returned his grandmother, rapping him sharply on the wrist with her fan. 'Our case is entirely different—and well you know it!'

This, as far as Richard was concerned, was a rather moot

point but, since there was little to be gained by prolonging the argument, he kept his silence, and followed the ladies across the hallway into the first of the two reception rooms.

As she crossed the threshold of the chamber, Helena was unable to prevent the gasp of wonder that escaped her lips. She was sure that she had never, in her whole life, seen so much brightness in one room. Four huge crystal chandeliers hung from the ceiling, each holding more than thirty wax candles. Ornate oil lamps hung at regular intervals all around the walls and, everywhere she looked, there were flowers. Small tables groaned under the weight of great urns filled with hot-house roses, lilies and carnations and, if this were not more than enough, there were four marble pillars reaching to the ceiling, each of them wound with garlands of ivy and rosebuds. Looking to the far end of the room, whose interconnecting doors had been drawn back to allow access into a second reception room, she was stunned to see that this room appeared to be larger, and even more sumptuously decorated than the first and from which, it seemed likely, access to the lantern-lit rear terrace and gardens could be gained. Gathering all her courage, she reached out and, giving Lottie's hand a little squeeze, she raised her chin and entered the room.

The waiting guests had gathered themselves into their usual groups of preference and, although they had quite happily passed the time exchanging the latest *on dits* with one another—whilst imbibing copious quantities of a rapidly dwindling supply of champagne—they were, all of them, equally curious to determine what manner of person this recently acquired 'daughter of a godchild'—as her ladyship had described Helena—would turn out to be. Needless to say, it had occasioned the countess, with her infallible instinct as to the workings of the minds of her fellow peers, very little difficulty to ensure that rumours of her grandson's romantic attachment to her newly discovered 'relative' had already been well and truly circulated amongst her most influential connections before she was ready to introduce the girl into society.

Finding herself confronted with such a splendid gathering of the rich and famous was, in the first instance, more than enough to cause Helena a good many flutters of uncertainty. But, never one to resist a challenge and, mindful of her mother's careful teaching, she pasted on her most beguiling smile, determined not to show any sign of nervousness.

As the evening progressed, still more guests arrived, filling every corner of both reception rooms and, eventually, spilling out on to the terraces. It soon became clear that a good many of the countess's acquaintances were proving themselves more than willing to allow themselves to be enchanted with Lady Isobel's débutante. Even the most rigorous sticklers amongst the ageing dowagers appeared to be in agreement that Helena's modest and unassuming manner was both charming and attractive.

Initially, Richard was inclined to be amused at what he could see was happening about him but then, as his awareness of the ripples of approval within the rooms increased, a very different sensation began to replace his amusement. Since he, himself, had barely had opportunity to recover from the thunderbolt with which he had been struck earlier, it had come as no surprise to him that Helena's very fetching appearance would be likely to have a not dissimilar effect on most of the other males in the room. The very fact of which, as Richard soon began to realise, was not at all to his liking. And, any satisfaction that he might have felt at Helena's success within his grandmother's select circle was rapidly being diminished by his rising sense of irritation at the way in which some of the elderly men were ogling her, in quite the most outrageous fashion!

He need not have concerned himself on Helena's account, however, since she, having been obliged to play hostess to her father's business acquaintances for the past three years, was well accustomed to the somewhat extravagant disposition of gentlemen of a certain age when finding themselves in the company of comely young persons of the opposite sex. She had learned, some time ago, that these excessive displays of gallantry by some elderly gentlemen were merely tentative attempts on their part to recapture a little of the exhilaration of some half-forgotten memory from their salad days. And since this, in Helena's view, was clearly intended to bolster the perpetrator's own growing lack of self-esteem, she could hardly help but feel flattered by these relatively harmless attentions and had very soon learnt to deal with the cheek-pinching, hand-patting and so on that accompanied the droll behaviour. Consequently, she was perfectly at ease with the ageing brigadier-general who had recently attached himself to her.

Having taken the earliest opportunity to grasp hold of her hand, Sir Arthur Levenshulme had lost no time in raising it reverently to his lips, pressing fervent kisses upon the tips of her gloved fingers. Following which effusive gesture, he had tucked the hand firmly into the crook of his arm and, refusing to relinquish his prize, had then taken it upon himself to guide its owner amongst the throng, thus ensuring that all the most illustrious guests should be given ample opportunity to become acquainted with her.

To Richard, however, who, along with Helena's cousin Lottie, had been following in their wake for some time, it seemed that the general was making rather too much of a habit of stroking and patting the captive hand on his arm and, as the earl's indignation increased, it began to occur to him that Helena, too, might well be finding her escort's attentions equally excessive. And, since it seemed to him that she was, in all probability, feeling somewhat overawed at finding herself in such exalted company, it was not long before he came to the conclusion that the poor girl might well be feeling far too timorous to attempt to extricate herself, lest such action should precipitate an unpleasant scene. No sooner had this likelihood presented itself to the earl than it was followed by a fierce desire to drag the elderly officer out on to the terrace and wipe the beatific smirk off his face.

The sheer unexpectedness of this violent sensation caused a start of dismay to run through him and, in an effort to distract his mind from these disquieting thoughts, he cast around the room for some sort of diversion. To his relief, he caught sight of his cousin Charles entering the room with both Fairfax and Braithwaite in train and, hurriedly delivering Lottie into the care of a nearby archdeacon and his good-natured wife, he made his way across the room to greet his three allies.

'Lucky dog!' whistled Standish, when Helena was pointed out to him. But then, having registered the growing enthusiasm with which she was being received within his grandmother's circle, he laughingly suggested that, in view of their earlier conversation, his cousin would do well to set about establishing some sort of prior claim on the girl without further delay, since the magnetic power of such combined wealth and beauty would, without doubt, find the heiress besieged by offers before he had time to turn around.

'Added to which,' he then observed, 'it would seem that having your name attached to Miss Wheatley's for the next month or so will do your cause no harm at all.'

Since the bulk of his attention was still focused on Helena, Richard merely grunted in reply. However, suddenly mindful of the promise he had given his grandmother, he excused himself and, making his way purposefully through the throng presently gathered about Helena, he placed a proprietorial hand on her elbow and declared, in as light-hearted a tone as he could muster, 'Come now, Sir Arthur, you have monopolised Miss Wheatley for quite long enough now. Time for one of us younger fellows to be given a look-in, wouldn't you say?'

If the general was at all offended, he certainly chose not to show it. Surrendering his far from unwilling captive, he raised her fingers to his lips once more, saying, 'Much obliged to you, ma'am. Might have known that it wouldn't be long before one of these young whippersnappers came along and stole you from me!' Then, flicking a mischievous grin in Richard's direction, he cautioned him, 'See that you take proper care of this little jewel, young-feller-me-lad, or you could have me to answer to!'

'Pistols at dawn, I've no doubt!' responded the earl, with the briefest of smiles then, taking Helena's arm, he steered her to the side of the room, murmuring, 'I really must apologise for not coming to your rescue more promptly.'

'My rescue?' Helena stared up at him in astonishment. 'I am afraid I fail to follow your lordship.'

'Well, I dare say you were beginning to feel as if you had been thrown to the wolves!'

'Thrown to the wolves! How do you mean?'

He gestured impatiently. 'Sir Arthur—it seemed to me that you might be finding it difficult to excuse yourself, so I judged that you would be glad of a reprieve.'

Helena shook her head reproachfully. 'Then your judgement is clearly at fault, my lord,' she replied. 'I felt no need to "excuse" myself, as you put it. As far as I was concerned, Sir Arthur was all that he should have been and—unless I have mistaken the matter—being on his arm did seem to be giving me a great deal of added consequence which, I was given to understand, was the object of this evening's assembly.'

'Not entirely,' retaliated Richard, slightly taken aback that what he had deemed to be a gesture of chivalry was being construed as some sort of interference. 'The agreement was meant to be mutually beneficial, surely? Whilst launching you into society was, certainly, part of the bargain, this evening's major objective—from my grandmother's point of view, at least—was intended to help furnish rumours of a possible—future announcement—between the two of us. I fail to see in what way your spending the entire evening in the company of any mountebank who cares to attach himself to you—!'

At Helena's sharp intake of breath, he broke off abruptly. 'I beg your pardon,' he said stiffly. 'That was indefensible—and not at all what I intended.'

A small frown appeared on Helena's brow. 'Then I should like to know precisely what it was that you did intend, my lord!'

Unfortunately, whatever sentiment it was that Richard had meant to convey was interrupted by the sudden arrival of Lottie Daniels who, her face pink with excitement, was tugging urgently at her cousin's arm and craving her instant attention.

'Oh, Nell!' she burst out. 'Look who I have come upon— you will scarce believe it!'

Mystified, Helena turned to see what, amongst this huge company of strangers, could possibly be causing Lottie such delight. However, as soon as her eyes came into contact with the laughing gaze of the stockily built, sandy-haired young man who stood beside her cousin, Helena was equally over-joyed to behold the familiar face and, holding out both hands in glad welcome, she cried, 'Doctor Redfern! Quite the last person I should have expected to see in this gathering!'

Grinning widely, the young man reached out, grasped her hands in his own and exclaimed, 'As I myself, dear lady! We had scarcely entered the room when I caught sight of Miss Daniels, who insisted upon bringing us to you directly!'

Markfield had no difficulty in recognising the newcomer as one of his late cousin Simon's ex-university friends. The Redfern family had, at one time, owned quite a sizeable property not far from the Standish estate and, as his grand-mother had recently informed him, it would appear that Thomas Redfern was fast becoming acknowledged as one of the capital's more sought-after physicians.

'Good to see you again, Redfern,' he said, thrusting out his hand. 'You are well, I trust?'

The physician returned the earl's salute, saying, 'Dreadfully sorry to hear about Simon, old chap—we seemed to lose touch after my unit was sent out to Portugal.' Then, his face bright-ening, he added, 'But what an amazing turn of events! To think that my Miss Wheatley should turn out to be the daughter of her ladyship's godchild!'

'You have known the family for some time then, I take it?' enquired Richard, who was finding himself unaccountably irritated at the other man's somewhat possessive terminology.

'Indeed I have,' affirmed Redfern and, having observed that Helena and Lottie were now in animated conversation with his sister, Jenny, who had accompanied him, he took hold of the earl's arm and edged them both out of earshot.

'I was with the medical unit that brought Miss Wheatley's brother back to England,' he confided. 'In point of fact, I owe the family a great deal.'

'How so?' asked Richard, his curiosity roused.

'It is Giles Wheatley that I have to thank for my present success,' replied the physician quietly. 'At the time of his son's illness, I was merely a junior surgeon in the Army Medical Corps, but when my father died, leaving both my mother and sister dependent on me, circumstances obliged me to resign my commission and take up an appointment at St George's Hospital. When young Wheatley was moved back home to allow him end his days with his family, his dear mother was most insistent that I should continue with my treatment of her son. Subsequently, not only did Mr Wheatley seek out a suitable property in which to set me up in my own practice, but he also advanced me the necessary wherewithal to help get it off the ground. Needless to say, both Jenny and I count ourselves fortunate to number the Wheatleys among our dearest friends.'

Pausing, he shot a frowning glance in Helena's direction, adding, 'Although, I have to say that to meet up with Miss Wheatley at such a prestigious gathering comes as something of a surprise to me, especially since it was only a few days ago that I was called to attend her father. I find it rather odd that neither she nor Miss Daniels thought to mention their relationship with your family to either Jenny or myself.'

Although the earl was not at all surprised to learn that Helena had refrained from broadcasting her recent involvement with his family, since it was clear that she was hoping that any association with him would prove to be as short lived as her previous ill-fated ventures, Redfern's rather proprietorial attitude in regard to her activities irritated him somewhat.

Although it was a great temptation to him to ask the doctor why he should consider it his right to be informed of his patient's daughter's movements, in the event Richard merely nodded and uttered an inconsequential reply. He then moved to pay his respects to Redfern's sister, with whom he had also been acquainted in his youth.

Jenny Redfern, who was several years her brother's junior, was a vibrant young woman, with thick dark hair and expressive brown eyes. Not a beauty, by the usual standards, but with her quick mind and infectious sense of humour, she was highly popular within her own circle of friends. Her association with the Wheatley family had begun at, more or less, the same time as her brother's, starting with the odd supper invitation and gradually developing into more frequent contact between the two families. That Redfern would take over as the Wheatley family's physician had been a foregone conclusion and, although Mrs Wheatley's illness and subsequent death had brought about the diminishment of the family's social activities, both of the Redferns had continued to be regular and welcome visitors to the house in Cadogan Place ever since. Her own father's death having brought about a distinct lessening of the Redfern family's circumstances, Jenny was very well acquainted with hardship and, no sooner had her brother begun to make his mark, she had determined to do what she could to help other unfortunates who, through no fault of their own, had found their ways of life similarly shattered. Hence her involvement in the Wesleyan Chapel soup-kitchen project.

Dipping Richard a curtsy, she extended her hand with a smile. 'I dare say you will scarce remember me, your lordship. I was still in the schoolroom when you and your cousins used to visit us at Bagworth.'

'Nonsense!' retorted Richard, with a quick grin. 'I remember you perfectly well—hair forever escaping from its pins and always into some scrape or other!'

'No change there, then,' laughed Redfern.

Wrinkling her nose at him, Jenny pointed out that he was a fine one to talk since, even though they had arrived some twenty minutes earlier, they had still not yet made their presence known to their hostess.

'Good heavens, you are right!' exclaimed Redfern, hurriedly taking hold of his sister's arm and turning to go. 'We must away and rectify that error at once!' But then, just as he was about to lead his sister off to find the countess, he paused and, flashing a quick grin at Helena, he said, 'Perhaps, with your permission, we may return and join you for supper?'

The sight of Helena's delighted smile and eager nod of agreement brought a pensive frown to the earl's brow. All at once, it occurred to him that Miss Wheatley's long-term acquaintance with the family's physician might well have developed into a far more meaningful relationship. No sooner had this uncomfortable thought entered his head when, hard on its heels, came the equally disquieting notion that, perhaps, the real truth behind Helena's reluctance to comply with her father's wishes was that she had already given her heart to another!

Unfortunately, the sudden arrival of his friends, all demanding that he present them to Helena and her cousin without further ado, afforded him no further opportunity to dwell on these somewhat unsettling conjectures.

Chapter Eight

Even though it had seemed that, had it not been for Lottie's untimely interruption, Markfield might well have been about to apologise for his inexplicable outburst, his earlier criticism of her conduct had badly dented Helena's self-assurance. Having had more than enough time to ponder over his words, however, she could not help but feel morally bound to concede that—despite the fact that his insufferably high-handed attitude had been totally unwarranted—it was more than possible that there was some grain of truth in his accusations. It came to her as something of a shock to realise that she had allowed the un-anticipated novelty of finding herself the recipient of so much praise and admiration in one evening to affect her judgement, an unpardonable state of affairs for which she was now begin-ning to feel deeply ashamed.

The unexpected arrival of the two Redferns, coupled with the subsequent interchanges within the group, had, unfortu-nately, made any further discourse between herself and the earl well nigh impossible. And indeed, having observed his rather enigmatic expression during her animated conversations with the doctor and his sister, it had not been long before she had begun to wonder whether she might have made the most terrible mistake in allowing herself to become this deeply involved with the Standish family. Not only had her peaceful, settled existence been turned upside-down, but she had, in addition, been almost on the brink of committing the most grievous error of actually starting to admire the man—whose motives, she had to keep reminding herself, were no purer than those of her previous suitors!

Nevertheless, no sooner had the earl's friends joined the group, than the pall of gloominess that had been threatening to envelop her swiftly evaporated, for she very quickly discovered that it was impossible to take exception to these highly amiable young men. Thus it was that, in no time at all, Fairfax, who was well known amongst his peers for his light-hearted, throwaway brand of humour, had both Helena and her cousin chuckling away at his rather comical observations regarding one or two of the more starchy-looking individuals present.

Richard, watching, was unable to avoid a sharp pang of envy at the apparent ease with which everyone but himself, it would seem, could bring such a glowing smile to Helena's face. And, as he recalled the inexcusable allegations he had flung at her earlier in the evening, a shudder of revulsion ran down his spine. What the devil could have got into him to challenge her in such a way was past understanding.

Hearing the pensive sigh that had emanated from his cousin's lips, Standish, who was standing close by and, mistakenly believing that he was aware of its cause, murmured, 'Cheer up, old chap! Everything looks to be going swimmingly. Haven't heard a word said against the girl all evening. Rumours of your possible attachment to her are already beginning to circulate. You just sit it out for a few weeks and—who knows—with a good harvest, you may yet come about!'

His cousin's oblique reference to the earl's ongoing difficulties regarding his growing debts swiftly returned Richard's thoughts to the problems that had kept his mind so fully occupied earlier.

'God willing!' he returned gruffly and would have said

more, had not the sight of his grandmother, making her way purposefully towards the group, jolted his mind back to his current predicament.

'Ah, here you are, Richard!' beamed the dowager, as soon as she had reached his side. Then, lifting her hand, she beckoned Helena over to join them. 'It would appear that we have achieved something of a success this evening, my dear,' she told her, a self-satisfied smile on her face. 'Naturally, we must make every effort to build upon that. Lord Ledburn has been kind enough to offer us the use of his box at Covent Garden for tomorrow evening's performance and, since I have been given to understand that Prinny himself will be in attendance, it is infinitely possible that if I can but manage to attract his attention, he may do us the honour of inviting us to join him!'

'The Prince Regent!' Her eyes now wide with apprehension, Helena stared at the countess in dismay. 'You cannot possibly mean to introduce me to his Royal Highness!'

Her ladyship raised one imperious eyebrow. 'But, of course,' she replied calmly. 'To be seen just once in the Royal box will give you far more countenance than you could hope to gain from even a dozen routs and assemblies.'

'I had not thought to find myself mixing with the Royal set,' faltered Helena, shooting Richard a beseeching look. 'I am not sure that I would know how to proceed.'

'Nonsense, child! You will do absolutely splendidly!' retorted Lady Isobel as, with a purposeful flick of her fan, she summoned one of her ageing gallants to come and escort her to the supper room, recommending that Markfield make a push to hurry his party into doing likewise, 'Lest the best of all those highly priced refreshments disappear before any of you have the opportunity to sample them!'

Her heart sinking as she watched the elderly countess wend her stately way across the room, Helena could not help feeling that events were moving far too quickly for her liking. This latest development was far beyond that which she had originally set out to achieve in her efforts to save her father from further disappointment.

'Try not to look so worried, Miss Wheatley,' came Richard's resonant voice at her elbow. As far as he was concerned, Helena had proved herself more than capable of holding her own in any circle but, having registered her obvious consternation, it appeared that some sort of reassurance on that point would not go amiss. 'After seeing the remarkable way in which you stood up to her ladyship the other day, I cannot help but feel that his Royal Highness will be as putty in your hands!'

Even though Helena was quick to dismiss such an unlikely scenario, Markfield's intended words of encouragement brought a swift smile to her lips. 'A most redoubtable lady, your grandmother,' she ventured, turning to face him.

'She certainly takes great pains to give that impression,' replied Richard, with an answering smile. 'But, I have to admit that I have always been of the opinion that she is nowhere near as hidebound as she would have everyone believe.'

'In my limited experience,' returned Helena, looking up at him with a challenging gleam in her eyes, 'very few people are!'

Richard started and then, as a slight flush rose in his cheeks, he said stiffly, 'You must allow me to beg your pardon for that wretched display of bad manners earlier!'

Helena shook her head. 'There is really no need, your lordship,' she assured him earnestly. 'On reflection, I am ashamed to admit that I was so taken up with the unexpected adulation that I was beginning to lose sight of the purpose of it all.'

'I find it hard to imagine that such adulation comes as any sort of novelty to you,' countered Richard, with a teasing grin.

Their eyes met and, for one breathless moment, time seemed to hang on a thread until, suddenly conscious of his surroundings, Richard forced himself to tear his gaze away from hers and, swallowing hard, managed to compose himself sufficiently to suggest that perhaps they had better follow the rest of their group into the refreshment room.

Helena was at a loss to understand what had happened in that moment. An extraordinary tingling sensation had run through her entire body, leaving her trembling with shock and it was some moments before she was capable of uttering any sort of sensible response.

Struggling to conjure up something to say that might lighten the charged atmosphere that seemed to have developed between them, she was struck with a sudden inspiration and, turning towards him, she said, 'I have not yet had the opportunity to thank you for the flowers that you so very kindly sent me. They are truly beautiful and quite my most favourite varieties.'

Gratified to learn that his supposition had not proved him wrong, Richard's eyes lit up. 'It was my pleasure, entirely, Miss Wheatley.' He smiled. 'I had a feeling that I recognised the perfume you were wearing and had them sent up from the estate—the woods and fields are full of primroses and violets at this time of year.'

To his surprise, Helena heaved a great sigh and said wistfully, 'How I envy you!'

Richard's brow puckered. 'Envy me, Miss Wheatley? How so?'

'Why, for being able to take off for the countryside whenever the fancy takes you, of course.'

He was about to protest that, if she seriously believed that this was how large estates were run, then her education must be sadly lacking but then, curious as to her reason for having made such a remark, he said, 'That rather sounds as if you yourself hankered to do likewise.'

'Oh, but I do!' she replied instantly. 'Ever since I was a child, I have pestered my father to purchase us our own country property. Sadly, he has always maintained that our twice-yearly visits to my Uncle Daniels's village should be more than enough for anyone.'

Captivated by the fervent look on her face, his eyes crinkled and he laughed. 'But not for you, I take it?'

'Absolutely not!' she exclaimed. 'Hiring a cottage for a month in the summertime and two weeks at Christmas is hardly *living* in the country. My dearest wish is that my father will sell up his practice and move out of town to some peaceful retreat where he could just relax and take things easy for once in his life.'

Still smiling, he felt constrained to point out that even small estates did not run themselves.

'No, I must suppose not,' she rejoined. 'And I imagine that running a large estate such as yours must be an even greater responsibility?'

His smile faded and, as his most recent quandary again invaded his thoughts, a pensive look came into his eyes. 'An unlooked-for responsibility, as far as I am concerned,' he replied, 'and one that I would happily have given my right arm not to have acquired.'

After silently digesting this somewhat unpleasant image for a moment or two, Helena asked, hesitantly, 'Were you very close to the cousin who died, your lordship?'

A faraway look came into Richard's eyes as he sought to answer. During their boyhood, the Standish cousins, Simon, Charles and he himself, had spent a great deal of time together on their grandfather's estate. From climbing the trees in the parkland to fishing for trout in the winding river that ran through the property, they had all learned to know and love every inch of the place. It had been very hard for him to come to terms with Simon's death, especially in view of what he had lately learned from his grandmother about his elder cousin's dissolute lifestyle.

'Simon and I were inseparable as youngsters,' he said slowly. 'But then, gradually, as various events overtook the pair of us— my father's death and my own military service—we seemed to see less and less of one another. Nevertheless, his death came as a great shock to me and I have to admit that not a day has gone by when I have not wished it otherwise.'

'Had you not been obliged to return to England, would it have been your intention to stay in the army?'

He shook his head. 'I could have stayed on, I suppose, but, as it happens, I had always rather fancied setting myself up as a racehorse-breeder—out of the question now, of course.'

At once, Helena's eager expression returned. 'A stud farm! What a marvellous idea! I once paid a visit to one when we were staying at my uncle's house near Lambourne. Horses are such beautiful creatures, are they not? Imagine having one's own string.'

'You like to ride, then, I take it?' he asked, concluding that the Wheatleys probably had their own stables and wondered if it would be worth sending down to Markfield for one of his thoroughbreds, in order that he might invite her to ride with him.

'Whenever I get the chance!' she replied fervently. 'Only hired hacks these days, I am sorry to say. Sadly, however, since my cousin is still something of a novice, we seldom venture further than Green Park.'

'Not to the Row, then?'

She gave a regretful shake of her head. 'Jason sometimes used to allow me to accompany him there when I was younger—we had our own mounts in those days, of course—but after he died, there was seldom any opportunity.' She paused, then, on a sudden impulse, laid her hand gently on Richard's sleeve and murmured, 'I do understand what it is to lose someone close, believe me, your lordship.'

At her touch, a quiver of shock ran through him and, for an instant, Richard found it impossible to reply. Horribly conscious that her impetuous and somewhat forward gesture had affronted him, a warm flush began to spread across Helena's cheeks, but, the instant she started to remove her hand from his arm, his own came up, capturing her fingers in his warm, firm clasp.

'I know that you do, my dear,' he said gruffly. 'And, if you were as fond of your brother as I was of Simon you, possibly better than most, will also understand why I must do whatever is necessary in order to put Markfield Hall back on its feet. The house has been in the family for generations—it is the place where we played together—grew up together. Every single memory I have of Simon is centred there. The idea of allowing it to fall into disrepair is unthinkable!'

Trembling, Helena stared up at him, her eyes wide with concern. 'Then you must sign my father's contract,' she heard herself imploring him. 'I know that he would be more than happy to advance you—'

Almost as if she had struck him, Richard let go of her hand and stepped back. His lips twisted and a look of pain crossed his face. 'That, at present, is not an option,' he replied shortly. Then he forced his lips into some semblance of a smile and said jauntily, 'Come now! Surely you cannot have forgotten our agreement already? A purely temporary arrangement for our mutual benefits only. It would not do for us to lose sight of our objectives, so there will be no further mention of monies changing hands, I beg of you!'

There was an awkward pause and then, with a rueful grin, he added, 'It would seem that I owe you yet another apology, Miss Wheatley. For me to burden you with my troubles—!'

'Oh, no more apologies this evening, if you please, sir!' Helena broke in, her voice wavering slightly. 'My mother was often wont to say that a trouble shared is a trouble halved.'

As he stared down into her wide blue eyes, so full of compassion, Richard's heart lurched and he mentally cursed himself for having ruined what had been turning out to be a hugely enjoyable interlude. Unable to prevent himself, he reached out for her hand once again and, lifting her fingers to his lips, he said softly, 'You really are the most unusual female, Miss Wheatley. The fellow who eventually succeeds in winning your heart must consider himself most fortunate indeed!'

Much flustered, Helena made every effort to extract her hand from his grasp, only to have him tuck it firmly in the crook of his arm, after which, having pointed out that both her cousin and their friends appeared to have deserted them, he led her towards the doorway, reminding her that the delights of the supper room still awaited them.

The remainder of the evening played itself out in something of a daze, as far as Helena was concerned. She had very little idea of what she ate or drunk, and, much later, when she was safely back within the sanctuary of her own bedchamber, she could not, for the life of her, call to mind the face of a single person to whom she might have spoken or even whether the responses that she might have given had made any sense at all!

The only thing of which she could be certain was that, at some point during the course of the evening, no matter how hard she tried to deny it, the most appalling thing had happened. In failing to keep up her guard, she had fallen victim to her own sense of compassion and had actually allowed herself to warm towards a man who would never have given her a second glance had it not been for her father's fortune! So much for her clever plan of remaining coolly detached!

As she stared at her decidedly woebegone reflection in the looking-glass, she tried desperately to recall exactly when or how this miserable state of affairs had come about. As far as she could remember, the earl had paid her no more attention than she might have expected during the early part of the evening, although it had seemed that, whenever she chanced to look in his direction, she would catch him staring at her with a very pensive expression on his face. At the time, she had supposed that he must have observed some horrendous fault in her behaviour and had straight away set about trying to curb her natural exuberance but then, when he had had the effrontery to fling those unworthy criticisms at her, she had not known whether to strike him or to run away and hide! Luckily, her inbuilt sense of decorum had prevented her from carrying out either one of these actions.

How she could possibly have gone from practically detesting the man one minute to being in perfect empathy with him the next baffled her. Apart from the earlier rather disagreeable interchange, they had exchanged very few words throughout the course of the evening. Until that final conversation which, she was bound to admit, had been proceeding very agreeably until she had committed the apparently unpardonable error of offering him financial assistance! But then, despite his having kissed her hand and making what one could only consider to be a most personal observation, he had taken great pains to avoid any further communication with her. Indeed, now that she came to think of it, he seemed to have gone out of his way to ensure that the two of them were always part of some group or other. Even in the carriage on the way home, he had been very withdrawn. Polite and courteous, of course, but, to a man of his breeding, that sort of behaviour would come as second nature; he had still managed to make it perfectly plain that he could hardly wait to take his leave.

The problem with which she was now confronted, however, was not in relation to Markfield's conduct, but her own. The thought of having to go on meeting him, with the express purpose of advertising their supposedly imminent betrothal, did not rest easy with her, especially since she could not help feeling that, having allowed herself to view him in a different light, it would be well nigh impossible to return to her former state of cool indifference.

But, what was she to do? She knew that any sudden curtailment of her association with the Standish family was bound to have the most disastrous effect on her father's fragile health. What possible reason could she give him for wanting to bring the relationship to a close at this early stage?

She could only hope that some sort of solution to this vexing dilemma would present itself to her very soon, otherwise she was afraid that she might well find herself very much in the suds!

Richard, too, had been pondering over the disquieting events of that first evening. Since there had been quite a crowd at their supper table, it had not been difficult to ensure that any exchanges between Helena and himself were kept, not only to an absolute minimum, but also at a relatively impersonal level. Not that such a course of action had proved particularly rewarding, as he ruefully reminded himself, for it had been quite impossible for him not to register the several perplexed glances that she had cast in his direction; nor had the gradual lessening of her earlier vivacity escaped his notice. How he had managed to keep up this detached attitude throughout the remainder of the evening, especially on the homeward journey—during which he was well aware that his manner had been particularly off-hand—he would never know! Added to which, although he had made up his mind that he would still continue to do his best to fulfil the terms of the, as yet, unsigned contract, an uncomfortable feeling in the pit of his stomach was warning him that all future transactions between Miss Wheatley and himself would need to be conducted on a strictly businesslike footing. Since she had laid down the terms of her requirements quite clearly and was merely biding her time until her father was deemed well enough to be told that she and Markfield did not suit, it was clear that to allow himself to become emotionally involved with her at this particular point in his life was the very last thing he needed!

Chapter Nine

Contrary to Helena's somewhat nervous expectations, the proposed introduction to the Prince Regent on the following evening failed to materialise. It was true that no sooner had the curtain fallen at the end of the first act of a rather dreary opera than the countess had risen to her feet with the intention of visiting his Highness's box. However, upon discovering that a good many of the theatre's other patrons had decided to do likewise, she had changed her mind and hurriedly returned to her seat.

'Another time, perhaps,' she proclaimed, as she flicked open her fan and proceeded to flap it vigorously in front of her face which, in the process of fighting her way back through the press of people in the passage outside, had become somewhat overheated. 'As a matter of fact, in view of the number of invitations I received this morning, it would seem that we are managing perfectly well without Prinny's patronage. In any event, I have no mind to mingle with that sycophantic set of hangers-on—obsequious toadeaters, the lot of them! Why folk cannot allow the poor fellow to enjoy a simple evening out without forever pestering him with their petty trivialities, I simply cannot imagine!'

Biting her lip to prevent herself from laughing aloud at what seemed to her to be blatant hypocrisy on her ladyship's part,

A Marriageable Miss

Helena shot a quick sideways glance at Markfield, only to find that he, too, appeared to be having great difficulty in controlling his amusement.

He, as it happened, had been fighting a losing battle with himself to keep his eyes trained on the stage in the face of Helena's tantalising nearness. With her hair swept up into a soft chignon and her gown of pale chartreuse crepe cut low to reveal her neck and shoulders in all their smooth and creamy glory, it was as much as he could do to maintain his normal mien of casual urbanity, especially in view of the faint wafts of her delicate perfume that seemed hellbent upon drifting in his direction.

The sight of her mischievously laughing eyes as she turned her face in his direction was, however, just too much for him to cope with, in his present frame of mind. Rising briskly to his feet, he made for the door of the box, declaring, 'It seems to be getting rather warm in here—I'll just go and see if I can find us something cool to drink!'

Lottie, seated on the far right of the box, reached across and tugged at her cousin's sleeve. 'Could we not get up and walk about, too, Nell?' she pleaded. 'It is so dreadfully stuffy in here and the smell from all those oil lamps at the front of the stage is beginning to make me feel quite queasy!'

Since she had no real knowledge of what the correct procedure might be on occasions such as this, Helena, turning to the countess, enquired, 'Would it be in order for the two of us to stroll up and down the corridor for a few moments, ma'am? My cousin is not feeling quite up to par.'

'Then by all means take her outside,' averred Lady Isobel, with a dismissive wave of her hand. 'That dreadful crowd may well have thinned by now and I cannot suppose that you will come to any harm—provided that you stay together and remain within earshot, of course. No more than five minutes, mark you. His lordship is sure to be back with the drinks directly.'

Unfortunately, the two girls were soon to discover that the narrow passageway at the rear of the boxes was still heavily congested and, opting to move in the direction that took them away from the vicinity of his Highness's box, they found themselves at the top of the staircase that led down to the foyer.

'If we made haste,' suggested Helena, after casting a concerned look at Lottie's decidedly pasty-coloured cheeks, 'we could probably step outside and snatch a few gulps of fresh air. Might that set you up for the second half of the performance, do you suppose?'

At her cousin's weak nod, Helena took hold of her hand and together the pair made their way through the thronging mass of theatregoers on the staircase down to the ground floor. They had all but succeeded in their venture when, as luck would have it, they found their way barred by a decidedly rattled-looking Lord Markfield.

He, greatly irritated at having been obliged to shoulder his way through the press of people gathered about the theatre bar in order to achieve his objective, had been in the process of making the return journey to the box whilst endeavouring to keep his tray of drinks still intact when, to his utter disbelief, he had caught sight of Helena and her cousin, apparently heading for the exit.

'Now, where might you two be off to?' he enquired, fixing Helena with an accusative stare. 'I trust that you are not attempting to engage in yet another of your renowned withdrawal tactics?'

Helena froze and, in the space of seconds, her attitude went from one of feeling rather like a child who has been caught with its hand in the biscuit box to one of deep resentment. That the earl should stoop so low as to use that which had been shared with him in confidence as some sort of weapon against her was, to her, thoroughly reprehensible and almost beyond belief!

'In point of fact,' she said icily, flashing him a look of such contempt that he was, momentarily, stopped in his tracks, 'it just so happens that my cousin is feeling unwell and I was merely attempting to take her outside for a breath of fresh air!'

Richard drew in a deep breath. The unaccountable feeling

of frustrated irritation from which he had been suffering since the start of the evening having been exacerbated by the rude jostling he had received at the drinks bar, the unexpected sight of Helena and her cousin apparently about to flee the building had brought him almost to breaking point, hence his rather tactless turn of phrase.

Nevertheless, even though he was prepared to admit that there was a slight possibility that he could have been mistaken in his surmise, meaning that an apology was in order—an occurrence that seemed to Richard to be repeating itself with a somewhat monotonous regularity, insofar as his dealings with Helena were concerned—his present mood was such that he found himself reluctant to accept what he considered to be a rather far-fetched excuse. His eyes kindling, he was just about to challenge the validity of her words when a low moan from Lottie caused him to switch his attention away from Helena and on to her cousin.

One look at her pasty-coloured cheeks had him instantly galvanised into action. Thrusting his tray into the hands of a passing attendant, he directed the man to deliver the drinks to Lady Isobel's box. Having divested himself of this encumbrance, he then turned back to Lottie who, in the face of her cousin's anger, was now looking distinctly out of countenance.

'I do wish that you had confided in me earlier,' said the earl, by now deeply concerned. 'Had I known that you were feeling unwell, I would have brought you downstairs myself. You must allow me to escort you outside for a breath of air.'

With that, he lifted Lottie's unresisting hand and, studiously ignoring Helena's affronted gasp, placed it on his arm and proceeded to escort her through the doorway out into the street beyond. Since it was impossible for him to miss the expression of rigid indignation that appeared on Helena's face, as she stood back to allow them to pass, he was unable to prevent the deep sense of remorse that overtook him. Nevertheless, since it was clear that seeking relief for Lottie's obvious discomfort was, at this moment, of far greater importance than concerning himself with her cousin's bruised ego, he stiffened his resolve and concentrated his efforts on getting the ailing female through the crowded foyer and out of the building—doggedly shoving all further thoughts of possible apologies to the back of his mind.

Helena, following the pair through the swing doors, was consumed with resentment. She had expected an instant apology from the earl for the hurtful and unjust accusation he had thrown at her. Instead of which, it had been Lottie who had claimed his attention! If this was how he intended to behave towards her in the future, she would jolly soon bring their relationship to a close! To think that she had actually begun to imagine herself halfway to falling in love with the selfish, inconsiderate brute! But then, as she saw how tenderly he was supporting her rapidly wilting cousin whilst attempting to fan her face with his pocket-handkerchief, Helena's fury evaporated at a stroke and she was overcome with shame. Poor, dear Lottie's need was, without a doubt, far greater than any petty grievance that *she* might harbour. How she could ever have thought otherwise was now beyond her comprehension!

Stepping forwards, she took hold of Lottie's free hand and, patting it gently, said, 'I think that we ought to go home at once, my love. You will feel better once you have had a little lie down.'

With a weak shake of her head, Lottie emitted a mewl of protest. 'Oh, no, Nell, please!' she gasped, frantically dabbing at her lips with her own damp and much screwed-up handkerchief. 'Whatever will her ladyship think?'

'Her ladyship will think just as Miss Wheatley does,' interposed Richard soothingly. 'It is clear that you are not well enough to return to your seat. If you will give me but a moment, I shall have the carriage brought round.'

With that, he signalled to the doorman who, flicking his fingers at a nearby pageboy, sent him scurrying around the corner to where the line of waiting carriages was parked.

Minutes later, the countess's barouche drew up in front of the theatre and the earl, after lowering the window slightly to allow in a little fresh air, settled Lottie into a corner seat.

'If you would be good enough to sit with your cousin for a few minutes,' he said, as he handed Helena up into the carriage, 'I will collect my grandmother and we will have you driven home without further delay.'

'Your lordship has been most—' began Helena but, before she could even begin to express her gratitude to him for attending so swiftly to her cousin's needs, the earl had closed the carriage door and was walking swiftly back towards the theatre.

Although she was left feeling rather foolish and not a little embarrassed at his abrupt departure, she had no time to dwell upon it, since Lottie, full of apologies for having spoilt everyone's evening, soon claimed her attention.

'No, no, dearest,' she said in reply. 'You really must not repine so. It is of no consequence whatsoever. Like you, I found the atmosphere in there quite stifling. Apart from which, I feel sure that her ladyship must have been as bored with that stupid opera as I was, for I swear that I caught her nodding off more than once during the performance! So, I beg of you not to give the matter another thought, my love. As soon as we get home, I shall have Mrs Pearson make you up one of her soothing possets and you will feel as right as rain in no time, I promise you.'

Markfield's return, with his grandmother in tow, quickly put a stop to any further protests from the still-drooping Lottie and, no sooner had they settled themselves in their respective seats than, at a signal from the earl, the carriage moved off.

'You really should have said something sooner, you silly child!' remonstrated Lady Isobel as, after ferreting through the contents of her reticule, she fished out a bottle of sal volatile and passed it across to Helena. 'Wave this under her nose for a moment. It usually serves!'

Inwardly castigating herself for not having had the forethought to tuck her own bottle of this simple remedy into her evening bag, Helena did as she was bid. Just one sniff of the pungent fumes was enough to produce a choking cough from Lottie who, although far from fully recovered, hastily waved the bottle away.

'Enough, thank you!' she gasped, as she dabbed at her streaming eyes.

The countess gave a satisfied nod. 'There,' she said, having retrieved her bottle of spirits and returned it to the rest of the jumble in her oversized handbag. 'I knew it would do the trick—I never travel without it. Restores the constitution wonderfully well. Nevertheless, since you are still looking a little pale, my girl, I recommend that, the minute you get home, you take yourself straight off to bed. Markfield will call in the morning to see how you do.'

Then, turning to Helena, she added, 'You and I, my dear, will need to get our heads together over all the invitations I have received on your behalf. It might be advisable if you return with his lordship after his visit tomorrow morning in order that we may decide which events will best advertise your growing attachment.'

Growing attachment! thought Helena, with an inward grimace. *Little does the elderly dowager realise how far from the truth that is!* Then, conscious of Richard's eyes on her, she hurriedly directed her own gaze out of the window on her side of the carriage, feigning an intense interest in the passing traffic and steadfastly refraining from looking in his direction.

He, too, was beginning to doubt the wisdom of ever having entered into this bogus relationship, which seemed destined to be beset by far more pitfalls than he could ever have imagined when he had first agreed to it. The constant emotional turmoil that he had recently found himself undergoing was, surely, far more than any sane man could be expected to deal with and, as of this moment, he was not entirely sure that he would be able to summon up the necessary stamina to ride the thing out. On the other hand, the gradual lessening in requests for immediate settlement of accounts over the past few days did seem to be giving credence to the fact that word of an impending engagement between himself and the daughter of one of London's richest stockbrokers was already going the rounds. Thank God he was still sufficiently in charge of his senses to realise that any sudden curtailment of his perceived courtship of Helena would have the most disastrous effect upon his already tenuous financial state. Suppressing those other unsolicited emotions, however, looked set to present him with a far more difficult task than he could ever have imagined!

Chapter Ten

Two days later, riding alongside his grandmother's landau as she took Helena and the now fully recovered Lottie for their first carriage outing through Hyde Park, it soon became apparent to Richard that their appearance seemed to be causing a good deal of curious speculation from promenaders and carriage-folk alike.

Reining in beside the landau, for what must have been the fourth or fifth time in a passage of less than a hundred yards, in order for his grandmother to conduct yet another protracted conversation with one or other of the occupants of a passing vehicle, the earl, shooting a quick glance at Helena's surprisingly composed countenance, could not help but wonder what she was making of all this unforeseen attention. Despite his determination to remain coolly aloof from her, he would have needed to be totally blind not to have noticed that she was looking particularly fetching this afternoon, in her skilfully styled lilac-coloured carriage gown, with the wide brim of her matching bonnet framing her lovely face to perfection. Doing his utmost to keep his eyes on the carriageway and not on her, he was only too conscious of the fact that, had he not been bound by this disastrous agreement, such delectable temptation as she was proving to be might easily have been regarded as something of a challenge. As it was, however… Clenching his jaw, he tried to focus his attention on the animated chatter that was going on about him.

She, having been achingly aware of the earl's reserved demeanour since the disastrous theatre trip, had made up her mind that, despite Markfield's obvious lack of enthusiasm for the project, she would do her best to comply with whatever demands the countess might choose to make. With her father still being kept in a state of mild sedation, the few short conversations that she had been allowed to hold with him had, fortunately, precluded any necessity of discussing the unsigned contract.

Nevertheless, she knew that as soon as Dr Redfern deemed him well enough to resume his normal way of life, the matter was likely to be brought up straight away. By which time, hopefully, she would have devised a plan by which she might extricate herself from what was becoming a highly stressful association with the Standish family. Until that happened, there was little she could do but sit back, try to give the impression that she was enjoying herself and endeavour not to allow all the unanticipated admiration that had suddenly become her lot to affect her judgement. Fortunately, in that respect, her innate good sense told her that all this newfound interest in her had merely come about as a result of the details of her father's extensive fortune being passed along the social grapevine. Never having previously encountered this particular brand of sycophancy, she could not help but feel rather amused at the lengths to which one or two of the individuals to whom she had been recently introduced were prepared to go to bring themselves to her notice. Compared with such patently false and effusive behaviour, Markfield's current somewhat taciturn attitude towards her might even be considered rather refreshing!

Besides which, having spent the best part of the morning doling out chunks of bread and mugs of soup to the several dozen down-and-outs who haunted the chapel basement in Justice Walk on a daily basis, she was inclined to think that many of the countess's acquaintances seemed to be little more than spoilt, over-pampered gossipmongers who appeared to have nothing better to do with their time than pull one another's reputations to shreds. She could not help thinking that it was a great pity that some of them could not find something more worthwhile to do with both their time and their money! In fact, when it really came down to it, out of the countless number of the so-called 'polite society' to whom she had been introduced, the only ones—apart from Lady Isobel and the earl himself, of course—who had treated both Lottie and herself with a kindly courtesy that was neither condescending nor ingratiating had been Markfield's two ex-army comrades and his cousin Charles, all three of whom had behaved in the most charming and friendly manner towards them.

Having arrived at this rather disheartening conclusion, it was impossible to conceal her smile of delight when, on glancing casually across the park, she observed that Standish himself, clad in the most elegant riding jacket and mounted on a handsome bay, was riding down the Row in the direction of his grandmother's carriage.

'A fine afternoon, ladies,' he said, doffing his hat respectfully, when he had finally reined in beside them. 'I'll join you, if I may?'

Then, after exchanging a few words of greeting with his cousin, he proceeded to take up his position on Helena's side of the carriage, Markfield, he had been surprised to observe, having elected to ride on the opposite side, at their grandmother's right hand.

'I was so sorry to hear of your indisposition on Saturday, Miss Daniels,' he said, casting a smile at Lottie, who was seated opposite Helena and the countess. 'I trust that you are now fully recovered?'

'Oh, yes, thank you, sir,' came Lottie's stammering response. Unlike her cousin, she had not yet fully mastered the art of polite conversation and to find herself being singled out in such a manner still had the effect of causing her to blush quite dreadfully.

'I'm very glad to hear it,' he replied, with a sympathetic nod. 'These theatres are apt to get oppressively hot at this time of year, I've found.'

Then, turning his attention to Helena, he went on, 'It was a pretty boring piece of work, anyway, if my memory serves me aright. I myself had the misfortune of attending a performance earlier in the week and must confess that I failed to understand the plot entirely—and as for that soprano!' Leaning towards her, he lowered his voice slightly. 'I swear I was forced to stick my fingers in my ears on more than one occasion!'

Hearing Helena's soft chuckle of amusement at Charles's airily unrepentant condemnation of the opera house's lead singer, the countess leaned forwards and shot her youngest grandson an admonishing glare. 'You know very well that the purpose of our visit was not to watch some trumpery opera,' she reproved him. 'We went in order that we might be seen by as many people as possible and, all in all, I would say that we succeeded in our aim!' Then, looking up at Markfield, she added, 'Would you not agree, Richard?'

The earl, who had been engaged in a slightly surreptitious contemplation of Helena's beaming countenance whilst, at the same time, envying the ease with which everyone—apart from himself, it would seem—had the ability to cause her face to light up in that entrancing way, found himself having to hurriedly redirect his attention to his grandmother's question. Having rather lost the thread of the conversation, he was reduced to making a trite comment regarding the press of people outside the Prince Regent's box.

'Be that as it may,' returned the dowager, 'our presence cannot have failed to make some sort of an impression and, given our reception during the past hour, I have the distinct feeling that today's little excursion has set a good few more tongues wagging. Furthermore, we have Lady Kettlesham's supper party this evening, which is certain to add a little more grist to the rumour mill! It will, doubtless, turn out to be one of her usual tame sort of affairs, although I understand that she is to include dancing on this occasion. That usually gets the wheels spinning very nicely, I've always found!'

Manfully stifling the groan that threatened, Richard deigned not to respond. But then, finding himself unaccountably eager to witness Helena's reaction to his grandmother's words, he was unable to avoid casting yet another covert glance in her direction.

Although she was sitting quite still, her expression perfectly composed, he could tell by the rigid set of her shoulders and by the fact that her hands were clasped tightly in her lap that she was not completely at ease with the situation in which she now found herself. His heart contracted and, sighing inwardly, he forced himself to redirect his attention to the carriageway. Had he been in a position to do so, it would have given him the greatest pleasure to inform his grandmother that he was putting an end to this dismal charade but, financial considerations apart, this would necessitate him having to renege on his promise to Helena and, until her father began to show some sign of recovery, he could not find it in himself to add to her difficulties. Nevertheless, since he was already having to summon every ounce of his will-power to keep his wayward emotions in check, the thought of having to continue with this fabricated courtship was enough to make him want to turn tail and head back to the relative tranquillity of his Surrey estate! For, despite all his best efforts to maintain a cool head, it was becoming disturbingly clear to him that every minute he spent in Helena's company looked set to steer this ridiculous scheme towards a very different conclusion from that which had been originally agreed upon.

The sound of his grandmother's voice calling for the coachman to pull over once again jerked him back to reality and he was obliged to rein in to allow her to greet yet another of her associates.

'Sally Jersey!' she exclaimed, giving an enthusiastic wave to one of the occupants of a smart phaeton that was approaching them. 'The very person!' Then, turning to Helena, she exhorted her to do her very best to impress her ladyship, adding *sotto voce*, 'Her ladyship is considered the most amenable of the Patronesses at Almack's and I have known her since she was a girl, so I have every hope of persuading her to oblige us.'

Having commanded her driver to draw up alongside, Lady Jersey greeted the countess with a welcoming smile. 'So, you are back on the town, Lady Isobel—and with a new protégée in tow, I hear! I dare say you are hoping for vouchers?'

Then, consumed with curiosity to view for herself the young lady about whom she had heard such glowing reports during the past few days, she leaned forwards and directed her attention towards Helena who, holding her breath, forced herself to sit in unruffled silence as her ladyship's frowning gaze travelled from the top of her bonnet right down to the tips of her shoes and back again to scrutinise her face.

'She's certainly pretty enough to take,' said Lady Jersey finally, as she sat back in her seat. 'Her father's occupation is something of a drawback, however—although I have it on authority that, apart from being extraordinarily well heeled, the fellow is also extremely well thought of in his circle—which does, of course, put the whole matter in a slightly different light!' Pursing her lips in thought, she paused for a moment, as she endeavoured to come to a decision. 'I dare say that under your sponsorship the girl will do,' she murmured, almost to herself. Then, with a decisive nod, she went on more positively, 'I shall have the vouchers sent over to Standish House tomorrow morning. I trust that you have not forgotten that our supper dances are held every Wednesday evening throughout the Season?'

At Lady Isobel's affirmative nod, she then turned her attention towards Standish and the earl who, having drawn their mounts to one side during the interchange between the dowager and herself, were now in the process of exchanging sardonic grins at the prospect of being obliged to rig themselves out in the regulation satin knee-breeches that were the obligatory mode of apparel at the highly regarded venue.

Favouring them with one of her famously flirtatious smiles, Lady Jersey informed them that both she and her sister patronesses would be more than delighted to welcome two such well set-up gentlemen into their elite company. Then, after signalling to her driver to move on, she cried, 'Now I really must be on my way—you will remember to have someone arrange your subscriptions, won't you? I forget the charge, but no doubt Mr Willis will advise you.'

And, with a casual wave of her hand, she continued her progress along the carriageway towards the exit at Stanhope Gate.

'Still monopolises the conversation, I see,' grunted the countess. 'And, as for asking me if I remembered when the balls were held! Does she suppose that I am in my dotage?'

Not waiting for a reply, for none was expected, she called to her coachman to turn the carriage and make for home, muttering to Helena that, if they didn't leave at once, they would scarcely have time to change in readiness for the coming evening's entertainment.

'I'll be off, too, if you'll excuse me,' said Standish, as he wheeled his horse round and made ready to leave. 'Delighted to have met up with you this afternoon, dear ladies, and look forward to seeing you again in the not too distant future.' Then, with a quick wave of his hand, he rode back towards his lodgings in Knightsbridge.

Richard, seizing the opportunity, transferred his position to Helena's side of the carriage and, as soon as they were on the move again, leaned over to enquire as to her father's current state of health.

'Doctor Redfern tells us that he is improving daily, sir,' she replied, conjuring up a smile of sorts. 'He says that he has every reason to hope that Papa will soon be his old self again.'

'He calls regularly, then—the doctor?' asked Markfield, adopting what he hoped was a casual tone.

'Oh, yes! Every day,' she returned. 'Sometimes, more than once, if he can spare the time. We count ourselves most fortunate that he keeps us on his list, in view of his growing popularity.'

Doubtless because he, too, gets his bills paid on time, thought Richard sourly, as he recalled Helena's use of that very phrase in regard to the celebrated Madame Devy. But then, despite his earlier resolve to keep a tight rein on his feelings, it proved impossible to prevent the hot spurt of jealousy that ran through him at the thought of Redfern's constant attendance at the Wheatley residence.

Fortunately, since the journey from the Hyde Park gates to Cadogan Place was less than two miles, the countess's well-sprung landau covered the distance in record time and they very soon found themselves at Helena's door, relieving the earl of the necessity of commenting further on the doctor's dubious visiting practices. Quickly dismounting, he handed both ladies out of the carriage and escorted them up the steps where Hayward, with his usual impeccable sense of timing, was waiting to admit them.

Although Lady Kettlesham's soirée proved to be everything that the countess had predicted—a somewhat staid affair, with random groups of people standing about sipping champagne and making desultory conversation—their own entry into the salon set enough tongues wagging to render the dowager bliss-fully contented for most of the evening. Lottie, unfortunately, having complained of a headache upon their return from the park, had elected to stay at home.

When the promised dancing did begin, it turned out to be of the country variety; a succession of sets and quadrilles, none of which promoted very much in the way of conversation between partners. In view of the fact that it had been quite some time since she had engaged in such an activity, Helena found that she was obliged to devote the whole of her attention to the performance of the, sometimes, fairly intricate measures.

Nevertheless, despite the fact that she and the earl took to the floor for no more than the permitted two dances, they were neither of them left unaware of the undercurrent of interest that continued to filter through the room throughout the evening. In between the dances, Markfield was all that he should have been, finding seats for both the countess and herself and bringing them the requisite platters of sweetmeats and glasses of lemonade. His occasional attempts at conversation, however, were at best perfunctory, leaving Helena with the distinct impression that he would much rather have been elsewhere. But, since he was continuing to observe the terms of their agreement, she knew that she had no right to expect anything more of him, although she could not help comparing the rather cool manner he had adopted of late with the teasing, light-heartedness of his former self. Having spent most of the afternoon reflecting upon what might be the possible cause of such a drastic change of temperament in so short a time, she could only suppose that it must have been some inexcusable lack of decorum on her part that had brought it about—which rather provoking thought had her hurriedly straightening her shoulders and tucking her feet out of sight beneath the hem of her skirt, lest he should have even more reason to deplore her conduct!

A sudden ripple of excited murmurs spreading throughout the room caused her to shelve her somewhat mutinous thoughts whereupon, on looking over to the doorway to see what might be the cause of this unexpected animation, her curiosity was immediately aroused by the fact that everyone's attention seemed to be centred upon the couple now standing at the doorway. Behind her, Richard, who had, until that minute, been leaning negligently against a convenient pillar nearby, suddenly stiffened.

Conscious of his unexpected movement, Helena turned her head to ascertain the cause, only to observe that his eyes, too, were fixed upon the couple who had just entered. Turning back, she studied the pair who, as far as she could tell, were nothing out of the ordinary—although it was fair to say that the lady, whilst she was no longer in the full bloom of youth, was certainly very striking. With her rich dark tresses artistically arranged in clusters of artfully swirling curls on top of her head, she was dressed in a gown of deep-red slubbed silk that, from Helena's point of view at least, seemed to hug her highly curvaceous figure just a shade too closely. It was clear to see that it was she who was the real object of everyone's attention.

Turning towards Lady Isobel, Helena observed that the countess was eyeing her grandson with a somewhat speculative look.

'Who is that lady who has just come in?' she whispered. 'Everyone seems to be staring at her.'

'She is Lady Kettlesham's sister—Rachel Cummings by name,' replied the countess tersely, casting another frowning glance in Markfield's direction. 'Widow of the late and clearly unlamented Sir Frederick Cummings.'

'But why is her presence causing such a stir?' asked Helena, perplexed. 'Not that it seems to be bothering her, I must say—in fact, she looks as though she is rather revelling in the attention—although her escort appears somewhat less at ease, don't you think?'

'More fool him to have accompanied her here!' retorted Lady Isobel. 'The creature is nothing but a lightskirt!'

'Lightskirt?' faltered Helena. 'I'm afraid I don't follow you, ma'am.'

'So I should hope, my child!' was the dowager's curt response. 'Hardly a fit subject for tender ears like yours!'

Temporarily nonplussed, Helena allowed her eyes to travel back to Richard who, although he had, by this time, managed to recover something of his former aplomb and had regained his stance against the pillar, still had his gaze focused on the recent arrivals—or to be more correct, as she very soon realised, on the dark-haired lady. Although Helena had never come across the actual expression 'lightskirt' before, it had not taken her long to hazard a guess that the term must refer to one of those women who practised the rather unsavoury occupation into which rather too many of her regular female visitors to the soup kitchen seemed to find themselves driven.

Her brow furrowed in thought, she stared across at the stunningly attractive brunette, finding it almost impossible to believe that any high-society lady would feel the necessity to involve herself in the sort of dubious activity in which the likes of Bet Mooney and Cissie Pritchard were forced to claw a living. It was clear that the ruby necklace she was flaunting, for instance, was worth a small fortune, so too that matching pair of bracelets and earrings. Such a woman, surely, had no need to debase herself in the way that those other poor souls did. Rather more puzzling, perhaps, had been Markfield's strange reaction to her unexpected arrival. If this Lady Cummings really was the sort of woman that the countess had given her to understand, what could possibly be the earl's connection with her?

However, no sooner had she really put her mind to the matter, than a violent blush suffused her face and she was obliged to bring her fan into quite vigorous use. Fearful that Lady Isobel would spot her sudden discomposure, she edged the chain of her reticule off her wrist and allowed the purse to fall to the floor at her feet, hopeful of using its retrieval to explain away her high colour.

Unfortunately, she was forestalled by Richard who, stepping forwards, reached down and, picking up the fallen article, handed it back to her.

'Allow me,' he said, executing a swift bow.

Despite his concern over Rachel Cummings's unexpected arrival, Helena's suddenly altered demeanour had not escaped the earl's attention and he was hoping against hope that he might be mistaken as to its cause. However, when she failed to meet his eyes and merely took back the reticule with a muffled 'thank you,' he was obliged to concede that his somewhat unguarded reaction to Rachel's unexpected arrival had not escaped her notice.

Frowning with unsuppressed irritation, he returned to the relative security of his pillar, telling himself that, regardless of how Helena might or might not choose to interpret his behaviour, any conclusion that she eventually reached could hardly be of any consequence, since it could not affect the arrangement in hand. Her views on gentlemen's indulgences did not enter the equation; whether or not he chose to keep a mistress was his business, not hers and, as far as he was concerned, she had no right to pass judgement on his activities when they could not possibly affect her.

As his annoyance diminished, however, he began to realise that his reaction to Helena's attitude had not emanated from anything that she had said or done but rather from some unaccountable feeling of guilt on his part. Never having experienced feelings of this sort before he had met Helena, he was at a loss to understand why it should suddenly matter now. He was beginning to wish he had never allowed himself to be drawn into the affair with the Cummings woman.

She, having set up home in the village of Chelsea the previous year, following the demise of her elderly husband, had become noted for throwing the most lavish of parties, entirely designed to appeal to the more liberally minded members of the *ton.* Finding himself at something of a loss one evening, shortly after his return from the Continent, Richard had accepted an acquaintance's invitation to accompany him to one such entertainment and, unaccountably, as it now seemed to him, had found himself utterly beguiled by the lure of unspoken promise in his hostess's dark, sultry eyes. Up until a week ago, his visits to her had been on a more or less regular basis but, after setting up this recent agreement with Helena, he had had every intention of putting an end to the liaison.

But why on earth her blessed sister had chosen to invite the woman here this evening, with so many prestigious guests in attendance, was beyond his understanding—it not having escaped the earl's notice that several of her ladyship's most devoted paramours had already sneaked out of the salon in order to seek sanctuary in one of the adjacent card rooms. This rather sudden depletion of male guests now made it highly unlikely that Rachel would fail to spot his own rather obvious presence. He could only hope that she would not take it upon herself to come over and greet him in person since, finding oneself obliged to present one's *chère amie* to one's elderly grandparent—who, as well as being a stickler for convention, was nobody's fool—must rate as one of the most socially unacceptable situations in which a man might ever expect to find himself. And, if that were not quite enough for him to cope with, there was the additional problem of what might be going on in Helena's head to compound the difficulty!

To his chagrin, however, he perceived that Lady Cummings was, indeed, heading in his direction. Although he was almost overcome by the desire to take to his heels and run, he resolutely stood his ground and forced himself to return her greeting with a stiff bow.

'How delightful to see you again, Ricky, my sweet!' she addressed him huskily, as she fluttered her long dark lashes up at him. 'You are quite the last person I should have expected to see at one of my sister's tedious routs!'

It occurred to him that, having simply spotted him lounging against the pillar, she might well have been under the impression that he was unaccompanied. Taking her arm, he endeavoured to draw her to one side, saying, 'This is most improper, Rachel. My grandmother is sitting scarcely two yards away from us!'

'So I observed,' she said, pursing her lips and shooting him a mischievous smile. 'Along with the little heiress that I have heard so much about, I perceive. Although, if your somewhat less than enthusiastic welcome is anything to go by, I must assume that you have no intention of introducing me to your illustrious companions!'

'I most certainly am not!' he replied curtly. 'And I would be highly gratified if you would refrain from any more of this foolish nonsense and return yourself to Lord Ruskin at once!'

Her eyelashes fluttered impishly. 'But you haven't paid me a visit for over a week now, Ricky,' she reproved him, with a coy little moue. 'And I cannot help but recall your enthusiasm at our last meeting!'

'I have been somewhat occupied of late,' he grunted, a faint colour staining his cheeks as he shot an apprehensive glance in Lady Isobel's direction. To his unbounded relief, it appeared that both she and Helena were deeply engaged in conversation. If he could just persuade Rachel to move further down the room!

'Ah, yes! Preparing yourself for parson's mousetrap, I hear!'

Flicking him playfully with her fan, Lady Cummings then turned her attention to the seemingly oblivious Helena. After casting her eyes calculatingly over what little she could see of her face and apparel, a little curve of satisfaction appeared on her lips. Then, lifting her eyes to the rigid countenanced earl, she offered him the benefit of one of her most seductive smiles and murmured softly, 'I see no problem there, Ricky, my love. I feel sure that a week or so in that sweet virgin's arms will soon have you clamouring for something a little more—shall we say—invigorating!'

'For God's sake, madam!' ground out Richard who, having witnessed her flagrant disregard for propriety, was now becoming thoroughly revolted, not only with Lady Cummings, but also with himself for ever having allowed himself to be captivated by what he had lately come to realise were decidedly overblown charms. 'You go too far!'

In reply, she simply let out a throaty chuckle and then, leaning much too close for decency, she bade him a whispered '*Au revoir,* my sweet!', after which, exhibiting the most provocative sway of her hips, she sauntered casually back to the hapless Viscount Ruskin.

As his eyes followed her progress across the floor, Richard's face was tight with anger. Apparently quite impervious to the disdainful looks and low mutterings of disapproval being cast in her direction, she rather gave the appearance of one who had grown bored by the whole proceedings. Having reached the doorway, where her highly embarrassed sister had been doing her best to entertain her abandoned escort, the unabashed Lady Cummings merely offered her a swift peck on the cheek and, after waving an ostentatious 'farewell' to the now stunned assembly, took hold of her *cicisbeo's* arm and exited the room.

A pensive frown upon his face, Richard did his utmost to ignore the speculative stares that were being cast in his direction, as he found himself reflecting that, all things considered, perhaps it was just as well he had been in a position to view the creature's true nature, since it had been his intention to visit her later that same evening, in order to terminate their relationship. Now, however, thanks to her blatant disregard for propriety, the woman had earned herself no more than a curt note informing her of his decision. What the devil he had ever seen in her, he was hard pressed to bring to mind.

Rather to his surprise, the anticipated reproach from his grandmother failed to materialise, although the dowager's manner towards him for the remainder of the evening was noticeably lukewarm. A good deal more disconcerting, perhaps, was Helena's failure to respond to any of his resolute attempts to engage her in conversation in anything other than a polite but somewhat preoccupied manner, causing him to suspect that it would not be long before his name was added to her growing list of failed suitors, an outcome that, for reasons that had nothing whatsoever to do with his monetary problems, the earl shrank from dwelling upon. Fortunately for his increasing sense of unease—owing to the fact that Lady Cummings's unexpected attendance seemed to have put rather a damper on the whole proceedings—the party broke up shortly afterwards.

As it happened, Lady Isobel had counselled Helena to refrain from making any mention of the incident and, after

pointing out that 'we females have ever been obliged to accept
the unaccountable proclivities of the opposite sex! It is the way
of the world and, as such, is unlikely to change', had urged her
to try to put the matter out of her mind.

Which was all very well, Helena could not help thinking, as
the countess's barouche wended its way through the late-
evening traffic back to Cadogan Place. Whilst it was true that
the event had given her cause to view Markfield in a rather different light, she still found it difficult to visualise him in the role
of out-and-out libertine. Not that she was actually conversant
with the precise meaning of the term, since her entire experience in that area was restricted to what she had picked up
during her occasional perusals of Lottie's somewhat lurid taste
in literature!

Nevertheless, one thing of which she was quite certain was
that, having already been subjected to some rather discourteous treatment by one such rackety individual, she was quite
determined never to find herself obliged to suffer such humili-
ating indignity again! And yet, setting aside the fact that Markfield had always treated her with the utmost respect, the rather
disconcerting discovery that he was in the habit of forming as-
sociations with women such as the atrocious Lady Cummings
had the effect of bringing about the most peculiar constriction
of her throat, not to mention an odd stinging sensation at the
back of her eyes.

Contrary to what the earl might have supposed, Helena's
education in worldly matters had not been entirely confined to
her time at Miss Haversham's Seminary for Gentlewomen.
Indeed, having spent much of the past two years in constant
contact with a class of individuals whose lives ran on very different lines from those of her present companions, it would
have been almost impossible for her not to have picked up a
certain amount of information about the parlous conditions in
which these people existed. Miscarriage, rape and abortion
were terms she came across on an almost daily basis and she

could hardly help but be aware of the fact that the sickening bruises that appeared, with depressing regularity, on the arms and faces of the likes of Bet Mooney and Cissie Pritchard had come about as a result of the rough handling that they had received at the hands of their dockside clientele.

Unfortunately, however, whilst it was true that a good many of the 'facts of life' were much less of a mystery to her than might have been imagined, Helena's understanding of what actually took place between a man and a woman was still rather vague. Added to which, since the browbeaten apathy of the women who queued at the kitchen daily bore no resemblance to the close and loving nature that had always formed part of her own parents' relationship, she had been forced to conclude that this rather questionable type of activity must be something peculiar to the lower orders, brought about as a result of their being forced to scrape a pitiful existence in such hopeless and straitened circumstances. To discover that those whose lives lacked for nothing should also choose to indulge in these doubtful practices was quite beyond her understanding. And that Markfield, for whom she was beginning to form such a high regard, might also be included in this number was something that she could scarcely bear to contemplate. On the other hand—if her ladyship were to be believed—this type of behaviour appeared to be regarded as perfectly commonplace within their circle!

She sighed, wishing with all her heart that her mother had still been there to offer her the wise and friendly counsel that had always been of such comfort to her in the past. But then, as she strove to find some sort of answer to her quandary, it suddenly crossed her mind that perhaps Jenny Redfern, who was several years her senior and a good deal more worldly wise than she was, might be able to shed some light on the vexing subject and vowed to tackle her friend on her very next visit to Justice Walk.

Apart from the occasional comment from the countess with

regard to the rather poor selection of refreshments on offer at the soirée, along with the observation that, in her opinion, one of the fiddlers had been sadly out of tune, all three passengers were singularly quiet throughout the return journey.

However, no sooner had the carriage drawn to a halt outside Helena's house than Richard had thrown open the door and leapt nimbly down, thus enabling him to be in a position to offer his assistance to Helena well before the footman had managed to scramble from his perch.

At his sudden and unexpected action, a glimmer of amusement lit up her eyes and she might well have laughed out loud, had she not been conscious of his extremely sober expression. Thanking the countess prettily, she bade her 'goodnight', then, placing her hand into Richard's, she allowed him to assist her down from the carriage.

Although he had spent the whole of the short journey from the Kettlesham mansion in Ennismore Gardens to Cadogan Place beset by the most inexplicable urge to assure Helena that any relationship that he might once have had with Lady Cummings was now over and done with, the earl still managed to retain sufficient aplomb to realise that this was hardly the moment for a discussion of that sort.

'I should like to call on you tomorrow morning, if I may,' he said, as he escorted her up the shallow flight of steps that led to the front door, which was opened almost as soon as his hand touched the knocker.

At his words, a wave of regret washed over Helena. 'I'm most dreadfully sorry, my lord, but I fear that I shall be otherwise engaged until well after luncheon tomorrow.'

Although his heart seemed to drop into his shoes at her reply, the earl gave a little shrug. 'No matter,' he replied, carefully assuming an air of nonchalance. 'It is of no importance.' Pausing briefly, he then went on, 'You will be available in the evening to attend the supper dance at Almack's, I trust—given that Lady Jersey sends the vouchers as promised, of course.'

To his relief, she inclined her head in affirmation, saying, 'Perhaps you would be good enough to ask Lady Isobel to send me a note advising me of their arrival and at what hour I might expect her carriage?'

'It will be my pleasure,' he replied, executing a swift bow then, bidding her 'goodnight', he turned smartly on his heel and made his way back to the waiting barouche.

As she watched the carriage disappear round the corner into Pont Street, a pensive frown appeared on Helena's face and, for several minutes, she stood silently mulling over the possible reasons for his proposed visit. Could he have been going to inform her of his intention to curtail their arrangement? she wondered. Or, perhaps his colourful lady friend had expressed her disapproval of his involvement in the scheme and ordered him to bring it to an end? However, having given a little more consideration to that particular option, she was obliged to concede that it was highly unlikely that anyone, either male or female, would be able to persuade Markfield into doing anything that he chose not to do.

A discreet cough from the open doorway, where Hayward was still waiting to help her off with her evening cloak, caused her to spin round in some confusion.

'Oh, do forgive me, Hayward,' she said, giving him a bright smile as she stepped over the threshold. 'I'm afraid I was miles away!'

Richard's difficulties, it would seem, were not yet over. No sooner had he taken his seat in the barouche than his grandmother leaned forwards and, tapping him sharply on his knee with her folded fan, insisted that she should be given an explanation of his part in the 'disgraceful display of bad manners' that she had had the misfortune to witness at the soirée. 'And, please don't try to fob me off with some feeble Banbury tale!' she begged him. 'For I was not born yesterday, as you are well aware! Surely that dreadful creature cannot be one of your fancy pieces?'

Fixing the dowager with a steely glare, Richard took a deep breath. 'In the first place,' he ground out, 'I would like to make it clear that I do not have "fancy pieces", as you term them. Whilst it may be true that I did once number Lady Cummings among my acquaintances in the past, any such association is now at an end. Furthermore, any display of bad manners you may have witnessed was not on my part. In fact, all things considered, I believe I exercised sufficient diplomacy to defuse a situation that might well have developed into something a sight more distasteful—rather successfully, as it turned out!'

'Humph!' returned his grandmother, suitably chastened, but only very slightly mollified. 'It is highly fortunate that the Kettlesham rout did not loom large on the social calendar. I only chose to accept the invitation because I felt that it would provide a suitably gentle stepping stone for Helena's entry into society. I can only pray that this evening's débâcle has done nothing to damage all our carefully laid plans!'

Ruefully echoing a silent 'Amen' to her prayer, Richard leaned back against the squabs and devoted the rest of the journey back to Standish House to wondering whether Helena did indeed have a prior engagement for the following morning or if it was just simply a ploy to avoid having any sort of direct confrontation with him. Given that their initially quite amicable relationship had already foundered, due to his clumsy mishandling of the situation, he could not help feeling that this evening's unfortunate débâcle could only have worsened matters. Added to which, it was gradually beginning to dawn upon him that, despite his determination not to allow his heart to rule his head, it was beginning to look as if the damage had already been done. How to deal with this highly disturbing circumstance was yet another problem to add to his growing list!

Chapter Eleven

The Wesleyan Chapel in Justice Walk had formerly been used as a court of law by the much revered Fielding brothers, John and Henry, for the trial and sentencing of the various felons of their day. The basement of the building, which had, at that time, been used to house those unfortunate prisoners who were waiting to be tried, was now in use as a centre for the dispensation of a daily allotment of simple provender to the neighbourhood's growing number of homeless and destitute.

Owing to the fact that the chamber was without windows, apart from a small barred opening situated on the wall some three feet away from the entrance, it had been necessary to restrict its use to mornings only, since the elected committee in charge of the scheme had agreed that to spend even a single penny of their pitifully small resources on the purchase of candles to light up the dark and gloomy atmosphere of the room's cavernous interior would be a shocking waste. Hence, thanks to some considerable ingenuity on the part of one of their number, the good ladies had hit on the reasonably satisfactory method of having a pair of trestle tables set up just inside the open doorway and adjacent to the small barred aperture. By positioning themselves behind these tables they managed to dole out ladles of the hearty soup that, for a suitable remuneration, was prepared on a daily basis in the kitchens of the Swallow, a small inn across the alleyway. The barred opening, barely two feet square, also managed to serve a useful purpose, since it had been discovered that the gaps between the iron bars were just wide enough apart to enable sizeable chunks of bread to be passed through to the, seemingly, never-ending queue of ravenous clients.

Whilst the lack of light and heat did not present much of a problem at this time of the year, the working conditions gradually deteriorated as the days grew shorter. Nevertheless, there were seldom any complaints from the dedicated team of volunteers since, no matter how cold their toes and fingers grew, every last one of them was only too aware that, unlike their impoverished clientele, they had warm and comfortable homes to which they would shortly be returning following the completion of their tasks.

On Helena's first visit to the soup kitchen, her immediate reaction to the plight of the desperate individuals who had held out their battered mugs and bowls for her to fill would have been to distribute the contents of her own purse before sending home for further supplies. Jenny Redfern, however, had very quickly prevented her from doing any such thing, warning her that, no matter how well intentioned her motives were, since she could not possibly give a share of her own largesse to every one of the waiting crowd, to single out even a few of them for preferential treatment would merely cause resentment amongst the others and could well lead to ugly scenes. In the beginning, Helena had considered this edict somewhat harsh and unfeeling, but had very soon grown to appreciate its necessity. And so, whilst it had been impossible for her not to develop soft spots for certain of the regulars over the years, both she and her cousin had learned to execute their duties with as much dexterity and benevolence as the unprepossessing conditions would allow.

Owing to the increasing press of humanity that arrived well before the kitchen was ready to begin its daily business, the alleyway, being a cul-de-sac, had been deemed too narrow to accommodate the influx of carriages that brought the volunteers to their destination. Most of the ladies, therefore, had adopted the habit of alighting from their vehicles in Cheyne Walk and covering the remaining short distance on foot, having instructed their various coachmen to return at one o'clock to collect them.

This morning, the two girls arrived to find the basement in the usual hubbub of activity, with the same half a dozen or so of the waiting men more than willing to involve themselves in the setting up of the trestle tables and the fetching and carrying of the first cauldron of soup and the baskets of freshly baked loaves that were supplied by a nearby bakery.

'Good morning, ladies!' one of the men called out, as Helena and her cousin approached.

'Good morning, Mr Corrigan!' returned Helena, with a smiling nod. She had warmed to Rueben Corrigan from his very first appearance at the counter for, despite the man's impoverished state, he always remained determinedly cheerful and did his best to keep himself clean and tidy. Unfortunately, due to his having walked all the way to London from Dover, following the disembarkation and disbanding of the army unit with which he had served, the soles of his boots had virtually disintegrated and, although he regularly replaced the makeshift cardboard inners, it was clear that, until he could find a way to earn some money and have his boots properly attended to, all thoughts of continuing his journey to his home in the north of England would have to be postponed.

In addition to providing a substantial meal for these unfortunates, the ladies of the trust also made it their business to seek out positions of gainful employment for as many returning ex-soldiers as they possibly could since, like Helena, most of them had lost close relatives in the war. Having already coaxed her father into taking on two fairly superfluous extra hands to help out in the garden and stables that were situated at the rear of her Cadogan Place home before Rueben had shown up, Helena continually found herself wishing that she could find some suitable employment for him, especially since he, unlike a good many others in his position, continued to make every effort to find himself work.

'Still no luck, I take it, Mr Corrigan?' she asked, giving him a sympathetic smile.

''Fraid not, miss,' he replied, with a regretful shake of his head. 'Heard they was taking men on at Chelsea Wharf yesterday morning but, even though I were down there well before six o'clock, the place was already swarming. In the event, it were only four they wanted so I weren't the only one disappointed.' Grinning ruefully, he then added, 'Cost me my place in the queue, though, and soup were all gone by the time I got to the counter!'

Helena's eyes filled with concern. 'Oh, Mr Corrigan!' she exclaimed, her tender heart aching with pity for his undeserved plight. 'I'm so very sorry! I do wish I could find something for you.'

'You good ladies already do more than enough for the likes of us chaps,' he said gruffly, before hurriedly turning away to hide his embarrassment at having almost allowed his emotions to get the better of him.

Along with a good many other members of the sisterhood, Helena was of the opinion that not nearly enough was being done, by either the government or any of those institutions who, it was felt, might easily have sought to involve themselves in the plight of these sadly neglected returning heroes. It was little wonder, she thought, that so many of their number had formed themselves into troublemaking bands who seemed to have little better to do with their time than roam the countryside stirring up resentment and unrest amongst the local workers.

Well aware that, since she was a mere woman—whose opinions held no sway whatsoever—there was nothing she could do to alter this highly unsatisfactory state of affairs, Helena let out a soft sigh and, picking up a carving knife, turned her attention to slicing one of the many loaves of bread into hefty-sized chunks, this being her allotted task for the day.

Jenny, hearing the sigh, was momentarily sidetracked from her own occupation of piling the bread chunks into one of the emptied baskets, ready for the doling out that was due to start at any minute.

'I hope that sigh doesn't signal that this work is beginning to bore you, Helena,' she said, casting an anxious look at her young friend.

'Good heavens, no!' protested Helena. 'I was merely thinking how unfair everything is.'

'Not everything, surely,' laughed Jenny. 'From what Lottie has been telling me, you and she would seem to have been leading a rather exciting life these past few days!'

'Hectic, perhaps,' Helena admitted, with a slight shrug. 'But exciting, no—I wouldn't have said so.' Then, pausing, she eyed her friend thoughtfully. 'However, that has put me in mind of something that I wanted to ask you—that is—' Colouring, she bent her head back to her work. 'Something rather odd occurred last evening and I was wondering whether you might be able to throw any light on the matter.'

'Fire away, then,' returned Jenny, her natural curiosity immediately aroused.

In a decidedly hesitant manner, Helena, her cheeks flushing rosily, managed to relay the somewhat puzzling events of the previous evening. At the end of her discourse, she looked across at the other girl questioningly, only to find her friend staring back at her with a rather quizzical expression on her face.

'Her ladyship seemed keen to have me believe that such—er, activities—were quite commonplace among members of the opposite sex,' she went on, hurriedly. 'But, I find it hard to believe that gentlemen such as my father or your brother could ever indulge in such practices!'

Shaking her head, Jenny gave her a rueful smile. 'They would hardly make us privy to such information even if they did, my dear,' she said kindly. 'I myself have learned that the way gentlemen conduct themselves when out of sight of their nearest and dearest can often be very far removed from the behaviour we normally expect of them—"deceivers ever", as the bard was wont to say!'

Helena's eyes widened. 'You cannot be referring to Doctor Redfern, surely?'

'Thomas?' mused Jenny, with a hesitant frown. 'Difficult to tell, as it happens. Although I doubt if he could spare either the time or the energy for that sort of amusement, his appointments book being as crowded as it is these days. One cannot be sure, of course, for he is a man, after all is said and done! But, that apart, it surely can't have escaped your notice that his sights are set in quite a different direction!'

'I'm afraid I don't follow you,' returned Helena, looking puzzled.

'You mean you haven't noticed?' asked Jenny, with a surprised lift of her eyebrows. Pausing momentarily to dust the flour from her fingers before moving across to the soup table to begin the lengthy business of serving the waiting throng, she cast her friend a swift sideways glance, then gave a rueful grimace. 'Oh, dear! There I go again! Letting my over-active imagination run away with me, as usual. Pay no attention, I beg you!'

Considerably confused as to the meaning behind Jenny's enigmatic remark, Helena was finding it difficult to concentrate on her work. Could his sister have been trying to intimate that Dr Redfern had formed some sort of *tendre* for her? she thought, as she distractedly sliced away at the crusty loaf in front of her. As though she didn't have more than enough complications in her life already! What with the constant worry over her father's illness, coupled with her own very mixed emotions in regard to Markfield, the mere hint of such an unwelcome situation developing involved her mind to such a degree that it was only when Lottie, who was piling loaves on to the table beside her, pointed out that the size of her bread chunks seemed to be increasing rather dramatically that she was hurriedly obliged to return her attention to the job in hand. Nevertheless, unable to ignore the fact that, this morning being a Wednesday, was also the day on which the doctor chose to attend his make-shift surgery in the inn across the alley, Helena could only hope that she had misunderstood her friend, since she was uncomfortably aware that for her to allow such a situation to develop would inevitably bring about not only the loss of her father's physician but also signal the end of what had been, hitherto, a most enjoyable and easy-going relationship between Jenny Redfern and herself.

It had been only very recently that the doctor, now highly sought after amongst the *ton,* had elected to neglect his upper-class clientele for a few hours each week, in order to utilise some of the valuable skills he had acquired during his time with the military, for the benefit of those who were a good deal less fortunate than his usual high-society patients. For this purpose, he had hired one of the small ante-rooms at the Swallow Inn opposite and, every Wednesday morning, now spent his time diagnosing symptoms, binding up injuries and dispensing helpful advice, along with copious quantities of free medication, some of which, he could not help feeling on occasion, were used for purposes other than that for which he had pre-scribed them. On the whole, however, his services were greatly appreciated by the countless number of grateful patients who queued outside his makeshift clinic every Wednesday morning for, without his selfless dedication, there was little doubt that a good many of them—the children in particular—might well have perished long ago.

At the end of each session, it had become his practice to join his sister and her friends at the chapel in order to assist them in their clearing-up exercise.

Fortunately, for Helena's peace of mind, the pressing needs of her allotted tasks proved more than adequate to prevent her dwelling further upon Jenny's puzzling words.

* * *

Consequently, it was not until some three hours later that, looking up from her final task of wiping down her table top, she was unable to prevent the slight flash of disquiet that ran through her when she beheld Redfern's cheerful visage grinning at her through the bars of the opening.

'Another busy morning, I see!' he called as, edging his way past the trestle at the doorway, he entered the basement. 'Word seems to be spreading. I would say that the queue was a good deal longer today!'

'You could be right,' sighed his sister. 'If they keep coming at this rate, we will soon be forced to look for larger premises.'

'Somewhere in the same vicinity, I trust?' interjected Redfern, somewhat uneasily, as he shot a quick glance over to where Helena and Lottie were busily engaged in stacking up the empty bread baskets, ready for collection.

Following the direction of his eyes, Jenny could not help smiling. 'We'll need to raise a good deal more money before we can even begin to contemplate such a move,' she pointed out, eager to reassure her brother that his weekly tête-à-têtes were not about to be suddenly nipped in the bud.

With a satisfied nod, Redfern made his way over to the other two girls to bid them good day.

Having viewed his appearance with some misgivings, Helena was thankful to find that, after a polite but sincere enquiry as to her father's health, the bulk of Redfern's conversation appeared to consist of a number of humorous anecdotes relating to the various eccentricities of some of his *ton*nish patients. Contrary to what she had expected, in view of his sister's comment, she was unable to discern any appreciable change in his manner towards herself, leading her to reach the conclusion that her normally rather astute friend Jenny had entirely misread the situation.

In no time at all, she found herself back to chuckling away at his droll tales in much the same manner as she had always done and, as she smilingly watched him divest himself of his jacket and roll up his sleeves in order to take over the heavier aspects of the clearing-up operation, she could only breathe a huge sigh of relief, happy in the knowledge that everything seemed to be exactly as it had always been.

His current set of anecdotes having run out, Dr Redfern then turned the topic to discussing the countess's soirée of the previous week and was soon genially enquiring as to whether Helena and her cousin were enjoying their current foray into high society.

'Have they told you that they are off to Almack's this evening?' put in Jenny as, having completed her tasks for the morning, she joined the group where, turning to her brother, she enquired, 'Didn't you once mention that Mrs Drummond-Burrell had offered you vouchers should Mama and I wish to attend? Is it possible that the offer is still open, do you suppose?'

At her words, Lottie's eyes lit up. 'Oh, do you think you might be able to come along, too?' she cried. 'I do wish you could. I find it really difficult to be among so many strangers all the time—do try to persuade them to join us, Nell!' she cajoled her cousin.

'The more the merrier, as far as I'm concerned,' returned Helena, who had been viewing the prospect of having to spend yet another evening in Markfield's decidedly non-communicative company with very mixed feelings, particularly after the highly unsettling events of the previous evening.

'Oh, do say we can, Thomas,' begged his sister. 'We had such fun last Friday!'

'Oh, I dare say I might manage to arrange something,' beamed Redfern, after scarcely a moment's thought. 'As it happens, I have been treating Lord Cowper for a stomach upset—merely a severe over-indulgence of cream pastries, in point of fact—and his wife has also offered to acquire vouchers for me, should I ever be in need of them. Perhaps we might pay a call on her ladyship on our way home to see if the offer still stands?'

It being agreed that the Redferns would do their level best to put in an appearance at the exclusive King Street venue later that evening, the girls collected their bonnets and, after waiting for his sister to lock the door to the basement chapel, the doctor then escorted her and her friends to Cheyne Walk, where their carriages awaited them.

'I'm so glad that you managed to persuade the Redferns to join us this evening,' said Lottie, as she settled herself against the comfortable squabs of the Wheatley carriage. 'I must confess that I was feeling quite nervous at the thought of attending this famous assembly hall. Having read so much about it in the *Ladies' Magazine,* just the idea of putting a foot wrong under the watchful eyes of those dreadful Patroness ladies has been worrying me to death! Hopefully, the doctor will be able to obtain his vouchers and then we shall, at least, be amongst friends.'

'Given that Lady Jersey remembers to send ours to the countess,' replied Helena with a light laugh, although she was secretly hoping that the promise to do so might have slipped her ladyship's mind. Quite apart from being obliged to 'run the gauntlet' of supercilious criticism she had heard so much about, there was now the added complication of Thomas Redfern who, despite what Lottie had said, had needed neither persuasion nor encouragement to join them. In fact, unless she was much mistaken, he had accepted the invitation with rather more alacrity than she cared to think about!

Chapter Twelve

As luck would have it, the promised vouchers arrived without mishap and Lady Isobel's barouche arrived at eight on the dot as arranged. The famed assembly rooms, however, proved to be something of a let-down as far as the wide-eyed Lottie was concerned for, although they were even more crowded than either she or Helena had expected, they were also a good deal shabbier than they had been given to suppose.

'Why on earth is there such a clamour to get on to the subscription list?' whispered Lottie, as her astonished eyes took in the faded curtains and the peeling plaster that adorned the pillars.

'Simply because of its exclusivity, my dear!' retorted Lady Isobel, whose sharp ears had caught her remark. 'You should think yourself very lucky to be here, you know, for the Patronesses are very particular about whom they allow in. The membership rules are very rigid and should anyone dare to flout them they would very likely find themselves banished for life! Now, the first thing we have to do is present ourselves to the committee. There is no need for you to say anything—I will speak for you—just curtsy and smile and you will both do very nicely!'

Blanching with fright, Lottie clutched at her cousin's arm. 'Oh, Nell! It is far worse than I expected! I do wish I hadn't come!'

But Helena merely smiled and gave her hand an encouraging squeeze, since she was privately of the opinion that all this pompous rigmarole was nothing more than inflated snobbery on the part of its originators. Squaring her shoulders, she applied her mind to trying to keep up with the countess, which, given that they were being jostled on all sides, was not the easiest thing to do.

Luckily, both Markfield and Standish, who had been waylaid at the entrance by Mr Willis, the Master of Ceremonies, with a courteous reminder that no subscriptions had yet been received for their party, soon managed to shoulder their way through the press of people to clear a path for them. With their assistance, the ladies very quickly found themselves standing in front of the raised podium where five of the Patronesses were seated.

As he stepped forwards to perform the introductions, Lady Jersey greeted Richard with a welcoming smile.

'Good evening, your lordship,' she cried merrily. 'I am so glad you decided to join us this evening—eligible gentlemen such as yourself and Mr Standish are getting to be rather a diminishing commodity these days!'

Since he was not at all sure that he cared to be referred to as a commodity of any sort, diminishing or otherwise, the earl merely bent his head over her ladyship's hand. He was well aware that the main reason the current batch of unwed males tended to avoid putting in an appearance at Almack's was— apart from a natural preference for entertainments of a more lively sort—due to a concerted determination to steer clear of the highly dedicated matchmaking tendencies of its committee. Especially since these tendencies were also the common factor that brought droves of overly ambitious mothers, along with their fresh-out-of-the-schoolroom daughters, into the capital at the start of every Season. Not for nothing were the assembly rooms mockingly referred to as 'The Marriage Mart' by the town's young dandies!

Thanking providence that his grandmother had gone to considerable trouble to set in motion the rumour that he was already spoken for, Richard stood to one side while the rest of the committee cast its fastidious and unforgiving eyes over its newest members. From what he had, thus far, managed to learn about Helena's attitude to the so-called *belle monde*, it would not have surprised him to learn that she was probably viewing the whole procedure with a feeling bordering on disdain—a feeling that he was obliged to concede that, at this moment, was not entirely dissimilar to his own. Shooting her a swift sidelong glance, as she executed the most elegant curtsy, he was unable to suppress the sudden longing that filled his heart. Dressed in a stunningly simple tunic-style gown of the palest peach-coloured satin that seemed to mould itself to her curves, Helena, her expression unreadable, now stood proudly erect as she waited for the Patronesses' to reach their verdict.

Clenching his jaw, Richard inhaled deeply, trying to ignore the rapid pounding of his heart whilst, at the same time, doing his utmost to convince himself that these inexplicable emotions that beset him whenever he was anywhere near her were just part and parcel of the normal virile male response when confronted with such loveliness. A state of affairs that a brisk gallop and a cold shower usually took care of but, since he had practically ridden his horse into the ground shortly after dawn that morning, in addition to having swum across the Thames and back at a secluded spot near Hampton Wick, it would seem that these tried-and-tested remedies were, given the present wayward reaction of certain parts of his anatomy, meeting with a singular lack of success!

The sharp dig of his grandmother's elbow in his arm snapped him back to reality. Starting, he became aware that all five ladies on the podium were looking directly at him, as though they expected something from him. Conscious that he had been so wrapped up in his reverie that he had failed to pay attention to what had been going on around him, a slight flush stained his cheeks as he looked down at his grandmother, his eyes mutely questioning.

'They're waiting for you to ask for permission to dance with Helena,' she hissed, the beginnings of an embarrassed flush on her face.

His brow clearing, Richard stepped forwards and, with his usual grace and style, performed the required ritual, whereupon each of the ladies in turn did him the honour of nodding their agreement to his request.

'And, in addition, you may also have our permission to dance with any of the young ladies to whom Mr Willis chooses to introduce you,' said Lady Jersey, as she favoured him and his cousin with the full radiance of her smile.

'Well, thank the lord that's over!' muttered Charles, as soon as they were out of earshot of the podium. 'Reminded me of being sent before the beak at Eton! I could almost hear my knees knocking together!'

'Probably the effect of these damned satin breeches,' returned Richard, suppressing a grin. 'Haven't worn such an uncomfortable get-up since God only knows when!'

Owing to the fact that a good many of the other gentlemen and indeed not a few of the older ladies had taken themselves off to one or other of the side rooms where the card tables had been set up, the initial press of people had thinned somewhat, making it relatively easy for the earl to commandeer a suitably placed set of chairs for his party.

As he handed her into her seat, Helena managed a brief smile of thanks, the feeling of exasperated disbelief that had beset her from the moment she had set foot in the hall only just beginning to evaporate. Never having wanted to be part of this upper circle of society, the entire rigmarole had struck her as being absurdly pretentious and utterly farcical, not to mention embarrassing. Why any mother would want to couple her daughter with any of the posturing and preening individuals who were presently doing the rounds was completely beyond her, for a more abject-looking set of obvious fortune-hunters she yet had to set eyes upon!

Unfurling her fan, she peeped surreptitiously over its fluted rim to where Markfield was standing, in conversation with his cousin. She could not help thinking that, unlike most of the other males present, the earl looked rather dashing in his long-tailed coat and knee-length breeches, it not having escaped her notice that the complementary white stockings he was wearing had the added effect of displaying his firm calf muscles to great advantage.

Having spent the best part of the afternoon agonising over just how she was going to act towards him when he called to pick them up this evening, she found that she need not have concerned herself with the pointless exercise, for it seemed that whatever had been troubling his lordship for the past few days had ceased to be an issue. Gone were the stiffly correct manner and taciturn demeanour and, in their place, were smiles and pleasantry, making it difficult for her to carry on with her own intended attitude of polite detachment. In fact, within minutes of his having handed her into the countess's barouche, many of her earlier doubts and reservations had seemed to vanish into thin air as, almost without thinking, she had found herself responding once more to his good-natured bonhomie.

Watching him now, as he leant down to have a word with his grandmother, she stifled a sigh, having reached the conclusion that, if what both Jenny and the countess had intimated were to be believed, there was little point in her continually repining over the issue since—quite apart from the fact that it was really no business of hers how Markfield chose to conduct his life—it had already been made abundantly clear that any arrangement between herself and the earl was intended to be of a temporary nature. None the less, as a series of highly disturbing images of him entwined in the arms of the dreadful Cummings woman persisted in hammering at her senses, she found it impossible to stem the feelings of melancholia that accompanied these bothersome fantasies. Unfortunately, as she was well aware, until her father's condition improved sufficiently for him to face up to being told of yet another doomed relationship, she had no recourse but to carry on with this dismal charade. A circumstance which, in the normal way of things, ought to be well within her capabilities—if only she could learn to still those painful longings that continued to beset her and school her pulse to behave less erratically whenever Markfield happened to turn his head in her direction!

She was so wrapped up in her thoughts that she failed to hear the earl's initial request that she stand up with him for the set that was presently forming.

'Miss Wheatley?' he repeated, looking down at her questioningly. 'The music is about to begin, if you would do me the honour?'

She gave a quick start and, as the realisation of what he was asking her gradually dawned, she leapt hurriedly to her feet, a rosy blush covering her cheeks.

Although the orchestra had already struck up the opening chords of the music, they had no difficulty in finding themselves a place, since there was little for the waiting couples to do at this point but raise their arms, while the top couple twirled and sashayed their way down through the arches.

'I trust that you were not too much put out by that ridiculous inauguration ceremony?' said Richard, as he reached out to take hold of her upraised hands.

'Not at all, my lord,' she replied, steeling herself to disregard the wild beating of her heart as their fingers touched. 'As a matter of fact, I must confess to finding the whole affair quite tedious.'

'I rather got the feeling that you were not particularly impressed,' he said, letting out a soft chuckle. 'You looked so deadly serious standing there, I couldn't help but wonder what was going on in your mind.'

She gave a little shrug. 'I was merely thinking what a great pity it is that such powerful women should choose to exercise their influence on such a petty and pointless rigmarole, when they might easily use it in far more beneficial ways.'

Although he was intrigued at her reply, the movement of the

dance prevented him from questioning her further and he was obliged to wait until they had performed the steps of the next measure before he was again in a position to pursue the matter.

'Beneficial to whom?' he queried, when they had again joined hands. 'I'm not sure that I follow you.'

Helena hesitated, not entirely sure of the suitability of embarking on such a serious topic while engaged in so frivolous an activity as dancing. But, since he had asked and since it was a subject so close to her heart, she was unable to resist the challenge. 'Well, they might start by taking an interest in the lamentable plight of the hundreds of displaced soldiers we have in our midst!' she returned, in a somewhat defiant manner.

'Displaced soldiers!' He stared down at her in confusion. 'Hardly a subject for a young lady to concern herself with, surely?'

'And, why not, may I ask?' she retorted defensively. 'Given that I have spent the better part of the past two years doling out bread and soup to such neglected souls, I think I might claim to have acquired a fairly knowledgeable grasp of the situation!'

'Well, I'll be—!'

He paused, temporarily at a stand. But then, as he recalled what he knew of her history, his eyes softened and he said, 'In dedication to your brother's memory, I imagine? On behalf of my fellow comrades in arms, allow me to salute you!'

And, raising her hand, he bent forwards and pressed his lips to her fingers, causing her considerable confusion.

'After the sacrifices that have been made on our behalves, it is little enough for any of us to do,' she replied breathlessly, when she had finally regained sufficient command of her senses to say anything at all.

Having taken note of the rather bewitching colour that had flooded her cheeks at his gesture, Richard was conscious of a sudden lightening of spirit. 'Might I be so bold as to enquire whether you were engaged in these duties earlier today?' he asked. At her nod of acquiescence, his lips curved in a satisfied smile. 'And that was why you were unable to receive me this morning, I take it?' he ventured hopefully.

Having discovered that the intense gleam in his eyes was causing her heart to behave in the most erratic manner, Helena was relieved to find that the movement of the dance required her to disengage her hands from his, in order that she might follow the rest of the ladies down the outside of the set.

'Partly,' she replied over her shoulder as, swinging away from him, she made her way up the line towards the top of the set. Taking a quick peek through the line of moving dancers on her left, to ascertain that her partner was keeping pace with her, she reached the top of the set where, holding out her hand in readiness for Markfield's grasp but reluctant to subject her senses to yet another bombardment, she kept her eyes firmly away from his and forced herself to direct her gaze over his right shoulder.

All at once, she stiffened and paled and, as a sudden trickle of apprehension ran through her veins, she tried desperately to steady herself but, unable to control her trembling limbs, she felt herself falling and, had not Richard thrust out his arms to catch hold of her, she would have slid to the floor.

The mishap having obliged the line of ladies in Helena's wake to slow their progress, the resulting confusion quickly brought the dance to a chaotic finish upon which, following a hurried signal from the Master of Ceremonies, the musicians were obliged to bring the tune to a somewhat haphazard end.

'Miss Wheatley?' Although the deep concern in Richard's voice was apparent, Helena, now totally mesmerised by the expression of unconcealed venom on the face of the man who had been the cause of her sudden apprehension, was finding it almost impossible to tear her eyes away from his. For her sneering tormentor was none other than the despicable Viscount Barrington—the man from whom she had fled the Vauxhall Gardens in disgust and the very last man she might have expected to encounter in such hallowed surroundings!

'Helena! Please!'

The returning colour in Helena's previously deathly white cheeks having encouraged the highly concerned Richard to suppose that she was now on the road to recovery, he resorted to giving her a little shake. 'Take deep breaths,' he urged as, placing his arm around her shoulders, he endeavoured to persuade her to move away from the eyes of the curious onlookers. 'Try to make the effort, dear girl. I must get you back to your seat.'

As his words gradually penetrated her dazed mind, Helena blinked and, with considerable effort, forced herself to drag her gaze away from Barrington's still mocking, contempt-filled countenance. Taking a deep breath to steady her nerves, she admonished herself crossly, telling herself that it had merely been the shock of seeing the man standing there with that dreadful expression on his face that had been the cause of her momentary agitation. There had been absolutely no need for her to have behaved in such a ridiculous manner. After all, no matter how contemptible he might be, the viscount was hardly likely to go so far as to create an ugly scene in this holy of holies!

But then, as Markfield's persistent tug again claimed her attention, she suddenly became aware that all the other couples were making their way off the dance floor, leaving the earl and herself the focus of everyone's attention.

'Oh, my goodness!' she stammered, her cheeks now flushed with embarrassment. 'I do beg your pardon, my lord—I fear that I must have been overcome by the heat!'

'Then we must get you back to your seat at once,' grated the earl as, finally allowing himself to breathe once more, he placed his hand on her back and gently but firmly propelled her in the direction of her seat. 'And then I need to go and procure you some sort of a cooling drink.'

Although both his words and tone were equally solicitous, Helena, having caught sight of his rather grim expression, could not help feeling that he must be thoroughly mortified at her dismal lack of conduct—and at such a highly esteemed venue, too! And just as they were beginning to get on so well again, she thought miserably, as she allowed him to lead her across the floor and settle her back into her seat where, unable to meet his eyes, she found herself incapable of offering him more than a slightly muffled, 'You are very kind, my lord.'

His worried frown still in place, the earl, with a hurried bow, made off in the direction of the refreshment room.

No sooner had he disappeared from view than Lady Isobel, her face wreathed in satisfaction, leaned over and whispered into Helena's ear. 'Very neatly done, my dear, I could hardly have planned it better myself—if that doesn't get all their tongues wagging, I'm sure I don't know what will!'

Choking back her indignation at the suggestion that she had actually engineered the whole dismal affair in order to advance the dowager's scheme, Helena found herself incapable of drumming up a suitable reply. Instead, she merely inclined her head and, despite the fact that she was still feeling decidedly unnerved by the viscount's unexpected appearance, she lost no time in perusing the faces of the groups of people who were milling about the room, waiting for Mr Willis to announce the resumption of the dancing. Of the dreaded Barrington, however, there was no sign. Thinking it unlikely that he had already left the premises, she could only conclude that he must have taken himself off to one of the assembly hall's several card rooms. She crossed her fingers in the fervent wish that he would find himself sufficiently entertained to remain there and not suddenly decide to put in another appearance and attempt to engage her in conversation or even—she suppressed a shudder—request that she dance with him! Quite apart from the fact that she could not bear to be in his company, she had the feeling that to refuse such an offer in this sanctuary of sanctuaries was likely to be looked upon as the height of bad manners and, since she had already blotted her social copybook once this evening, she felt disinclined to repeat the experience!

Discreetly plying her fan, she peeped sideways at the countess and, observing that she was now deep in conversation with one of her cronies, she then turned her head in her cousin's direction, only to find Lottie's soft brown eyes regarding her with some anxiety.

'Whatever happened, Nell?' came her urgent enquiry. 'One minute you were dancing and the next thing I knew was that everything had ground to a halt and everyone seemed to be staring in your direction! You haven't crossed swords with his lordship again, have you?'

'Certainly not, dearest. I was slightly overcome by the heat, that is all,' returned Helena, feigning nonchalance, for she could see no point in adding to her cousin's already nervous state by informing her of Barrington's presence. Then, summoning up a smile, she added, 'Lord Markfield has very kindly gone off in search of some refreshments for us.'

Lottie nodded, but remained unconvinced. Having caught sight of Markfield's decidedly forbidding expression, as he had passed by her on his way to the refreshment room, she wondered whether it might not be just as well to warn her cousin that, in her opinion, she could well be about to find herself at the receiving end of the earl's disapprobation! Casting a hurried glance about her to ensure that the earl was not within earshot of her remarks, she was about to whisper her misgivings into Helena's ear, when her attention was suddenly diverted by the sight of Dr Redfern and his sister making their way across the room towards them. Her face lighting up with delight, she at once thrust aside any qualms she might have had regarding Markfield's possible irritation and, nudging her cousin's arm, exclaimed, 'Oh, do look who's coming to join us, Nell! Now we can be comfortable again!'

Pasting a welcoming smile on her face, Helena could not help feeling that, until she was certain that she discovered what lay behind his sister's somewhat baffling allusion, being comfortable in Redfern's presence was likely to prove rather difficult, insofar as she was concerned. Stifling the sigh that threatened, she did her utmost to focus her attention on welcoming the newcomers and set about presenting them to the countess. As if it were not sufficiently taxing to be beset by the constant feeling that Barrington was lurking somewhere close by, she found herself thinking, the idea of being obliged to fend off unwanted advances from the family physician was enough to make her feel like grinding her teeth in despair!

Some time later, however, although his promise of acquiring cooling drinks for them had eventually been fulfilled by the arrival of a waiter bearing a tray of glasses, of the earl himself there was still no sign. Her ladyship had taken to muttering tetchy imprecations under her breath and Helena who, having spent most of the time tormenting herself as to the reasons behind his prolonged absence, now held herself entirely responsible for his failure to return. Having done her best to dismiss the highly embarrassing incident on the dance floor from her mind, she was unable to fully recall the exact train of events that had followed her initial shock at seeing Barrington. She remembered Markfield urging her to pull herself together, along with his helping her back to her seat, considerations for which she had felt entirely grateful at the time, although she was bound to admit that his subsequent haste to remove himself from her presence had left her in little doubt as to his feelings over the incident. Biting back the tears that threatened, she could only suppose that his lordship, disinclined to subject himself to any further public discredit at her hands, had elected to steer well clear of her for the duration! Just how much worse could this dreadful evening possibly get, she wondered forlornly as, conjuring up a counterfeit smile, she rose to her feet to allow Charles Standish to escort her, for the second time in Markfield's absence, out on to the dance floor.

'Can't think what can be keeping Richard,' he said, looking towards the doorway with a puzzled frown. 'It's not like him to be so neglectful of his duties. Grandmama is not at all happy about it, I can tell you!'

Reflecting that it was unlikely that her ladyship could be feeling as wretched as she herself did at this moment, Helena merely shook her head and tried to focus her attention on the complicated movements of the cotillion.

Chapter Thirteen

Although Helena was unaware of it, Richard's feelings of despair were running very much in parallel with her own. With the recurring image of her wide-eyed, ashen-faced expression occupying his brain, his abiding aim was to get hold of a reviving drink and get back to her as quickly as possible. As to what had been the cause of her sudden attack of giddiness, he was unable to fathom for, although she had claimed to have been overcome by the heat, it had been impossible for him to miss the unmistakable look of panic in her eyes. Upon reflection, it occurred to him that perhaps his reference to her dead brother had been responsible although, despite his admittedly short acquaintance with her, Helena had hardly struck him as being the kind of female who indulged in the sort of vapourish fits for which his Aunt Adelaide was renowned! Shaking his head, he could only hope that, whatever the reason for the puzzling vertigo, a cooling drink would quickly restore her to her former doughty self.

Heading straight for the refreshment room, he had all but reached his goal when, to his consternation, he found himself being set upon by a noisy, laughing group of his ex-army comrades, newly arrived from the Continent that very day. At any other time and under any other circumstance, he would, of course, have been more than happy to see his old friends and catch up on their news. But, Helena's welfare having occupied his whole attention since the moment he had left her side, he became desperate to have done with the long drawn-out procedure of over-zealous backslapping, accompanied by loud and raucous laughter, that the unexpected reunion seemed set to involve.

Unfortunately, until he had gone through the pantomime of greeting each of the half-dozen individuals by name and given them his promise that he would meet up with them on some unspecified date in the near future, the men refused to allow him to abandon their company, each of them insisting on sharing his various experiences with him and all of them demanding to have his recent ennoblement explained to them in the fullest detail. Only when he was finally able to excuse himself was he able to set about fulfilling his earlier undertaking of having drinks delivered to his grandmother's party. That task accomplished, he was making his way back towards the doorway when, without warning, he found himself face to face with none other than the iniquitous Viscount Barrington!

'Barrington,' he acknowledged with a cursory nod and, since he had no wish to converse further with the notorious scoundrel, he stepped briskly to one side, only to discover that the viscount who, having grinningly aped his action, appeared set on impeding his further progress.

'A word, if you have a mind, your *lordship*!' drawled Barrington, laying particular emphasis on the term denoting Markfield's recent elevation to the peerage.

'I'd just as soon not be seen in your company, if it's all the same to you,' grunted Richard, impatiently standing his ground as he waited for the other man to move out of his way.

A pained expression appeared on the viscount's face. 'Oh, come now, sir!' he replied, in protest. 'That's no way to greet such a close friend of dear Simon, surely? I was merely wishing to—ah—commiserate with you on your cousin's unfortunate passing.' These words having elicited no response, he frowned then, lowering his voice, added somewhat derisively, 'But, perhaps it would be more in keeping if I were to congratulate you on your *present* success—such a tasty little armful and a fortune to boot! Do share your secret, old man!'

Although Richard managed to control the violent surge of anger that Barrington's scabrous references had brought about, he was quite unable to prevent the involuntary curling of his fists, as the probable cause of Helena's unusual agitation suddenly came to him. Fixing the viscount with a look of pure disdain, he ground out, 'Whilst I'm bound to admit that wiping the fatuous grin off your face would afford me the greatest satisfaction, Barrington, I fear that this is hardly the place in which to indulge in such pleasantries. Unless you are prepared to meet me elsewhere, I must request that you either move aside at once or suffer the consequences!'

For the briefest of moments, the viscount, his eyes glittering with unconcealed rage, seemed to toy with the idea of accepting Markfield's challenge but then, as reality dawned—along with a sudden recollection of the rumours he had heard regarding the earl's prowess with both sword and pistol—his cheeks reddened and, with obvious reluctance, he stepped slowly to one side.

Although Richard was well aware that he would have had no difficulty in carrying out his threat, he was rather relieved that he had not been obliged to do so since, as he had often heard his father remark, there was little satisfaction to be gained from thrashing a fellow who was well below one's own weight. Nevertheless, he could not help feeling somewhat concerned that Barrington—whose usual haunts, he had been given to understand, were inclined to be of a rather less salubrious variety than this present venue—should have chosen tonight, of all nights, to put in an appearance at the assembly rooms. Even more disturbing was the thought that Helena had already caught sight of her despised ex-suitor, any recurrence of which the earl was determined to prevent at whatever cost.

Tossing a contemptuous glance in the other man's direction as he passed him, he said, 'Let me advise your lordship to quit the building while you still have all your faculties intact. I'm inclined to think that the Fancy Club or Dot Finnegan's place would be rather more to your taste than this present venue!'

Although Barrington merely glowered at him in reply, Richard was sufficiently confident of his own powers of persuasion to suppose that the viscount would heed his warning and make himself scarce and, since his mind was rather more occupied with his concern about Helena's immediate well being, he quickly dismissed the matter from his mind. A hurried glance at a nearby wall-clock, however, alerted him to the length of time that he had been absent and he was aware of a slight pang of unease as he hurried back into the ballroom.

'Where on earth have you been all this time, Richard?' hissed Lady Isobel, eyeing him balefully, the moment he got within earshot of her seat. 'What is the point of me dragging Helena along to all these functions if you are going to disappear for hours on end?'

'My apologies, ma'am,' returned the earl somewhat abstractedly, his attention being more closely concerned with the worrying discovery that both seats beside the countess were now unoccupied. 'I must assure you that my absence was entirely unavoidable—where are our guests?'

'If you care to use your eyes, you will see that both your supposed intended and her cousin are out on the floor!' her ladyship retorted crossly. 'Which is where I had supposed you would be—having gone to all that trouble to acquire the blessed vouchers! Thank heavens I had the foresight to persuade Charles to come along to make up the numbers!'

Heaving a sigh of relief as, for one awful moment, it had crossed his mind that Helena's not being there might well have had something to do with Barrington's unexpected appearance, Richard turned his attention towards the dance floor and ran his eyes across the groups of dancers presently engaged in a lively

quadrille. He was able to spot his cousin almost immediately—
Standish men having always stood a good head above the rest
of the crowd. To his consternation, however, he soon realised
that the young woman whose hand Charles was clasping was
not Helena, but her cousin Lottie Daniels!

Although his hurried scrutiny of the other dancers very soon
revealed Helena's whereabouts, the discovery that she was
being partnered by none other than Thomas Redfern did
nothing to assuage his mounting irritation.

'We must hope that the good doctor has not stolen a march
on you!' observed his grandmother sourly, as she registered his
forbidding expression. 'Having already twice done his duty by
her, Charles could hardly petition Helena for a third time, now
could he? In fact, we may count ourselves fortunate that Redfern
and his sister elected to join our party, since it transpires that
they are both sufficiently well enough acquainted with several
of the gentlemen present to furnish us with the necessary introductions. Indeed, had it not been for their timely intervention,
I fear we would have made a very poor showing indeed!'

The somewhat disconcerting discovery that Helena had, apparently, recovered sufficiently from her earlier setback to take
the floor with not just one, but several different partners, during
his absence was more than enough to quell Richard's inclina-
tion to parry his grandmother's scathing comments, his feeling
of righteous indignation being such that he was temporarily
deprived of speech.

Having expected some sort of riposte to her diatribe and, to
her surprise, receiving none, the countess eyed her tight-lipped
grandson curiously for a moment or two, before continuing,
albeit in a somewhat less reproving tone of voice. 'Be that as
it may, Richard, it is highly unlikely that your protracted non-
attendance will have escaped the notice of our ever-vigilant
committee. It is clear that you are going to have to make some
sort of a push to retrieve the situation, for I am sure that you
need no reminders as to our true motives for being here.'

Richard, striving to maintain some semblance of control, assured the countess that he would do his best and, having observed that the dance was about to reach its close, stood away to allow his cousin and the doctor to return their flushed and laughing partners to their seats. They were soon joined by an equally animated Jenny Redfern, in the company of the most recent of her conquests, the Honourable Philip Tindale, younger son of the Earl of Smethwyck.

'Tindale, Redfern,' returned the earl, with a brief nod in ac-knowledgement of the other men's greetings, his thoughts being more directly concerned with the problem of how to get Helena on her own, in order that he might apologise for his lengthy absence but, rather more to the point, to try to ascertain whether her earlier spell of faintness had, as he suspected, come about as a result of her having spotted Barrington in the crowd.

'Perhaps you would care to take a turn about the room, Miss Wheatley?' he said, stepping forwards and reaching out his hand to her.

Having been expecting him to steer well clear of her, lest she should cause him any more embarrassment, Helena was too taken aback to utter more than a shaky, 'Yes, of course, my lord.'

'I really must apologise for leaving you in the lurch like that,' he began, as they started to make their way around the ballroom. 'I am afraid I was set upon by a bunch of my fellow officers and quite unable to make my escape.'

Although she felt a certain amount of relief at hearing these words, Helena could not help wondering what else had kept him away since, along with countless other onlookers, she was well aware that the 'bunch of fellow officers' of whom he had spoken had been taken to task by Mr Willis for their rather dis-orderly entrance into the ballroom well before Markfield had eventually chosen to put in an appearance.

'Please do not concern yourself on my account, my lord,' she replied. 'My cousin and I were amply entertained during your absence.'

Having been privy to the obvious pleasure she had exhibited when dancing with Redfern, Richard was obliged to bite back the sarcastic retort that had almost sprung to his lips and, whilst he ached to know whether the doctor's role in her life was anything more than just that of family physician, he knew that to pose such a question was completely out of order. That Helena was still at odds with him was blatantly obvious and, unless he could find some way of getting her to view him in a more favourable light, it was becoming rapidly apparent that their rather tentative arrangement would soon be on the verge of collapse.

Providentially, an announcement from the Master of Ceremonies that the final dance before the supper bell was to be the second waltz of the evening, soon furnished him with what he hoped might be a possible solution to that particular problem.

Disengaging her hand from his arm, he swung her round to face him.

'Our dance, I believe, Miss Wheatley,' he said, the hint of a smile lurking on his lips.

Stepping back in astonishment, Helena shook her head, protesting, 'But, this is a waltz, my lord and, as you are no doubt aware, I have not yet had the opportunity to learn the steps!'

'Oh, come now, Miss Wheatley,' he cajoled softly. 'What has become of all that doughty resolution you exhibited earlier? It's really very simple, I promise you.'

Thoroughly disconcerted by the challenging gleam in his eyes, Helena hesitated. Having been obliged to decline both Tindale's and Redfern's requests to partner them in the highly acclaimed dance some time earlier, she had been given ample opportunity to study the dancers' movements at some length and had come to the conclusion waltzing did, indeed, look absurdly simple. Added to which, the mere idea of Markfield holding her in such a close manner as the dance seemed to require was extremely tempting. Nevertheless, disinclined to make yet another foolish exhibition of herself, she reluctantly stood her ground.

But then, as Jenny, skipped past her, crying, 'Oh, you simply must give this a try, Helena!' before practically throwing herself into Tindale's outstretched arms, she felt herself weakening.

The earl, observing her momentary hesitation, quickly seized the opportunity and clasped her by both hands. Before she had had time to collect her wits, she found herself being steered in the direction of the dance floor with Richard resolutely ignoring her attempts to free herself from his hold.

'Really, my lord!' she gasped, looking up at him in dismay. 'You cannot mean to force me into this!'

'Just relax and leave the rest to me,' he said reassuringly as, his eyes smiling down into hers, he placed his hand at her waist, causing sudden ripples of excitement to surge up and down her body. 'All you have to do is surrender yourself to the beat of the music—I won't let you down, I promise you. Now, left hand on my shoulder and—off we go!'

Then, without giving her any more time to dwell upon the consequences of his actions, he was propelling her backwards across the floor. Luckily for Helena's peace of mind, her innate sense of rhythm, coupled with her many years of musical training, came quickly bounding to her rescue. With a joyful leap of her heart, she submitted herself to the earl's highly competent leadership, whereupon she instantly found herself swept up in the compulsive beat of the music.

With every passing minute, her confidence grew and, thanks largely to Richard's patient and adroit handling, it was not long before she had mastered many of the turns. Thoroughly captivated by the seductively lilting rhythm of the music, her eyes were soon shining with unalloyed delight as, smiling up at him, she managed to exclaim, if a little breathlessly, 'Oh, Jenny was so right! Isn't this just the most glorious sensation imaginable?'

Returning her smile, his heart pounding with a heady mixture of excitement and deep satisfaction, Richard was bound to admit that it was—not so much the dance itself, as far as he was concerned, but rather the indescribable feeling of having Helena in his arms at last. Had one of his hands been free, he might have been obliged to pinch himself, if only to convince himself that this was real and not one of the bizarre dreams that had been tormenting him of late!

Content to let him lead her where he may, Helena, closing her eyes, soon became oblivious to everything but the heady, pulsating beat of the music and the lithe, swaying movements of the earl's body, so tantalisingly close to her own. In her enchanted dreamlike state, it seemed to her that they were joined together as one being, whirling and twirling about the room in absolute and perfect harmony. Utterly enthralled, she could not help wishing that the enchantment of the moment would go on for ever.

Sadly, all too soon, the closing chords of the music could be heard echoing across the crowded floor, bringing the dance to its inevitable conclusion. Helena was aware of the earl's arms tightening, pulling her yet more closely towards him as he swung her round in one final glorious, exhilarating twirl. Only when he had brought her to a dazed and breathless standstill could she at last bring herself to open her eyes, whereupon she found him staring down at her with such an unfathomable expression on his face that her heart seemed to stop in its tracks.

For one agonising moment, as they stood gazing into each other's eyes, Richard was beset by an almost overwhelming desire to pull her back into his arms and capture the luscious softness of her lips with his own. Fortunately, the sound of the supper gong, signalling the end of the first half of the evening's entertainment, brought him quickly to his senses. With a sudden start, he became aware of his surroundings and, drawing in a deep breath in an effort to steady his racing pulse, he conjured up a somewhat shaky grin, saying, 'An unqualified success in my opinion. What do you say, Miss Wheatley?'

Then, placing his hand at her elbow, he directed the still slightly bemused Helena back to her seat, where they found the others smilingly awaiting their return.

'Ooh, Nell!' whispered Lottie, her eyes wide. 'That was indeed a surprise—why did you never let on that you were able to waltz?'

'I was not aware that I could until a few minutes ago!' returned Helena, with a self-conscious smile. 'I just hope that I didn't make a frightful cake of myself!'

'Quite the reverse,' declared her cousin stoutly. 'I could scarcely take my eyes off you!'

Although his momentary aberration had left him feeling thoroughly disconcerted, Richard was no less resolved to ensure that Redfern was allowed no leeway in his pursuit of Helena. Having observed that the doctor had ceased his conversation with Tindale and was now heading in Helena's direction—*doubtless in expectation of being granted the privilege of escorting her into supper*—he thought sourly, he sent a discreet signal to his cousin to indicate that he should see to their grandmother's refreshments and, stepping forwards, neatly intercepted Redfern.

'I believe Miss Wheatley has already promised herself to me,' he said, as he held out his hand to a somewhat taken-aback Helena.

'But of course, sir,' returned Redfern, standing back with a good-natured grin. Then, with scarcely a moment's hesitation, he bowed and extended his arm to the blushing and much-overcome Lottie. 'Miss Daniels, if you would care to do me the honour?'

Despite being perfectly well aware that no such previous arrangement had been made between Markfield and herself in regard to the supper interlude, the expression of steely determination on his face, coupled with her recent experience on the dance floor, were more than enough to convince Helena that contesting his declaration might not be the wisest course of action to take at this juncture. Aside from which, she decided, the intermission would provide her with a much-needed opportunity to tackle him regarding the rather troublesome matter that had been brought to her attention during his absence.

Taking his proffered arm, she waited while he stood back to allow the rest of their party to precede them out of the room. Then, as soon as they were alone, she removed her hand and, turning to face him, she said, 'If you wouldn't mind waiting just a moment or two, my lord, I need to speak to you about the subscriptions.'

He stared down at her, his expression suddenly guarded. 'Subscriptions?' he repeated. 'What about them?'

'Doctor Redfern has informed me that he was obliged to pay a membership fee of ten guineas each for his sister and himself and it occurred to me that you also…'

She hesitated, uncomfortably aware of the narrowing of his eyes and the tightening of his lips but then, throwing caution to the wind, she pressed on none the less, 'You may scowl all you like, sir, but I simply cannot allow you to continue to incur these sorts of expenses on my behalf—my father was quite insistent that we should pay our own way during the course of this venture!'

'I prefer not to discuss the matter any further, if it is all the same to you, Miss Wheatley,' Richard growled as, taking hold of her elbow, he attempted to steer her in the direction of the doorway. 'I am not yet so down on my uppers that I cannot afford a few guineas' entrance fee!'

Helena, however, had no intention of being diverted from her chosen course. 'I beg your pardon, my lord!' she retorted as, resolutely standing her ground, she refused to budge. 'But I must remind you that the terms of our agreement state quite clearly that you are to be refunded for any expense that you incur on our behalves!'

'And *I* would remind *you* that I have not yet signed any such agreement,' returned the earl, a dangerous glint appearing in his eyes. 'Nor, indeed, do I have any intention of so doing and, since I believe we have already covered a somewhat similar ground on a previous occasion, the subject, as far as I am concerned, is at an end!'

Choking back her indignation, Helena stared up at him in disbelief. 'Well! Of all the arrogant…!' she gasped. 'Just because *you* have decided that the matter is closed by no means makes it so as far as I am concerned, sir! What right have you to dictate to me in such a high-handed manner?'

About to defend himself against her unexpected onslaught, Richard, suddenly confronted with the rapid rise and fall of the twin mounds of her magnificent bosom, found his attention so thoroughly diverted that he was momentarily deprived of speech. But then, furious with himself for having been so easily side-tracked, he hurriedly dragged his eyes away from the tantalising sight and, with a quick intake of breath, asked carefully, 'Might I ask in what way my refusing to accept money from a lady can possibly be thought of as either arrogant or high-handed?'

Helena gave a disdainful shrug. 'It would appear to be all of a piece with you,' she replied bitterly. 'First, you disappear for hours on end—coming up with the most trumpery of excuses when you finally do deign to return—and then you drag me on to the dance floor against my will! And now, it seems, I am not even to be permitted to speak unless you give your consent! If that is not arrogant high-handedness, I am sure I don't know what is!'

'But, I thought I had explained what kept me away so long!' he argued, staring down at her in bewilderment. 'Not that my absence appeared to have any effect on your own enjoyment, by all accounts,' he added, somewhat cynically. 'Unless my eyes were deceiving me, I would say that you seemed more than happy to have the popular doctor take you up in my stead!'

'*How dare you, sir!*' exclaimed Helena, her eyes kindling. 'Perhaps you would rather I had sat on the sidelines for almost an hour while you amused yourself elsewhere?'

Then, drawing herself up to her full height, she shot him a scornful look and, unable to contain her resentment, exclaimed scornfully, 'I suggest that you take stock of your own rather suspect behaviour before you criticise others, my lord! In view of that questionable episode at Lady Kettlesham's last evening, I wonder that you have the gall to accuse *me* of coquetry!'

At her words, Richard stiffened with outrage. 'Whatever

happened at Lady Kettlesham's last evening, is not, in my opinion, any concern of yours,' he said tersely. 'Furthermore, I was hardly accusing you of coquetry. I was merely concerned at how others might view your conduct.'

'*My* conduct…!' Now thoroughly lost to reason, Helena, scarlet-cheeked and her eyes bright with unshed tears, rounded on him. 'That is the outside of enough, sir! I will not stay here and allow you to insult me any further! Just as I suspected, you have proved yourself to be no better than the rest of your kind and, as far as I am concerned, this stupid farce is now at an end! You may notify her ladyship that any agreement that we may once have had is terminated!' And, before he could reach out his hands to stop her, she had turned and fled across the room towards the nearby exit.

Whilst the earl found himself to be thoroughly exasperated by Helena's unaccountable reaction to what he had regarded as a fairly straightforward statement of fact, every nerve in his body was urging him to hasten after her and beg her pardon for causing her such unintended distress. Straightening his shoulders and doing his utmost to ignore the hushed whispers and pointed glances that were being cast in his direction, he lifted his chin and strode towards the doorway and thence out into the corridor beyond.

Chapter Fourteen

Having reached the corridor, Helena paused and looked about her, undecided as to her next move. Already on the point of regretting her impulsive outburst, she could not yet bring herself to face Lottie and the others in the supper room. Whilst what she most wanted to do was to get herself back to the peace and comfort of her own home as quickly as possible, her head was in too much of a whirl to concentrate on how best to achieve that goal without drawing undue attention to her flight. Perhaps she could call on Mr Willis, the Master of Ceremonies, to assist her, she thought, as she stood in the dimly lit passageway. He had looked a kindly sort of gentleman and would surely help her to procure a reputable hansom cab? Fortunately, she had plenty of money in her reticule, her previous experience having taught her never to leave the house without sufficient funds to see her safely home again.

Getting a message to Lottie presented another problem, of course, but how that might be arranged, she could not think. Added to which, since she had a very clear image of Markfield tucking the cloakroom tickets into his breast pocket shortly after their arrival, Helena soon realised that the chances of her being able to retrieve their cloaks were somewhat less than nil!

Having tentatively toyed with the possibility of seeking Dr

Redfern's assistance, she had been obliged to put the thought aside for, whilst it was true that he had been careful not to display any overt partiality towards her throughout the evening, his evident disinclination to wander far from her side had not escaped her notice. Added to which, although she had only stood up with him for one dance, it had been impossible not to register the fact that, on each of the two occasions that Charles Standish had led her out, the doctor had been very quick to cajole poor little Lottie—who was no dancer at the best of times—into joining the self-same sets. To involve him in any sort of secret assignation might well be misconstrued as some sort of subtle invitation to encourage him to press his advantage, a situation that was to be avoided at all costs. Having only just managed to extricate herself from one, now apparently, undesirable relationship, she was determined not to find herself up to her neck in another!

Dashing away the tears that persisted in welling up into her eyes, she was finding it hard to believe that she had allowed herself to be so badly taken in. Markfield, it seemed, was no better than any of the others—an arrogant, supercilious beast, with a total disregard for anyone else's feelings. It was just as well she had found him out before she had allowed herself to fall completely under his spell!

She pressed her fingers to her aching forehead and glanced about her, in an effort to get her bearings. At the far end of the corridor, groups of people were still moving in and out of the supper room but, since she had no desire to join the rest of her party, she thought it best to move away from that area, in the hopes of finding either the ladies' room or some other unoccupied spot in which she might sit and rest her pounding head for a few moments while she considered what to do next.

Unfortunately, as she was soon to discover on peering round their doors, both of the rooms at this end of the corridor had been given over to card-playing, leaving only a tiny store room that, upon further investigation, proved to be crammed full of boxes, broken chairs and other unwanted bits and pieces.

Feeling utterly dispirited, she was just on the point of closing the storeroom door when there, in the darkest recess of the room, almost hidden amongst the discarded paraphernalia, she caught a glimpse of what looked to be a dilapidated *chaise-longue*, piled high with old curtains. Sending up a prayer of thanks for whichever Providence had seen fit to grant her this much-needed respite, she began to edge her way through the piles of clutter towards the seat.

She had barely taken two steps into the room, however, when she was staggered to feel a pair of hands grasping at her shoulders and then, before she had time to understand what was happening, she found herself being propelled roughly forwards and thrust, face downwards, into the pile of dust-covered velvet curtains on the *chaise*. Shocked out of her senses and struggling to breathe, it was some little while before she had recovered sufficiently to roll herself over on to her elbows, whereupon she found herself staring up into none other than the malevolently grinning Viscount Barrington!

'So, we meet again, Miss Wheatley,' he drawled softly, as he reached forwards and pulled her towards him. 'I do believe we have some unfinished business to attend to.'

Helena's mind reeled. Having spent most of the evening looking over her shoulder in a constant fret as to whether or not the viscount had left the premises, the bitter confrontation with Markfield had completely erased her earlier concerns from her mind.

'Let me go, sir, I beg you!' she implored him, as, still struggling to catch her breath, she tried to wrench herself from his hold. 'You cannot mean to keep me here against my will!'

'By the time I am finished with you, my dear,' he retorted, pushing her back on to the *chaise* and placing his hand over her mouth, 'I promise that both you and your father will be down on your knees begging me to marry you!'

Her eyes widening with disbelief as the implication of his words sunk in, Helena, kicking with all her might, fought to free herself from his hold until, limp and panting, she felt herself collapse beneath him. 'Waste of time and effort, all that pointless struggling,' grunted Barrington as, lowering himself on top of her, his free hand groped amongst the several layers of petticoats under her skirt. 'Best to save your breath for the pleasures yet to come, my sweet!'

Her head swimming, Helena, now utterly spent, was powerless to prevent the viscount's grotesque fumblings and, frozen with terror, she could feel herself slowly drifting into a state of oblivion.

Then, just as she was about to lose all sense of reality, a violent crashing sound jerked her back to consciousness, whereupon she discovered, to her intense joy and relief, that her breathing was no longer being restricted by the weight of Barrington's body. As a series of thuds and guttural croaks swiftly followed his unexpected departure, her mind gradually became more fully attuned to her surroundings.

'Helena?'

Markfield? Her eyes fluttered open and there, kneeling at her side, was the earl, his expression of fearful apprehension clearly visible, even in the room's half-light.

'Helena? Sweetheart? Can you stand?'

Sweetheart? Had the viscount's attack affected her hearing? Shaking her head and blinking rapidly, in an attempt to clear away the mists of confusion, she gazed up at him through the gloom.

'Barrington?' she whispered, as she gingerly raised herself into an upright position.

'He won't be troubling you again, I promise,' returned Richard, guardedly flexing the knuckles of his bruised right hand. Then, reaching forwards, he drew her gently to her feet. 'Are you—? Did he—?'

His voice wavered and, with a muffled groan, he pulled her into his arms. 'I'm so very sorry, my dear. I should have been more vigilant. Can you ever forgive me?'

As her heart leapt within her, Helena was scarcely aware of the words he had uttered. Finding herself wrapped in the security of his embrace was, as far as she was concerned, more than adequate compensation for any degradation that she might have suffered at the hands of the hateful viscount. Through the layers of clothing that separated them, she could feel the warmth of his body and the slightly unsteady beat of his heart. Powerless to resist the compulsion, she slid her hands around his waist and, pressing herself against him even more closely, she raised her head and looked intently into his eyes.

Although his sense of duty was telling him that what Helena was most in need of at this moment was a period of calm and comfort, Richard, meeting her limpid gaze, found himself again fighting an almost overwhelming desire to feel the inviting softness of her lips against his own.

Regrettably, his mounting need quickly put paid to any finer feelings that he had harboured earlier and, emitting a soft sigh of capitulation, he closed his eyes and lowered his head.

'May I enquire exactly what is going on in here, your lordship?' came Lady Jersey's frosty tones behind them.

Starting back in dismay, Richard swung round and, in a vain effort to shield her from view, thrust the equally shocked Helena behind him.

There, clustered together at the doorway and glowering at him with unconcealed disapproval on their faces, were all five of the club's notoriously unforgiving Patronesses. Moreover, these ladies were not on their own, but were accompanied by a rather surprising number of other inquisitive onlookers, among whom, as the earl was soon to observe, to his utter chagrin, was the dowager countess herself! Biting back the violent oath that was starting to form, it did not take him long to work out that it had been Barrington who—despite his bruised and battered appearance—had quite clearly lost no time in spreading word of the recent violent confrontation between himself and the earl. Any vague puzzlement that

Richard might have felt as to why the viscount should be so eager to advertise such blatant misconduct was soon to be clarified by Lady Jersey's next broadside.

'Viscount Barrington has already been so good as to inform my fellow Patronesses and myself of his courageous attempt to prevent you molesting one of our young ladies, sir! That one of our members should go so far as to forget himself and behave in so despicable a manner is quite beyond belief! And, under our very noses, too! Unless you are able to explain your actions, sir, we must request that you collect your party and leave our premises without further ado!'

Passing a weary hand across his forehead, Richard found himself momentarily unable to conjure up an acceptable explanation that would refute the dastardly viscount's scurrilous claim. What was becoming abysmally clear to him, however, was that, since Barrington had been devious enough to set about circulating such a highly calumnious version of the event, any attempt from him to reveal the truth of the matter was more likely to increase his accusers' belief in his own guilt rather than persuade them of his innocence. Apart from which and, rather more to the point, as far as Richard was concerned, was the necessity of protecting Helena from malicious gossip. He drew in a deep breath, reluctantly concluding that, despite the fact that it went against the most basic of his principles, there was, clearly, only one way out of this mess.

'It would seem that your ladyships have been badly misled,' he said, eyeing his detractors steadily. 'Whilst it is perfectly true that I was obliged to eject Lord Barrington from the room rather forcibly, I consider that my actions were wholly justified, since, far from molesting the young lady in question, as his lordship has suggested, I was, at the time he barged in upon us, in the process of proposing marriage to her!'

Steeling himself to ignore the barely concealed gasp of dismay from behind him, he then added, 'As Miss Wheatley will no doubt be prepared to confirm, should you care to ask her.'

And, keeping his fingers crossed, he stepped aside to reveal the scarlet-faced and somewhat dishevelled-looking Helena who, having listened to his astounding claim with mounting alarm, now found herself so utterly taken aback that she was incapable of speech.

'Miss Wheatley?'

Taking her unresisting hand in his, Richard, summoning up a smile of encouragement, looked down at her, saying, 'It would seem that our little secret is out, my love. Perhaps you would care to explain to their ladyships the true purpose of our clandestine rendezvous?'

On raising her eyes to meet his, the earnest entreaty contained therein caused Helena's breath to catch in her throat and, although her exhausted brain was struggling to digest the full implication of his words, it would have been well nigh impossible for her not to have registered the somewhat lowering fact that, in his valiant endeavours to protect her from shame and dishonour, the earl was even prepared to go so far as to sacrifice his principles on the altar of her good name.

All at once, it came to her that this whole appalling fiasco had been brought about as a direct result of her own wilful determination to challenge Markfield's authority. Horribly conscious of the fact that, had she not fled from his protection and attempted to hide herself away in this storeroom, none of the disastrous events that had followed could possibly have occurred and his lordship would not now be finding himself in the invidious position of being obliged to ask for her hand in marriage! Nevertheless, knowing full well that she was left with little choice but to go along with his outrageous claim, Helena forced herself to dredge up the remains of what little courage she still had left and, reluctantly entwining her fingers in his, she turned towards the murmuring crowd at the doorway and exclaimed, 'You have no right to cast such dreadful aspersions on Lord Markfield's integrity! He has spoken nothing but the truth! Had not the viscount chosen to invade our privacy and cause such wicked mischief, our little tête-à-tête would have been over and done with long before either of us had been missed. As it is, what was intended to be our own private secret until his lordship was able to speak with my father, is now, thanks to Barrington's malicious allegations, common currency!'

Then, turning back to Markfield, she said, 'I would like to go home now, my lord, if you would be so good!'

The earl, who was somewhat awed at the speed with which Helena had managed to summon up such apparent composure, hurriedly tucked her hand into his arm and strode purposefully towards the doorway. With a hasty signal to the assembled throng that the pair should be allowed through, Lady Jersey sank into a deep curtsy as they passed her, saying, 'Pray accept our deepest apologies for the misunderstanding, my lord, and allow me to be the first to offer you both my heartiest felicitations on your betrothal.'

Although she was still filled with a curious mixture of mortification and disbelief, Helena, lifting her chin resolutely, swept past the now hushed crowd with as much dignity as she could muster.

They had hardly gone more than half-a-dozen steps or so down the passageway, however, before their progress was brought to an abrupt halt by the anxious tones of Lady Isobel calling them from behind, urging Markfield to slow down.

'I cannot possibly keep up with you, if you insist upon dashing along at such a preposterous speed!' she huffed irritably, as soon as she had caught up with them. Then, without pausing for breath and, after casting a concerned look towards her grandson, she asked, 'I don't suppose you would care to explain to me exactly what that astonishing brouhaha was all about?'

'Not now, Grandmama, please!' groaned Richard, shaking his head in weary protest. 'We have to get Miss Wheatley home. Can't you see that the poor girl has endured more than enough for one evening?'

'Hmm. I dare say you have a point there, my boy,' returned

the countess, a pensive frown appearing on her face as she took in Helena's dishevelled appearance and unnaturally pallid cheeks. 'But I trust that you will do me the courtesy of clarifying the matter as soon as we get back to Curzon Street.'

'All in good time, I promise you,' he assured her as, after pushing open the door that led into the assembly room's foyer, he gently settled Helena on to one of the nearby sofas. 'For the moment, however, I would appreciate it if you would be so good as to sit with Miss Wheatley while I go in search of her cousin and collect our cloaks.'

'Very well, dear boy,' returned her ladyship with a brief nod as, taking her place beside Helena, she picked up her hand and began to stroke it reassuringly. 'And have no fear! No one will dare to pester the child while I have charge of her, you may be sure of that!'

On hearing the dowager's forthright reassurance, a sudden rush of guilt caused a momentary faltering in the earl's step as he returned to the doorway and he could hardly help the dismal reflection that, had he been a sight more attentive, he might well have been able to utter the same words himself! As it was, however, by allowing his damnable pride to outweigh the most basic of gentlemanly codes, he had exposed Helena to one of the gravest of dangers imaginable. And, it suddenly came to him that, despite all his former reservations on the subject, if marriage were the only way in which he could redeem himself in her eyes then he would be more than happy to take the chance and let the consequences go hang!

No sooner had the door closed behind him than Helena, jumping to her feet, swung round to face the dowager, exclaiming, 'Now we really are in the basket, ma'am! Markfield has led everyone to believe that he and I are engaged to be married! How on earth are we going to persuade them that it has all just been some frightful mistake?'

'Pray, do not allow yourself to worry about it, my dear,' returned Lady Isobel as, reaching out and catching hold of her hand, she pulled her gently back down on to the sofa. 'Richard is bound to have the matter well in hand. You may be sure that it will not be long before he comes up with some perfectly satisfactory solution to this inopportune predicament!'

Chapter Fifteen

But when, ten days later, Helena found herself standing clutching at her father's arm in the vestibule of St George's Church, Hanover Square, it had become worryingly evident to her that Markfield had not, thus far, managed to come up with any sort of solution at all, let alone a satisfactory one. Other than denying him at the altar—the idea of which was wholly repugnant to her nature—it would seem that she had been left with no alternative but to see the thing through to its fateful conclusion!

After having spent the whole of the morning following the traumatic events at Almack's closeted with Dr Redfern in Mr Wheatley's sick room, the earl had left town for his Surrey estate and, apart from two short visits when he had called in at Cadogan Place in order to sign various settlement papers and finalise last-minute details of the impending union, his presence had been conspicuously lacking. And, even though he had conducted himself in a perfectly proper manner on each of these occasions—such as bending over her hand and pressing his lips to her fingers in the time-honoured fashion—Helena had been left with the distinctly uncomfortable feeling that Markfield had resigned himself to the situation and was merely going through the motions.

During the whole of this seemingly endless period scarcely a dozen words had been exchanged between the pair—and every one of these had been in the presence of either Lottie or the earl's cousin, Charles Standish. And to complicate matters even further—if that were at all possible—Standish's constant attendance at her house during the past week had led her to suspect that Markfield had charged his cousin with the task of ensuring that no harm should befall his betrothed during his own enforced non-attendance.

Her father had, not surprisingly, been over the moon with delight at the unexpected announcement and, owing to his absolute determination to lead his only daughter up the aisle, his health had begun to improve with startling rapidity from that moment onwards. And now, as she looked across at his dearly beloved face, which held an expression that she could only liken to a cat that had been set free in a creamery, Helena was unable to prevent the sudden rush of tears to her eyes. At least *he* had achieved his heart's desire, she thought, as she forlornly contemplated the uncertainty of her own future happiness. Even after everything that had transpired during the past week, she was still finding it difficult to come to terms with the fact that, in a little less than an hour, she would be walking out of this same church on the arm of a man who quite clearly did not love her and for whom her own feelings were still in such a wild turmoil of confusion!

The sudden ripple of organ chords, signalling the start to the ceremony, quickly roused her from her somewhat morbid reflections and, as the poignant notes of the music echoed across the vaulted galleries, she took a deep breath and, her chin held high, she grasped hold of her father's arm and stepped through the vestibule doors into the church's lengthy aisle.

To her amazement, every single pew on both sides of the church was packed to capacity—most of the faces totally unknown to her and, even though she forced herself to return their smiles as she passed them, she could not help but wonder at who they might all be, since neither she nor her father had invited even half of their small circle of acquaintances. She could only suppose that they must all be here at Lady Isobel's request for, although she herself would have preferred to have had her Uncle Daniels conduct the marriage service in his little country church in Woodlands St Mary, the countess had refused to countenance the idea, having declared that the only way to knock their detractors' noses out of joint would be to put on the grandest, most prestigious display that society had seen since the wedding of Princess Charlotte herself! Needless to say, the reluctant bride, who would far rather have seen what she could only regard as an obscene amount of money being put to a far more practical use, had been inclined to view the excessive arrangements with a somewhat jaundiced eye. However, since her father—to whom, of course, had fallen the privilege of funding the entire venture—had given his wholehearted support to the project, here she now was, clad from head to foot in the most outrageously extravagant concoction of satin and lace ever to have been created and feeling more wretched than she could ever have thought possible.

But the moment her eyes finally lit upon her waiting groom, she found it impossible to control either her sudden intake of breath or the tumultuous pounding of her heart. Attired in an elegantly tailored swallow-tailed jacket of maroon superfine, his buff-coloured pantaloons hugging his thighs like a second skin, he looked so very handsome, standing there, with his smiling cousin in attendance. If only she could find some way of softening his heart towards her, she felt sure that she could eventually learn to settle for a marriage based upon mutual affection. After all, she reasoned, as she stepped to his side, wasn't this how the majority of marriages were said to function nowadays and why should she, with her very limited experience in such matters, look for anything more?

Markfield's eyes had been glued to her face from the moment she had appeared through the vestibule doors and his heart was now so full that he would have been prepared to swear that it was at bursting point. It was almost impossible to believe that this vision of loveliness was soon to be his wife; to have, to hold and—as he now knew without any shadow of a doubt—to worship with every fibre of his being. And, although she had made her feelings for him perfectly clear, he resolved that, as soon as they were married and away from all the fuss and palaver that the hastily organised celebrations had necessitated, he meant to do everything in his power to try to gain her love. He would woo her with so dogged a devotion that that she would eventually find his advances impossible to resist! Or so he had to keep telling himself, lest he lost his nerve entirely.

Now, unbelievably, she was here standing at his side, ready to take those all important vows and, although he did his utmost to catch her eye in an effort to offer her a reassuring smile, she refused to look in his direction and, instead, kept her gaze resolutely focused upon the prayer-book that the vicar was holding up in front of him.

And so, with the immortal and hallowed phrase, *'Dearly Beloved',* the wedding service at last began. Striving to ignore not only the cleric's somewhat nasal monotone but also the far more disconcerting sensation of Markfield's arm so close to her own, Helena did her level best to focus her attention on the unique and powerful words of the sacred text.

'...honourable estate...not taken unadvisedly...procreation...mutual society...just cause...impediment...'

One by one the highly revered phrases rolled off the vicar's tongue with relentless finality and then, *'Wilt thou, Richard Alexander Henry, take this woman...?'*

Markfield's deep and confident, 'I will.'

'Wilt thou, Helena Louisa, take this man...?'

Her own whispered and hesitant, 'I will.'

Then her father stepping forwards and passing her hand into Markfield's and he, still vainly trying to catch her eye, promising to love and cherish her, and she blindly repeating the self-same words and then Markfield placing the ring on her finger.

'*...let no man put asunder.*'

A prayer, a psalm, yet more prayers. The final blessing and, at last, the thing was done. For better or for worse, it seemed, she and Markfield were wed!

Recapturing her hand, Richard drew her towards him and lowering his head, sought to claim the bridegroom's first, tentative kiss.

Her heart pounding with excitement, Helena raised her face to receive the long-awaited touch of his lips, but since she could not bring herself to look him directly in the eyes, lest he might see and recognise the true strength of her feelings for him, she averted her gaze and allowed it to drift idly across the heads of the waiting congregation.

But then, as, all at once, the unexpected flash of a brightly coloured jewel in a feathered headgear caught her attention, her eyes were at once drawn to its wearer's face and, as the highly painted features of Lady Rachel Cummings swam into her view, she felt a cold fury descend upon her. *That he should have gone so far as to invite his mistress along to witness his wedding must, surely, rank as the greatest of insults to offer his future wife! So much for the 'avoidance of fornication' and the 'forsaking of all others'!*

Angrily jerking her face to the side, she was vaguely aware of Markfield's lips making brief contact with her right earlobe but, impervious as to any possible consequences, she extricated herself from his hold and indicated to the startled cleric that he should proceed with the signing of the registers.

Feeling somewhat embarrassed and not a little confused at the sudden and unexpected alteration in Helena's hitherto distinctly remote and withdrawn manner—which he had put down to bridal nerves—the earl, a puzzled frown on his face, accompanied the pair into the vestry where, reaching forwards, he took hold of her arm and spun her round to face him.

'What is it, my dear?' he asked anxiously. 'Are you feeling unwell?'

'I am perfectly well, thank you, my lord,' she replied, in a slightly unsteady voice as, disengaging herself carefully, she turned to the perplexed reverend and, in a rather firmer tone, reminded him that he had not yet invited the witnesses to join them.

'Please tell me what is troubling you,' Richard urged her, as soon as the man had scurried out of the room. 'If you have the headache, I am sure I can arrange—'

'I can assure you that my head is perfectly fine,' she interrupted him hotly. 'In fact, I would say that it is a good deal clearer now than it was an hour ago!'

'I'm not sure that I entirely understand you,' queried Richard. 'You are surely not intending to imply that you are beginning to regret this marriage already?'

'I doubt that it would bother you greatly were I to do so, my lord,' returned Helena, with a careless shrug. 'It is quite clear to me that you, at any rate, have no intention of abiding by any of the vows that we have just exchanged!'

He stepped back, an angry flush covering his face. 'I beg your pardon!' he gasped, in astonishment. 'What, in the name of God, can you possibly mean by that remark?'

'I doubt that the Almighty is likely to rush to your defence, my lord,' she retorted drily. 'In my opinion, you would be far better advised to take the matter up with your *"chère-amie"!*'

'Chère-amie?' Now totally at a loss, Richard raked his fingers abstractedly through his hair. 'I really cannot imagine what—'

Unfortunately, owing to the fact that the Reverend Aldridge happened to choose that very moment to return to the vestry, accompanied by the dowager countess and Giles Wheatley, the deeply confused earl was obliged to abandon his protestations and concentrate his attention on the signing of the registers.

As luck would have it, the newly-weds were to be allowed no further opportunity to indulge themselves in private discussion. Not only did huge crowds of well-wishers surround their open carriage every step of the way from Hanover Square back to Standish House, where the wedding breakfast was to be held, but, aside from the fact that they sat next to one another at the actual meal, where conversation of any sort was, of necessity, restricted to the commonplace, it seemed that the bridal pair were destined to be kept apart for almost the whole of the proceedings.

Having smiled and dipped and curtsied to every single one of the hundred and fifty guests as they jockeyed their way along the receiving line, Helena had allowed herself to heave a huge sigh of relief when, as the last of their number finally disappeared through the double doors that led towards the dining room, she realised that her worst fears had not been realised. At least the despised Lady Cummings had not been invited to attend the reception!

Insofar as Richard was concerned, it was as though he had found himself trapped in the grip of some hideous nightmare. As a result of all the hearty handshaking and back-slapping he had undergone, his head and shoulders ached and, thanks to the crowds in constant attendance around Helena, it had been impossible for him to get close enough to her to suggest that they might snatch a short respite for a few minutes.

He had racked his brain to try and figure out what she could have meant by that very pointed reference to his one time paramour. Having neither seen nor heard from Rachel since that fateful night two weeks ago, he could not begin to imagine why Helena should have suddenly got it into her head that he was still involved with the creature. *And why today?* he wondered, as he stared disconsolately across the room in the vague hope of catching even the merest glimpse of his bride. *At the blessed altar, no less! And, fat chance he had of getting to the bottom of the confounded matter while she seemed to be more than content to surround herself with a set of cork-brained fly-by-nights who, if he were any judge, were only there in the hopes of setting up some secret assignation with her. What he wouldn't give to put a bullet into every last one of them!*

'So this is where you've been hiding yourself, old man! The burdens of marriage getting too much for you already?'

Hurriedly putting aside his bellicose thoughts, he turned to greet the grinning Geoffrey Fairfax who, along with Sir Peter Braithwaite, had finally managed to track their friend down to the temporary refuge he had sought in one of the ballroom's many window alcoves.

'Just wishing the whole thing was over and done with,' he replied, with a weary sigh, as he once again cast his eyes across the room to where his wife was still heavily involved in flirting with one of her latest conquests.

Observing his friend's somewhat bleak expression, Sir Peter was anxious to point out that, since it seemed that a good many people were already beginning to take their leave, it would appear that Markfield's wish was soon to be granted.

'And, if I'm any judge,' he added bracingly, 'we'll be waving you off on your honeymoon trip before that grandfather clock in the hall strikes three.'

'Not going on a honeymoon trip, as it happens,' said Richard, with a dismissive shake of his head. 'It's true that Wheatley was keen to send us off on an extended tour of the capitals of Europe, but since one of my brood mares is about to foal any day now, I decided that she's far too valuable to leave to Grimthorpe to cope with on his own.'

'Not even going off for a few days?' asked Braithwaite, in surprise.

'Later on, maybe,' replied the earl, colouring slightly. 'When things have settled down a bit.'

For a brief moment, neither of his friends could think of a suitable response to this rather enigmatic remark.

Then, eventually, 'Well, I'd say that you've got yourself a real corker of a wife there, if you don't mind me using that expression!' offered Fairfax hurriedly. 'Added to which, it would seem that your money problems are well and truly at an end. Not a bad day's work, when all's said and done!'

'True enough,' returned Richard, somewhat non-committedly for, despite the closeness and long duration of their acquaintanceship, he had an uncomfortable feeling that his two friends would be less than pleased to learn that he had turned down all of Wheatley's various monetary offers. As a matter of fact, he had made a point of ensuring that every penny of the not inconsiderable dowry that her father had insisted on bestowing upon Helena should be instantly transferred into her own private account at the Thomas Coutts banking facility in the Strand. Luckily, the date of the wedding had happened to coincide with one of his estate's quarterly rent days, temporarily furnishing the earl with sufficient funds to meet his current expenses, albeit that his hasty withdrawal of this providential input had also meant setting back the late spring planting by some, as yet, indeterminate period!

To Richard's relief, however, his friend's speculation that the gathering was starting to draw to a close seemed to be proving to be the case as, one by one, a varied assortment of dignitaries and their wives drifted over to offer the earl their good wishes and bid him farewell. As the crowd around his wife gradually thinned, the earl, not entirely sure of the welcome he would receive from her, took a deep breath and strode across the room to stand at her side.

'It all seems to have gone pretty well, wouldn't you say?' he ventured, as he tried, without success, to catch her eye.

Helena's response was hardly encouraging. 'Highly impressive, my lord,' she said, in the tone of voice she might have used to speak to a total stranger. 'Lady Isobel is to be congratulated on her outstanding organisational skills.'

Privately, she was of the opinion that the whole affair—lavishly funded by her father, of course—had been a long and arduous drag from start to finish. Having spent the past half-hour or so trying to fend off several breathtakingly explicit suggestions from a number of the so-called gentlemen present, she had been left wondering what on earth she had let herself in for by marrying into the so-called *beau monde*. How these people could prose on about their 'standards of behaviour' and 'codes of honour' whilst, at the same time, conducting their lifestyles in such an appalling manner, was quite beyond her understanding. Little wonder that her mother had renounced her own noble connections in favour of a lesser but far more satisfying life in the lower echelons of society! If only her father had been well enough to share her concerns, Helena felt sure that he would never have allowed this sham of a marriage to have taken place. As it was, Rachel Cummings's attendance at the church had made it quite clear to her that Markfield, with the better part of her father's money now at his disposal, had no intention of altering his way of life simply to accommodate any eccentric whims and fancies in which his new wife might choose to indulge herself!

Biting back the sigh that threatened, she stole a quick sideways look at her new husband, who was now engaged in a serious conversation with her father and Lady Isobel. *If only I didn't feel so drawn to him,* she thought forlornly, as she endeavoured to return her attention to the ongoing business of bidding the last of the guests farewell. *He has made it quite clear that he doesn't love me, it is true, but I had hoped that, given time, some sort of mutual understanding might have developed between the two of us.*

'Time for us to leave, my dear.'

Startled out of her reverie, Helena was unable to prevent a momentary start at the unexpected touch of his hand at her elbow. A swift glance at her husband's rigid countenance, however, was more than enough to inform her that he had registered the recoil and had mistakenly assumed the worst. Biting down hard on her lip, she did her best to suppress the sudden pricking of tears that this painful realisation brought about.

'There, there, my pretty,' came her father's voice at her side.

'No need for tears. As soon as you have had time to settle in to your new home, Lottie and I will be straight down to visit you, just you wait and see!'

'Oh, Papa!' she cried, as she flung her arms around him and hugged him tightly. 'Just promise me that you will look after yourself—keep off the port and follow Doctor Redfern's advice—don't forget to take your medication—Lottie has all the instructions, so she can easily…'

Unable to carry on, her voice broke and the carefully restrained tears were at last allowed to flow unchecked. The somewhat dismayed Wheatley, having tentatively patted his weeping daughter on the back for several minutes, during which there was no appreciable lessening of the outburst, then cast a pleading glance in the earl's direction, as though asking him for guidance. Richard, who, with a pensive frown on his face, had been watching the whole sorry drama unfold before him, stepped quickly forwards and, gently extricating Helena from her father's grasp, wrapped his own arms about her and holding her firmly against his chest, murmured, 'Hush now, my sweet. Everything is going to be just fine, I promise you.'

The sudden shock of finding herself in Markfield's arms brought Helena's outburst to a shuddering halt and, as she gradually became aware of the warmth and strength emanating from him, the oddest sensations began to ripple through her body, causing her to pull away from him in mortified confusion.

'Oh, dear! What must you all think of me!' she gasped, as she frantically attempted to wipe away the remains of the tears that still lingered on her cheeks. 'Your handkerchief, if you please, Papa?'

But Richard, having pulled out the white silk kerchief that adorned the breast pocket of his jacket, had already anticipated her need.

'Allow me,' he said softly and, before Helena could summon up the wits to realise his intention, he had cupped her chin in his hand and had started to dab away at her damp and now rather highly flushed cheeks with the silken square.

'Perfect!' he then said as, thrusting the handkerchief carelessly back into its place, he gazed steadily down into her eyes. 'Like violets in the rain,' he whispered, before taking her unresisting hand in his and lifting it to his lips.

Markfield's inexplicably sensuous actions having had the effect of increasing her mental agitation still further, Helena's final 'goodbyes' to her father and Lottie were completed in something of a daze and, even after the earl had handed her up into his recently refurbished chariot and the coachman had whipped up the horses to set them on their journey, her mind seemed to be in no less of a turmoil.

That she had allowed herself to fall head over heels in love with the man who sat lounging on the seat beside her there was very little doubt. That another woman was mistress of that man's heart was equally indisputable. Unfortunately, since she had no idea how to deal with either one of these unsatisfactory states of affairs, it would seem that she had been presented with the most insoluble problem of all.

Chapter Sixteen

Although he could hardly help but be aware that, seated as they were in the intimate confines of a closed carriage, a more favourable opportunity to question Helena as to her inexplicable behaviour following the marriage ceremony was unlikely to present itself, Richard was not entirely sure how best to broach the troublesome matter. Since his brain had already begun to conjure up far more pleasant ways in which he and his bride might while away the next couple of hours, he could not bring himself to say anything that might damage their already fragile relationship.

'I trust that you won't find the journey too demanding, my dear,' he ventured instead. 'It's just a little over sixteen miles—two hours at most, I would hazard.'

'I dare say I shall cope,' she replied, somewhat indifferently, appearing to be rather more interested in concentrating her attention on removing the many rice grains that had lodged themselves in the trimmings of her skirt. 'May I ask where it is we are heading?'

Somewhat taken aback, he shot her a look of pure astonishment. 'I beg your pardon?'

'Well, I know that Papa was rather disappointed that you had refused his offer of a tour of the European capitals,' she said.

'Since then, however, no one has seen fit to inform me of any alternative arrangements that you might have made.'

'Good Lord!'

Clapping a hand to his forehead, Richard stared at her in dismay. 'Doubtless you are thinking that this is yet another example of my high-and-mighty arrogance!' he observed sardonically.

'High-handed!' she returned at once, doing her best to conceal the smile that had leapt, unbidden, to her lips. 'I said "high-handed", not "high-and-mighty".'

'Much the same thing, I should have thought,' he replied, with a disconsolate shrug.

'Not at all!' protested Helena. '"High-handed" implies imposing one's will over other people, while "high-and-mighty" merely suggests an excess of haughtiness.'

'I see,' said Richard, after a brief pause. 'And of which of these two admirable traits do I stand accused?'

Helena's brow creased in a troubled frown, for she could not help feeling that any further perusal of this particular subject matter might well do more harm than good. 'Well, if you really must have it,' she proceeded, somewhat hesitantly, 'both of them, I suppose.'

But then, as she caught sight of his utterly dashed expression, she at once wished the words unsaid. Despite all the pain that Richard had caused her, she loved him too much to seek to damage his self-esteem.

An awkward silence followed until the earl, uttering a slightly self-deprecating half-laugh, eventually riposted, 'Hoist by my own petard, by George!'

'Well, you *did* ask,' she felt obliged to point out. 'However, if I may now revert to the subject of our original conversation, I would remind you that you have still not acquainted me with our intended destination.'

Face to face with his new bride in the secluded confines of a swiftly moving carriage, Richard found himself having to concede that his recent concerns over the fate of his brood mare now seemed rather inconsequential when set against the broader canvas of a non-existent honeymoon trip.

Racking his brains for a plausible answer, he replied, 'Well, it did occur to me that a short respite from all the hustle-bustle of the last few days might not go amiss, before we make up our minds where we eventually want to go.' Then, improvising hurriedly, he added, 'I thought it might be useful to spend some time at Westpark House—in view of any possible alterations or redecorating…'

Conscious that Helena was now eyeing him with an expression that could only be described as bordering on utter disbelief, he swallowed hurriedly and his voice ground to a halt.

'I fear that I am obliged to admit that I haven't actually arranged a trip of any sort,' he acknowledged finally. And then, swivelling to face her, he reached out and grasped hold of her hand. 'I really must beg your forgiveness, my dear. I realise that I should to have given such an important matter rather more consideration than I appear to have done!'

At the earl's sudden and unexpected possession of her hand, Helena was forced to take in a deep breath, in an endeavour to counteract the rapid pounding of her heart. 'It is really of very little consequence,' she returned shakily but then, gathering courage, she tentatively squeezed his fingers and offered him a supportive smile. 'I dare say you have had many more important things to attend to.'

As their eyes locked, Richard felt a powerful tremor run through him. Struggling to regain his breath, his lips twisted in a brief smile. 'I confess it did rather seem so at the time,' he said, shaking his head slowly as he gazed down at her. 'But now, I am not nearly so sure.'

Unable to make sense of the unfathomable expression in his eyes, Helena's mind was barely able to function and, even though every single one of her instincts was screaming at her to draw back while she still had the chance, all rational thought seemed to have vanished into oblivion as a rapidly spiralling passion suddenly erupted from somewhere deep within her soul. Powerless to tear her eyes away from his, she could only gaze at him in breathless wonderment, her lips parted in quivering anticipation.

As he inhaled a trembling breath, Richard gazed down at her and could feel himself being drawn, slowly but inexorably, into the boundless blue depths of her breathtakingly captivating eyes. Completely beyond salvation, he let out an inarticulate moan and, reaching out, he pulled her towards him.

'Time for that thwarted kiss, I believe,' he whispered huskily as, wrapping his arms around her, he lowered his head and captured her lips with his own.

Hardly daring to breathe, as delicious quivers of ecstasy pervaded every inch of her body, Helena returned the kiss with every fibre of her being. Even though her heart was dangerously out of control, it seemed to her that, in that single euphoric moment, even the wildest of her dreams had become an instant reality. Sliding her hands across his chest and over his shoulders, she caressed the short hairs at the back of his neck, pressing herself tightly against him, in a feverish attempt to draw him still closer. At her unexpected intensifying of the kiss, a shuddering jolt ran through the earl and, with a strangled groan, he drew back, but only to begin a slow sensuous nibbling of her neck and earlobe, causing Helena's delight to escalate to even more dizzying heights. All at once, his hands were in her hair, sliding out her hairpins and laying waste to her carefully constructed coiffure. Allowing her head to fall back, she closed her eyes in dreamy wonder, as she felt Markfield's long, sensitive fingers ravaging through the tumbling curls, impatiently grappling with the fixtures of her pearl-studded coronet…

Suddenly, like an icy blast, reality hit her as her mind's eye was once again confronted with the unprepossessing vision of that other bejewelled headdress and, beneath its triumphantly waving feather, the self-satisfied smirk of her husband's lover!

Wrenching herself out of his hold, she scrambled as far away from him as far as the limited confines of the carriage would allow.

'This was not part of the agreement!' she panted, as the horribly vivid image continued to taunt her consciousness. 'I will *not* play second fiddle to that brazen-faced trollop!'

The abrupt curtailment of his amatory advances had the effect of leaving the thoroughly shocked Richard not only gasping for breath but also in a high state of arousal, a situation with which he was having the devil's own job trying to come to terms. One minute it had seemed as though every one of his hopes and desires were about to be granted at a single stroke and the next…

'Trollop?' he echoed, when his brain had at last recovered sufficiently to make sense of her words. 'What in God's name are you talking about?'

'You know quite well what I'm talking about!' she flung back at him, as she shakily strove to repair the damage to her coiffure. 'Your sainted mistress—that's who! The female *you* invited to watch you getting shackled to the wealthy cit's idiot of a daughter! What a very amusing experience that must have been for the pair of you!'

He blanched. 'Are you referring to Lady Cummings?' he asked, in astonishment.

'Well, she was the only one of your paramours that I actually recognised!' retorted Helena, with a defiant glare. 'I dare say that there could well have been an entire harem of your floozies there, for all I was aware!'

Despite the undoubted gravity of the situation in which he now found himself, Richard was unable to prevent the almost involuntary smile that flitted across his face as he strove to conjure up such an unlikely assembly. Was it possible that Helena could be displaying symptoms of jealousy? he wondered, a sudden hope leaping within him. But then, as he looked across and studied her clenched hands and downcast expression, he collected himself and reasoned that, whilst it might have flattered his vanity to assume such an implausible state of affairs, the more probable cause of Helena's angry outpourings was too many sleepless nights. Having suffered from more than enough of those of late himself, he was well aware of the distinctly anomalous effect they could have on one's mental processes—to which his somewhat over-eager conduct of a few minutes ago could well lay testament!

Shaking his head, he reached across and tried to separate her tightly entwined fingers. 'You can't possibly believe that even I would stoop so far as to invite an ex-paramour to attend my wedding,' he attempted to cajole her. 'If my memory serves me aright, it's barely fifteen minutes since I was striving to come to terms with the fact that you think me "high-handed"! Surely it's not possible for me to be "low-handed", as well?'

'Very droll, my lord!' she retorted, doing her best to shrug off his very determined advances. 'But it still doesn't explain the lady's presence!'

'Well, I assure you that she wasn't there at my request,' asserted Richard briskly. '*I* didn't see her, I can promise you that.'

'I'd say that she was pretty hard to miss, given the ghastly feathered concoction that she had stuck on her head!' returned Helena, with a defiant toss of her head.

'Very possibly,' acknowledged the earl with a triumphant grin, having finally succeeded in capturing hold of one of her hands. 'But then, you see, I had eyes for no one but my beautiful bride.'

Helena bit her lip in confusion, an embarrassed flush clothing her cheeks. 'But, somebody must have invited her,' she persisted, refusing to look at him.

'Not necessarily—a wedding is a public ceremony, after all—and churches are supposed to be open to all and sundry.'

'Especially "sundry", it would seem,' she returned, bristling.

His ensuing shout of laughter brought a swift, if albeit reluctant, smile to her face.

Still chuckling, he lifted her unresisting fingers and pressed them against his lips. 'Try to put it out of your mind, sweetheart,' he said. 'I give you my word of honour that I have neither seen nor spoken to Lady Cummings since the evening of the Kettlesham rout.'

Helena wriggled uncomfortably. 'Then you must think me the most awful gudgeon for having behaved in such a very foolish manner,' she said, in a small voice.

His eyes softened and, draping an arm across her shoulder, he drew her gently towards him. 'As a matter of fact,' he whispered, 'it so happens that I think that you're the sweetest, most adorable wife any man could possibly wish for!'

Her heart soared with elation. Could it be possible that everything was going to work out for the best, after all? she wondered hopefully. Whilst it was true that he had not actually mentioned the word 'love', it was beginning to seem that Markfield did, in fact, hold her in some sort of affection and—if his recent performance was anything to go by—he was certainly desirous of her! But then, as she recalled her own, rather wanton, behaviour on that occasion, a rosy blush crept over her cheeks. It was difficult for her to understand how a simple kiss could have the power to create such inner turbulence—not that there had been anything remotely commonplace about *that* particular kiss—at least from her point of view! Even the thought of it was enough to send her pulse rocketing skywards and leave her fighting for breath—brought about by her decidedly limited experience in such matters, she supposed glumly. She doubted that Markfield had been similarly affected. Given his greater age and likely wealth of experience, she thought it probable that he had had more than enough time to hone his rather breathtaking technique! But then, as she recalled the several somewhat oblique references to the 'joys of marriage' that she had heard whispered of late, she found that she did not care to dwell too long on her husband's past history.

Just as long as he has truly disentangled himself from the clutches of that beastly Cummings woman, she told herself firmly, she was certain that she would be able to learn to cope with whatever unusual demands he might choose to make on her. The very fact that both her mother and her Aunt Daniels had managed to survive such onslaughts—rather frequently, in her aunt's case, given the number of offspring she had produced—had led her to suppose that the whole business must depend upon the relative nature of the man concerned, and it was hardly fair to compare gentlemen of either her father's or Markfield's ilk to such creatures as the contemptible Viscount Barrington, or the foul-mouthed ruffians who took their pleasure from poor Bet and Cissie and their like.

Nevertheless, as the carriage ate up the miles towards their destination, she found it increasingly impossible to ignore the growing knot of apprehension that had lodged itself in her throat, for it was fast becoming clear that, whatever the truth of the matter, she would very soon find herself fully acquainted with it, and her nervousness regarding the unknown prospect that lay ahead was sufficient to cause more than just a flutter of uneasiness within her breast!

Finding himself deeply and irrevocably in love for the first time in his life was something of a new and rather daunting experience for Richard. Observing that Helena had finally closed her eyes, he tightened his hold and, leaning contentedly back against the squabs, he indulged himself in the luxury of an uninterrupted perusal of her lovely face: the remarkable length of the fringe of thick, dark eyelashes that swept across the velvet creaminess of her skin; the tiny scattering of pale freckles on the impertinently tip-tilted nose; the stubborn little chin; the perfect bow-shape of her lips—such infinitely kissable lips…

As the rather too-tempting reminder of the heady rapture so inopportunely ripped from his grasp brought about a disturbing contraction of his pelvic muscles, Richard hurriedly switched his attention to the sudden flare of colour that was sweeping across Helena's cheeks. Smilingly registering the soft rosy hue, he was unable to prevent the warm glow of gratification that spread across his chest, as he speculated on the probable cause of her discomfiture. The eager enthusiasm with which she had returned his kiss had filled him with un-mitigated delight and had at once brought home to him that there was a good deal more to the former Miss Wheatley than he had at first supposed—hidden talents indeed, as his grand-mother had unwittingly remarked! And, despite the fact that Helena had gone out of her way to make it clear that she felt nothing for him, her passionate response to his embrace had given him every reason to hope that, with time and patience, he might, eventually, persuade her otherwise. Just as soon as they had set foot in Westpark House, he swore that he would court her with such a fierce determination that she would be unable to find it in her heart to resist him!

Chapter Seventeen

'Thank you, Teddington, you may leave us now.'

'Very good, my lord.'

Having placed the decanter of port within convenient reach of his master's right hand, the butler bowed and quietly withdrew, to report his findings to the eagerly awaiting group of house servants who had assembled themselves at the dinner table below stairs.

'Scarcely a word out of either one of them during the entire meal,' he said, with a concerned shake of his elderly head.

'Not even a mention of my peach soufflé?' demanded Mrs Ellis, the portly cook, with an indignant snort. 'Took me nigh on twenty-five minutes to whip up that cream!'

'Oh, her ladyship was very complimentary about every single one of the courses,' soothed the butler, unbuttoning his jacket and taking his seat at the head of the table. 'It was just that there seemed to be a certain—how shall I put it—constraint between the two of them.'

'Oh, give the poor lambs a chance,' put in Mrs Wainwright, the housekeeper. 'Bless me, they've barely been in the house five minutes! I swear her ladyship looked fit to drop when I showed her up to her room—I did suggest that she might like to have a little lie down on the bed while that maid of hers sorted out the rest of her things, but she said that she needed to change out of her dress. I dare say she'll be fine, as soon as she's settled in—she's quite a taking little thing, to my way of thinking.'

'Didn't help, his lordship going straight off to the stables like that,' muttered one of the footmen sourly. 'Would've thought that Grimthorpe fellow would have had a bit more gumption than to drag him off before he even had time to introduce us all properly. Bad form that, if you want my opinion.'

'Well, we don't!' retorted Teddington, with a reproving frown in the young manservant's direction. 'Mr Grimthorpe has been dashing backwards and forwards for the best part of the afternoon, waiting for the master's return. Seems that prize mare of his has been giving him trouble.'

'Yeah, but even so,' persisted the unrepentant Hadley. 'Leaving his brand new wife for the sake of a blessed horse! I ask you!'

Such sentiments as were not entirely dissimilar to those entertained by his lordship's brand new wife at the time. With barely a hurried "So sorry, my dear—I'm afraid I have to go!", Markfield had hurried away with the troubled stable man and vanished from Helena's sight, leaving her to deal with the greeting and dismissal of the dozen or so servants who had been lined up inside the front door to pay their respects to their new mistress.

Luckily, her previous years of managing her father's household, albeit a good deal smaller than this present one, had stood her in excellent stead and, with the housekeeper's welcome assistance, she had accomplished her first task as Countess of Markfield with just the right mix of dignity and graciousness.

Having then been escorted up the stairs by Mrs Wainwright, she found that her allotted bedchamber had, as she had supposed it might, originally belonged to Markfield's mother, although the added discovery that the room adjoined his lordship's did nothing to curb her rapidly mounting feelings of resentment, especially when it transpired that the only discernible evidence of a keyhole appeared to be situated on her husband's side of the interconnecting door!

Nevertheless, she had been immensely relieved to find that her maid Fran who, having arrived an hour or so ahead of the newly-weds, had already made considerable inroads into the task of unpacking and transferring her mistress's personal belongings to their designated locations, the greater bulk of Helena's possessions having already been sent ahead to her new home earlier in the week.

Dismissing the housekeeper's suggestion that she might care to make use of the unexpected opportunity afforded her by Markfield's enforced absence to indulge herself in a little nap, Helena, having grown heartily sick of wearing the weighty and cumbersome cream-coloured corded silk gown in which she had spent the better part of the day, elected, instead, to change into a lightweight muslin afternoon dress. Since Mrs Wainwright had assured her that the dinner gong was unlikely to sound until five o'clock—and certainly not before his lordship had put in an appearance—and the little porcelain clock on the marble mantelshelf indicated that it was still only a quarter after three, Helena could see little point in trolling about the house in an evening gown for the next two hours or so. In fact, as soon as she had finished the tea that Mrs Wainwright had had sent up to her, it occurred to her that to use the time to familiarise herself with the layout of her new home would be a far more sensible option.

Westpark House, as she very soon discovered, after a thorough perambulation of the ground floor, was of relatively modern construction, built along elegant, but simple lines. A number of rooms led off from a large central hallway; to the right of the front door lay an imposingly furnished withdrawing room, whose double doors connected with the equally well-appointed dining room; to the left was a somewhat neglected library that seemed to double as a study or office and, behind this, overlooking a very pretty terrace garden, was situated a rather more casually furnished salon that gave the impression of having been used rather more frequently than its neighbours.

Tucked into the alcove below the central staircase she spotted a green baize door that looked as though it must lead down to the basement area—which probably housed the kitchen, cellars and staff quarters—but, since she had no desire to waste what little time she had at her disposal indulging in any more small talk with the servants, Helena chose to bypass this area, for the present. Having made a comprehensive study of the ground-floor layout, it was not difficult to assume the disposition of the two upper floors; two pairs of bedchambers, back and front, on each floor, she hazarded, making a total of eight bedchambers in all. Well within her capabilities, she thought as, with a relieved nod, she retraced her steps up to her own room, where she found that Fran, having sorted her mistress's belongings to her own fastidious satisfaction, was now in the process of tidying away the masses of tissue paper and empty boxes.

'I'll just pack this lot away, Miss—oh, dear! There I go again, my lady!' she cried, clapping her hands to her cheeks in mortification. 'Will I never learn?'

'I dare say it's bound to come, eventually,' chuckled Helena. 'You've seen us both through trickier situations than this during the past six or seven years or so, Fran, so please try not to worry about it.'

'I promise I'll do my best, Mi—my lady,' sighed the maid, returning her mistress's smile. 'I'll just go and fetch one of those footmen to carry these baskets and boxes up to the lumber room—or wherever it is they store things in a place like this.'

'Why don't you just tug the bell?' suggested Helena, nodding towards the tasselled rope at the bedside. 'As the Countess of Markfield's personal attendant, you're going to have to get used to giving orders on her ladyship's behalf, so now's your chance to begin.'

Staring at the bell rope as though it might leap up and bite her, Fran took a hesitant step forwards.

'Go on, just pull it,' encouraged Helena, giving the woman

a gentle shove but, when Fran still refused to budge, the likely cause of the maid's apparent reticence suddenly occurred to her.

'Look, if it will help,' she then suggested, as she walked across the room towards the adjoining door, 'why don't I just duck into his lordship's room for a few minutes and leave you to it? I dare say you'd rather not have an audience at your first order-giving ceremony!'

Fran's face cleared and, grinning broadly, she bobbed a neat curtsy. 'If you would be so good, Mi—my lady,' she said, as she watched her mistress exiting through the door into the next room.

To begin with, Helena was a little disconcerted to find herself standing in what was, all too clearly, a gentleman's bedchamber. Intimate signs of her husband were all around her, from the maroon banyan draped across the foot of the immense four-poster bed, to the set of horn-backed brushes, lined up with military precision on the mahogany dressing-table, along with a varied assortment of pots and bottles. There was even that indefinable smell about the room: a smell that was entirely Markfield.

Curious, she picked up one of the crystal bottles and, uncorking it, raised it tentatively to her nose. Essence of earl, undoubtedly, but difficult to put a name to! Lemon, certainly, and possibly verbena? Unable to resist the temptation, she bent her head and took another, more positive sniff. Most definitely Markfield and quite intoxicating, she thought dreamily, as she closed her eyes and cast her mind back to that incredibly breath-taking kiss that they had so recently shared. As the well-remembered fragrance drifted across her senses she could almost feel the compelling strength of his arms about her and the hot, insistent pressure of his lips on hers.

Letting out a trembling sigh, she re-corked the bottle and returned it to its place. How foolish it had been of her to automatically believe the worst of him, she thought, as her eyes travelled over the rest of the room: the twin leather chairs straddling the fireplace; the wardrobe, chest of drawers and marble-topped washstand; and, dominating the whole, that awesomely huge bed, complete with its plush jade-silk curtains and matching coverlet. Truly, a bed fit for a king, she found herself thinking. Well, an earl, at any rate, she then amended hastily. And, possibly, or rather, even probably—if that look in Markfield's eye had been anything to go by—his countess, too!

The sudden sounds of movement in the corridor outside had her scurrying towards the interconnecting door where, no sooner had she thrust it open than she was able to observe that her maid appeared to have had little difficulty in exerting her new-found authority. Every vestige of the former disorder and untidiness had been removed, finally allowing its mistress to stand back and admire the full splendour of her own bedchamber.

Decorated in a soft green shade, the walls reflected the serenity of the sweeping lawns that could be seen through the pair of wide picture windows that occupied most of the wall on the far side of the room. Delightedly resting her hands on one of the window-sills and drinking in the beauty of the terraced garden below, Helena supposed that the view from the windows in the adjoining suite must be identical to hers, but was obliged to admit that she had been too otherwise absorbed to pay that much attention. Besides which, the far more delicate design of the pale maple furniture, along with the lilac-coloured gauze-like curtains that festooned her windows and bed had the effect of turning what was, in fact, an almost identical room to her husband's, into a light and airy boudoir, rather than the sober and severely masculine bedchamber she had just vacated.

Aside from the shock of Markfield abandoning her to her fate the minute she had stepped over the threshold—a matter for which she intended to take him severely to task, whenever it eventually suited him to return—she could not feel that she had anything to complain about. In fact, insofar as she was able to judge, things seemed to be falling into place very nicely. Just that other, slightly bothersome sticking point to overcome and, once that had been dealt with, she was sure that everything would be plain sailing!

'Shall you wear the blue or the green for dinner, Mi—my lady?'

The sound of Fran's voice cut across her contemplative musings and she was obliged to give herself a little shake to clear her head before she turned round to acknowledge the question.

'I think the green tonight, Fran,' she replied, with a hurried look at the clock. Gone five already and still no sign of her lord and master! It really was too bad of him to treat her in such a cavalier manner! And just how much longer was she expected to sit up here in her bedroom? She was supposed to be the mistress of the house, for heaven's sake!

'Just keep it simple, please, Fran,' she instructed the woman, as she saw her reach for the hairbrush. 'All that fancy coiling and pinning you did earlier gave me quite a headache.'

'Ah, but you did look lovely, Mi—my lady,' replied her unrepentant abigail, as she skilfully swept up her mistress's shining tresses into a soft chignon at the back of her neck. 'I overheard several of the guests commenting on how lucky his lordship was to have got himself such a delightful wife.'

Feeling suddenly dispirited, Helena got to her feet and let out a weary sigh. She had been so wrapped up with congratulating herself on how splendidly everything was going that the original reason for the impetuous marriage had almost escaped her mind. But, now that she had been given an opportunity to study the reality, it came to her that, not only had it obliged her to desert her ailing father and abandon him to Lottie's somewhat less tender mercies, but it had also forced her into giving up her work at the soup kitchen. And, for what? Little more than the doubtful privilege of seeing her inheritance handed over to a heartless ingrate who seemed to prefer the company of horses to that of his new wife, if his current performance were anything to go by! And, if that were not more than enough for anyone to contend with, she thought dismally, it appeared that she was going to have to spend the rest of her days being referred to as 'Mi—my', by her maidservant!

Unable to prevent the unbidden tears that suddenly sprang to her eyes, she turned away from the dressing-table and walked swiftly across to the window where, leaning her forehead on the cool glass, she tried to summon up the will-power to take herself downstairs and demand that dinner be served at once.

As if in answer to her unspoken thoughts, the plangent tones of the dinner gong suddenly sounded out, their tremulous echo reverberating to every corner of the house.

Blinking back the tears, she lifted her chin, straightened her shoulders and made ready to leave. But, scarcely had the last vibrations of the gong died away than her bedroom door was suddenly thrust open to reveal a decidedly dishevelled Markfield who, hurling himself across the room, threw his arms around her.

'I'm so dreadfully sorry!' he panted. 'What must you have been thinking of me?' and then, totally ignoring the dumbfounded gasp of the maidservant, he bent his head and sought her lips.

Helena, however, had no intention of allowing her husband's well-practised charm to win her over twice in one day. Wrenching herself away, she glared up at him.

'May I ask where it is that you have been all this time, my lord?' she enquired, her tone decidedly chill.

A disconcerted frown crossed his forehead. 'Over at the stables, of course,' he explained. 'Surely Mrs Wainwright informed you—Grimthorpe was worried about Copperlady— she had a bad colic—we were obliged to send to Epsom for the veterinary.'

Pausing, he then added, 'I dare say it all sounds of little consequence to you, my dear, but I swear I did my best to get away sooner.'

One look at Helena's stony expression, however, was more than enough to convince him that there was little point in telling her that he had spent the better part of his time at the stables all but tearing out his hair in his utter frustration and fury at having had to abandon his new bride so abruptly. Those final, precious few moments in the carriage having encouraged him to believe that Helena was not quite as averse to his advances as he had originally feared, he had been so desperate to get back to her that the majority of the horse doctor's pontificating advice had sailed totally over his head.

'I trust she has recovered—this Copperlady—one of your brood mares, I take it?'

He nodded and, stepping forwards, reached out to take hold of her hands.

'Don't be cross with me, sweetheart,' he cajoled her. 'I swear it won't happen again.'

Not until the next time, I suspect, thought Helena as, repressing a sigh, she could feel herself succumbing, once again, to the irresistible appeal in his eyes and the compelling pressure of his hands on hers. *Why do I allow him to have this effect on me?* she wondered hopelessly as, with a brief kiss on her fingertips, the earl sketched her an extravagant bow and made for the connecting door that led to his chamber, saying, 'Ten minutes—no more!'

A quarter of an hour later, having changed out of his soiled garments into a black dinner jacket, his skilfully tied neckcloth of snowy white linen a fine testament to his valet's expertise, Richard proudly escorted his blushing bride through the doors of the impressive dining room she had inspected some hours earlier.

The grand banqueting table itself, she was relieved to observe, had had several of its leaves wheeled away and its two end pieces had been slotted together to form a table of a more intimate size, enabling the couple to sit a mere eight feet distant from each other.

It was clear to Helena that the cook had gone to considerable trouble to show off her culinary skills, thereby occasioning her new mistress to feel obliged to taste a little of everything, lest the woman take offence. And, as one after another, the courses and removes were set before her, in seemingly never-ending succession, she was obliged to resort to a number of different stratagems in order to give the impression that she was enjoying every mouthful.

In point of fact, she found the presence of so many attendants hovering around her rather unnerving, quite apart from the fact that it proved a decided hindrance to any sort of a private conversation between Markfield and herself. Whilst she, in the normal way, would have been perfectly content to have him enlarge upon the ongoing health of his ailing mare— or, indeed, any other matter upon which he might have cared to converse—the eight feet of highly polished mahogany that lay between them was more than enough to quell any desire she might have had to introduce a topic, since the very idea of having to listen to the sound of her own voice rebounding off the panelled walls was hardly conducive to friendly discourse. As for her husband, other than the hurried apology blurted out before dashing off to change, the only observations he had managed had been in reference to the meal itself—yet another sad indication of their future life together!

Had she but known it, Richard's silence had rather more to do with the odd sense of unease that he had, all at once, found himself experiencing, as his thoughts dwelt increasingly upon the upcoming nuptial scene.

Not that he had any reservations as to his own competence in that direction—as his many successful conquests in the past would, no doubt, have been prepared to stand surety! No, the difficulty that confronted him at present was in regard to his wife's total lack of knowledge—a situation that fell well outside his customary range of experience, since he had always been pretty careful to ensure that his amatory adventures only ever involved the sort of female whose familiarity with such matters was well on a par with his own—women such as Rachel Cummings, for instance.

Innocent virgins, he realised, as he stole a quick look at his silent wife, were, on the other hand, an entirely different matter, and one that would require a somewhat more delicate approach. Especially if one wanted to be certain of not making a great hash of the whole event, he cautioned himself grimly, reflecting that he'd made more than enough of those recently to see him well into his dotage.

Signalling to Teddington to serve the port, he clenched his jaw. If he was to have any hope of breaking through the barriers of reserve that Helena seemed to have erected between them, it was clear that he was going to have to subjugate his own wayward emotions and concentrate all his efforts on a slow, gentle seduction, the very prospect of which was distinctly at odds with his current desires!

Taking her husband's gesture as the sign for which she had been waiting, Helena rose purposefully from her seat, having told herself that there was little point in her sitting there in silence if it was Markfield's intention to drink himself into oblivion.

'If you will excuse me, my lord,' she said, with a quick glance at the decanter at his elbow, 'I will leave you to enjoy your port and retire to my room—it has been a long day and I am feeling rather tired.'

Richard rose hurriedly to his feet. 'I had rather hoped you would stay and join me,' he exclaimed. 'We have scarcely had a moment to ourselves all day…'

Her look of incredulity was sufficient to indicate that this particular phrase was not the most ideal to have chosen in the circumstances.

'Yes, well, I realise that I have been greatly at fault in that respect,' he said. 'But that's all over and done with now, surely? I thought we might take our glasses across to the sitting room and relax for a few minutes.'

'I don't actually care for port, my lord,' returned Helena, in a last-ditch effort to put off the fateful moment for as long as possible. 'And, it is getting rather late, so—if you have no objection?'

Despite his earlier good intentions, Richard was unable to prevent the sudden wave of irritation that washed over him at her rejection. Why couldn't she just accept his apology and be done with it? he fumed silently. It was not as though he had enjoyed walking out and leaving her—particularly not with the heady taste of that kiss still lingering on his lips. Perhaps it was time to exercise a little of that male dominance for which he had, until fairly recently, been well renowned.

'I hesitate to remind you, my dear,' he said as, pushing back his chair, he moved purposefully towards her, 'but, as you are no doubt aware, this is supposed to be our wedding night—an occasion which generally requires the observation of certain—how shall I put it?—formalities. Taking yourself off to bed alone is hardly in keeping with the moment, to my way of thinking!'

Helena backed away, her cheeks flooding with colour. 'I assure you that I have no intention of avoiding my—obligations, my lord—'

'And, for God's sake, stop calling me "my lord"!' interrupted the earl hotly, his fingers raking through his hair in frustration. 'My given name is Richard, as well you know, and I would be greatly obliged if you could bring yourself to use it, on the odd occasion!'

'Whatever you say, *Richard!*' retorted Helena pointedly but then, fearing that she had finally outrun his patience, she held her breath.

There was a brief pause, during which Markfield regarded her steadily then, with a slight twitch of his lips, he executed a polite bow and lifting her unresisting hand, tucked it into the crook of his arm and started to make for the door.

'You are quite right, my dear,' he said, as he led her through the hall towards the staircase. 'The hour is getting rather late—well past our bedtime, I hazard a guess!'

Trembling with a mixture of fear and expectation, Helena could do nothing other than follow where he chose to lead her. On reaching her bedroom door, she had every reason to suppose that he would accompany her inside. Instead of which, he halted and, spinning her round to face him, wrapped his arms around her and held her tightly against his chest.

'Please stop fighting me, my sweet,' he breathed into her hair. 'I simply cannot bear to be at odds with you. I'll submit to whatever penance you care to drum up for me—just don't shut me out of your life, I beg you!'

'Penance, my lord?' Helena stared up at him in confusion. 'I don't understand.'

He gave her a brief smile and released her. 'I realise that I've made a complete mess of things from start to finish, Helena, for which I truly beg your forgiveness. I want you to know that, from this moment on, I mean to do whatever it takes to make this marriage work. I just need to hear that you're willing to give me the chance.'

Totally lost in the glow of the absolute sincerity that shone from her husband's eyes, Helena was so full of love for him that she could scarcely breathe. No longer afraid of whatever mystery lay in store for her, for she felt that she could trust him with her very life, she reached out her hands and pulled him towards her, yearning for the feel of his lips on hers and the comfort of his arms around her once again.

His heart skipping several beats, Richard found himself in a wild state of euphoria. Having cast aside all his former cleverly conceived plans, he had been perfectly prepared to bid his wife a respectful goodnight and adjourn to the solitude of his lonely bedroom, with nothing more than a bumper of brandy to keep him company through the coming night. Instead—and he could hardly believe it possible—it seemed that she had forgiven him and, more than that, appeared to be actually inviting his caresses!

With a husky groan, he swept her into his arms and lowered his lips, revelling once again, in the captivating sweetness of that earlier embrace. Clinging to him, it seemed to Helena that the whole world had spun away, leaving the two of them suspended in a kind of enchanted oblivion, where nothing mattered but the heat of the spiralling passion within which they were both locked.

Gasping for breath, Richard reluctantly tore his lips away from hers and, hefting his shoulder against the bedroom door, thrust it open; lifting Helena in his arms, he strode swiftly to the bed and, without taking his eyes from hers, deposited her none too gently on its lilac-coloured counterpane. Ripping off his jacket, he tossed it carelessly to one side, likewise his waistcoat. Then, tearing at his neckcloth, he dragged it from his neck and sent it sailing across the room. With scarcely a pause, he kicked off his shoes and leapt on to the bed beside her, his fingers busy with the fastenings of her gown.

The raucous creak of a floorboard on the far side of the room cut across his senses like an icy shower. With a muttered oath he lunged to his feet and at once perceived the scarlet-faced figure of Helena's maid tiptoeing gingerly towards the door.

'What the blazes do you think you are doing?' he rapped out, barely able to control his fury.

'B-beg pardon, sir!' stammered Fran, utterly beside herself with mortification. 'I was turning down madam's bed when you—that is, I…'

At the earl's pointed gaze, her voice trailed away and she shrank back in embarrassment.

'Very well,' he barked curtly. 'Now go!'

Dipping a hasty curtsy, Fran scurried for the door but then, as a sudden thought occurred to her, she hesitated and turning, she held out her hand and faltered, 'It's just that I found this, sir—madam—and I know it isn't yours, Mi—my lady, so I just wondered what I should do with it?'

'What is it, Fran?'

Having rolled over and hidden her face in the coverlet in her humiliation at being discovered by her maid in such a wild state of abandon, Helena, her curiosity gradually overcoming her, raised herself into a sitting position and, screwing up her eyes, squinted at the shiny object dangling from Fran's fingers.

All at once, it was as if her very breath had been torn from her body; the room seemed to be closing in on her and she could feel herself sinking into some vast bottomless void.

A stifled moan escaped her lips, bringing Richard instantly to her side.

'What's wrong, my love?' he asked urgently, reaching out for her.

Thrusting his hands aside, Helena scrambled away from him, her face numb with shock.

'Get out!' she said hoarsely, her voice quivering with anger. 'Get out of this room and take your paramour's bauble with you!'

Then, leaning forwards, she snatched the offending object out of her maid's trembling fingers and hurled it at him.

Although Richard was at a complete loss as to why Helena had erupted in such a sudden fury, his reaction was instinctive, his hand coming up to catch the object in mid-flight. Uncurling his fingers, he stared down at it, in stupefied incomprehension.

There, in the palm of his hand, its ruby eye glinting up at him, lay one of Rachel Cummings's earrings!

Chapter Eighteen

As the insistent sound of tinkling chinaware broke into Helena's consciousness, a dejected groan escaped her lips and she made a futile attempt to block out the invasive noise by burrowing more deeply into the mound of pillows.

'I'm that sorry to have to wake you up, Mi—my lady,' came Fran's hesitant tones. 'But it's gone half-past ten and the cook and housekeeper are waiting downstairs for you to give them their orders.'

Like a bolt of lightning, awareness suddenly returned and, shooting up, Helena stared at her maid in wide-eyed consternation. 'You haven't mentioned anything about—what happened last night?' she breathed fearfully.

'Hardly!' retorted the woman drily, pulling open one of the drawers and extracting a soft shawl. 'What goes on between a husband and wife in the privacy of their bedroom is nobody's business but their own, to my way of thinking,' she added, and returning to the bedside, draped the shawl across her mistress's shoulders. 'Now, you drink up your chocolate and then we'll see what we can do about those dark rings under your eyes—else that lot down there will have a field day making much out of nothing!'

Having spent most of the night curled up in one of the

fireside chairs, still fully dressed and with her eyes pinned to the adjoining door, lest her husband should choose to return and catch her unawares, Helena was too exhausted to do anything other than offer a weak smile in reply.

'I think we'd best forgo the bath this morning, ma'am,' continued the maid, as she selected an assortment of undergarments from the chest of drawers and piled it neatly on top of the ottoman at the foot of the bed. 'The quicker you get downstairs and start taking up your duties, the less they'll have to gossip about.'

Spurred on by the woman's matter-of-fact attitude, Helena quickly gulped down the remainder of her hot chocolate and slid out of bed.

'There's hot water in the basin, waiting for you,' Fran advised her, indicating the marble washstand, on which reposed a pretty rose-patterned washbowl and its matching water jug, along with Helena's own toilet accessories. 'And I brought up a few bits of ice, as well—a cooling compress for those swollen eyes will make all the difference, you'll see.'

Barely twenty minutes later, thanks to Fran's deft administrations, her neatly dressed and fully coiffed mistress stood at the door to her bedchamber, willing herself to go down and face whatever lay before her.

Having already ascertained from her maidservant that his lordship had taken himself off to the stables some three hours earlier, her nerves were not nearly as strung up as they would have been had she been required to confront him head-on.

The violent altercation of the previous evening had left her feeling both physically and mentally drained. After taking one look at the ruby earring, so clearly recognisable as one of the pair that Lady Cummings had worn at the Kettleshams' rout, Markfield had flung it from him in angry refutation, disclaiming any knowledge of how it had come to be in her bedroom.

Nevertheless, despite the fact that his robust denials had

eventually dissolved into an anguished and frantic entreaty, Helena, by clamping her hands over her ears, had refused to listen to a word he said, the discovery of her rival's earring being the final insult in a day that had seemed to her to have consisted of one indignity after another. She was thoroughly ashamed of herself for having been so totally gulled by his charismatic love-making techniques and had sworn that, as far as she was concerned, he had played that card for the last time. No matter what he might do or say to try to persuade her otherwise, she would never again allow him to cozen her in such a despicable manner. To think that she had been so utterly captivated by the feel of his arms around her and the compelling pressure of his lips on hers that she had been within a whisper of succumbing to his persuasive overtures. But for Fran's timely interruption—!

A shudder ran through her and, drawing in a trembling breath, she straightened her shoulders, stepped out into the corridor and made her way down the stairs, steeling herself to face the uncertain rigours of her new position.

Having decided that she would conduct the interviews with the cook and housekeeper in a relatively informal manner, she turned in the direction of the cosy-looking sitting room that she had viewed briefly the previous day. After tugging at the bell cord next to the mantelpiece, she settled herself into a comfortable armchair near the window and, after offering up a silent prayer, sat back and waited.

Mrs Ellis, the cheerfully buxom cook, having spent the past quarter of an hour or so hovering at the top of the staff staircase in high expectation of the summons, was the first to arrive, anticipating the equally impatient Mrs Wainwright by a good thirty seconds.

'Good morning, my lady!' she cried, as she bustled in with her daybook and grocery lists, her crisply starched apron crackling as she moved forwards. 'You slept well, I trust?'

Then, accepting her mistress's invitation to sit, she proceeded to spread her lists in on the table in front of her before turning an expectant eye in Helena's direction.

'Lamb today, I should think, my lady, possibly with a smoked haddock roulade to start—Mr Pearson tells me that he has some fine French beans that are just ripe for picking—new potatoes, of course, and maybe a cherry almond syllabub to finish? How does that sound, ma'am?'

'It all sounds very nice, Mrs Ellis,' replied Helena, with just the slightest lift of an eyebrow. 'But rather as though you hardly needed to confer with me in the first place, it would seem.'

'Ah, well, that's true, ma'am,' said the cook, looking slightly abashed. 'Mr Richard—his lordship, that is, usually just lets me get on with it.'

'Well, since you have already gone to so much trouble to arrange this evening's dinner menu, Cook, perhaps we ought to leave it at that for today. In future, however, I do believe that a little discussion would be in order. Needless to say, of course, I shall always rely on your expert knowledge to assist me in my choices.'

Her chubby face wreathed with gratification at the implied compliment, the smiling woman gathered up her bits and pieces and sketched her new mistress a brief curtsy. 'Why, of course, ma'am—it will be my pleasure, ma'am.'

'Let's say tomorrow at ten, then,' nodded Helena, as the cook prepared to depart. 'Ask Mrs Wainwright to come in now, if you would, please.'

Having already been given ample time to weigh up the housekeeper's assets on the previous afternoon, Helena lost no time in assuring Mrs Wainwright that she was more than happy to leave the general running of the house in her capable hands for the time being.

'And, if I happen upon anything that I would like to change, I'm sure we won't need to come to cuffs over the matter,' she added, with a swift smile at the older woman.

'I should think not indeed, your ladyship,' returned the other, with an answering smile. 'And, may I say, on behalf of all the staff, ma'am, how very glad we all are to see the master happily settled down at last!'

'Why, thank you, Mrs Wainwright—how very kind of you to mention it.'

Feeling somewhat flustered at hearing such a fond reference to her husband, Helena sought desperately to change the subject.

'You have been with the family for a long time, I imagine,' she ventured, at last.

Her eyes lighting up, the housekeeper nodded. 'Why, yes, ma'am—thirty years this coming August, as it happens. Brand, spanking new the house was, when I first came here. I was just twelve years old and only a kitchen skivvy in those days, of course, and Captain and Mrs Standish—his lordship's parents—were just newly-weds themselves then.'

Despite her current antipathy towards her husband, Helena could not help feeling a certain curiosity about his early days.

'His lordship was born here, then, I take it?' she asked.

'Oh, yes, ma'am! I can remember the day as if it were yesterday. Such a fuss and palaver there was going on—what with the master being born scarcely six hours after Lord Leo's son Simon! Captain Standish's father—the old earl, that was—brought a whole hogshead of ale down to the kitchen for the staff to celebrate the two births—he was over the moon with joy at getting two grandsons at almost one and the same time.' She paused, reflectively. 'A grand fellow, he was, his old lordship—he'd be turning in his grave if he could see the state of his old home now!'

Helena nodded in sympathy. 'How did it come to be allowed to fall into such a state of disrepair?'

The housekeeper shook her head. 'An unfortunate combination of events, really. When the old earl died—six years ago, that would be—Lord Leo, Viscount Lexington, as he was then—being the eldest of his old lordship's three sons, inherited the title, but he was a very poor landlord, having always been a bit of a loose fish, ever since his wife ran off with one of the grooms back in '92!'

'Ran off with one of the grooms?' repeated Helena faintly. 'Why did his lordship not just go after her and fetch her back?'

'Oh, he did try, my lady,' replied Mrs Wainwright, with a pensive sigh. 'That was the start of it, really. He took after the pair like a maniac, grabbed hold of the leader's harness and brought the carriage up so sharply that the whole lot tipped over on its side. Poor Lady Julia didn't stand a chance, I'm afraid— that was when Lord Leo started all the drinking and gambling. Never took the slightest bit of interest in either the estate or young Lord Simon from that moment on—not until the lad turned seventeen, that is, when his father chose to introduce him to all his rakehell associates and their obnoxious pursuits!' She gave a disapproving sniff.

'I understand that the present Lord Markfield and his cousin Simon were very close, in those days,' put in Helena carefully. 'Am I to take it that he, too, joined in the general revelry?'

'Good gracious, no, my lady!' The housekeeper looked thoroughly shocked. 'The master has always been far too much of a gentleman to involve himself with that sort of set. He preferred to spend whatever spare time he had in his grandfather's stables, just as he does now, my lady—he's been totally besotted with horses ever since he was in leading strings!'

'But, the two of them were close—as children, I mean?' persisted Helena, unable to reconcile her husband's own description of events with what the housekeeper now seemed to be telling her.

'Oh, yes, ma'am,' replied Mrs Wainwright, with a satisfied nod. 'Almost inseparable, they were then—on account of the poor lambs both having lost their mothers at such an early age, I suppose—Lord Simon barely six years old when his mother was killed and then Mrs Standish dying in childbed the following year, just after the master's seventh birthday. Spent most of their time with their grandparents over at the Hall, after that, the pair of them did,' she added reflectively. 'Went off to Rugby together the following year and then on to Cambridge—joined at the hip, they seemed to be—until Lord Simon was sent down for getting up to some sort of mischief, that is—although I never did get to find out what that was all about.'

'And that was when the two of them started drifting apart, I suppose?' suggested Helena, her interest growing by the minute. 'Lord Markfield joined the military...?'

Mrs Wainwright nodded. 'His father—who was General Standish by then—bought him a cornetcy in the same regiment that he was in—the master didn't really seem that keen at the time, to my way of thinking, but he's always been the sort of lad who puts duty before self and, once he makes up his mind to do something, he just knuckles down and does his very best to make a success of it. He refused to sell out—even after the old earl died and then his father was killed at Vimiero. Fair knocked him sideways that did, I know, but I remember hearing him tell Lady Isobel that there was still a war to be won and that he had no intention of quitting until our lot had settled those Frenchies for good and all!'

A moment's silence followed, during which Helena reflected upon the rather different picture of her husband that the housekeeper had succeeded in conveying to her. A pensive frown crept across her brow as she wondered if it could be at all possible that she had misjudged him—his indignation and subsequent fury last evening had been extremely convincing, after all, and, if Mrs Wainwright's assessment of his character held any credibility, it seemed hardly possible that so principled a man would ever involve himself in the sort of devious chicanery of which she had held him guilty!

'It does seem most unlikely,' she murmured softly to herself.

'I beg your pardon, my lady?'

Helena started. She had been so wrapped up in her re-evaluation of Markfield's character that she had almost forgotten the housekeeper's presence.

'That Lord Markfield would quit his post!' she parried hastily. 'I was merely remarking how unlikely that would be!'

'Very true, my lady,' nodded Mrs Wainwright, in mournful agreement. 'Stuck it out right to the end, he did—too bad he had to come home and find that his uncle had sold off all the old earl's horses and let the Hall to go to rack and ruin. Fair broke Master Richard's heart—oh, I do beg your pardon, ma'am—I've been so used to calling his lordship by that name that it just slipped out!'

A stricken expression in her eyes, the mortified housekeeper got to her feet and, smoothing down the skirts of her black bombazine gown, dipped a hurried curtsy and made ready to leave, but Helena, putting out her hand, stayed her.

'Please do not concern yourself, Mrs Wainwright,' she begged. 'It is perfectly natural for you to think of his lordship as Master Richard and I really don't mind a bit. I would dearly love to hear more about his childhood, if you can spare me another few minutes of your time, some time in the near future?'

'Why, certainly, my lady,' returned the housekeeper, highly relieved that her careless slip had not been taken amiss. 'I'd be more than glad to do that.'

Having also risen, Helena accompanied the woman to the doorway. On reaching it, she paused momentarily, before asking, 'The old house—Markfield Hall—how far is it from Westpark?'

'The drive gates are about two miles up the road to the right,' volunteered Mrs Wainwright. 'But, if you were wanting to surprise his lordship over at the stables, my lady, your best bet is to cut across the lawn out here and follow the river path down to the old footbridge, which goes straight over the river into Markfield itself—you can see the back of the old Hall from there and the stables are just behind the walled garden. It's a very pretty walk and shouldn't take you more than twenty minutes or so.'

Having collected a wide-brimmed straw bonnet and a light-weight wrap, Helena slipped out of the house through the double doors of the sitting room on to the terrace beyond, and ran lightly down the steps and across the sloping lawn towards the path that bordered the little river that snaked its way between the two estates.

Just as Mrs Wainwright had said, the walk proved to be a most attractive one, with magnificent willow trees draping their freshly budding fronds into the water on one side of the path and a copper beech hedge sheltering neatly kept vegetable and herb gardens on the other. Even though it was still only mid-April, the air was still and the temperature pleasantly mild. Strolling dreamily along in the sunshine, Helena was soon drinking in the beauty that surrounded her; the huge drifts of wild daffodils adorning the grassy banks of the river and, most enchanting of all, the clusters of primroses, violets and celandines that nestled randomly amongst the roots of the hedgerows. She stopped and watched in awe as a pair of haughty-looking swans sailed majestically by, then laughed out loud at the antics of a noisy family of ducks as they jostled for position at the river's edge.

Just the sort of property she had always envisioned whilst endeavouring to persuade her father to sell up and move out of the capital, she recalled, as she let out a wistful sigh. His health could hardly have failed to improve had he chosen to surround himself with such serene tranquillity and now, she was not even sure that she was in a position to invite him down for a short stay! After last night's bitter confrontation, it would not have surprised her to learn that her husband had every intention of filing for an immediate annulment of their hasty marriage—a resolution with which she would have heartily concurred until less than half an hour ago. Her rather enlightening chat with Mrs Wainwright, however, had raised a host of doubts in her mind and she was now finding it impossible to reconcile the housekeeper's sturdy avowal of Lord Markfield's upright character with her own less than complimentary appraisal of him.

Nevertheless, it was difficult to see how she could have been so mistaken about everything—the Cummings woman *had* been in the church, after all and, despite the earl having pointed out that church services were open to the public, Helena still could not understand why any self-respecting female would feel the need to attend her ex-lover's marriage ceremony since, as far as she could see, any such action could well be likened to the rubbing of salt in an open wound!

Rather more perturbing, perhaps, had been the matter of that ruby earring. Despite Markfield's angrily vehement protests and denials, there had been no doubt in Helena's mind as to the trinket's owner, although she felt bound to admit that, had it not been for the fact that his earlier long-term absence over at the stables still rankled somewhat, she might easily have persuaded herself to take her husband's word on the subject. As it was, the earl's protestations had finally ground to a halt and, turning furiously on his heel, he had made for his own chamber where, after slamming the door behind him, she had actually heard the click of the lock as he turned the key.

Summoning up the nerve to face him after all the bitter antagonism that had flowed between them was not going to be easy, she told herself, as she approached the rather ancient-looking footbridge. If, as was beginning to look increasingly likely, her husband turned out to be totally innocent of all that she had accused him, then an abject apology would seem to be in order. Having recalled Markfield's expression as he had flung himself out of the room, however, Helena could only view such a prospect with increasing apprehension. And yet, as she well knew, if the fault lay at her door, she would just have to steel herself to admit the possibility of a mistake.

But that still did not explain the presence of the earring! Could it have fallen out of her husband's pocket during an earlier inspection of her room? she wondered. Perhaps he had retrieved the earrings from Lady Cummings at their final meeting, she then conjectured—but why, then, would he need to deny all knowledge of its existence? It was all so very perplexing!

The footbridge, as she was soon to discover, spanned the river at its narrowest point, just before it altered its course to curve sharply westwards, thereafter to meander its way between Charles Standish's Southpark property and the main Markfield estate. Mrs Wainwright had mentioned that there was a second bridge some three-quarters of a mile beyond this one but, since she had made up her mind that it was up to her to make the effort to effect some sort of a reconciliation between herself and her husband, Helena could see no virtue in postponing the inevitable any longer than was absolutely necessary.

Despite the fact that the distance between the two banks was little more than eight feet, she could not help but feel a moment's unease at the sight of the river rushing along beneath her feet through the many gaps in the bridge's woodwork. No sooner had she reached the far side, however, than she was taking herself to task for behaving in so juvenile a manner—doubtless the estate workers who crossed the bridge on a daily basis would have been highly amused to witness the tottering steps of their new mistress!

Richard, doing his best to keep his mind on his work and off the disastrous events of the previous evening, had an uncanny sense of Helena's presence long before he could bring himself to turn around and confront her.

The amount of brandy he had consumed the previous evening, in an effort to blot out the image of his wife sprawled on the bed in fervent anticipation of his lovemaking, had resulted in him suffering from the most blinding headache. Now, every time he tried to redirect his attention towards trying to fathom out how the offending jewel could have found its way into his wife's bedroom, a searing pain shot through his head, rendering him incapable of any kind of constructive thought. He had managed to get as far as questioning Fran, the maid-

servant, as to precisely where she had come across the bauble—
snagged up in one of her mistress's bed curtains, apparently—
but beyond that, he was totally mystified as to how it could
possibly have come to be there.

The fact that he had allowed his angry frustration to get the
better of him galled him intensely, but he doubted that there was
a man alive who would have regarded so unpropitious an interruption with any sort of equanimity. It was bad enough that his
ardour had been dashed for the second time that day, but to find
himself accused of—what? He was not entirely sure of the
charge. Did Helena seriously imagine that he had invited his
ex-paramour to share his soon-to-be-wife's bed with him during
the past week? Good God in heaven! To the best of his knowledge the room had been shut up ever since his mother's death
and only his forthcoming marriage had caused him to unlock
the door and order its total redecoration and refurbishment.

The only other explanation that his fuddled head had been
able to conjure up was that both of these ploys—Helena's tale
about having seen Rachel in the church and her maid's
supposed discovery of the earring—had been drummed up by
his new wife in some sort of desperate attempt to avoid an
unwanted consummation of their marriage!

All of which both irritated and puzzled the earl deeply, since
he had been utterly convinced that Helena's responses to his
caresses had been genuine. The idea that he might have
imagined such eager enthusiasm was almost laughable—and
he was sufficiently acquainted with the ways of the opposite sex
to be reasonably certain that the former Miss Wheatley was far
too much of an innocent to be versed in the subtle art of teasing.

Nevertheless, if that was the way she wanted it, he decided,
with a disaffected shrug, then that was the way it would have
to be. He had never been obliged to resort to taking a woman
by force before and he was certainly not about to start now.

'What a fine-looking animal!'

Helena's cheerful call cut across his thoughts and, carefully tethering the thoroughbred colt he had been in the process of training to the nearby gatepost, Richard turned to face her. The discovery that she managed to look so fresh and infinitely kissable after so tempestuous a parting, when he felt so damnably haggard, gave him yet another reason to stay well clear of her. It would seem that the previous night's débâcle had not overset her in the slightest!

'Arabian stock,' he explained, eyeing her curiously. 'I was hoping to have them ready for next week's auctions.' He paused, then, unable to stop himself, he blurted out, 'I hardly expected to see you here this morning.'

'Well, at least you haven't asked me if I slept well,' she returned drily. 'It has been the question on almost everyone else's lips this morning!'

A reluctant smile tugged at the corner of his mouth. 'It's just that they are all rather keen to find favour with you,' he assured her. 'It's been a good many years since Westpark had a—'

He had been about to say 'mistress' but, in view of the present contention between them, hurriedly substituted, '—lady at its helm.'

The replacement not having escaped her, Helena merely gave a brief nod but, not entirely at ease with the way in which her husband's eyes seemed to have rested upon her lips, reviving unwanted memories of those heady kisses, she blinked and moved hurriedly across to the five-barred gate where, by stepping up on to the lowest bar, she was able to rest her folded arms across its topmost strut and direct her attention to the young colt cropping contentedly at the grass scarcely two feet away from her. 'He's very beautiful,' she exclaimed, as soon as she had regained control of her wayward emotions. 'How many horses do you actually have here?'

'Only twelve in the actual stud—three stallions, six mares and three colts—plus the usual assortment of carriage horses and other working animals, of course.'

Holding his breath, Richard stepped towards her, his fingers positively itching to feel the warm softness of her body once more in their grasp. 'What's brought you here, Helena?' he asked softly, hoping against hope that, having taken stock of their parlous situation, she had decided to put aside their differences and attempt a fresh start.

But, not entirely confident of her ability to withstand any advances he might be about to make, Helena, leaping down from her perch, sidestepped him neatly and waved her hand in the direction of the house. 'I just wanted to take a look at the Hall,' she replied, somewhat breathlessly. 'After all, it *was* your reason for seeking out my father in the first place, as I recall. I just had a fancy to see what all the fuss was about!'

'Be my guest,' returned Richard, giving an impassive shrug of his shoulder. 'I doubt that you will be particularly impressed—last week's rain hardly helped matters.'

The speed at which recent events had occurred had rather curtailed his former enthusiasm for reviving the grandeur of the family home and, in view of the latest disappointments he had suffered, its very presence now served only as a mocking reminder of how he had come to be in such an unenviable position in the first place.

'Oh, I dare say it can soon be put to rights,' Helena said dismissively. 'Now that you have Papa's money, there is no end to the improvements you will be able to make.'

Ignoring his extended arm, she strode off in the direction of the Hall's rear entrance, feeling a growing need to keep as much distance between herself and her husband as was humanly possible. How it was that he always had such an overwhelming effect upon her senses, she was at a loss to understand, but it was becoming very clear that she was going to have to watch herself very carefully if she meant to avoid any sort of repetition of the previous day's heartrending experiences!

Fighting back his frustration, Richard hurried after her and managed to catch up with her just as she was proceeding down the passageway that led into the great hall.

'Oh, how perfectly dreadful!'

Helena's shocked whisper smote at his heart.

'Not a pretty sight, is it?' he sighed.

And, indeed, it was not. Its roof open to the elements in a good many places, the once-grand entrance hall revealed its rather sorry state in all its depressing entirety; the once highly coveted Gibbons panelling that covered all four walls up as far as the roof beams was badly cracked and bulged out in many areas. Scarcely an inch of woodwork had escaped the long years of neglect, and the irreplaceable carvings were now, seemingly, water damaged beyond repair. And, if that were not more than enough with which to contend, evidence of a recent heavy rainfall had left a great many pools of water littered about the marble-tiled flooring, filling the air with a damp and fetid odour.

As she incredulously took in the ruined shell of the hallway, a lump began to form in Helena's throat and tears filled her eyes.

'It's absolutely appalling,' she choked. 'How anyone could treat such magnificent craftsmanship with so little respect is quite beyond my understanding!'

Then, spinning around, she confronted Richard with an indignant glare. 'You cannot allow such destruction to continue!' she stormed at him. 'You must cease what you are doing immediately and set about putting it all back to rights!'

'Later in the year, possibly,' he responded. 'I have more important things to think about at present.'

'But, surely, this is why you have been so urgently in need of money?' she persisted, staring up at him in frowning incredulity. 'You cannot mean to tell me that now that you have my dowry in your hands you have no intention of using it to repair this lovely old place?'

At the implied criticism Richard felt himself stiffening in protest, but then his shoulders slumped and he turned away from her. 'I do not have your money,' he countered, in weary resignation. 'I had intended to inform you but—er—other events—rather forestalled me.'

A look of horror crept into Helena's eyes. 'What are you trying to tell me?' she whispered fearfully. Surely the man could not have gone through such a massive fortune already?

'I was unable to bring myself to accept it,' he went on, giving a careless shrug, as he started to make his way back towards the rear passageway. 'You will find every single penny of your dowry in your own named account in Mr Coutts's bank in the Strand. I have no intention of touching a penny of it!'

'But what about the house?' she demanded, as she hastened after him and grasped at his hand. 'Surely you don't intend to stand by and watch it fall into total disrepair?'

Richard stilled, willing himself to ignore the compelling feel of her hand on his. 'As things stand at the moment I fear that I have rather lost interest in the whole project,' he returned, as he reluctantly extracted himself from her hold and continued on his way. There hardly seemed much point in adding that, since Helena had made it rather clear that she was unable to return his love, he was not sure that he could bring himself to care very much about anything at all.

Chapter Nineteen

'Well, "hail, fellow, well met"—as the saying goes!'

The welcoming tones of his cousin Charles greeted Markfield as he stepped back out into the sunlight but, on perceiving Helena close behind the earl, Standish executed a courtly bow in her direction and, giving her a swift grin, added, 'And, good morrow to you, fair maid—if I might make so bold!'

Finding herself unable to resist his cheery countenance and boyish bonhomie, Helena was quick to return his smile. 'Good morning, Charles—I trust that yesterday's proceedings did not overtire your mother too greatly?'

'Back on her day-bed, as snug as a bug,' he replied jauntily, his eyes darting between her and the earl with unconcealed curiosity. 'Although, I must say that I hadn't expected to find either of you over here this morning.'

'Helena expressed a certain eagerness to take a look at the place,' returned Richard carelessly. 'What's brought you over?'

'Just thought I'd take a look and see if Friday's rainfall had done any further damage—the quicker we get those tilers back on the job the better, to my way of thinking.'

Having made a point of avoiding all mention of the final marriage settlements to anyone but Helena, Richard was averse to having his rather strange arrangement held up for general discussion, since he had no wish to find himself suddenly bombarded with requests for account settlements quite yet a while. With the stock auctions coming up, he had every hope of being able to recoup some of his original investment with the sale of the three thoroughbred colts he had reared.

'All in good time,' was his hurried response, although he did attempt to shoot a quick cautionary glance in his wife's direction as he spoke.

But Helena, having registered his cousin's undoubted interest in the project and being only too keen to garner his support, chose to ignore her husband's veiled instruction.

'It would seem that his lordship is far too involved with his other schemes to spare the time to attend to the refurbishment of useless old buildings,' she informed Standish airily. 'It is beginning to look as though I shall need to attend to the matter myself!'

Equally taken aback by her statement, both men stared at her in astonishment.

'Well offered, dear cousin!' began Standish, being the first to recover. 'Although, I fear that you cannot possibly have had time to consider what will be involved. It's rather more than simply choosing new curtains and cushions, you know. There are a host of things to consider when undertaking a project such as this—qualified craftsmen will need to be hired—as well as a whole army of workers and cleaners and all that sort of thing—hardly a lady's domain, I should have thought. Much better to leave it all to Richard, don't you think?'

'Not if he is disinclined to spend any time on it,' retorted Helena, throwing her husband a defiant glance before adding, 'It would appear that we are quite likely to have to wait until doomsday itself, before his lordship regains his interest.'

At his cousin's gasp of disbelief, Richard put up a hand to silence the expected disputation. 'Helena is perfectly correct,' he said quietly. 'Recent events have rather overshadowed my own former regard for the Hall but, since she has expressed an interest in the reconstruction, I see no harm in allowing her to pursue that interest. Quite apart from the fact that, since it is her own money that she will be using, I am hardly in any position to dictate to her how she spends it!'

Perceiving that Standish appeared to be far too taken aback by this statement to do anything other than goggle at him in a shocked silence, the earl gave him a wry smile, before adding, 'Don't worry, Charles. I dare say it will all come right in the end.'

'In the end!' Standish gestured hopelessly towards the building behind them. 'But the building is falling to pieces now! And I was under the impression that the whole idea of this agreement of yours was to acquire enough money to put everything back to rights?'

Wooden-faced, Richard chose not to respond to his cousin's somewhat barbed reference apropos his recent marriage. Helena, however, was of a different mind.

'You are quite right to be concerned, Charles,' she asserted. 'But, I promise that you have no need to worry unduly. And surely it matters not one whit who organises the project—as long as the renovations continue. As to the problems you mentioned, I dare say I shall be able to count on the pair of you to set me on the right track, should I run into difficulties?'

Barely conscious of Standish's instant 'yes, of course', she turned an eager face in her husband's direction and raised a questioning eyebrow.

'How you choose to dispose of your own money is no concern of mine,' he replied stiffly. 'And, as to the Hall's renovations, as far as I am concerned, you may both do with it just as you wish. As I have already told you, I have other far more important matters to deal with at present. Now, if you will please excuse me?'

And, with a curt bow that encompassed the two of them, he swung away and strode off towards the stables, leaving a stunned and confused Standish staring after him.

'Well, I'll be da—!' he began, then hurriedly recollecting himself, he turned back to Helena and said apologetically, 'I do beg your pardon, Helena—I trust that I may I call you that, now that we are cousins?'

At her subdued nod, he continued. 'I fear that my careless remarks must have been the cause of that outburst. I should have realised that today of all days was hardly the moment to bring up the matter of the building programme. But, I swear that I had no idea that Richard had become so averse to continuing with the renovations. Hitherto, he had always been so keen…'

His voice trailed away and his eyes travelled across to the ivy-clad wall of the Hall at his rear. 'It would have been splendid to see it back as it was when our grandparents were in residence,' he said sadly. 'We three boys had such fine times there.'

Snatching her own gaze away from the stable door through which her husband had disappeared, Helena squared her shoulders and stiffened her intent. 'And so you shall,' she exclaimed defiantly. 'I meant what I said, Charles. I swear that this blessed building will be returned to its former glory, even if it takes every penny I possess!'

'Well, I trust it won't come to that, my dear,' returned Standish, with a swift smile. 'But, you can certainly count on my support, I promise you that—any little thing that I can do to further the cause, you only have to ask—short of actually plastering walls, of course—I flatly draw the line at any sort of manual labour!'

'I trust we won't need to resort to such extreme measures,' retorted Helena gaily, doing her best to enter into the spirit of Standish's light-hearted repartee, for she was well aware that he was doing his best to take her mind off Markfield's precipitant departure. 'Perhaps you would care to accompany me back to Westpark for lunch and we can discuss some of the details— if you are prepared to take your chances over that dreadful footbridge, of course?'

'You might like to put that at the top of your list of essential repairs,' laughed Standish, as he held out his arm to her. 'Before one or other of us has the misfortune to take a header into the river!'

* * *

Standing in the shadow of the stable-door jamb, Richard, now thoroughly deflated, watched the pair depart. Trust Charles to turn the situation to his advantage, he thought, with a rueful shake of his head. If he had not known better, he might well have suspected his cousin of setting up some sort of flirtation with Helena! It was true that the two of them did seem to be on very friendly terms, but the earl concluded that this had probably come about as a result of his own enforced absence from town when, having experienced a slight feeling of unease regarding Viscount Barrington's possible reaction to the marriage announcement, he had charged Charles with keeping an eye on his bride-to-be. Nevertheless, it was pretty galling to have to stand by and watch one's wife skipping gaily off hand in hand with some other fellow when she could barely raise a smile for her own husband!

Scowling slightly, he strode across to the paddock, untethered the colt and proceeded to carry on with the unhurried training procedure that his beloved grandfather had so carefully instilled into him. If only women were as easy to handle as horses were, he thought longingly, as the colt nuzzled his pocket gently, in search of the expected treat. But then, as he recalled Helena's determined stance and spirited responses, he could not refrain from letting out a wistful sigh, concluding that it was becoming very clear that toeing the line was not exactly in her nature. Never having been one to turn his own back on a challenge, however, it came to him that he was going to have to put in a good deal of extra effort if he wanted to gain her trust and—more important—her love.

Holding out the piece of apple that he had been saving for the end of the session, his lips curved in a satisfied smile as the colt reached forwards and took it from his hand. 'Slowly and gently,' he murmured softly. 'That's always the best way to achieve the desired result, isn't it, my lad?'

* * *

Keeping firm to his objective, Richard then set about wooing his wife in the most dedicated fashion. After greeting her with a welcoming smile in the drawing room that same evening, he was quick to compliment her on her appearance before leading her to her seat at the dining table, whereupon he proceeded to regale her with a series of light-hearted anecdotes from both his school and army days. Any questions that she plied him with, he answered with a cheerful grace, although he was careful to change the subject whenever it happened to drift in the direction of the proposed building programme.

Whilst Helena was finding herself quite entranced with this new persona that her husband seemed to have adopted, she could not help feeling slightly wary of it all. Was this some new ploy of his to bend her to his will, she wondered as, almost mesmerised, she followed his actions as he refilled his wineglass and raised it in her direction, before slowly lifting it to his lips. A little ripple of uncertainty ran through her for, despite the great distance that separated them, his very masculinity seemed to surround her, pinning her to her seat and rendering her quite helpless. And, even though she could not help but be aware that he had hardly taken his eyes off her throughout the entire meal, she had found it impossible to prevent her own glance from continually straying in his direction, obliging her to tear her eyes hurriedly away from his the moment they locked together. If this was seduction, she found herself thinking, as her pulse began to race and she felt the slow spiral of heat rising from within, the Earl of Markfield was certainly proving to be a veritable master of the craft!

The question was: should she surrender to her emotions and allow that smouldering look in his eyes to take her over the threshold into that unknown paradise she had so narrowly avoided the previous evening, or should she hold fast to her reason until a full and proper explanation of how that Cummings woman's earring had so mysteriously found its way into her bedroom?

As it turned out, the choice was not to be hers. To her surprise—and utter chagrin, if the truth be known—at the meal's end, Richard rose from his seat and, after leading her back to the drawing room, raised the tips of fingers to his lips, kissed them briefly and asked to be excused.

'I'm feeling a trifle jaded, my dear,' he drawled. 'Rather a short night and a long day, with an equally heavy one tomorrow, I fear—I think I will just take myself off to my bed, if you have no objection?'

'N-not at all,' Helena stuttered, in some confusion. 'I was c-contemplating something similar myself, as it happens.'

A slow smile curved across his lips. 'Then I will wish you a pleasant night, my dear.'

With which parting remark, he turned and walked smartly out of the room, leaving Helena staring after him in a speechless rage. *Well, of all the…! Having spent the entire evening flirting with her and bringing her almost to the point of tossing away her inhibitions and succumbing to his will, he had simply changed his mind and thought better of it!*

Not entirely sure whether to burst into a fit of hysterical laughter or allow the hot tears that were forming in her eyes to have their way, Helena collapsed on to the nearest chair. *Well, if that's the way he means to go on,* she told herself, as she resolutely suppressed the waves of deep disappointment that her husband's apparently casual rejection had caused her, *he is about to discover that it's a game that two can play!*

Chapter Twenty

Early the next morning, his horse blowing heavily after its challenging gallop across the South Downs, Richard swung back into the stable yard, only to find his access to the stables partially blocked by a pair of large wagons, the contents of which were in the process of being unloaded by several teams of workmen.

Quickly dismounting, a furrow of irritation gathering on his brow, he tossed his reins to the waiting stable hand and stared in growing perplexity at the busy hive of activity going on all around him, until finally, his eyes fell upon a small, scrawny-looking man, clearly the instigator of the unanticipated commotion.

'Mr Jarvis!' he exclaimed, in astonishment, as he strode quickly towards the man. 'I had not thought to find you here this morning!'

'Ah, good morning, your lordship,' beamed the other, Ned Jarvis by name and a master slater by trade. 'We got here as soon as we could—her ladyship was most insistent that we needed to get on with the job before the next rainfall.'

'Her ladyship?' Richard queried, even more confused. To the best of his knowledge, his grandmother was still in London, recuperating after the wedding reception.

'That's right, m'lord,' returned Jarvis, as he signalled a

further instruction to one of his minions. 'Called in on her way to the coaching office, her ladyship did—caught me right in the middle of my breakfast—'

Richard stilled and a cold rivulet of unease ran down his spine as he realised that the ladyship the man was referring to was not the dowager countess, as he had supposed, but to the new Lady Markfield—his wife! But the coaching office? Surely to God Helena hadn't taken it into her head to walk out on him already? Inhaling deeply, he let out a slow breath.

'And did her ladyship manage to catch the stage, do you know?' he asked, striving to keep his tone neutral, despite the sudden rush of apprehension that was starting to threaten his ability to think straight.

'Oh, you've no need to concern yourself there, sir! Saw her climb aboard the stage with my own eyes, I did—the Blue Boar being right opposite my yard, as you know. Bang on time—eight o'clock, as usual. Her ladyship is probably disembarking at Hyde Park corner this very minute, even as we speak, sir!'

'Yes, I dare say you're right.'

Richard's eyes swivelled over to where Jarvis's workmen were busily unloading the stacks of slates into wheelbarrows prior to ferrying them across to the rear of the Hall. He was finding it difficult to draw breath, let alone make sense of what the craftsman was telling him. Unable to bring himself to question him as to the amount of luggage her ladyship might have been carrying—or indeed, whether or not she had been accompanied by her maid—he was overcome by a most urgent need to get back to Westpark and check for himself—hopefully, Mrs Wainwright would be able to throw some light on what had gone on in the house during his absence.

Turning towards the stables, he took two steps and then came to a sudden halt as, with a muted oath, he remembered that the grooms would have taken the thoroughbreds out for their morning exercise. Having set out for his own ride shortly after dawn, in a vain attempt to direct his thoughts away from the tormenting image of Helena curled up in her bed in the adjoining room, he had ridden his mount practically into the ground, rendering the poor creature out of commission for the next hour, at the very least—and far too long for him to wait to discover what new blow Fate had seen fit to hurl at him!

Striding quickly away from the stable yard, he made at once for the river path, breaking into a run as soon as he was out of sight of the workmen but, on reaching the footbridge, was faced with yet another impasse. Busily engaged in hacking out the bridge's rotten planking was another gang of labourers, rendering any imminent crossing totally out of the question!

'Very sorry, your lordship,' called out one of the men as he approached. 'Won't be able to use the bridge for an hour or so yet—but we'll be as quick as we can, sir.'

Muttering violent imprecations, Richard turned away and set off up the path in the direction of footbridge that crossed the river into his cousin's property, which lay some three-quarters of a mile further upstream.

What in God's name was going on? he asked himself, as he once more broke into a run. In the two hours since he had set out for his ride, his entire world seemed to have been tipped off its axis. Not only had his wife of one day walked out on him, but it would appear that she had added fuel to the fire by reinstating the abandoned building programme, knowing full well that he was unable to pay the contractors. So much for his arrogantly conceived plan of a slow and careful wooing! Perhaps he would have done better just to shelve his high-flown principles and demand his marital rights, as a good many other men would have done in the circumstances! A well and truly bedded wife might have had second thoughts about taking off and running back home to her father!

But then, with a quick shake of his head, he cast that notion aside. Quite apart from the fact that the taking of any woman against her will was totally foreign to his nature, it was difficult not to forget that it had been as a result of such a brutish attempt that Helena had found herself under obligation to agree to his marriage proposal in the first place.

At which consideration, a shudder of dismay ran through him, causing him to quicken his pace. If she had really gone off to London on her own and if Barrington should happen to catch sight of her, she could well be in serious danger, for the viscount was not the sort of man to bear his grudges lightly and, after the hiding Markfield had dealt him…!

As the possible consequences of his past actions crowded into his brain, Richard's sense of foreboding increased and, as he tore up the path towards the Southpark footbridge, he could hardly contain his growing feeling of dread.

At last, he reached the bridge which, being more than twenty feet across at this point, was of a much sturdier construction than the one on the lower stretch of the river. Urging himself forwards, his lungs almost fit to burst, he managed to stumble halfway across, before a severe lack of wind, caused by his badly neglected physical condition, forced him to a standstill. Pausing to catch his breath, he became aware of the approaching sound of horse's hooves.

Straightening up, his eyes hit upon his cousin riding towards him on the opposite bank.

'Quick, Charles!' he gasped, as he launched himself across the short distance that separated them. 'I need your horse—I have to get back to Westpark right away!'

'Steady on, old man!' exclaimed Standish as, hastily dismounting, he thrust his reins into the earl's outstretched hands. 'Is something amiss? You look totally done in!'

'It seems that Helena's taken herself back up to town,' croaked the earl abruptly, as he swung himself hurriedly into the saddle and turned the mount in the direction of his home.

'Well, yes, I know all about that!' cried his cousin, clutching at the horse's bridle. 'But why all the sudden panic?'

Richard froze and, his eyes narrowing, he stared down at Standish.

'What do you mean—you know about her leaving?'

'Why, yes, of course—Helena and I discussed it all yesterday. She was aiming to go to that soup kitchen of hers in Chelsea and persuade a parcel of her down-and-outers to come back here and work for her—I offered to take her up myself, of course, but she insisted that I needed to stay here and set some men on to repairing that old bridge of yours before she got back. I was just going down to see how they were getting on.'

'I see,' said Richard who, having regained both his breath and his composure, was beginning to feel slightly foolish at having allowed himself to get into such a panic-stricken state. A feeling that quickly turned to one of irritation as he hurriedly dismounted and returned the reins to the clearly bewildered Standish.

'Seemingly, my fears are unfounded, then,' he growled as he turned to leave. 'I had visions of her coming face to face with that bounder Barrington—it's a pity that neither of you saw fit to inform me of your arrangements!'

'But you professed to want nothing to do with any of it!' protested his cousin. 'And, if I may say so, the fact that you and your wife appear not to be on speaking terms is hardly an excuse to treat me as some sort of whipping boy!'

'No, you are quite right, Charles,' returned Markfield, with a weary sigh. 'Please excuse that remark—I seem to have lost the ability to think straight recently.'

'This marriage of yours is not going according to plan then, I take it?' asked Standish, staring curiously at his cousin.

Throwing back his head, Richard let out a bark of derisive laughter.

'Certainly not to any plan that I have ever heard of!' he retorted grimly. 'We manage to keep up a reasonable show in front of the servants, but that's about it—though you can't have failed to notice that my new wife has rather a low opinion of me.'

A puzzled frown flitted across Standish's brow.

'Well, she certainly didn't mention anything of the sort to me,' he countered. 'We spent most of the afternoon discussing what needed to be done to the Hall and she seemed most enthusiastic that it should be returned to its former state without any further ado—just as you would have done yourself, I imagine, had you not been fool enough to—'

He stopped and a flush covered his cheeks. 'Forgive me, old man,' he stammered. 'That was uncalled for, I know, but I cannot help thinking that you might have made a grave mistake in handing the reins over to your wife!'

'With hindsight, you may well be proved right,' acknowledged the earl heavily. 'But it's done now and I have no intention of sticking my nose into whatever arrangements the pair of you might have cooked up together—I dare say I can rely on you to ensure that the work is up to the necessary standard?'

'Absolutely, old man,' exclaimed Standish, thrusting out his hand. 'I promise that nothing will be done without my express agreement. I'm as keen to see the Hall back to its old self as you once were!'

'Probably still am, if the truth be told,' revealed Richard, as he clasped his cousin's hand between both of his. 'Just got knocked slightly off kilter, that's all, but I'm perfectly happy to leave it to you to oversee. You're just as familiar with the place as I am, after all. Apart from which, I shall be up to my eyes, for the next week or so, with other matters that are rather more pressing—at least, as far as I'm concerned.'

Assuring his cousin that he would be more than happy to stand proxy for him, Standish remounted, and with a cheery smile and a friendly wave, the two men parted—Standish to inspect the ongoing progress at the footbridge and Richard to make his way back to Westpark, where yet more revelations lay in wait for him.

Having confirmed that Jem the coachman, had taken both Helena and her maid off to Epsom to catch the London stage, Mrs Wainwright directed her master's attention towards the library where, as she informed him, her ladyship had left him a note.

A single sheet of paper, folded in half and propped up

against his inkwell, briefly intimating her intentions, merely
confirmed what both Charles and the housekeeper had already
told him. Rather more to the point, as he very soon realised,
upon casting his eyes across the desk towards the large stack
of bills that normally sat there, was that the formerly rather
large pile had diminished quite considerably. Anger surged up
within him as he thumbed through the remaining requests for
payment, to discover that every bill that pertained to the refurbishment of Markfield Hall had been extracted. Clenching his
fist, he brought it down on the surface of the desk with such a
mighty thump that the inkwell toppled forwards and tipped its
contents right across the blotter in front of him.

His shoulders slumped in despair, his eyes followed the
spreading inkstain until, with a strangled oath, he leapt out of
his seat and strode across to the sideboard, whereon a selection
of drinks was displayed. Pouring himself a full bumper of
brandy, he tossed back the fiery liquor in a couple of hefty
gulps, refilled the glass and threw himself down into one of the
leather chairs that straddled the fireplace, staring into the flickering flames with the grimmest of expressions on his face.

*A damned gigolo! That's what this marriage had turned
him into. There was nothing for it but to wave a fond farewell
to all his high-flown principles of honour above all, since it was
clear that he was now little more than a kept man, totally
dependent upon his wife's charity!*

How he had ever been fool enough to suppose that his wife
could be sweet-talked into falling in love with him, he could
no longer imagine. It was bad enough that she regarded him as
an adulterer, but to find out that she had rifled through his
private correspondence was, as far as he was concerned, pretty
much the final straw. Never mind that she had very likely taken
the bills in order to settle the accounts—the fact that she had
gone through his papers at all was quite the outside of enough
and, to his mind, utterly indefensible!

Not that there was much he could do about any of it, he

thought moodily, as he glared into the bottom of his now empty glass. Although his head was distinctly muzzy, one thing remained abundantly clear to him. He was left with little choice but to buckle down and endeavour to give the outside world the impression that this sham marriage was working. Thank God he had more than enough to occupy him over at the stables at the moment, what with the stock auctions coming up next week. If he could just channel his concentration into preparing those three colts for sale, there was every chance that he might be able to ignore the relentlessly intrusive images of Helena's highly provocative curves and breathtakingly kissable lips that constantly bombarded his brain, day and night alike, conjuring up wildly erotic fantasies that were more than enough to drive any sane man out of his mind. And, if all else failed, he thought as, with a dour smile, he poured himself yet another hefty serving of brandy, he could always succumb to the family trait and drink himself into oblivion!

Several hours later, Sadie, one of the housemaids, entered the library with her usual intention of setting a taper to the fire in readiness for his lordship's return from the stables, only to find her master fast asleep, his long legs sprawled inelegantly across the arm of his chair, his hand still clutching his empty glass and his snores resonating softly throughout the room.

At about the same time as Sadie was tiptoeing out of the library in an effort not to disturb the earl's inebriated slumber, two park drags rumbled up to the Hall's rear entrance carrying Helena and her newly acquired workforce: fifteen reasonably fit ex-soldiers, picked personally by Rueben Corrigan, and eight women, Cissie Pritchard and Bet Mooney amongst them.

Every one of them filled with a mixture of excitement and varying degrees of trepidation as to what they might have let themselves in for, having only too gladly accepted Helena's offer of employment. In addition to a fair wage for their efforts, the promise of a full set of clothes and a new pair of boots had been enough incentive for a good many more volunteers for her scheme. Helena, however, had not held back in her descriptions of the vast amount of hard work to which they would be required to commit themselves and, placing her trust in Rueben's judgement of his fellow colleagues, had left the final decision to him to pick the most suitable men for the job.

Lottie and Jenny, both full of awe and admiration for her plan, had helped her select the women and, after having paid a hurried visit to her rapidly improving father and a rather more extended one to the bank, Helena had sent Rueben off to hire the drags, while she, Bet and Cissie had visited all the cobblers in the vicinity to purchase every single pair of boots that they were able to make available at such short notice. A varied selection of workclothes had been packed into two large hampers that were strapped to the rear of the coaches and, to a chorus of cheers and whistles from a somewhat envious but still highly interested crowd of spectators, the drags had set off for Markfield.

Seated next to Fran, inside the leading coach, Helena leaned back against the comfortable squabs with a contented smile on her face. It still amazed her that she had been able to achieve so much in so short a space of time—such was the power of money, she supposed, as she recalled the bank manager's face when she passed over the twenty-seven unpaid bills that she had found on Markfield's desk and instructed him to see to their immediate payment. It was true that she did harbour a slightly niggling sensation of guilt for having taken them without having first consulted her husband but, after she had inadvertently caught sight of the one on the top of the pile, it had been quite beyond her strength of will to resist poring through the rest. Besides which, having reasoned that Markfield had expressly commanded her to 'do as she pleased' in the matter, she had been very careful to remove only those that pertained to the Hall's refurbishment. In any case, she kept telling herself, surely his lordship would be over the moon to discover that the settlement of so many unpaid bills had been taken out of his hands?

As she sat back and tried to envisage the look of admiration that would appear on Markfield's face as she described her day's activities to him, she found herself overcome by a decided lowering of spirit. She was beginning to have the most uncomfortable feeling that no matter how much the earl might congratulate her for her efforts at securing a workforce in so short a time, he was not going to be altogether happy when he discovered that she had taken it upon herself to investigate his private correspondence. The fact that dealing with much of her father's paperwork during his recent illnesses had become almost second nature to her could hardly be used as an excuse for her to make free with her husband's personal papers.

Climbing out of the carriage, she took note of the slates that were stacked neatly against the rear wall and, casting her gaze upwards, was glad to see that Mr Jarvis had been as good as his word and had made substantial inroads to the work over the central hallway. Turning to look at the stables across the way, however, she was surprised to note that all the doors were closed and the only sign of activity, as far as she could discern, was a single stable hand busily engaged in sweeping the yard. Her heart sinking, it became clear to her that, contrary to what she had supposed—given his usual practice of remaining at his work until the light began to fade—it appeared that Markfield had already left the premises and was, in all probability, well on his way back to Westpark even now. By the time she got back, his lordship would have had more than enough time to work himself up into a towering fury, after having discovered her improper actions!

Fran's hand on her elbow jerked her back to her present difficulties and she turned to face the hushed and expectant group of people who were awaiting her directions.

'I am afraid that you will find the entrance hall something of a disgrace,' she told them, as she led the way through the back door of the house. 'But I am told that there are several habitable rooms in the east wing—I have arranged for some mattresses and bedding to be delivered up there and I understand that the kitchens are in quite good working order.'

'Doubt if it'll be much worse than the 'ovel I were stuck in back there, miss,' averred Bet, with a cheeky grin. 'An' scrubbin' floors will be a darn sight more agreeable than what I been puttin' up with these last few nights, I can tell you!'

'And far better pay, I wouldn't mind betting!' returned Helena with a valiant smile as, keeping her fingers crossed that Charles had managed to fulfil the considerable list of tasks that she had set him the previous afternoon, she started up the stairs that would lead her troop of recruits to the rooms that would serve as their quarters for a good many weeks to come.

An hour or so later, when she had at last been able to tear herself away from helping Cissie and Rueben sort out the various unexpected hitches that had arisen as a result of the sudden influx of so large a group of people into a property that had suffered so much neglect, Helena, accompanied by an equally weary Fran, made her way back to Westpark in the fast fading daylight.

'At least we can now cross the river in safety!' she exclaimed in delight, as she stepped on to the now fully functional footbridge. 'I have to admit that I was in fear of my life when I was obliged to use it yesterday.'

On reaching the far side, she turned and looked back at the Hall, from where a score of brightly flickering beams of light cast their cheerful glow out of several of the upper-storey windows. 'I do hope that they will all be comfortable,' she confided in her companion as, arm in arm, they scurried through the deepening dusk along the riverbank.

'A good deal better than they've been used to, by all accounts,' countered Fran, somewhat disparagingly. 'And I dare say you won't thank me for saying this, my lady, but his lordship is going to have a right fit when he sets his eyes on you!'

Helena bit her lip. Her mind had been so full of other things during the past few hours that she had allowed herself to put aside all thoughts of her own difficulties, especially those in regard to her likely reception by her husband. 'We did get ourselves into rather a mess, I'm afraid,' she said, with a rueful glance at her companion's dirt-streaked face. 'There was a good deal more grime and dust than I had reckoned on—thank goodness that nice Ben Fuller managed to get the kitchen range working! At least there will be plenty of hot water for them all.'

'I trust the same will apply to ourselves, when we get back,' grumbled Fran who, having risen to the status of lady's maid a good many years earlier, had rather balked at some of the activities in which she had been obliged to involve herself in today's project. But, having taken one look at the state of the rooms in which she expected her workers to sleep, Helena had simply rolled up her sleeves and set about helping to remove the festoons of dust-impregnated cobwebs that seemed to have gathered in every possible nook and cranny of the place, not to mention sweeping floors that hadn't seen a brush in more than five years, leaving her maidservant with very little option but to follow her mistress's sterling example.

Although Mrs Ellis was a good deal taken aback when the new Countess of Markfield strode into her kitchen covered in a varied assortment of grime and filth, she managed to contain her astonishment long enough to assure her mistress that there was more than enough hot water in the range's back boiler for both her ladyship and Fran to take their much-needed baths.

'I'll get Mrs Wainwright to see to it right away, ma'am,' she declared, rising hurriedly from her seat and thrusting her feet back into the shoes that she was in the habit of removing at the finish of each workday, whilst signalling to the scullery maid, who was still busily engaged in wiping down the draining boards.

'I am truly sorry to have to disturb you at such a late hour, Mrs Ellis,' said Helena, unable to stifle a slight gasp as she caught sight of the woman's badly swollen ankles and instantly making a mental note to get extra help in the kitchen as soon as possible. 'But I'm afraid we will require something to eat, as well. Just a snack will do. We can eat it here in the kitchen, if you have no objections—I imagine that his lordship has already dined?'

'No trouble at all, ma'am,' averred the cook, as she shuffled towards the pantry. 'There's a whole rabbit pie, a nice roast capon and a leg of ham—all of them totally untouched—seeing as how the master took himself off to his bed around four o'clock this afternoon and, according to his man, Shipman, he's been dead to the world ever since!'

'Good heavens!' cried Helena, in some alarm, as she started for the door. 'His lordship has been taken ill? Has anyone sent for the doctor?'

'Now there's no need for you to go getting yourself all of a quiver, my lady,' Mrs Ellis assured her calmly, as she proceeded to carve several thick slices off the succulent looking ham-bone that she had fetched from the pantry and arranged them neatly on the two plates in front of her. 'It appears that Master Richard—his lordship, that is—indulged himself rather too liberally with the brandy bottle this morning and was obliged to retire to his room with a slight—er—stomach disorder. Mrs Wainwright gave him one of her special physics and, like I said, he's been sleeping like a babe ever since!'

'She means the man was rolling drunk, my lady,' intimated Fran, giving a disapproving sniff, as she headed into the scullery to wash her hands and face prior to sitting down at the kitchen table to eat her meal.

Helena's heart seemed to sink right down to her half-boots as she followed her maid's example. Exactly what sort of creature was this man that she had married? she wondered. Not only a rake, but a drunkard, too, it would seem! Probably an inveterate gambler, as well, just as his uncle and cousin had been, she thought dolefully. Not that any of these shortcomings appeared to have the slightest effect on the way her pulse reacted whenever he happened to walk into a room…or touched her hand…or cast a smile in her direction. And as for his kisses! He had left her speechless, breathless and unable to construct a single sensible thought. Even her belief that her husband was an accomplished philanderer appeared to have done nothing to prevent her from falling completely under his spell, which was decidedly demoralising, when she remembered her previously pompous attitude towards him.

And then, as, once again, the increasingly discomfiting recall of her casual perusal of the earl's private paperwork invaded her thoughts, a shudder of apprehension ran through her, thoroughly stifling her appetite. Getting to her feet, she said, 'I seem to have developed a slight headache, I fear. I believe that I will take my bath first, after all, if you don't mind. Perhaps you would be good enough to have my supper sent up in an hour or so, Mrs Ellis?'

Then, turning to her maid who, her meal only half-eaten, had also risen to her feet in preparation to accompanying her mistress to her room, she added, 'Do finish your meal, Fran— I can easily ring when I need you.' And, without further ado, she swept out of the kitchen, leaving the pair staring at one another in frowning consternation.

Back in her bedchamber, she discovered that the preparations for her requested bath were already well advanced and, having finally dismissed the last of the trio of maidservants who had toiled up and down the stairs carrying jugs of hot water on her behalf, she deftly divested herself of her grimy clothing and sank gratefully into the soothing warmth of the violet-scented water.

Still mulling over the several possible excuses that she had hit upon to justify her misdemeanour, she reasoned that it was possible that the earl might not be quite so angry when he learned that so many of his outstanding bills had been dealt with. Although, having recalled his instant withdrawal every time a conversation touched upon money matters, she was well aware that her approach to the subject was going to have to be very delicate.

Now fully refreshed, she stepped out of the bath and, not bothering to ring for her maid, dried herself and, after running a comb through her still-damp curls, slipped into the matching white silk nightdress and peignoir that Fran had laid out for her before their departure early that morning.

Straightening her shoulders, she marched resolutely across to the door that separated her husband's room from hers, having made up her mind that the best time to tackle him would be whilst he was still slightly under par, so to speak—not strictly ethical, perhaps, but, given Markfield's predilections insofar as money matters were concerned, Helena was inclined to suspect that striking while the iron was cool might, in the present circumstances, be far the best bet!

Not wishing to alert him to her presence before she had had time to compose herself fully, she reached out and turned the handle gently, only to discover, to her chagrin, that the door was still locked!

Biting her lip in frustration, she glared at the offending mechanism, wondering what sort of fiendish mind had conjured up a system whereby it was possible for a husband to bar his wife from entering his room, but not the reverse! Vowing that she would have one of her own workmen fit a bolt on her side of the room at the earliest opportunity, she swept across to her bedroom door, edged it open and, after peering carefully in both directions in order to ensure that there were no stray footmen wandering about in the vicinity, she scuttled hurriedly down the passageway towards her husband's chamber.

Chapter Twenty-One

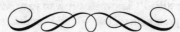

His head feeling as though it was about to shatter into a thousand fragments at any minute, even the soft click of the door handle was, to Richard, highly reminiscent of the deafening sounds of the British cannon on the field at Waterloo. Struggling to rise, but finding himself incapable of doing so, he flopped weakly back on to his pillows, having arrived at the conclusion that, although he was unable to recall the exact details, it appeared that he must have received a mortal wound. The throbbing pain in his head was such that, as far as he was concerned, only instant death could provide a merciful release. He had tried opening his eyes on several occasions, to find that the piercingly blinding lights—presumably blasts from the mortar explosions—made matters a thousand times worse.

'Richard?'

He grimaced and let out a faint groan. Wasn't it bad enough that he was lying here, dying in agony, without having to suffer the added anguish of imagining that he could hear Helena's voice, calling to him from across the void?

Helena? Impossible! Waterloo had long since passed before she had come into his life! Making every effort to marshal his chaotic thoughts into some sort of coherence, he struggled to rationalise the enigma.

'Richard?'

Tentatively prising one eye open, he reeled back in disbelief as a pulsating flash of light exploded across his vision to reveal the ethereally white-clad figure standing at his bedside. *Dear God*, he found himself thinking, as a feeling akin to panic swept over him, *surely they haven't sent down an angel to lead me there*!

Helena, having observed that he was awake at last, reached out and took hold of his hand. 'Please, don't be cross with me, Richard,' she began. 'I know that it was very wrong of me to interfere with your papers, but—'

'Papers?'

His eyes now closed tight against the invasive light and his head pounding fit to burst, Richard found himself growing more confused by the minute. *Did one actually need papers to be granted admittance into Heaven*? he thought in wonder, as he managed to croak out, 'You must do whatever you think best, dear angel—the whole matter is entirely in your hands.'

Frowning slightly, Helena leant across the bed and laid her hand on his forehead which felt, as she found to her considerable dismay, decidedly damp and clammy. Since her experience of badly inebriated gentlemen was somewhat less than nil, she was at a loss as to the proper course of action. That the earl was in some sort of distress was obvious, but she could not decide whether to send for Shipman to deal with the problem or to ring down for another of Mrs Wainwright's willow-bark remedies.

Her concern increasing, she lowered herself on to the bed beside her husband, her eyes quickly registering his pain-ravaged expression and the tight compression of his lips, both of which clearly denoted the torment that he was undergoing and, although she could not help but feel that he had no one but himself to blame for his present distress, she was unable to prevent the sharp wave of pity that ran through her. As she tenderly stroked his damp hair away from his forehead in an attempt to soothe away the worst of the pain, a tight lump formed in her throat and the hot sting of tears began to gather behind her eyelids.

The gently comforting feel of the cool hand on his fevered brow came as utter balm to the still highly befuddled Markfield and it was not long before this most pleasurable sensation, along with the soothing murmurings of reassurance that accompanied the soft caresses, lulled him into a peaceful trance-like state, which had the effect of making him only too glad to lie back and entrust his deliverance to the tender mercies of this angelic vision of loveliness.

But then as, with a startled gasp, Helena became conscious that the earl's free arm seemed to have found its way across her waist and was now tightening and pulling her more closely towards him, she saw that his eyes, far from being shut tightly as they had been earlier, were now wide open and staring—albeit with a slightly puzzled expression—deep into her own.

'Unbelievably lovely,' he murmured softly, as he turned his head and buried his face in the mass of unbound chestnut curls that had spread themselves across his pillow during her ministrations. 'Who would have thought that an angel would be so accommodating?' With which bizarre observation, his eyelids drooped and he gradually drifted off into a heavy slumber.

Realising that it would be impossible to extricate herself from his hold without waking him, especially since several locks of her hair were still tightly pinioned beneath his head, Helena resigned herself to staying where she was—at least until her sleeping husband chose to change his position which, she reasoned, he was bound to do at some point. Apart from which, she had to admit that the warmth of his arm slung loosely across her back was rather comforting and, after such a long and tiring day, she could not help feeling that it could do no harm just to lie back and close her own eyes for a few minutes…

Several hours later, just as the first pale streaks of dawn were beginning to light up the morning sky, Helena awoke from the most refreshing sleep she had experienced for some time. Stretching languidly, she rolled over, recoiling with a sudden shock as her fingers encountered the satiny soft nakedness of her husband's arm draped in careless elegance across the pillow next to hers. She was horrified that she had not only allowed herself to fall asleep in his arms, but had also—or so it would appear, given the tumbled state of the bedclothes—actually snuggled down beneath the covers right next to him! Desperately hoping that her hasty movements had failed to disturb her husband's tranquillity, she edged her way cautiously off the bed, tiptoed across the floor towards her own room and unlocked the adjoining door, pausing only momentarily before extracting the key and thrusting it resolutely into the jewellery box on her dressing table.

In future, I shall be the one who decides on the locking or unlocking of that door, she vowed as, sliding between the far less welcoming sheets of her own bed, she lay shivering in the early morning chill and cast her mind back to her husband's final words. Surely, he could not have been so utterly foxed that he had mistaken her for that ghastly Cummings woman, she reflected moodily, as she waited for sleep to overcome her.

Having woken with a crippling headache only to discover that—contrary to what he had been happy to believe the previous night—his soul had not been wafted into Heaven by an angel bearing an uncanny resemblance to his new wife, Richard was obliged to concede that the highly erotic vision of a semi-clad Helena lying asleep in his arms, which had seemed so incredibly real at the time, had to have been yet another example of those frustratingly tormenting dreams with which he had been plagued every night for the past week or so. And, rather than suppressing his emotional fervour, as had been his intention, it would seem that the time-honoured standby of drowning his sorrows in an overindulgence of spirits had actually exacerbated the problem—as well as having presented him with the most diabolical hangover he had ever had the misfortune to suffer! Pressing his fingers against his eyes in an attempt to shut out the faint streaks of daylight that were already beginning to light up the room, he swore to himself that—in addition to steering clear of strong liquor for the foreseeable future—he would need to make sure that he kept himself well out of range of Helena's spellbinding influence.

Concentrate on his work! That would surely do the trick, he decided firmly, as he reached out and pulled at the bell-cord to summon his valet. Get those colts ready for sale and, by God, yes! He would enter all three of his racing thoroughbreds in next week's Epsom stakes. Having held back from getting involved in any of the actual racing this early in the season, he had put all his effort into increasing the strength of his fledgling stud but, as it now occurred to him, putting his thoroughbreds through their paces now would certainly draw a lot of useful attention to their finer points and might well encourage potential breeders to approach him—not to mention necessitating his absence from the estate for several days at a time.

Entering the dining room in a far more cheerful frame of mind, he was decidedly put out to find his wife already ensconced at the table, contentedly spreading butter on her third slice of toast.

A slight flush spread over Helena's cheeks as he came towards her and, whilst she prayed that he would make no mention of last night's occurrence within hearing distance of the butler who was hovering at the doorway, she could not help hoping that the earl would pass her some sort of private sign to indicate that he had not failed to register her presence during at least one of his moments of lucidity.

Rather to her disappointment—not to say mortification—Richard halted at the threshold and, with a strangled, 'I beg your pardon—please excuse me!' he turned tail and made at once for the door that led out to Westpark's stable area.

For several moments, Helena was too shocked to do anything other than but stare at the now empty doorway, in a transfixed silence. But then, as a growing sense of affront gradually began to dawn upon her, she thrust back her chair, leapt to her feet and started after the earl, intent upon taking him to task for having treated her in so discourteous a manner.

Halfway down the hall, however, she hesitated and came to a halt, with the sudden realisation that, given the severe depth of his intoxication, any recollection of last night's events that Markfield might retain was likely to be decidedly hazy. That being so, it would hardly be in her best interests to do anything that might jog his memory. Far better that she put the matter out of her mind and kept out of his way for a while.

With that thought in mind, she sped up the stairs to her room, hurriedly collected a bonnet and, was soon making her way across the lawn towards the river path, intent on getting to Markfield Hall well before his lordship even had time to saddle his mount.

This plan would have been perfect, had it not been for the fact that Jem, having been made aware of Markfield's unexpected fall from grace the previous afternoon and, being well acquainted with the earl's requirements when he was out of sorts, had taken the precaution of saddling the highly spirited Titan several minutes before his grim-faced master strode into the stable yard.

'Good man!' exclaimed Richard, as he relieved the groom of the reins and leapt into the saddle, inwardly cursing at the searing explosion of pain that the sudden movement brought about. He was about to swing his mount towards Westpark's main gate, in order to take his usual route to the Hall, when he checked and, looking down at the groom, enquired, 'The footbridge—did the men manage to repair it, do you know?'

'Good as new, sir,' Jem assured him. 'I used it to fetch Titan over yesterday afternoon—made a fine job of it, did Mr Standish's men.'

'Excellent!' replied the earl, wheeling the gelding around. 'That'll save a good few minutes every trip.'

Lifting his crop in farewell, he set off in the direction of the riverside path, doing his best to ignore the spasms of pain that every jarring step seemed to bring about. Slumping low in his saddle, he slowed his mount to a gentle walk and kept to the grass in order to alleviate the throbbing ache in his head, vowing that he would never touch another drop of liquor if he lived to be a hundred! Although, how the hell he was going to be able to keep his hands to himself for the next few days without some sort of diversion, he was hard pressed to imagine. Even with all the extra work he was about to take on, he knew that there was still a limit as to how much time he could spend in the stables and, even if he were to arrange to have his meals brought over to him, he would still be obliged to return to Westpark to sleep.

Sleep! The very idea brought a wry grimace to his face. How was he supposed to sleep when such irresistible temptation lay practically within touching distance of his bed? Especially now, when he was actually starting to believe that his dreams had become reality, he was not at all sure that he could trust himself to stay away from her!

Realising that they were approaching the footbridge, he raised his head, only to have his heart thud to a sudden halt, as his eyes fell on Helena's trim figure strolling gracefully up the path scarcely ten yards ahead of him. Clearly unaware of his presence, the grass having muffled the sound of Titan's hooves, she had removed her bonnet and was swinging it by its ribbons, humming softly to herself as she walked.

Straightening up in his saddle, he gave the reins a brisk shake and, edging his mount over on to the stony part of the path, he urged him into a slow trot.

The sudden and unexpected sound of an approaching rider caused Helena to let go of her bonnet strings and leap for the safety of the hedgerow.

'You idiot!' she gasped, as Richard drew up beside her and started to dismount. 'Now see what you've done!'

Ignoring the earl's warning shout, she ducked under Titan's head and dashed over to the riverbank, in a vain attempt to prevent the breeze lifting her straw bonnet off the grass and tossing it over the edge.

'I dare say that's your idea of a joke!' she exploded, as she turned back towards him, her eyes flashing with fury. 'Did you really need to creep up on me so furtively?'

'I was not in the least furtive!' he retorted as, cursing under his breath, he strode past her and stared down at the rushing waters below. Helena's bonnet, as he was soon able to ascertain, had not sailed off with the current, but had snagged itself against the roots of one of the willow trees, some ten feet or so below them.

'And, it was quite my favourite, too,' she murmured sadly, coming to stand next to him. 'Now, I suppose I shall have to return home and get myself another before I can go on.'

It was her unforeseen use of the word 'home' that finally decided him. Unbuttoning his jacket, the earl shrugged it off and, tossing it to one side, started to clamber down the sloping bank her errant headpiece. 'No problem,' he ventured stoutly, his fingers clutching at a clump of reeds, as one of his boots sought for some sort of toehold. 'I believe the bonnet is within my reach.'

'Good heavens, no! I'd really rather you didn't!' gasped Helena, her eyes wide with concern. 'If you should slip—oh, do come back, Richard, please—I beg of you!'

At the sound of his name on her lips, Richard's heart swelled and he vowed that he would retrieve the blasted hat for her, if it was the last thing he ever did!

As it happened, reaching the snagged object did not present him with much of a problem but, no sooner did he have it in his hands than he realised that returning to the footpath was going to prove a far more complicated matter. His downward progress had been helped to a large extent by the looseness of the muddy scree, which would be of little use in any upward scramble. Scanning the terrain both to his left and to his right, he could see that the same difficulty presented itself all along the riverbank, indicating that just one ill-judged foothold might easily be the means of pitching him into the rock-strewn river below.

Grinding his teeth, he muttered several violent imprecations. So much for his juvenile attempt at heroics! The last thing he needed was to have to ask Helena to run back to the Hall and fetch help. Looking up, he could see that she was now on her knees, peering down at him over the edge of the bank. In her hands she held a coil of rope.

'I found this in one of your saddle bags,' she called down to him. 'If I throw one end to you, you could tie it around your waist. Then, if I tie the other end to Titan, perhaps I could get him to help to pull you up.'

Richard grimaced. 'Great idea, in principle,' he grunted. 'Trouble is, Titan has a slightly obstinate streak and it's doubtful whether he'll let you anywhere near him.'

'No harm in trying, anyhow,' retorted Helena, as she disappeared from his view. 'He didn't kick up too much of a fuss when I took the rope out of the saddlebag.'

Several minutes passed, during which time Richard made numerous valiant but unsuccessful attempts to hoist himself up the slippery bank. Then, to his astonishment, he saw the end of the rope flipping down towards him and, although there was no sign of Helena at this point, he could not mistake the swish of Titan's black tail as his rear end gradually began to appear at the top of the incline, indicating that she had, by some incredible means or another, managed to persuade the huge gelding to back up to the very edge of the riverbank.

'Now, tie yourself on to the end of the rope,' he heard her voice commanding him and, although he did not hold out a great deal of hope of her plan meeting with much success, he coiled the rope securely around his middle, carefully looping the bonnet's ribbons into the finished knot.

'Ready!' he called, still slightly amazed by the fact that she had managed to persuade the rather self-willed Titan to comply with her wishes.

All at once, he felt a tug at his waist and, scarcely able to believe what was happening, he reached up and grabbed hold of the rope, only to find himself being pulled, surely but steadily, back up to the top of the incline.

With his feet back on terra firma once more, he turned thankfully towards the source of his rescue where he saw Helena hurriedly sliding down from his charger's saddle! Quickly untying the rope from his middle, he grasped the bonnet in his hand and stepped forwards, holding it out towards her.

'A little worse for wear, I fear,' he said, giving her a slightly rueful grin before glancing down at his heavily soiled shirt and breeches and adding, 'As, indeed, am I, it would appear!'

Ignoring both the bonnet and his mud-splattered garments, Helena, her eyes wide with incredulity, stared up at him for a long moment, took one shuddering breath and then, to his utter dismay, dissolved into a flood of tears, before throwing herself at him and proceeding to pummel his chest with her clenched fists.

'You stupid, stupid idiot!' she cried. 'You could have fallen into the river and been swept to your death on the rocks!'

'Well, I didn't and I wasn't, so no more tears, if you please,' he returned, forcing a light laugh as, capturing her hands between his own, he found himself filled with a sense of wild elation to learn that Helena had actually been concerned for his safety. 'And all thanks to your quick thinking—although, how the devil you got Titan to allow you up on his back defeats me!'

'It's amazing what an apple and a pocket full of biscuits will do,' replied Helena, somewhat self-consciously, as she tried, without success, to free herself from Richard's hold. 'I really brought them to give to your colts, but he seemed perfectly amenable to doing as I asked, once he discovered my store of goodies.'

'Well, I'll be—!' exploded the earl, casting the now peacefully cropping Titan a scornful look. 'And, there's me been deceived into thinking him a one-man horse all these years, when it seems that he'll do anything for a piece of apple!'

'Oh, no! I shouldn't think so,' she said, with a vehement shake of her head. 'I'm sure that he only followed my commands because he sensed that you needed his help—horses have that sort of second sight, I'm told.'

'So I believe,' he said, smiling down at her flushed face. Gently releasing her hands, he pulled her towards him and held her close. 'Nevertheless, I consider that you are the one to whom I owe the most thanks.'

Locked in the warmth of her husband's caress, Helena would have been more than happy to remain there indefinitely had not the sound of Charles Standish's voice, hailing them from the far side of the river, destroyed the harmony of the moment.

'Enough of that, you pair of lovebirds!' he called laughingly. 'I was just about to come over and collect you, Helena. Your people are awaiting your instructions and I wasn't sure what plans you had for them this morning.'

Mentally cursing his cousin for so untimely an interruption, Richard released Helena and bent down to retrieve his discarded jacket.

'Back to work, then,' he said, catching hold of Titan's trailing reins and holding out his arm to her. 'I'm really sorry about the bonnet—I trust it isn't totally beyond repair?'

'Oh, I dare say that it will serve for the present,' replied Helena with a casual shrug, as she strove to regain her composure. Having made every effort to tug the now sadly misshapen article into a more recognisable shape, she crammed it on her head, and then attempted to tie the heavily begrimed ribbons into some semblance of a bow. At which, her lips began to twitch and, before she knew it, she was chuckling aloud.

'What a sight, the pair of us are,' she gurgled, looking down at the front of her bodice, where a good deal of the mud from Richard's shirt had deposited itself during their recent close contact. 'Lord and Lady Muck, to the very letter!'

Such unexpected levity when confronted with her decidedly bedraggled appearance only served to underline the earl's growing admiration for his wife and, even though her hat was crooked, her hair was coming adrift from its pins and her nose and cheeks were liberally speckled with dirt, to him she had never looked more beautiful and desirable.

Grinning broadly, he stood back and swept her a highly theatrical bow, at the same time drawling in an extremely affected tone of voice, 'To work, then, your ladyship—it appears there are estate matters that demand our attention—and to keep one's workforce waiting is considered pretty bad form, don't you know!'

With an answering smile, Helena tucked her hand into the crook of his arm and allowed him to escort her over the bridge to meet up with the clearly mystified Standish.

'What on earth have you been up to?' he exclaimed, after taking an astonished look at their highly dishevelled appearances.

'Just a minor disagreement,' replied the earl, as he shot a smiling glance at his wife.

'Ending with a satisfactory conclusion, I trust?' enquired his cousin, looking from one to the other for some sort of confirmation. 'You certainly did not look to be at odds with one another a few moments ago!'

'Oh, we weren't at odds with one another,' the blushing Helena put in hurriedly. 'It was just my bonnet!'

'Yes, I can see how it might have brought about something of a difference of opinion,' said Standish, as he eyed the offending article.

Helena could not help but burst out laughing at the expression on his face. 'Let me assure you that it didn't start out like this when I left home. The fact is that the wind swept it out of my hands and trapped it in the roots of a willow tree. His lordship was good enough to go to its rescue and I was simply—er—expressing my thanks, just as you arrived.'

'Perhaps you would prefer to go back to Westpark and change, before you face your eager minions?' he then suggested, but Helena shook her head.

'Certainly not! I dare say I shall look a good deal worse than this by the time I've swept out a few rooms.'

Standish's brow furrowed. 'But, I thought that was what you brought that pack of "down-and-outs" here for? Surely you don't intend to involve yourself personally in the clearing-up operation?'

'But, of course I do!' Helena stared at him in some surprise. 'You cannot suppose that I will simply stand around dishing out orders, right and left, surely?'

After a short pause, during which the silent Standish eyed her with undisguised amazement, she added quietly, 'And I would be grateful if you would refrain from referring to my people as "down-and-outs". I'll have you know that all of these men are displaced soldiers and the women, for the most part, are those who have been left widowed and destitute, as a result of their husbands having been killed while serving their king and country!'

With that, she swung away from the two men and marched off in the direction of the Hall, leaving a transfixed Richard staring after her, his heart swelling with a mixture of emotions that included awe, admiration and respect—but, most of all, an even deeper love than he could ever have believed possible. Had they been allowed just a few minutes longer, before that magical spell had been broken by Charles's intervention, he was almost certain that he and Helena might well have resolved their differences. Letting out a soft sigh, he wondered how long it would be before another such perfect moment would present itself.

Having heard the sigh and taken note of the changing expressions on his cousin's face, Standish, taking his elbow and urging him forwards, remarked gently, 'Things still not working out between the pair of you, old chap? Could've sworn that you both looked quite—how shall I put it?—*besotted* with each other back then.'

'Had it not been for your blasted interruption,' grunted the earl, as he shrugged off his cousin's hand and strode up the path in his wife's wake, 'we might well have been about to reach some sort of understanding.'

'Oh, lor!' groaned Standish, hurrying after him. 'Sorry about that—I'll try to be more careful in future.'

Richard halted and, with a rueful grin on his face, turned to face his cousin.

'No offence, Charles,' he said awkwardly, holding out his hand for the other to shake. 'Fact is, I soaked up rather too much of the old grape juice yesterday and I'm now like the proverbial bear—with a very sore head. Forgive my lapse of manners?'

With a quick smile, Standish grasped the outstretched hand, exclaiming, 'I only wish there was something I could do to help—I hate to see you looking so low.'

'The fact that you are here at all is good enough for me,' returned Richard gruffly. 'Just two of us Standish boys left now, so we're going to have to stick together!'

Chapter Twenty-Two

Thoroughly exhausted but highly pleased with the results achieved by her hotchpotch force in just a single day, Helena stood in the rear courtyard, smiling up at the Hall's now gleaming windows. It was clear that Rueben Corrigan's choice of workers had proved surprisingly beneficial to her cause.

It had transpired that several of the men, including Rueben himself, had been apprentice carpenters before an over-zealous sense of patriotism, along with a youthful craving for adventure and excitement, had prompted them to volunteer themselves for military service, some eight years earlier. Having then found themselves required to participate in some of the most savage acts of violence known to man, in the process of which they had lost many of their friends and comrades, these initially exuberant young countrymen had been forced to contend with the biting cold of the Spanish winters, along with the overpowering heat of its summers. They had endured unbelievable privations during eight long years of bitter campaigning, often subsisting on scavenged victuals for weeks on end, only to find themselves—following Napoleon's final capitulation—cast adrift with callous indifference, with no thought or consideration as to their future welfare and even, in a great many cases, left to make their own way back to their homeland.

Totally disillusioned, huge numbers of these displaced ex-soldiers had been forced into a life of crime in order to survive; many of them had banded together and were presently engaged in terrorising whole communities throughout the land, instilling unrest among workers and inciting them to rise up against their employers.

Others, such as Rueben Corrigan, Ben Fuller and their like, had made every effort to find work and, despite continual setbacks, had succeeded in keeping themselves on the straight and narrow, their only succour often being the daily ration of bread and soup served out by the various soup kitchens set up by the many small charitable organisations throughout the kingdom.

'A splendid day's work, Mr Fuller,' exclaimed Helena, beaming her appreciation at the wiry young man standing by her side. 'If every day progresses as well as this one has done, we shall have the old house back on its feet in no time at all.'

'It's certainly a fine old building,' nodded her companion, standing back to admire the newly repaired window-frame that he had just finished fitting. 'That panelling in the great hall is quite magnificent. My old master, back in Leicestershire, would probably give his eye teeth just to get a peek at it—a great admirer of Gibbon's work, was my Mr Tobias.'

Nodding absentmindedly, since her attention had been diverted by the sudden sight of her husband approaching from the stables, Helena's heart executed a joyous leap but, upon observing that the earl had been diverted by a call from his cousin who, while leaning out of the window of the Hall's morning room on the first floor, from where he had been directing various operations, was eagerly relating his part in the day's activities, she took a deep breath and attempted to focus her mind on what her companion was telling her.

'Did I hear you say that you were apprenticed to a Mr Tobias, Ben?' she asked, her mind flitting back to a recent article that she had read on wood-carving. 'That wouldn't have been a Mr Hector Tobias, of Enderby, would it?'

'Why, yes, indeed it would, ma'am,' he replied. 'Didn't serve my full time, of course—on account of my brothers persuading me to join up with them—both dead now, sadly—and precious little chance of him taking me back on again, at my age.'

'Your old master is said to be somewhat of an expert, I believe?'

'Oh, a proper wizard with the carving knives, he was, ma'am,' returned the young man, with a wide grin. 'The local folk used to say that he would have given that Gibbons fellow a run for his money, if he had still been around!'

Nodding thoughtfully, Helena studied Fuller's enthusiastic expression for a moment or two then, making up her mind, she asked him, 'Do you suppose he would be interested in coming down here to Surrey to take a look at our panels, with a view to replicating those that have suffered the worst damage?'

Fuller's eyes widened. 'I should think that sort of thing would be right up Mr Tobias's street, your ladyship—I'll get a letter off to him right away and thank you for thinking of him, ma'am! Now that the roof and the window frames are finished, we can get on with stripping off the panelling and sorting out the good from the bad.'

With another smile, he dipped his head and was on the point of turning away from her when, glancing upwards to feast his eyes on the now completed roofwork, the smile was instantly wiped from his face, to be replaced by a look of total dismay.

Uttering a violent *'Look out, sir!'*, he flung himself across the courtyard towards the earl.

Hearing the warning shout, Richard spun round and took a step forwards. Seconds later, at the very moment that Fuller cannoned into him, hurling them both to the ground in a tangle of arms and legs, a huge shower of roof slates shattered all around the pair of them, sending a myriad of splintering shards in all directions, as the heavy slate made violent contact with the courtyard's paving-stones.

For almost a full minute, there was a heavy pall of silence as those who had witnessed the accident endeavoured to make sense of what had happened but then, as realisation dawned, all hell broke loose as, first, Helena and then a score or more of the other workers dashed over to remove the debris that had descended upon the pair.

Ignoring the cuts and scratches to her hands, Helena frantically thrust aside the broken bits of slate, only to reveal the terrifying sight of her husband's face, his features totally obliterated by a mixture of blood and dirt!

'Gently, gently!' she beseeched, as the anxious band of willing helpers strove to extricate the seemingly lifeless pair from beneath the pile of rubble. *Don't let him be dead,* she prayed silently, *please don't let him be dead! Dear God, I love him so much!*

Catching hold of Richard's hand, she held it to her lips, as the men, having lifted the earl free, carried him across to the other side of the courtyard and laid him reverently down on the lawn. Scarcely able to breathe for fear of what she might learn, she knelt down and pressed her head against his chest. As the blessed sound of a racing heartbeat thundered into her ear, she let out a wild sob of exultation and threw her arms around him. *He was alive!*

All at once, Richard's eyes flicked open and, lifting his hand, he swiped the congealing blood away from his nose and mouth and stared up at her.

'What the hell happened?' he asked hoarsely, as he gradually became aware that he was no longer trapped beneath the man who had thrown himself at him and that the arms that were pinioning him to the ground, were in fact, Helena's!

'There was an accident,' she said breathlessly, making a valiant attempt to straighten herself up, only to find that her husband had wrapped his arms across her back and was intent upon keeping her where she was. 'A pile of slates fell from the roof—Mr Fuller tried to—!'

'Yes, I remember now,' he replied testily, hurriedly letting go of her and struggling to rise to his feet. 'The young fellow who pushed me to one side—where is he—was he hurt?'

His eyes travelled across the grass, to the spot where the men had laid Ben Fuller. He, unlike, his master, lay unmoving, a weeping Cissie Pritchard doing her best to suppress the flow of blood that was seeping from the ugly gash on the side of his head.

Although he was not aware of any pain, the blood that he could see on his hands seemed to suggest to Richard that he, too, had suffered some sort of damage. Reaching up, his fingers probed every part of his head and face and found nothing. It was not his blood! As realisation dawned, he strode quickly across to his injured rescuer and knelt beside him on the grass, motioning Cissie to one side and, extracting his own handkerchief from his pocket, he pressed it firmly against the jagged injury.

'It needs to be held tightly, to prevent further loss of blood,' he explained, to the curious onlookers, beckoning to Helena to assist him in the removal of his neckcloth, prior to binding it securely around the injured man's head. 'I have had some experience of sabre slashes and I would say that this cut is in need of being stitched as quickly as possible—I assume that someone has had the forethought to send for a doctor?'

'Mr Standish rode off for one, just as soon as he saw what had happened,' volunteered one of the bystanders.

A sudden hush fell as Fuller's eyes drifted slowly open and a strangled moan emitted from his lips. 'Set up,' he whispered, fixing his gaze on Richard. 'S-set up.'

'Not advisable to sit up just yet, old chap,' returned the earl softly. 'Best to stay on your back until the doctor has dealt with that cut—you've lost quite enough blood already. Just lie still, until we can get help, there's a good fellow.'

Lifting a shaky hand, Fuller clutched at Richard's sleeve. 'S-saw—ro…' he slurred breathily. 'S-saw…' Then his hand fell, his eyes closed and he lay silent once more.

'Out of luck, I'm afraid!'

Hearing Standish's voice, the crowd stood back and allowed him through. 'Both local doctors are out on calls,' he informed his cousin, as he sought to regain his breath. 'I sent a lad over to Hilverton to see if their fellow is available, but I don't hold out much hope—if we can't stop that bleeding…' His voice tailed off and he turned away in distress. 'I can only thank God that he stopped you getting the brunt of it, Richard.'

'All the more reason to do our best to save the poor fellow,' said Richard. Then, although he knew that it was a forlorn hope, he looked up and called out, 'Is there no one amongst you who knows how to set stitches?'

'I have a little experience,' came a soft voice at his elbow.

Spinning round, Richard stared at his wife in astonishment.

'You cannot possibly—' he began, only to have her hold up her hand to silence him.

'I saw many such procedures during my visits to St George's, when Jason was first brought home,' she assured him quietly. 'In addition, both Charlotte and I were often called in to assist Doctor Redfern at the Swallow Inn, when he was unable to manage a young patient on his own. I am willing to try.'

'But, such a wound as this! I cannot possibly allow it!'

He gestured to the figure lying comatose at his feet.

'Would you rather stand by and watch the poor fellow bleed to death, then?' she pressed him urgently. 'I am well aware that you consider my experience limited, but what other choice do we have?'

Following a low murmur of approval from the crowd of workers, Rueben Corrigan stepped forwards.

'I know it ain't for me to say, sir,' he blurted out, twisting his cap nervously in his hands, 'but I guess young Ben here would be willing to take whatever chance he could get— t'would be a right shame to see him die like this after surviving eight years on the battlefield. I say let her ladyship have a go—we know that she'll do whatever is in her power to save him and, should she fail in her endeavours, sir, I can assure you that there's not one amongst us who would hold her to blame.'

Stepping back, he then added, ''Sides which, I've always

been inclined to believe that it's the Almighty who makes the final decision in matters such as this.'

'Not a lot of point in us interfering then, is there?' muttered Standish under his breath, but Richard, having caught his words, shot him such a condemnatory look that his cheeks flamed and he turned away, looking decidedly abashed.

Realising that there was little time to lose, Richard found himself obliged to make an instant decision.

'Do we have suitable facilities for such a procedure?' he asked Corrigan, knowing that it would be pointless to try to transport the injured man back to Westpark, where ideal conditions would prevail.

But it was Bet Mooney who stepped forwards this time. 'Kitchen's as clean as a whistle,' she informed him, as she sniffed back her tears. 'Table's been scrubbed many times over and, thanks to young Ben here, we've no shortage of hot water.'

'Right—four of you sort out a stretcher—rip out one of the doors, if need be, and let's get this lad down to the kitchen!'

Turning to Helena, the earl reached out and took her hands in his, frowning as he discovered how cold they were. 'Are you sure that you feel up to this, my dear?' he asked softly. 'No one will think any worse of you if you decide that you can't go through with it.'

'He saved your life,' she replied shakily, unable to prevent the tears that sprang into her eyes as she recalled the total desolation that had swept over her when she feared that she had lost him. 'There is nothing in the world that I would not do for the poor man, after that.'

Another indication that she felt some real affection for him, thought Richard, hope flaring in his eyes as he looked down at her. There had been several moments lately when he had almost believed…

But then, realising that this was hardly the time for such speculation, he heaved back a sigh and, tucking her hand into his arm, he led her towards the house in the wake of the stretcher party, with the words, 'Tell me what you need, my dear. I can send off to Westpark for anything you think you might require.'

Helena paused for a moment, thinking hard. Then, with a decisive nod, she replied, 'Whisky or brandy. As much as you can spare—for both cleansing and patient-numbing purposes—needles and thread my women will have here, of course—basilicum powder, if Mrs Wainwright has any, sheets for tearing into bandages and—oh, yes, of course—some more oil lamps. We will need as much light as possible!'

'I'll get on to it right away,' he returned and, lifting her hand to his lips, he kissed the tips of her fingers. 'Sadly, whilst I know that this is hardly the time to mention it, I just wanted you to know how much I—'

'We're ready now, if you please, ma'am,' interrupted a tentative voice at his elbow. 'We've managed to get Ben on the kitchen table, but he's thrashing about something awful, ma'am—you'd best come at once, if you would.'

Steadfastly ignoring her husband's groan, Helena regretfully extracted her fingers from his grasp and turned to greet the waiting Cissie. 'Well, then,' she said, as she conjured up a valiant smile, 'we had best get on with it.'

She had only gone a few steps down the path before she suddenly stopped in her tracks and, turning back, she implored him, 'Wish me luck, Richard, and say a little prayer for me, if you would.'

At the sight of her troubled expression, as she made her simple request, it took Richard every ounce of his resolve to stop himself from leaping forwards, wrapping her in his arms and carrying her away from this appalling task she had set herself. But, given their present situation, the best he could offer her was a supportive smile and a few words of encouragement.

'With every beat of my heart, dear one,' he said, his eyes dark with unsuppressed feeling.

Scarcely daring to believe that she could have heard aright,

Helena's heart leapt into her throat and, unable to tear her eyes away from his burning gaze, she took a hesitant step towards him but then, conscious of Cissie's insistent tugging at her arm, she offered him a faltering smile, turned reluctantly away and allowed herself to be propelled towards the doorway.

Grappling with the powerful feelings that were threatening to overcome his resolve, Richard watched her disappear then, with a wry grimace, he, too, turned and hurried off in the direction of the stables. At the very least, he intended to make certain that her requests were carried out to the letter.

Wiping a weary hand across her forehead, Helena took a deep breath and, standing back from the table, peered across at the clock on the kitchen dresser. Ten to one! It had taken her nearly three hours to close up Ben's wound—although it was true that much of that time had been involved in calming him down. Luckily for him, he had still been in a deep swoon when she had poured the fiery spirit into the gash to wash away the dust and grime that had accumulated as a result of the accident, and she had been able to set the first half dozen or so of the twenty-five stitches without too much difficulty. But then, as soon as his eyes had reopened, he had begun threshing about like a madman, mumbling all sorts of nonsense about saws and stands and ropes and goodness knows what else.

Charles, who had elected to stand behind her and hold up one of the oil lamps, had advised her to ignore the incoherent rambling and concentrate on finishing her task.

'Poor chap's delirious,' he told her, with a pitying shake of his head. 'Hardly surprising, considering the amount of blood he's lost. The quicker we get this done and get him to his bed, the better his chances of recovery, if you ask me.'

Having opted to accompany the earl back in the gig, along with the supplies, Mrs Wainwright had proved herself to be an indispensable asset, shooing away all but the few helpers whose assistance was necessary and disposing of the bloodstained cloths without so much as a single murmur of complaint.

Richard had spent much of his time ripping good linen sheets into long bandages and rolling them up for future use, but had had to leave this occupation on several occasions, in order to help hold down the patient to prevent him from getting up from the table, as had seemed to be his constant intent. With neither laudanum nor opiates available, either of which they could have done with in order to render him unconscious, they had been obliged to resort to pouring quantities of brandy down the poor man's throat in an endeavour to placate him but, in Helena's opinion, the spirit seemed to be doing more harm than good. On one occasion, Fuller had actually lashed out at Standish, causing the earl's cousin to back away in vexation, demanding that the two men supposedly holding the patient down attend to their business and pointing out that such a move could easily have caused him to drop his lamp and set the place alight! At Helena's frown, he had the grace to mumble an apology, but thereafter kept himself well out of reach of the struggling worker.

But, at last, it was done. The stitches were set, compresses and bandages had been applied and all that was left to do now was to pray that she had stopped the bleeding and that the injured man might be kept free of infection—both of which could prove decidedly tricky, given the primitive circumstances in which the workers were living. Mrs Wainwright was all for moving him across to Westpark right away, where she would be able to keep a managing eye on him, but Standish was quick to point out that jogging the patient about in a carriage so soon after the operation might easily undo Helena's careful handiwork. And so it was agreed that a truckle bed would be brought over from Westpark and that Fuller would be housed in what had originally been the housekeeper's room, which lay just beyond the kitchen and, upon inspection, proved to be reasonably acceptable.

A slight argument then ensued as to which of the four of them was going to spend the rest of the night overseeing the patient, but since Helena was quite determined to see the job through, there was little that any of the others could say to dissuade her.

Standish was persuaded to take Mrs Wainwright back to Westpark and then return to his own home, along with Richard's proviso that they would both return after breakfast and take over the watch.

Rueben, Bet and Cissie and those helpers who had not yet retired were sent off to bed, with the suggestion that they might care to regard the rest of the day as a holiday, in order that they might all recover from the shock of the accident and, at last, Helena and Richard were left to themselves in the makeshift bedroom.

'I'll drag in one of those free pallets and we can take turns to rest on it,' suggested Richard. 'Sitting up all night in a chair can be dashed uncomfortable.'

'That sounds as though you are speaking from bitter experience,' she replied shakily and, as she watched him setting up the makeshift bed, she suddenly began to feel quite shy of him.

He gave a soft laugh and, taking hold of her hand, led her over to the pallet. 'Military accommodation is not always up to scratch, my dear,' he said. 'But I assure you that I usually managed to find somewhere to sleep—and now it's time for you to do the same.'

At her attempted protest, he lifted up his hand and pressed a finger against her lips. 'Not another word, I beg you. You have done more than your share for the moment and I insist that you try to get some rest. You may rely upon me to keep a faithful watch and wake you up again in two hours time.'

As exhausted as she was, with scarcely enough strength to keep her eyes open, Helena was still torn between the need to do her duty by her patient and an aching desire to spend some time alone with her husband. Nevertheless, since she could not

help but agree with his judgement that an hour or so's rest now
would help to ensure Fuller's ongoing well-being, she obe-
diently lay down on the straw mattress, revelling in the ten-
derness the earl displayed, as he carefully tucked a blanket
around her and pressed a soft kiss on her brow, before removing
himself to the chair by the fireside. One minute her sleepy eyes
were smilingly contemplating his shadowy outline, as she
drowsily watched him settle himself into a more comfortable
position, and the next she was fast asleep.

Chapter Twenty-Three

By inching his way along the stable wall and pressing his ear against a narrow gap in the door's woodwork, Charles Standish was just able to make out the low murmur of his cousin's voice, uttering what sounded like soothing words of encouragement. And, if the laborious snorts and whinnies that were also issuing forth from within the building were anything to go by, it would seem that Copperlady had finally decided to drop her foal, the likelihood of which came as no great surprise to the silent listener, since it had been he himself who had presented the mare with a cascara-impregnated apple, some two hours earlier, before driving Mrs Wainwright back to Westpark.

With a satisfied nod, he edged himself cautiously away, happy in the knowledge that such a momentous event as ensuring the safe arrival of another thoroughbred foal to his collection was enough to guarantee Markfield's absence from Fuller's bedside for some considerable time—time enough for Standish to silence the fellow for good and all, if he could just persuade the sainted Helena out of the room for a few minutes!

Had it not been for that meddling swine of a joiner, who had chanced to look up and spot him whipping back the dangling cord—just as the stack of heavy slates showered to the ground—the 6th earl might well have met his Maker, as had been Standish's meticulously organised intention. As it was, the clodhopping fool had gone and spoilt the whole effect by having taken it into his head to leap forwards at the crucial moment and barge Markfield out of harm's way, thus taking the full brunt of the damage upon himself!

That the interfering swine had managed to survive the on-slaught was, in itself, something of a miracle—particularly as Standish had made no attempt whatsoever to contact any of the local doctors—when, in a state of trembling dismay at what had occurred, he had dashed across to the stable to collect his mount and had ridden off, as fast as the horse's legs were able to carry him. His apprehension as to what might be happening having eventually overcome his initial panic, however, he had crept back to view the ensuing scene from a safe distance and only when conditions seemed to indicate that the man was at his last gasp had he judged it safe to return and attempt to give the im-pression that he was as deeply concerned as were the rest of the onlookers at their workmate's plight.

But now, unfortunately, it had become glaringly obvious from his earlier behaviour that, unless something was done to stop his mouth, the Fuller chap was hellbent on divulging what he had witnessed, thereby putting paid to all of Standish's care-fully laid plans. Having spent the past four years in the dedi-cated pursuit of what had been a long-held aspiration, however, there was no way on earth that he was going to allow a useless down-and-out to scupper his ultimate goal!

The death of his grandfather, followed in quick succession by that of his father and then each of his two uncles, all in the space of five years, had brought home to Standish the realisa-tion that, were it not for the existence of his two older cousins—for whom he had harboured the most bitter resentment ever since he had been in short coats, owing to their constant habit of leaving him out of their games, along with their persistent teasing—the Markfield earldom, along with its entire estate and bordering properties, would devolve upon himself!

Having confidently assumed that Richard's death might reasonably be left to the well-renowned expertise of the French artillery, it had taken him almost three years to accomplish his objective of putting a period to Simon's life. After a series of ingeniously created 'accidents', from which the 5th earl had managed to emerge unscathed, Standish had finally succeeded in eliminating his cousin when, after having plied him with a plentiful supply of strong liquor—to which a hefty dose of laudanum had been secretly added—he had bet the inveterate gambler that his horsemanship was not up to taking him over a nine-foot hedge—a challenge that the devil-may-care Simon had been unable to resist and the one that had, ultimately, led to his death.

That Richard had arrived home from the war both safe and sound had brought his remaining cousin no joy at all and, since the new earl was cut from an entirely different pattern from that of the previous one, every one of Standish's attempts to bring about his downfall had, thus far, met with a decided lack of success. A moderate drinker, who regarded gambling as a pastime for fools and charlatans, the ex-major had learned to keep his wits about him at all times—especially in the matter of his riding equipment, it seemed—the attempted sabotaging of which had merely led to one of the grooms receiving a rather severe set down, after the sharp-eyed Markfield had spotted the partly severed saddle strap, while tightening his mount's girth.

Having also failed in his endeavour to nudge his cousin under the wheels of an oncoming beer dray, on a busy city thoroughfare one particularly foggy day less than a month ago, Standish had been close to reaching the end of his tether when, to his utter dismay, the matter of Markfield's marriage had suddenly reared its ugly head. Although, as it happened, on first being told about the possible arrangement between his cousin and the Wheatley girl, it had seemed to him to be the God-given answer to his prayers, especially since he had been growing increasingly conscious of the earl's growing mountain of debts.

Having no wish to be saddled with such an adverse encumbrance upon his own succession, he had reached the conclusion that it might be just as well to allow the current incumbent a certain amount of leeway to enable him to sort out the worst of his financial problems before proceeding with any more attempts to further his demise.

The unfortunate incident at Almack's having precipitated his cousin's hasty marriage, Standish had then been at his wit's end to conjure up ways to keep the newly-weds at loggerheads with one another. Spurred on by the thought of the fifty-thousand-pound dowry sitting waiting for him in his cousin's bank account, he had concentrated his whole attention on ways to keep the pair apart for, after all of his efforts to secure the succession for himself, the very last thing he needed at this stage in the game was another claimant to the earldom!

Having filched one of the wedding invitations from the huge pile on his grandmother's writing desk, he had sent it to Rachel Cummings, marked with a scribbled *'Do come, my love'* at the bottom of the card—safe in the belief that no woman on earth would have the power to resist such a pointed request. In addition, he had set about bribing one of Rachel's maidservants into 'borrowing' the pair of earrings that Markfield had bought her mistress, intimating that his lordship was thinking of having their design copied into a matching necklace for her ladyship. Tossing the earring on to Helena's bed had presented him with very little difficulty, since Mrs Wainwright had been only too keen to show off the newly furbished room to him, taking great pains to point out the immense amount of trouble to which his lordship had gone on behalf of his bride-to-be!

That both of these tricks had served their purpose in setting up what ought to have proved an insurmountable barrier between the pair had become very quickly apparent, although it would have been well nigh impossible for Standish to have missed the simmering undercurrent of emotion that seemed to flow between Helena and his cousin every time he saw them together. This, coupled with Markfield's recent abnormal drinking habits and unusually brusque manner, was enough to convince him of a pressing need to redouble his previous efforts—particularly after having witnessed the pair involved in so close an embrace that very morning; the kind of embrace that, in Standish's eyes, bore all the hallmarks of a soon-to-be fully fledged love affair! To allow any continuance of such closeness could very quickly sound the death knell to his ambitions.

Having remembered his despised cousin Simon catching him out with a very similar trick during his childhood—although a basket of ripe peaches had been the relatively innocent missile on that occasion—Standish had spent much of his afternoon stacking a pile of heavy tiles on to the very tip of the Hall's upper parapet after wedging the tail-end of a strong cord beneath the first of these tiles. By positioning himself at the window on the first floor, he had managed to lure Richard over to an almost perfect spot beneath the carefully poised stack. He had hardly been able to contain his glee when, with one single quick twitch of the dangling cord, he had brought the whole stack of tiles tumbling from its perch.

But, now it seemed, his entire campaign was in danger of being knocked completely awry. Not only had he failed to put a convenient end to his cousin's life, he was now in grave danger of losing his own, should Fuller be given any opportunity to describe what he had witnessed!

After tapping gently on the door of the makeshift bedroom, he let himself in and, after greeting the startled Helena with a warm smile, he whispered, 'How's the poor fellow doing? Any improvement?'

'Not really,' she sighed, with a sorrowful look in the direction of the bed, where the softly moaning Fuller lay tossing restlessly to and fro. 'But at least there is no sign of fever—for which I am eternally thankful. I only wish that one of those doctors you called on would put in an appearance and administer some form of pain-relieving sedative.'

'Yes, indeed,' he replied, giving a sympathetic nod. 'Dashed bad luck that they both had to be out on difficult cases, but I dare say one or other of them is sure to turn up pretty soon.'

'Oh, I do hope so!' she exclaimed fervently. 'I would hate to think that my crude efforts might cause more harm than good and I will not be really happy until Mr Fuller has been examined and properly dealt with by a professional.'

'That is perfectly understandable, my dear, and I fully appreciate your concern.'

After eyeing her downcast expression carefully for a minute or so, Standish then had a sudden brainwave.

'You look as if you could do with a breath of fresh air,' he ventured. 'Why don't you pop outside for a few minutes? You know you can rely on me to stand guard for you—and I can always call you back, should anything untoward occur.'

'Oh, thank you, Charles—you are very good!' she said, rising at once to her feet. 'Richard was obliged to go over to the stables over an hour ago—I understand that one of his mares is about to drop her foal.'

'Yes, I did see the light as I passed, but judged it better not to interrupt.'

Striving to hide his impatience, Standish took her arm and ushered her towards the door. 'You take your time, my dear,' he said, with an encouraging smile. 'Your patient will be perfectly safe in my hands.'

Slipping out of the door, Helena closed it gently behind her and made her way towards the back door, eager to join her husband and hoping that his 'patient' was faring rather better than her own. On reaching the courtyard, however, she was greeted by the sudden chill of the night air and, with a little shiver, turned back to fetch her shawl.

Noiselessly entering the room, she reeled back in disbelief, as her eyes took in the terrifying scene before her. Despite the fact that his back was towards her, there was no mistaking the fact that Standish was doing his utmost to suffocate the groaning and writhing Fuller by pressing a pillow to his face!

'Stop! Stop!' shrieked Helena as, diving across the room, she grabbed hold of Standish's coat sleeve, causing him to stumble backwards and let go of the pillow. 'What, in God's name, do you think you are doing?'

As soon as he had regained his balance, however, Standish flung himself around and started towards her, his eyes glittering with unconcealed rage and his face contorted with such a hate-filled expression that Helena found herself backing away from him in breathless terror.

'Oh, no, you don't, my dear,' he snarled, as he reached out and grasped hold of her wrist and attempted to drag her towards him. 'You had your chance—you should have trotted over to see your beloved spouse, as I advised—too late now, I fear!'

'But…I don't understand,' she gasped, clutching at the bedpost, in a frantic effort to avoid whatever dreadful punishment he had in mind for her having caught him out in his murderous act. 'Why are you behaving in this way, Charles?'

'H-he—m-meant—to—k-kill—his—l-lordship!' came Fuller's strangled croak as, weakly thrusting aside the pillow, he struggled to raise himself on to his elbows. 'I s-saw it all— he—he p-pulled a cord and—'

'Keep your mouth shut, you!' snapped Standish abruptly, but then, as his eyes covered the distance between the terror-stricken Helena and the rapidly recovering man in the bed, he very quickly became aware of the rather hazardous position in which he had, inadvertently, placed himself. Too far away from Fuller to prevent him having his say, he was unable to release his hold on the wildly struggling Helena, lest she escaped from the room and sought assistance.

Scarcely stopping to think, he let go of her hand but, before she managed to take even a single step, he had leapt forwards and fastened both of his hands around her neck, causing her to release her hold on the bedpost and try, instead, to wrench his fingers from her throat. Feeling his hold tighten, she found herself in a desperate struggle to take even the smallest of breaths and, as the room started to spin and grow dark about her, she could feel herself drifting away from the world.

'Let her go, Charles!'

So intent was he upon his task that Standish had failed to take note of Richard's stealthy entry into the room and it was not until he felt the earl's fingers flexing around his own throat that he was made aware of his lordship's presence. Releasing Helena instantly, he flung her away from him as, gasping for breath, he made a vain attempt to free himself from Markfield's steel-like grip.

Hooking his hand over the back of Standish's collar, Richard dragged him backwards and then, after swinging him around to face him, raised his fist and dealt his cousin a punishing uppercut, the force of which had the dazed man slumping to the floor, whining in agony.

In two strides the earl was at Helena's side where, lifting her to her feet, he cradled her in his arms, groaning, 'Oh, my dearest darling! What has he done to you? Forgive me, please—I should never have left you!'

'I—I'm fine, Richard—truly,' she did her best to reassure him, although it was impossible to disguise the hoarseness in her voice. Yet, despite that fact that she was still finding it difficult to breathe properly and that her heart was still beating nineteen to the dozen, she could not be entirely sure whether these irregularities were symptomatic of the terrifying shock she had just experienced or to the fact that her beloved husband was holding her so closely to his chest, stroking her head and calling her his 'darling' and his 'precious one'. But, as she snuggled more closer to him, she was in no mood to stop and fathom out the causes, she simply revelled in the joy of being in his arms once more, his words and actions only seeming to confirm what she had hardly even dared to hope.

'He's gettin' away, sir!'

Fuller's urgently croaking cry instantly wrenched the reluctant Richard out of his almost surreal state of jubilant exhilaration. He had been so lost in the ecstasy of having Helena in his arms again, his body responding in joyful anticipation as he surrendered himself to the sweet warmth of her soft curves pressing so invitingly against him, that the cares of the outside world had all but wiped themselves from his mind.

A muted curse escaped his lips as he forced himself to release his hold and, stepping away from her with a muttered apology, he swung on his heel, turning towards the door just in time to catch sight of his cousin's hasty retreat. He was about to start after him, in order to take him to task for his inexplicable attack on Helena when the sudden realisation came to him that, in his great eagerness to comfort his stricken wife, he had failed to discover exactly what had brought about Charles's totally uncharacteristic behaviour.

'I don't suppose you can tell me what the hell went on here, while I was gone?' he said, directing his question towards the man in the bed who, having lost a great deal of blood both before and during Helena's emergency treatment, had, for the past fifteen minutes or so, been hovering between a deep-rooted need to keep himself alert and a pressing desire to sink into the comforting oblivion of unconsciousness.

He gave Richard a weary nod.

'I…already…told…her ladyship,' he said, haltingly. 'Stan-Standish was aiming to k-kill you.' He wriggled himself up into a sitting position and, after he had taken several deep breaths, his voice grew a little stronger. 'I looked up and saw this cord—dangling from under a huge stack of slates, it was— seemed rather odd to me, but then, when his hand caught my eye—tugging at the cord—I tried to warn you, sir, but the whole lot came tumbling down…'

Charles had tried to kill him?

Unable to believe what he had heard, the earl cast a questioning look over at Helena, who having been deprived of the comfort of her husband's arms, had sought the security of the fireside chair.

She nodded.

'I caught him trying to suffocate Fuller,' she told him. 'I suppose he was trying to prevent him telling what he had seen. But then, of course…' She paused and a slight shudder ran through her, before she forced herself to go on. 'Once he realised that I was just as much of a threat, he—he…'

A great lump came into her throat, making it impossible for her to continue. Great tears welled up in her eyes—tears that she had, thus far, succeeded in keeping at bay—and, turning away from him, she hid her face in her hands and proceeded to sob her very heart out.

With a quick exclamation of dismay, Richard was on his knees beside her, wrapping his arms around her and cradling her gently against his chest. An anguished moan emanated from somewhere deep within him as he rocked her to and fro.

'Oh, God,' he choked, as he buried his face in her violet-perfumed hair. 'This is all my fault! How, in God's name, am I ever going to persuade you that I love you after having left you to face all that?'

'You could try telling me!' came a muffled croak from somewhere in the region of his heart and, starting back in disbelief, he looked down to find Helena staring up at him, her eyes wide with wonder and a trembling smile on her lips. 'Is it true?'

'That I love you?' Choking back a sound that was halfway between a laugh and a sob, he bent his head and captured her waiting lips, intent on savouring every breathtaking moment of the magical event.

'As true as every precious hair on your head,' he averred, as soon as he had recovered sufficient breath to continue. 'I believe I fell in love with you the very first time we met and I seem to have been falling deeper and deeper with every day that passes.' Pausing, he leant forward to press his lips against her brow. 'No chance that you might return my regard, I suppose?' he whispered provocatively, as he transferred his lips firstly to her earlobe and then to her cheek.

'Oh, Richard,' she sighed, snuggling up against him, 'I can't even begin to tell you how much I love you. To think that I might have died without ever having—oh, my goodness!'

Pushing herself away from him, she cried, 'Enough of this! Shouldn't you be trying to find Charles, before he does any more damage?'

'Yes, I suppose so,' he groaned, getting reluctantly to his feet. 'But why he should have suddenly taken it into his head to do away with me, I simply cannot fathom.'

Helena stared up at him, in some surprise. 'Why, for Markfield, of course, you great gudgeon! With you gone, the entire estate would be back to its original size and he would be the only one left to lay claim to the title!' Pausing, as a sudden dreadful thought occurred to her, she then whispered fearfully, 'You don't suppose that he could have had anything to do with your cousin Simon's death, do you?'

'Oh, hardly!' returned Richard, with a brisk shake of his head. But then, as he started to recall what he had heard of Simon's accident, he could not help but begin to wonder a little. 'I suppose I'd better try to track him down,' he said, as he made for the door. 'But, first of all, I think it might be wise to ensure that you have one or two of the others down here to—er—keep you company.'

Well aware that he had been about to say 'protect you' but, not wishful of causing her unwarranted alarm, he had quickly sought a more suitable choice of words, Helena merely nodded and smiled her loving thanks at him.

'It's probably time I changed Ben's dressing now, anyway,' she said, 'and I should be glad of someone else's help, if either Bet or Cissie would care to volunteer their services.'

'Good as done,' he replied, as he went out and closed the door firmly behind him.

Chapter Twenty-Four

Having taken less than twenty minutes to locate Standish, a puzzled Richard stood silently in one of the shadowy recesses of the main hall, at a complete loss as to his cousin's present actions. As far as he could make out, Standish appeared to have moved all the smaller pieces of furniture from their designated places against the walls and was in the process of assembling this collection at the foot of the staircase.

Frowning, the earl stepped forward. 'What are you up to, Charles?' he called softly.

With a startled curse, Standish dropped the small table he was holding and wheeled round to confront his cousin.

'Clear off, Richard,' he yelled at him. 'Just leave me be, will you? I have no desire for your company at the moment!'

'Perhaps I might help?' suggested Markfield, strolling over towards a pair of heavy Jacobean chairs and proceeding to drag one of them across the floor towards his cousin's jumbled assortment. 'Where would you like me to put this?'

'No, no! That sort of thing won't do at all!' retorted Standish, with a dismissive wave of his hand. 'That heavy dark oak will take far too long to catch—'

Eyeing his cousin angrily, his words came to an abrupt halt. 'Just go away, Richard,' he scowled. 'I don't need your help.'

'I rather think you do, Charles, old man,' replied Richard gently as, having worked out his cousin's intention, he inched his way forwards towards the haphazardly arranged pile of furniture. 'I really can't allow you to burn the place down, you know.'

'Why not?' sneered Standish. 'It means nothing to you—I even heard you say that you'd lost all interest in it. You're no better than the previous pair. Uncle Leo sat back and allowed the Hall to fall into a shambles and, even though I badgered Simon to do something about it, he simply laughed in my face!'

For a moment, Richard was lost in confusion but then, as he studied the strange glitter in his cousin's eyes and the fevered expression on his face, it became increasingly clear to him that his cousin Charles's mind had become badly unhinged.

'Uncle Leo is the one to blame for leading Simon astray,' he ventured carefully. 'When we were boys—'

'When we were boys,' scoffed his cousin, as he lowered himself on to one of the stair treads and reached across for the tinderbox that he had placed there. 'When you and he were boys, you mean! As I recall, neither of you had any time for me, when I was a boy!'

'There *are* four years' difference between our ages,' Richard felt constrained to remind him. 'Such an age gap hardly signifies now that we're adults, but to a couple of ten or twelve-year-olds, four years can seem a huge difference. You could hardly expect us to allow you to accompany the pair of us when we were engaged in pursuits that were dangerous, even for a couple of tearaways like Simon and me.'

'That didn't stop you playing your filthy tricks on me!' retorted Standish belligerently.

'Tricks?' frowned his cousin. 'I don't recall ever having played tricks on you.'

'Well, Simon certainly did! What about that basket of rotten peaches he perched on the roof of the gazebo?'

'Oh, that!' returned Richard, with a short laugh, as he took another small step forwards. 'As I recall, that trick was intended for me, in repayment for the trip-wire I'd arranged just outside his bedroom door that morning. Just tough luck that you happened to come along and pull the string before I got there. Really spoiled Simon's day, that did—although I do recall that we both went to considerable trouble to clean you up before we took you home to your mother.'

His stared across at his cousin, his eyes softening in recollection. 'You have to remember that the reason Simon and I were so close was because we had both lost our mothers when we were quite young, Charles, and, even though Grandmama did her best to make up for our loss, we were both rather envious of you still having yours.'

'Well, you're welcome to the old bat now!' exclaimed Standish, his attention momentarily diverted. 'She's nothing but a pain in the neck, as far as I'm concerned! And you can quit trying to butter me up, Richard—you always were a bit of a do-gooder, as I recall. If only you had had the decency to get yourself killed at Waterloo, everything would have worked out according to plan.'

'Well, you can hardly expect me to apologise for that, old chap,' reasoned Richard lightly, taking the opportunity to move forwards another few inches. 'Surely, any blame for my survival should be directed towards the incompetence of Boney's fighting forces?'

Glaring at him, Standish let out a hollow laugh. 'It's perfectly obvious that you lead a charmed life,' he said. 'Even when I succeeded in edging you off the pavement into the path of that dray in Bond Street last month, you managed to leap out of its way without a scratch!'

'Good Lord!' gasped his cousin, blinking back his shock. The somewhat disturbing incident was still quite vivid in his memory but, having assumed that it had been merely the press of people on the pavement that had caused his sudden lurch into the roadway, he had endeavoured to put the matter out of his mind. 'I always had the feeling that there was something decidedly fishy about that business!'

'And then you had to go and mess everything up by getting involved with the Wheatley girl,' continued Charles, ignoring Markfield's remark.

About to take another step forwards, Richard faltered. 'Helena?' he breathed softly. 'What has she to do with all of this?'

'Should have thought that was pretty obvious!' sneered his cousin. 'Your ridiculous arrangement suited me down to the ground to begin with—especially since it meant that you would be able to carry on with the rebuilding programme. Plus, I had come up with several rather clever ideas on ways to deal with you once the Hall was back in shape. Only, then, of course,' he finished bitterly, 'you had to go and marry the stupid wench and ruin everything!'

Richard, his hands fisting tightly at his sides, was experiencing an almost uncontrollable desire to charge through the barrier that separated the two of them and render his cousin permanently senseless. But, heavily conscious of the fact that, in taking such a course of action, he would lose any chance he might have had to discover the full extent of Charles's duplicitous chicanery, he forced himself to heave in a deep breath before asking, in fairly measured tones, 'What difference did that make to your plans? If you intended to do away with me anyway, I fail to see where Helena fits into your equation. The property and title are both entailed, so you were bound to have inherited.'

'Not if you had already done the business and begotten the next Standish heir!' snarled Charles as, reaching into his jacket pocket, he drew out a small leather pouch and proceeded to unwrap the band that secured its neck. 'Even persuading the Cummings woman to attend your wedding didn't seem to have the desired effect of setting the pair of you at each other's throats—although by your manner the next morning, I did have every reason to suspect that my rather neat placing of that same lady's earring in your new wife's bed had managed to achieve a reasonable modicum of success!'

Learning that his cousin had been the cause of the distasteful scene between himself and Helena on their wedding night
was the straw that finally broke Richard's resolve. Reaching the
barrier, he began to drag away the various tables and chairs, his
fury mounting with every breath he took. 'By God, Charles,'
he ground out, 'I'll see you pay for that!'

'Not in this world, old chap!' returned the other calmly as,
leaning forwards, he proceeded to sprinkle the pouch's black
powdery contents over the assembled pile in front of him.
'Markfield Hall should be mine by rights and, if I can't have
it, I intend to make damn sure that nobody else does!'

Having instantly recognised both the sight and smell of gun-
powder, Richard started back, his eyes wide with alarm. 'For
pity's sake, Charles!' he shouted. 'Don't be such an idiot!'

But it was too late. Charles had already opened his tinderbox and, having struck his flint and set light to one of the small
strips of cotton inside, he gave a careless laugh and tossed the
flaming rag on to the gunpowder-sprinkled woodwork.

The blast from the ear-shattering detonation that followed
his actions hurled Richard halfway across the hall, only to result
in his head striking against the solid leg of the very Jacobean
chair with which he had been attempting to confound his cousin
minutes earlier, rendering the earl immediately unconscious.

The thunderous noise of the explosion permeated throughout the entire house, shocking the sleeping workers into instant
wakefulness and bringing them to the upper gallery in a concerted and panic-stricken rush.

Helena, a sickening dread filling her heart as she tore down
the passage, with Rueben and Cissie hard on her heels, was
amongst the first to enter the hall itself.

The sight that met their eyes, however, although quite
shocking to behold, was not quite the total devastation for
which Standish had hoped. Some of the furniture that had failed
to shatter into pieces had started to burn, it was true, but the

amount of fire they caused was minimal. It was the blast from the explosion that had caused the most harm, ripping out several of the newly repaired windows and destroying much of the lower staircase. On attempting to go forwards through the palls of black smoke to inspect the damage, Helena found herself being pulled away by Rueben who, having spotted the mangled remains of the earl's cousin amongst the smouldering debris at the foot of the stairs, was determined that his mistress should not catch sight of the abomination.

In directing her away from the horrific scene, however, he was unable to prevent her eyes from alighting upon Richard's still form, as he lay sprawled awkwardly across the floor tiles, the back of his head smack up against the leg of a very solid-looking chair.

Uttering a low wail of distress, Helena skidded across the hall and landed on her knees at her unconscious husband's side.

'Oh, no! Not now!' she wept, as she tenderly lifted his bleeding head into her lap, stroked his blood-streaked hair away from his temple, her shaking fingers probing carefully for his wound. 'Please God! Don't let me lose him now, just as we've found out how much we love each other!'

As her distraught tears fell upon his cheeks, Richard's eyelids flickered and slowly forced themselves open but then, as his befuddled eyes gradually focused themselves upon his weeping wife's face, they widened and he breathed, 'My beloved angel! You've come back to me!'

At his words, a slight flush covered Helena's cheeks. Although she was fully aware that her husband must still be in a state of shock and hardly responsible for this temporary disorder of his mind, she could not help but recall that she had spent the better part of the night before last locked in his arms, whilst he had murmured that self-same epithet over and over again! Hurriedly putting the recollection aside, she held him tightly in her arms, scarcely daring to believe that, apart from a rather painful-looking cut on the side of his head, he appeared to have escaped the worst of the explosion.

Richard's eyelids drooped and a slight frown sifted across his brow, as he did his utmost to unravel the confusion within his brain. Then, suddenly, his eyes flew open and, as they latched on to Helena's, his lips began to curve in a slow seductive smile.

'I remember that there was a distinct smell of violets,' he murmured softly. 'I couldn't seem to get it out of my mind—it *was* you in my bed that night, wasn't it, dear heart?'

As her cheeks flamed for the second time, she could only nod and shyly return his smile, for she was not entirely sure exactly what he did recall of that night's strange happenings.

Gingerly fingering his swollen abrasion, he slowly raised himself into a sitting position and then, as he gazed lovingly into her eyes, he shook his head in disbelief.

'What a fool I am!' he groaned. 'To think that I actually had you there in my bed next to me and was too damned foxed to realise it!'

Lifting her hand, he pressed her fingers to his lips, saying, 'I'll do far better next time—you have my word!'

As Helena dropped her eyes, and blushed yet again, he let out a little chuckle and, rising to his feet, put out his hand to help her up.

'First things first, however,' he said, as he frowningly surveyed the damage all around him. Then, beckoning one of the men over to him, he took him to one side, in order to confirm his supposition that his cousin had, indeed, perished in the explosion.

The arrival of the doctor who, after checking the earl over, affixed a court plaster to his wound and pronounced him fit enough to carry out his normal occupations, also revealed the full extent of Standish's wily duplicity—although Richard was no longer surprised to learn that his cousin had made no effort to contact any of the doctors after Fuller's accident, since it was now clear that he had banked on the man dying without recovering consciousness. Hence his desperate attempt to silence the young worker for good, Helena's interruption presumably being the catalyst that had finally tipped him over the edge into total insanity.

Although the earl could not help but feel a deep sadness that his young cousin's thinking had become so warped during his own extended absence from the family estate that he had actually been prepared to kill to ensure his own succession to the property, it was impossible for him not to cast up a prayer of thanks that all of his efforts had failed.

And now, as he looked across the hall, to where Helena was already engaged in the business of directing the clearing-up operations, he felt his heart swelling with so much love that it seemed it might almost burst and he swore that never again would he allow anything to come between him and his beloved angel.

As she lay curled up in her husband's arms that night, Helena was filled with a deep and drowsy contentment, coupled with an absolute certainty that Richard's love for her was as real and true as hers was for him. Having heard the full story of Charles Standish's treachery she, too, had been sickened to learn that the young man for whom she had begun to develop quite a fondness had turned out to be such a treacherous fraud and, whilst she was deeply sorry that he had gone so far as to take his own life, she could not help but feel profoundly thankful that he had been the one to die and not her beloved Richard.

Raising her head, she pressed a teasing kiss against her husband's throat, causing him to tighten his hold and hurriedly capture her lips with his own. But then, as he felt himself being swept up in yet another current of breathless exhilaration, he reluctantly drew away from her and, mindful of the rapidly approaching daylight, murmured, 'You really need to get some sleep now, my love—we have a full day's work ahead of us, remember.'

'A good many full days, it would seem,' she replied with a soft laugh, as she snuggled even closer to him. 'And, if tonight's performance is anything to go by, a good many full nights, too, I would imagine!'

'You tempting little minx,' he growled huskily, pulling her swiftly into his arms once more. 'Who would have thought that an angel would be so very accommodating!'

Epilogue

Almost a year to the day of the explosion the Earl and Countess of Markfield decided to hold a celebratory ball. The renovations to the Hall were now complete and to commemorate this happy event—in addition to the happy event who lay sleeping peacefully in his cradle in the newly furbished nursery wing—the idea of so grand a celebration seemed entirely appropriate.

Thanks to Helena's prompt intervention, Ben Fuller had survived his injury, the rapidly fading scar on his left brow being the only reminder of that dreadful time. Having managed to persuade his old master, Hector Tobias, to come down from Leicestershire to examine the Hall's damaged panelling, it seemed that the elderly woodcutter could hardly wait to get down to work and restore it to its original magnificence, adding insets of his own exemplary carving, in those cases where the damage was too far gone to repair. In addition, after seeing some examples of his ex-apprentice's work, he had agreed to take Fuller back on again—on condition that he didn't decide to go off and join another war!

Several of the other men, Rueben Corrigan amongst them, having managed to save much of the generous wage that Helena had allotted them, had opted to go back and seek employment in their own home towns—Richard having assured them that should they be unsuccessful in their search, he would always be glad to find work for them on the estate.

Bet and Cissie, along with the other females who had come from Chelsea, had been happy to remain at Markfield, working either in the kitchens or the laundry room—although Cissie, who seemed to have developed a certain affinity with the dairy herd, had elected to become a milkmaid!

As soon as the earl had deemed it suitable to move himself and his family into the grander quarters of Markfield Hall, Helena had taken advantage of Westpark's lack of tenancy to finally persuade her father to quit his London residence and retire to the countryside. And so, under the doughty Mrs Wainwright's care, there he had ensconced himself and was often to be seen casting a line into the little river that ran between the two properties or merely sitting and smiling his contentment, as he watched the passing wildfowl at play.

Southpark, once Charles Standish's property, had also become vacant, due to his mother, Mrs Adelaide Standish— gladly accepting her nephew's kindly offer to provide her with a generous annuity—having chosen to spend the rest of her days in the company of her widowed sister in Bath. The redecoration of the house having met with Lady Isobel's approval, it had been agreed that it should be kept for her future use, should she ever feel the need to remove herself from Standish House.

Richard's stud farm had grown into a thriving enterprise, much as it had been in his grandfather's day, and his racing thoroughbreds had succeeded in winning many a useful purse throughout the past year, helping to fill both the estate's coffers and the earl's pockets alike—a source of great satisfaction to Richard, since it made him more or less independent of his wife's unstinting generosity—this having proved to have been the only sticking point in what had become an otherwise perfect marriage.

Possibly the most unexpected development that had occurred as a result of Helena's leaving London, however, had been one that had caused her an occasional moment of deep mortification, it having turned out that Thomas Redfern's numerous visits to Cadogan Place had been on behalf of her cousin Lottie and not herself, as she had, at the time, supposed! It appeared that the doughty doctor had decided that the vicar's daughter possessed all the necessary qualifications to make him the most excellent of wives. Giles Wheatley, on being informed of this happy news, had immediately made over the lease of his London house to the young couple, in addition to providing his overjoyed niece with a handsome dowry.

And so, as, with a smile of deep satisfaction on his face, the earl led his wife out across the floor for the first dance of the evening and the great hall rang once again with the happy sound of music and the appreciative murmurings of the one-hundred-and-twenty guests who looked on with such approval, he could hardly wait to draw his countess into his arms to whisper into her ear how utterly ravishing she looked in her ball gown of white silk and silver gauze; how extremely proud he was of her and—most importantly of all—how very deeply he loved and adored his dearest angel of a wife.

Helena, for her part, had never been as happy as she was at that moment and, as she raised her glowing eyes to meet her husband's ardent gaze, she felt bound to admit that the contract that her father had drawn up had not been such a bad idea after all—despite the fact that the earl had never got round to signing it!

millsandboon.co.uk Community

Join Us!

The Community is the perfect place to meet and chat to kindred spirits who love books and reading as much as you do, but it's also the place to:

- **Get the inside scoop from authors about their latest books**
- **Learn how to write a romance book with advice from our editors**
- **Help us to continue publishing the best in women's fiction**
- **Share your thoughts on the books we publish**
- **Befriend other users**

Forums: Interact with each other as well as authors, editors and a whole host of other users worldwide.

Blogs: Every registered community member has their own blog to tell the world what they're up to and what's on their mind.

Book Challenge: We're aiming to read 5,000 books and have joined forces with The Reading Agency in our inaugural Book Challenge.

Profile Page: Showcase yourself and keep a record of your recent community activity.

Social Networking: We've added buttons at the end of every post to share via digg, Facebook, Google, Yahoo, technorati and de.licio.us.

www.millsandboon.co.uk

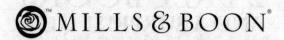

www.millsandboon.co.uk

- All the latest titles
- Free online reads
- Irresistible special offers

And there's more...

- Missed a book? Buy from our huge discounted backlist
- Sign up to our FREE monthly eNewsletter
- eBooks available now
- More about your favourite authors
- Great competitions

Make sure you visit today!

www.millsandboon.co.uk

2 FREE BOOKS
AND A SURPRISE GIFT

We would like to take this opportunity to thank you for reading this Mills & Boon® book by offering you the chance to take TWO more specially selected books from the Historical series absolutely FREE! We're also making this offer to introduce you to the benefits of the Mills & Boon® Book Club™—

- **FREE home delivery**
- **FREE gifts and competitions**
- **FREE monthly Newsletter**
- **Exclusive Mills & Boon Book Club offers**
- **Books available before they're in the shops**

Accepting these FREE books and gift places you under no obligation to buy, you may cancel at any time, even after receiving your free books. Simply complete your details below and return the entire page to the address below. You don't even need a stamp!

YES Please send me 2 free Historical books and a surprise gift. I understand that unless you hear from me, I will receive 4 superb new books every month for just £3.79 each, postage and packing free. I am under no obligation to purchase any books and may cancel my subscription at any time. The free books and gift will be mine to keep in any case.

Ms/Mrs/Miss/Mr_____ Initials _____

_____

Surname _____
Address _____

_____
_____ Postcode _____

Send this whole page to: Mills & Boon Book Club, Free Book Offer, FREEPOST NAT 10298, Richmond, TW9 1BR